THROUGH THE EYES OF IRIS

Thomas Henry Bennett

Iris was neither woman, nor man. The difficulty was not so much assigning my status, it was accepting it. The brain bestowed could not relinquish its hold and I could not resent it for being so resilient. And the body which carried around the brain I could not control; that empty shell which was nothing without the brain gifted, was helpless.

Iris was born a woman but stillborn, lost to logic, to watching, to understanding, to analysis without feeling, touch, emotion, love; without recourse at all. Now, as Iris looks back, I look forward. Only by looking back can I look forward, back to all Iris was and I became, in order to look forward.

So I document Iris as I document myself.

Iris was an officer of the court. I had a law degree from Cambridge. Iris was a lawyer, sliding and wailing within the innards of a silk purse to a bed of status and financial security others could only aspire to. What an advert Iris used to be when I achieved in a world once dominated by the masculine ilk.

For Iris was someone in the City of London, hacking at the coalface, hacking away for the biology I looked down upon every morning I took a shower, every time I cleansed my skin, every time Iris valued pretence and slapped paint on my face.

Neither man nor woman - who would know of Iris?

Who would want to?

The following events are as close to a recollection as I can muster. Mistakes as to fact and detail, belonged to Iris.

Today, they belong, to me.

I.

The Northern Line smells of damp, decay and the rain soaked detritus of human beings moulded to corners as Victorian sleepers below, make the unsteady minions above, jump.

Welcome.

Welcome to the daily slog into institutions composed of worker ants ensuring the whole adds up to more than the sum of its parts. Welcome to London as daily, interminably, this miserable visage of decomposition; this tube that transports us from the carbon-blackened boxes we call home, frees us from the rain until we arrive ready to call shots others can easily call for us.

Suddenly, commuters spill from the tube when its sliding doors open. A suit becomes frustrated as he loses a square inch of train reluctantly taking him to work. As he tries to get back on, all he has are the pin-stripe backs of the recipients of his lost property - shiny-suited money-peddling monkeys, who cannot let him on. He looks at his watch, he asks others to move down, the door begins to close, he seizes his chance and drops his shoulder into the crowd. But it doesn't move and hope turns to frustration which turns to anger which turns to violence. Pity the poor chap who gets the punitive slug to the back of the head as the doors close and the train crawls away. With no way to retaliate there is no sympathy to be had.

Who notices anyway?

Who, in London, ever notices anybody else?

Who has time to notice anybody else?

London devolves upon its occupants; London falls upon its prey. For many years Iris has watched and suffered the slow mutation from the wide-eyed to the myopic, supported by a collective denying support for each other. The tube - a microcosm; the tube - a brief passage but indicative of the whole. Events chain and collate the sum total of all the dissatisfactions of the day. Pity the poor man who gets the punitive slug to the back of the head, taking out an unknown angst on those who take out an unknown angst, so embellishing the whole. Though pity can be such a gentle emotion, London is neither gentle nor is London anything other than an ethereal overlord forcing all into a corner where the only reflection is of oneself. How selfish a

4

town. How selfish a people. How selfish the collective, regardless of the people.

I slide my hand into my bag, feeling for my book. A gentleman gives me a seat. I use the word gentleman loosely, for through the linear eyes of the male I am a blonde, he is masculine and these temporary seats are for the worthless yet pretty. Which one am I as he strikes up a conversation with a friend while both try to look down my top and quantify my breasts, qualify my breasts and so unveil my breasts. They are just breasts - lumps of flesh diluting with age hanging off a rib cage and predisposed to droop. I love the juxtaposition for I so despair for these irregular balls of flesh I try to hide them. For these deluded males the marginal possibility of ever seeing the things gets Iris a seat. What is it to be a man, for they live in a perfect, albeit perfectly circular world - government is flesh and flesh - it is sexual government.

A masculine world, squatted in by femalia. At least this is the way men see it. It is a masculine world for as long as this is the way men think it is. Iris is meat; Iris is fodder - though the object can object, light falls in through a lens and they cannot help but stare. I am being dissected, clothing peeled, measurements taken. Discretion subsides as comfort takes over. Following my curves causes the imagination to rise. This seat is not comfort and the act is not pure. To park my backside is to invite favours and favours will arrive. These actions aren't motivated by kindness. Want and how to get it coincide. Man turns predator and woman must submit - sized up by a butcher, slaughtered by my sex; this seat, these men and Iris - a microcosm of the whole. A microcosm of London.

I try to ignore them. I try not to think of them. Alas Iris is trapped by analysis as I imagine a wife sitting on another train in the network, or a wife clogging up the narrow streets of London in a Land Rover. I wonder if she is as knowing as I am. I wonder if she realises that the man she married forgets the church on leaving the church, forgets the ring as he hides the ring and remembers only to serve himself - to service, himself.

More of peripatetic London try to get on the train. Body odour mixes with deodorant coloured by petrol which infuses the rank air outside. Faces are tinged coal black as millions of sticky molecules attach to skin, cloth and fabric. As cells divide and conquer my lungs are turning cancerous with every second of each minute I live and work in London. Both inside and out I am being attacked and infected with disease.

At Kennington the tube half empties as those who work in the West End alight while those who get on are like the rest of us - little worker ants making money for each other in a system none of us is supposed to question. The English middle class circles - professionals at every turn - accountants, bankers, lawyers, stockbrokers, insurance brokers, financial advisers, pension fund managers, economists, traders. As the financial wheel turns and the service economy which sustains us envelops all else, our daily exodus to little fiefdoms within the City of London gives each of us time to think of how we can increase our empire, thereby feeding the ego which dare not see this shameful life for what it is.

As for Iris, it gives me time to cement my prejudice, for papers are ruffled by pin-stripes, glistening magazines are ruffled by girls, perceptions are allowed in by my psyche and distortion gives it words. The thoughts of all are categorised into neat boxes as I travel through time, just as much a victim of the town in which I have chosen to live as any I choose to package in my own, neat way.

Or do I?

Do I not just float like so much burnt paper above a flame? Can Iris be part of a world I understand, question, assimilate then segregate? Through the eyes of Iris or Iris through the eyes of all?

I listen to my suitors as they speak of a trip to Amsterdam and a brothel where the victim's wallet was stolen and he was forced to have sex with the thief. I become envious. What secrets do these men cling to? How many little adventures at night-time and with how many women?

How much of my soul would I have to relinquish in order to allow them a pleasure they will subsequently express to my detriment?

I look down at my body. How easy it would be to give in and let them have it; how quickly they will elope once the job is done. But they cannot have Iris, for no man ever has. The breach of my innards is as repugnant to me as it is to a man. And sometimes I think I am a man in a woman's body. Oh, and how I wish, sometimes - just sometimes, I were a man.

I change tube at Bank and catch the Central line to St Paul's. So do these dotards. When they let me past one smiles at the other and I smell their product, gagging as an acrid stench is accompanied by juvenile giggling. And then they have gone, sucked up by the crowd. Whether I will see them again is moot. I can guarantee their type at any time. I can guarantee man, at any time.

The office lurks. The office - covered by the shadow of St Paul's Cathedral; St Paul's Cathedral - coloured on a cold wet day by acidic, discolourant rainwater, sometimes effecting the veneer of purity, sometimes not. Either way it is covered in detritus, just like Iris.

Oh, what measures must I take to wash off the attitude I convey?

But who has time in London?

Who notices anyway?

My day starts in five minutes and Iris must perform. I must disregard the anger and disregard the whole. Under the shadow of omnipotence is the devil's work conducted; under the shadow of the devil does the God of capitalism frequent. Secular life displaces the old and St Paul's Cathedral, magnificent but lost, looks to me like a rag-ridden leper on a trillionaire's yacht.

Iris is an international finance lawyer. Iris is supposed to be superior. We are lauded for being superior. For the vain; for the secular worshippers of the theology of profit, they think - they know they are superior. Still, trapped in the system, they all moan, decry, dissemble and denigrate. They all do. But why complain? Why rock the boat to portend drowning? The system calls for acceptance and like a frozen lichen stuck to the hull of a listing ship, I accept. We are called to submit to any and all directions and go to where we follow. Why fight without the means to conquer as some do? Why not assist an enemy until it is an enemy no more?

It doesn't do to be seen as a force for disruption in the City of London. The tender balance between happiness and departure in every sausage factory is one we worker drones recognise and disrupt at our peril. We accept its trappings, we dismiss its failings, we fall in line and follow the dollar brick road.

I see my boss in the distance.

Edmund Rose coughs as he leaves his cab and expectantly looks up at the building in which he has spent most of his career. Oh, I rue the day I took the job here. What offended and what offends is the hypocrisy. This very public testament to achievement; a careerist's lodestar; a world-class finance lawyer - those evenings spent drowning in gin, the covetous attentions upon younger men - soiled and oiled in every dingy homosexual recess in London. No finer man. No bigger gloss.

Truth resiles with this duplicity. Edmund Rose carries duplicity under his arm as a gift to all. His real achievement is having never been caught. One may ask his wife and children; one may ask the lawyers in the know. The presentation of truth to the City of London delineates the façade. Every day Edmund Rose ascends a ladder to a tightrope along which his corpulence plods, looking down upon the jaw-snapping hungry below. Every day he gambles with exposure, risking all he has achieved on pain of being exposed as a homosexual in a brutish, unforgiving world. Should he fall he falls into the jaws of bigotry, of hatred, of detestation.

But the façade is all. I too, am the façade. Edmund Rose hired Iris to practise deception, to misrepresent normality, to culture acceptance. Though Rose gambles continuously, delivering himself unto exposure and to the elements which can destroy him, Iris lends to the air beneath that thin rope with separations of confusion, dissemblance and denial. I am part of the inner fabric of one man's excess. Should he be exposed and he will be exposed, I will fall with him. I knew it then. I know it now.

One day he will have to account for his expense. Risk subsides as time devalues risk. It is plain. It is obvious. Though Edmund Rose is as repugnant to me as a book is to a fool, even I, Iris, realise that Edmund is expendable. I, am expendable. And Edmund Rose will be expended. And I will too. So his secret has become my secret. His secret is best kept within the innumerable, angular and bare walls of the office. The fact that Edmund Rose is a fifty-eight year old homosexual is best kept within. Differences in the City of London are not tolerated. Form is everything and substance is nothing at all.

I recall that a new partner joins us today, chosen by Edmund through his gin-riddled world of moral jaundice and recruitment to order. He will be young; he will be pretty. With the power to select, Rose recruits men in his own image and Iris awaits the introduction without inclination. Soon he is hovering outside my room. Without really knowing why, I try to look busy and while I detest the thought of doing so, it may have some beneficial effect. As Edmund takes stock I catch sight of his companion and see a small man with boot polish black hair and a rounded gut badly covered by piece three of a three-piece suit. I hear an accent, possibly Irish, and an office laugh. How I hate office laughter - arriving a nanosecond before a natural laugh and a nanosecond after a comment which would otherwise be regarded as utterly unworthy. The laughter gives his insecurity away and the insecurity puzzles me. Rose normally recruits in his own image pursuant to relationships which have developed pursuant to anonymous sex in saunas, nightclubs and bars. Such men feel comfortable with Rose and there is little need for the act. The new man needs to act.

I beckon them in.

Edmund's clothes are the same garments he wore the whole of last week. He smells too, with rancorous breath at three yards and I daren't go any closer to save greeting the projectile spittle flung from his cogitating mouth. Behind him a head bobs incongruously, like an escapee apple flung deep into a swimming pool and I see a man anxious to get his face in mine, a man anxious to deliver unto me another false City greeting, laced with another sardonic, City of London smile.

His name is Brodie.

Strange name. Very strange name. And a strange-looking man too, as I listen to an overenthusiastic welcome and visit body language suggesting the opposite. This man is not a homosexual I decide. So what is he doing here? With the exception of Iris, this department is occupied by up and coming homosexual lawyers and Rose puts this cherubic Celt in charge of them and in control of me?

I feel confused.

I am as nice as pie.

"Of course I'll drop by for a chat," I say.

"Let me sort out my work for the day and I'll pop in for a coffee. I can tell you what I am doing. I can tell you the type of work I do. Perhaps we can work together. I'll look forward to it."

He smiles and I suspect he can sense my façade. I assume his sensitivity and begin to splinter concern. Sensitive males augur disaster as they always assume the worst. Tainted males, as impenetrable as granite, worry me, and for good reason. What confusion rambles around their heads, what disjointed perspectives, what skewed foresight. Homosexuals are just bitches and need each other, even if it is just safety in numbers. Delicate males are different. Monomaniacs, are different.

Edmund Rose decides to show off, telling Brodie how much the current deal in Milan is worth. My mind turns to Brodie. I wonder if he knows what a nest of homosexuality he has decided to lead. I hope he is open-minded. I hope, though I fear not, that Brodie defeats the norm. It is Rose's judgement I question. Can he really have dissembled City of London mores in blind disservice to reason? Why is Brodie here? Why a possible infidel-adjutant to this very private Sodom and Gomorrah?

At 10.30 a.m. Brodie is stocking up his bookcase. With his back turned I notice the hind-quarters of his head and the careful way he has crafted his hair in order to hide a square inch of scalp. Alas, it is a lost cause for darker freckles on his underlying skin show through the thinning strands of his blackened hair.

Aware of my presence, Brodie turns around. His eyes follow my curves but far from coming forward, he takes a step back on realising I am a couple of inches taller. Then he tries to hide his wedding ring as he slips his left hand into his pocket, feebly shaking my outstretched hand with his right. A pattern enters my thoughts. As I accept his invitation to take a seat, I seem, intuitively, to confirm my first impressions - vanity, insecurity, pride, social-myopia, inferiority complex. I resolve once more to watch my step, for someone's personality clash is ripening, maturing, growing, gestating. I hope it isn't me he chooses to violate. The last thing I want is this potential little Napoleon sending me to winter in Southern Russia.

I qualify my ignorance, telling him I was unaware of his arrival. It is to do with Milan and the deal Edmund and I have with the Italians. I ask about his previous firm. Brodie cuddles his seat and looks uncomfortable. I can sense, then see the answer before his pinprick green eyes.

"Known Edmund for a few years now. I am a good friend of his son. We met as students at Cambridge."

Two thoughts. Here is an insecure egotist - why else mention Cambridge? The second I find more interesting - I had, in part, made some small assumption that Brodie had guessed Edmund's sexuality. This is, or must to a degree, be incorrect.

I admonish myself. How on God's earth would anyone not intimately involved with Rose know what lies behind the veil? He is pre-eminent in the City of London and has an unimpeachable professional reputation. He is also protected by the environment in which he excels. Rose is Eton, Cambridge, a member of The Maundeville and shares a background with the great and good in every walk; every unquestioned pantheon of English life. Protection if it is ever needed, is just a phone call away. Edmund Rose can indulge himself in whatever way he likes, be it men, be it boys. No one here will remonstrate. Lawyers never bite the hand that feeds them - lawyers feed the hand to stop the biting. And the City of London protects its very own provided discretion is the norm.

"Edmund speaks highly of your legal talents."

Brodie looks at my breasts. I wonder if he knows how I understand that look and the inflection in his voice. I doubt it. He is a man, after all, and I am convinced, with that look, that Brodie is not a homosexual. What chance the background his accent evinces culls the recess of morality into which fall tolerance and understanding?

We talk work for a while. Then he gets personal. I try not to pry but Brodie is insistent as he tells me of his life as a grammar school boy in Ireland, his family, his elder brother who is a professor of psychiatry and a younger brother from whom he claims to be estranged.

I wonder what Brodie would think about boys without consent. Will Edmund Rose tell him? Will he find out anyway and what will he do, for Brodie seems a coarse Irish moralist. A distant brother is one thing but a pederast boss?

"I am having a few drinks tonight next door - my way of saying 'hello' to the department. I would be delighted if you could join me."

He eyes me closely. Nerve endings start twitching all over my body. I desperately search for an excuse but search in vain. As my toes start crawling into the soles of my feet I come to face the reality that I simply cannot avoid saying 'yes.'

"Splendid. Edmund promises me that everybody will be there."

My thoughts turn to my flatmate, James, as I lip-read Brodie trying his best to ingratiate me into the invasive tediousness of his work-world. I decide to invite James for he is absolutely first class in such situations and besides, I get a second opinion of this basic little Celt. My faculties may be critical and my perception high-powered but James is a simple soul at heart. While I see complexity he can spot the simple without knowing why complexity should have a place.

See, my world has been my domain for so long that all but the tender tips of feelings have long since gone. I am Iris - a sad reflection of all of the dull documents I have ever crafted and a poor cousin to the spontaneity of man. A dry wasting cynic I am; a tacit admission that life imitates all before it.

I curse this petty Irishman as he moves onto yet another anecdote about Cambridge.

"So I shall see you later?"

Once more I am courteous. I despise myself. Iris instructs me to decline before it is too late. It is too late. Why do I say 'yes' when I should say 'no'? Am I truly a coward or just guilt-ridden for playing the game in search of an easier life? London infects as the will to acquiesce is stronger than the stealth required to envelop self-respect. London has got to me just like it gets to everyone else – eventually. Different as I may think I am, Iris too, I am one of many. But I must cling to my differences - I must float, I must hover.

I will have to try harder to resist.

Iris, will just have to try harder.

II.

Cold Krug waits for me, beckoning me to the bar. Rose is welded to a stool with a bottle to himself, talking to a figure I do not recognise. With a glass in my hand he calls me over, introducing me to a banker.

The business chit-chat is dull. I sense that my value to this banker is not in the content of my conversation but in the shape of my body, the colour of my hair and the contours of my face. My repulsion lies not with him, though he is fat, flatulent and fatuous. My repulsion is with the concept - the very idea.

I pretend to listen though I look around. I see no sign of Brodie or James. Butting in, I let Rose know that James will be in attendance. A twinkle appears in his eye though his subliminal thoughts give way to persona and instinctively he returns to the act.

To this banker and to the finance world, Rose represents the establishment - a clever man with the background and the position to make the myopic assume he is straightforward and trustworthy. The homosexuality isn't an issue because the secret is denuded by manner. Whether it is weakness which stops him from declaration or his intuitive sense of what may happen should his inclinations of midriff become public I do not know. Although the man is an uncouth, walking, living, breathing, lie, it is an economy of deception he is exceptional at keeping.

"Iris; let me join you. This looks like one conversational merry-go-round we won't get on."

I turn and look all the way down my button nose at Brodie, who has somehow managed to creep up beside me. Once more he seems threatened by my height.

"This preoccupation with business has got to be bad for the ego. We must let them get on with laying golden eggs. Come, join me."

Brodie drags me to a parting in the crowd.

"I've worked in the world of finance for over ten years now and in all that time the biggest deals and the most superficial relationships are cemented over expensive champagne and some vague recollection in the morning of an agreement the night before. The trick, if you want the business, is to remember every drunken syllable and telephone the target first thing. As his cerebellum stews in the juices of excess, remind the victim of all the things you laughed about, adding just enough information so he remembers the confidential information he should have kept to himself. The balance of power changes in that one call. Only the knowing can dance between the raindrops Iris. Only the knowing."

Brodie smiles. I wait for him to come closer - Fagin, tapping the side of his nose; words within meaning and meaning within words - people are tools manipulated into favourable decisions and favourable decisions beget success. Brodie extols his secrets as if they are precisely that. And in doing so, he gives himself away, for in doing so Brodie exposes himself as an outsider. As we look at Edmund Rose, Brodie little understands that Edmund and this rapidly disintegrating banker are from the same ilk. The deal was sold before the market took hold, for human nature proffers adhesion to what one knows and by background, learning, trust and by association, Edmund is in control as is his compatriot. Understanding is subliminal but it is an understanding based on mutuality and not difference. Brodie's analysis is based upon dichotomy - us and them, the hunter and the hunted, matter and doesn't matter. The Establishment, however, knows and seeks out its own.

I ask Brodie of his intentions.

"Not so much intentions Iris - intentions and strategy."

I wonder why he chooses to tell me what other ambition-riddled monkeys choose to keep to themselves.

"A man's reach should always extend beyond his grasp. All else is a no-brainer. I admit that I want to be successful. Who in this part of the world doesn't? Success comes to those who grace the game and embrace the challenge."

He brings his face closer to mine. His eyes become intense.

"And I intend to take whoever wants to come along with me for the duration."

I start giggling like a little girl. I look away. With my peripheral vision I see that his stare remains intense as Brodie's champagne glass empties for a third time. It must be the alcohol. The man couldn't possibly be this shallow without chemical imbalances affecting his insight. Maybe Brodie is shallow. More dangerous still, he is plain old stupid. Not academically stupid; what I mean is, by utilising all of the nerve endings, synapses and sections of brain required in order to do his job - well, all one has left behind in the other cavities of the brain is a draught, a moral vacuum, a moral-free zone, a cavity devoted to delight in the subjugation of others.

My glass is empty. While Brodie reaches for the Krug, I notice Edmund leading a previously sentient man toward the exit. Though the banker is capable of raising a smile, he staggers and mutters incoherently while Edmund slaps him on the back. I feel sorry for the man and my sorrow is compounded a few moments later when I look through the ochre-stained windows of the bar and see a hunched figure vomiting against the outside wall. The banker looks possessed, haunted - exorcising his excesses as his Medusan eyeballs roll around a skull fit to implode.

Comparatively sober, Edmund hails a cab. The cabbie is reluctant but forthcoming at the sight of a crisp, fifty pound note. In the banker goes with a tan leather briefcase not far behind, as we watch one mature human being licking the taxicab window on his way past.

I hear laughter in my left ear - discreet laughter. Brodie is gorging himself on his own facetiousness.

"God makes them sheep and has them sheared Iris."

Without thinking I look at Brodie - a sly eye-line once more travelling down my nose. He notices but tries to hide the acknowledgement. Behind him I see James entering the bar, followed by Edmund with banker vomit on his shoes and carnal desire all over his abhorrent face. I make my excuses to Brodie who seems put out by the swiftness of my flight. Unfortunately Edmund sees James at the same time, trapping James by the bar, whereupon his grubby fingers produce a pristine crystal cut glass and his disfigured mouth evicts an insect black smile.

James excuses himself much to Edmund's annoyance and heads toward a fruit machine.

"Straight or Dorothy darling?"

"I've told you - James is straight."

"Shame. Must tell you about last night…"

Suddenly the twinkle in Edmund's eye departs. He becomes pious and almost angelic. We are joined by Brodie. Brodie is basic albeit pleasant but utterly incongruous. Rose has turned to stone - gone is the brief bum foolery of a queen, replaced by a seriousness of impression and a cavalcade of empty words. He even changes the pitch of his voice. Brodie laps it up and doesn't seem to notice. This Irishman is so caught up with himself, so caught up with this impression-voodoo I wonder if he has any self-respect at all. What must Brodie return to inside his tumbleweed head when he goes home at night?

"You must come, you simply must. It is the best club in the West End."

With Brodie out of earshot, Rose makes plans to go to a table-dancing club for men, by men. Why he thinks I will be impressed I have no idea - the concept is repugnant to me. Previously when I was press-ganged to attend, I was treated as a joke, a fag-hag, an addendum, a sexual pariah. My last memory was Edmund trying to pay a dancer one thousand pounds for an hour while another punter was on all fours giving a bald Dutch queen a blow job two feet from the bar. The image stays and I use James as my excuse. Edmund will not take 'no' for an answer.

An hour or so later I am light-headed and Edmund's hand is in the small of my back, pushing me out of the bar. Semi-drunk, I have little time to think of Brodie and as the cab arrives I stumble through its black door and park myself on the back seat, while my head narrowly avoids the spins and I try to muster some resolve.

"I've got this terrible feeling," James whispers, as Edmund reaches over to try and feel the inside of his leg, "that we are in for another one of those nights."

The sentiment really doesn't console me. I have had quite a night already and my disjointed thoughts flit between the incumbent smell of Edmund in the morning and a meeting room in Milan full of smoking bankers playing nicotinic odds with coffin nails.

"Room for one more? Thought you'd left without me."

Brodie catches the cab door as James tries to pull it to and invites himself unwanted to our unwanted party. Through semi-closed eyes I see Rose look, suggesting with expression what is on the tip of my tongue. For his part, Brodie seems enthusiastic, almost thrilled at the prospect of ingratiating himself so quickly through the mist and tangential focus of alcohol.

"Where are we off?" he asks.

Edmund hesitates.

"Wardour Street" James replies, knowingly.

Without obvious explanation, a glint appears in Edmund's eye. In a flash, his hand falls from his hip and touches the inside of James' thigh.

"I'm warning you," James replies, smiling - almost benevolent.

Brodie looks at Rose who momentarily gets a hold of himself and tries to look away. But the dark deserted streets of Fleet Street fail to offer something to distract and as control and want go their separate ways inside Edmund's head - a head being egged on by the moral, social and practical redundancy of alcohol, his eyes flick around the cab like those of a petulant child on the point of challenge. Once more James' thigh gets a stroke and once more, James brushes Edmund's hand aside.

"What is he doing?"

The whispers belong to Brodie. They resonate throughout my head as I understand his tone for its lack of understanding.

"Why is Edmund grabbing his leg?"

I pretend I am asleep. I am most certainly awake and part of Iris is smiling. This is Edmund's worst nightmare coming true, though he will not grasp the full extent of the ambiguity which could lead to long feared consequences. Here is a minion - this commonplace Irishman being shown the outer cusp of what, by any person's standards is a licentious world and what, to this moral misnomer, must be an extant view of hell.

In disbelief I watch as Rose starts unbuttoning his shirt. As the call for freedom takes over, even James starts to look concerned. Edmund Rose is getting smaller with every excruciating second. Brodie's eyes have expanded to the size of banquet plates.

"I'm going to have a ball even if no one else is."

Edmund undoes the top two buttons of his fitted shirt. Sweat patches have soaked and formed, creeping like burst vessels toward his corpulent chest. His stomach exhibits signs of perspiration too as sweat-ridden hair sticks to the inners of his shirt, visible through the off-white material clinging to the outer reaches of a startlingly rotund, middle England gut.

A sad, misguided mutation - this is Edmund's attempt to look relaxed, with it, urbane. All Iris sees is a sad individual pouring his secrets away and falling slowly before a man who can utilise all he sees and all he is about to see. A clever and thoughtful man is thus sublimated to another - a drunk, a lecherous ageing dandy, leaving both sides of his character to the arbitrary discussions of the next ill wind.

I don't know whether to laugh or cry - not for myself but for these antitheses, namely the one sitting beside me and the other one opposite. As I weigh the dilemma which has long since left Edmund, I watch with open eyes as Edmund looks at Brodie, whose eyes instantly hit the cab floor, at James, whose disjointed thoughts take an age to switch on, and then at Iris, whose recompense is a slow wink and a rubbery smile.

I try and guess Brodie's next move. In a way he is trapped. If he leaves now, he is telling us he cannot countenance what his late night imagination won't let him consider - he is a homophobe; he is backward; he is a bigot. If he stays, he will witness such scenes which his upbringing, his sense of morality, his very righteousness, will turn his stomach over. In a sense and no doubt unknowingly, Rose has turned the argument beautifully. How far is this egotist, this shallow, blinkered, chameleonic career-boy, going to descend in the name of his own progress? And if he accepts the subliminal blackmail and stays along for the ride, how will the inner wrench of placing the very fabric of his soul on the altar of his career seek retribution from those, such as myself, who seemingly accept this moral hideousness and turn the other cheek?

Brodie cannot but realise that Edmund Rose has duped him. Whatever they had in common has been reversed in this vaudeville. He will also know, on the other hand, that Rose has not exclaimed this state of affairs to the market and the market could eat him alive for his differences. Brodie can see that he has leverage, he has power. Should he wish to use it, Brodie has blackmail.

III.

We arrive at doorway located off Compton Street. It is attended by two large, hairless but extremely muscled bouncers without the voices to match the steroids which have enhanced their form. They know Edmund by name and Edmund shares their jokes as I do my best to walk in a straight line down some damp stairs to the basement. Behind me I can hear Brodie taking deep breaths. Edmund, visibly excited, scuttles off to the bar in search of more champagne.

"Did you know Iris? Did you really know?"

I cannot answer and pretend I do not hear.

Brodie asks again and James speaks for me.

"Both of us know. But she can hardly sound off. The man is powerful and protected. Think about who he is."

One yard from the tip of Brodie's nose is a table surrounded by four suits and on the table is a muscle-Mary wearing a small white towel dipping his flaccid yet elongated penis into a punter's pint glass. I count Brodie lucky not to see another punter protrude his index finger and slide it into the man's anus.

Through his silk trousers I can see Brodie's legs shaking.

", relax. There is nothing, absolutely nothing you can do. These men won't threaten you."

"They are not, men."

"Don't be ridiculous. You must have come across this in the City of London before."

I watch Brodie thumb his wedding ring. I recall him trying to hide it earlier in the day. A man walks past James and pinches his backside.

Brodie snarls.

"Isn't he touchy?"

"Are you going to take that?" Brodie shouts.

James shrugs his shoulders.

"Look around you. The place is populated by men who work in precisely the same environment as you do. Some of these guys are married, some of them are outwardly straight or indifferent and all of them live this double life in which shitholes like this are a private world in which they can let themselves go. I guarantee that if you stay for more than an hour you will see someone you know. You don't have to accept it. All the same, you are here - look on it as an experience."

"And you," Brodie asks, looking at me.

"Do you accept it?"

James is my advocate, my spokesman, my foil.

"There is nothing for either of us to accept or not accept. The fact is, you have chosen to work for a man whose moral spectrum is different from yours. And you will have to learn not to think in terms of acceptance or non-acceptance. Make yourself blind."

"I, am fucking leaving."

Vernacular rises as Brodie protects his dignity and what little self-respect he has left by reverting to the local plainsong which bottoms the personality subterfuge he has spent years layering on top. I hope James isn't going to continue with justifications. I creased when he mentioned moral spectra. He affirms what a career prostitute Iris is as I consider, in turn, the true depth of Edmund's depravity.

I wonder where he has got to. I need not have asked as he appears with four grubby glasses and two bottles of Moet, beckoning us to a table. Iris sits down first with James behind, followed by Brodie.

Rose is oblivious. Caution and risk have subsided and need has taken over. From his pocket he produces a wad of five hundred pounds and lays it on the table. We are set upon by two dancers who see all his money can get them and how little they have to do for it. Edmund picks up a fifty pound note and stuffs it down the string circling the back of the closest dancer, till it pokes from the valley separating his hairless, angular, oily, buttocks. Immediately these sentinels of capitalism realise who is and isn't in the money and both men, putting the obviousness of their eyesight aside, ignoring the momentous ugliness of Edmund Rose, start cavorting while Edmund extends drunken swathes and careless roundhouses at their backsides.

Once more Brodie looks away.

"What do I say to him?" James asks me, discreetly.

"He has suffered enough."

James goes about his business and makes a mess of it. Brodie shrugs his shoulders as I sense a mercenary taking over. James is now superfluous and redundant. Edmund moves me aside. He has spotted a man at the bar he finds attractive. I see his eyes as they survey the game, with lust, want and longing colouring his troglodyte features. But his dancers, aware that the attentions of their benefactor are waning, struggle hard to put themselves in Edmund's eye line. As Edmund struggles to see we cannot see Edmund for the physical intervention of thrusting, dripping, greased crutches in his face. When, finally, I catch a glimpse of him he is salivating so much that spit is dribbling down his chin, following his concave gullet and matting the greying chest hair collecting either side of his drooping chest. The money goes completely when he is allowed to put his hands down the front of each dancer's crotch pants.

Rose feeling the testicles of two young men is too much for Brodie. It is over the top for James. He gets up and takes himself wearily off to the bar. Brodie is already there.

"What is the matter my dear?"

"Aren't they just simply sweethearts?"

I smile for a second, however, I have his attention and tell Edmund that Brodie is uninitiate and alarmed beyond reason.

"He is a friend of my son. Cambridge too. I'm sure he will understand. How could he not understand?"

"But one can't simply land on innocent people - people who are blind to a wider and imperfect world. Brodie is living out his worst nightmare. The repercussions could be catastrophic."

Slowly Edmund gets the point as he realises that the fuller consequences of his actions can come back to infect him. He tries to bluff.

"So it is a baptism of fire. Others have seen it. You, my dear, are one of them. We all have secrets deep down. Name me one person you know in our business who hasn't got a mistress, a lover, a boy, a girl or a line of cocaine in their top drawer at work. Not one of them. We are all sinners darling – all of us. Besides, he can't hurt me."

I consider the arrogance implicit in his last statement. I know very well that Brodie can hurt him.

Strangely I consider myself. I wonder why I am trying to advise this utterly repugnant human being how to protect himself in the face of a threat most people would be happy to see succeed.

"What if I ameliorate his evening?"

"Ameliorate is hardly the word."

"My dear, I accept that the man could conceivably be in shock. What if you move on to an environment he could more easily accept? I am invited to a dinner party predominately inhabited by bores. What do you say? You make a discreet exit and I give you an address in Chelsea?

You simply attend the party late - it has a few hours in it yet, and mention my name. Maybe the excursion will loosen Brodie's relationship with his memory."

"Take this money."

He hands me a fistful of cash.

"And pay off the bar. I'll see you at Heathrow first thing in the morning. Don't be late."

Rose kisses me on the cheek. I feel revolted. I dread to think of the morning. I dread to think of Milan.

In the distance I can just make out the figures of James and Brodie, well hidden in the corner of the room. I swear I see Brodie smile and my mood improves immediately. I get their coats and spring the surprise of our sudden departure upon them. This club is not for any man, or woman, with an unswerving mind. There is little room for logic here, for logic cannot travel around corners, whereas the darker recesses of male imagination has no obstacles to wanton depravity. Maybe this is the nature of Edmund's liberation. I thank God we are not made the same way.

IV.

A short cab ride and we are walking up the very regal steps of a stucco-fronted terrace on the affluent borders of Chelsea and Kensington. Discussions are to do with what we have just seen. James and I sense the conversation is an absolutely necessary way of Brodie dealing with a new modus operandi.

"It is not just that it is unclean, Iris. There is the moral or immoral aspect to homosexuality but to pleasure oneself with such a flagrant disregard to the sensibilities of others is more than gross.

"I am not saying homosexuality is wrong. I tell you that to put it on the shoulders of others who make a choice not to have anything to do with it, is wrong. I don't care if Rose copulates with animals as long as he doesn't try it in front of my children. Let his instincts be what they may be - why should they have to appal me?"

"You must give him a little latitude," James replies.

"I am not a homosexual but I do not wish to stop anyone else. And I am confident enough in my own sexuality to look at the process objectively. Rose does not have that choice."

"Why can't he find himself a partner and settle down with discretion? Why choose the alternative option?"

"He has no option. If he chooses the quiet life it is worse, as those who seek to put him down will see his supposed weakness through a transparency the secret itself unveils. If he can get away with licentiousness then why shouldn't he? Depravity isn't just for the young."

As I ring the door bell, I wonder how well James really knows Iris. While I carry around this feminine exterior, I too, hold secrets which mark me out. Yet I choose a quiet life. I do not have relationships with men for I do not want relationships with men. I find the sight of my body vulgar and I do not wish to be the victim of the wiles of men I know so well. Maybe Edmund is luckier than I am. At least he does have an outlet. I do not. My choice is a quiet life because I cannot express physicality with either sex. My exterior tells the world one thing while my interior - the thoughts of Iris and to the extent they are not suppressed, my feelings, tell Iris to forsake the world, as it holds little for me. How can it? A man and a woman in a woman's body seek not the physical at all as the inner and outer contradictions I suffer are, to me, all I know and to the rest of the world, an attractive curiosity. Escape from contradictions of the physical and emotional are impossible, for both are me, for both are Iris.

"Good evening."

I hear Led Zeppelin travelling around our middle-aged host, who is a silhouette in the doorway. Musing on contradiction I hear Jimmy Page on guitar, see the black outline of a cravat, a double cuff shirt and Ralph Lauren chinos. Brodie smiles. James grimaces. We have descended into another civilisation.

"And you are friends of?"

I enjoy the very English way he asks - ineffectual and not really wanting to imply that entry is a matter of establishing credibility first. Cul-de-sac turns to thoroughfare when we mention Edmund's name.

"Oh, you're a friend of Edmund's", he says, hooting like and owl.

"Do come in."

I marvel at the breadth of personage Edmund keeps. It can't just be to do with Eton, Cambridge, the City. I suspect that Edmund has the benefit of a large gene-pool conclave of individuals characterised by the same outlook, mores and expectations. And over the years he has created a large enough impression on enough similar people to fill an opera house.

"Hang your coats up on the right. Come through. Drinks are in the kitchen; music in the lounge. Please, feel free to do as you please."

As we walk into the kitchen, Brodie and James are still arguing.

"The point is not to do with genes. It is to do with how we choose to treat those with sexual predilections for members of the same sex. Once we have accepted that you are what you are, it is a matter of making a choice as to how we treat someone who is different. And with homosexuals, because they are different from most of us, most men choose to reject them. See the point is in the idea of difference. It is human nature to reject difference when we don't understand it."

"But there is difference and downright ungodliness."

Brodie gravitates to religion - the great intangible.

Iris defers. I want them to stop arguing. I want them to look around. A party of well-heeled money-frumps in Chelsea yields the oddest assortment of mutation. Each person has something to say; each garment, each look, each expression, each inflection in the voice, means a little about the individual. And the study of how they live is every clue as to the way they think. Understanding this is all to Iris - to try and get the travel key to reach inside the heads of all I see. I watch and I watch and want to watch so understanding the innards of every goldfish bowl, every psyche, every closet of character I peer at and into.

Ignoring the music, which is crass, meaningless, tack, I take myself on a tour of the house. But I grow bored. Then, as I walk the landings of this opulent abode, so clearly a mixture of new money and old, I hear a couple having sex in one of the bedrooms. As I listen to confirm, I am seen by this satiated twosome when they furtively tiptoe down the stairs. I wonder if they are married but fear they are not - on entering the living room I see these illicit lovers cuddling up to partners of clear long standing.

I confess my loss as to why this man should prefer clandestine liaison with an upper crust louse over the beautiful creature sitting next to me. Therein lies the truth in this microcosm of the whole. By their standards, by standards I have no part of, his wife's accent and manner is ill-befitting the social world from where this man emanates. Money meets beauty and considerations of mutual intelligence and compatibility are royally ejected from the equation. Money meets beauty and the mutual massage transpires. Drunken sex follows as she allows her body to be used in the pursuit of the need not to think any more once his money is reallocated to her account. And he, of course, needs to confirm his status with a trophy wife, notwithstanding her vacuous, materialist, intellect.

What is his consolation, I wonder?

He looks like a banker or a stockbroker. He can exercise and exorcise his intellect at work while she can exercise her reproductive capacities and validate his worth by looking good in the Range Rover with two, spoilt, good-looking kids in the back.

What further compensation does he require for the task of taking on someone he can't relate to?

There is always the excitement of someone else - the illicit gain-share to be had upstairs at parties, on business trips abroad - women swayed by the sight of a gold card, a double cuff shirt, champagne, Cuban cigars, an English accent and the hearty laugh of a man for whom money allows him to dictate his own destiny. His worlds are complete for he has the best of all worlds - the pretty wife with whom he cares not to share anything other than temporal pleasantries; the stimulating job entitling him to his status as a god of all before; the illicit pleasantry of sexual subterfuge whenever the urge takes over.

Men - men.

How they use the environment so to calculate a maximal advantage. How women fall for it. How women have sublimated what is plain and obvious while men have no need to sublimate at all. His fortune lies precisely in his fortune. And his wife accepts the power of money now that the power of her beauty has gained for her all the trappings of wealth and the necessary evil of deferring morality for the sake of keeping the trappings of wealth. I don't know who to pity. Should I pity him? Well I don't. Should I pity her? Well how can I pity her? For she is just one of a cast of thousands who seek out fortune, get it and accept its plunder. To blame her or to pity her is pointless. One can't pity another for sins they all extol. They are what make them human; they are what make Iris, inert.

"Drink, Iris?"

Following James into the kitchen, I see Brodie chatting to a pretty girl, probably a lickspittle wife-in-waiting. By the smile on her face and the affected manner I guess she hasn't realised that Brodie is both married, though this isn't normally an obstacle to entrapment, and just a monkey-boy lawyer, which is.

James, on the other hand, sees a roomy woman pouring herself a drink. She is alone and James seizes his chance. Casually he saunters over, his brain working out the best way to impress. I see him whispering consecutively in her ear. He smiles, leaving her to mull.

Both he and I know she is now trapped by her own curiosity. She has at least two comments to choose from, both of which should be followed up with some enquiry as to their relevance. Once she enquires she is lost. Provided James has chosen the right woman, it will be a question of our flat or hers. After a few seconds deliberation, she is suitably intrigued to join us.

Her accent is plummy and Home Counties.

"It is a London thing," James assures me, when her back is turned.

"In a city bedevilled with selfishness, the object of the exercise is to look like you are indulging an object who hasn't grasped the truth. To get a London woman talking of herself, when she is inevitably obsessed by herself, is the key. After all, when no one else wants to listen to you and one finds a man who actually seems to care, the release results in gratefulness to the point of distraction."

No sooner has she swallowed the bait than she is regaling him of her unhappiness at the estate agents in South Kensington where she works.

"Not that I need the money," she says. "I do need something to do. But they are so beastly toward me at times, I don't know why I bother."

I roll my eyes toward the ceiling and console myself with a large vodka. The simplicity of the human spirit; the need to be loved; the need to feel wanted; the fall of all the defences London erects and the speed of their demise, staggers me. I used to think it was complex. But with the alcohol which floods her veins waking the dependency instincts of childhood, when mummy and daddy came running as soon as the howl was let out, simplicity re-asserts itself with consummate ease. All she has is someone to talk to within a conversation with a selfish, subliminal agenda. She is, however, confused. And her confusion is her weakness. And her weakness will either depress when she returns home tomorrow morning without a phone number, panties in her handbag, stubble rash on her chin, or she will just plod on, as most do, unable to grasp and unable to counter.

Finally James moves in for the kill. His body language is languid and open, his eye contact is constant and the gentle touches of his hands, soothing her, fooling her, are as good as any.

Five minutes later and the contract has been formally executed as a deed without consideration. He has been leading up to it slowly, moving his face closer to hers as her physical perspectives diminish and all she can see is a mirage she desperately wants to kiss. James is a drug and she craves a fix to envelop her so that she can forget all that is complex in her unremarkable life and let her senses float in the ether - in that thought-void arising when they consummate their relationship with a long and glorious kiss. Still he teases her. Timing lives with the tease. Her horizons must extend beyond the kiss. All she must feel the moment his lips finally drift onto hers is how much more of herself she wants to give him.

There. It is done. Her glass is placed on the kitchen table beside her and his remains in his hand. She has forgotten her gin; she has discarded herself. I turn and fill my glass with vodka as Iris resorts to drink.

The urge to take away my perspective now lies in the bottom of a glass. I am alone as usual. I understand that feeling sorry for myself in these few moments is but a by-product of all that I have drunk and if I were to stop my equilibrium would return quickly. But I want a few moments to feel sorry for myself. I look long and hard at the orange liquid filling my glass and swirl. The distraction is pointless. I am feeling morose because sometimes I want to feel morose - it is as simple as that. It forms part of the addiction of alcohol not that Iris is addicted. These are thoughts I can't countenance when sober and therefore must release when drunk.

I think of Edmund Rose. He may be debauched, he may be to some, vile. At least he is utterly human in the sense that his spirit, his need to live and breathe life, now without regard for consequence, is something I cannot do. Is he not contradictory - a sober personality recluse but a drunken hedonist? Has he gone too far? Is his judgement awry? Is his analysis with regard to Brodie, simply wrong?

Brodie on the other hand, is plain and dangerous. And yet, at least compared to me, he has feelings he is willing to act upon. Fine, they may not be what I can value, maybe they are so foolish they fall on the side of mental illness. But he has life, he embraces life and isn't caught, as I am, in these endless and terminal rounds of analysis of everything, searching for my place in every environment and my differences from every environment. This isn't a recipe for feelings as one would naturally understand them. This is a recipe for inaction and standing. Life is being lived all around me and I, Iris, have no life.

I see a reflection of my face in the glass panel opposite. I see a reflection of my body. This body, for most women, would be a gift and a blessing. I should be using it to obtain for myself and the biology given to me the right to a man and a consequent comfort I am not, through absolutely no fault of my own, able to have. My name is Iris. I am gifted with being an extremely attractive woman. But I do not have a woman's mind. I watch – yes that is the very word - I *watch* the world as it unfolds around me but I cannot take part. How I do sometimes wish that my inner thoughts had some relationship with my outer appearance.

I look through my reflection and out of the kitchen window. Though it is late there are many lights on opposite and I think of all the people trapped in this hideous city wanting the same thing - the very thing I cannot have. I see a woman drawing her curtains. I see her silhouette undress until a male figure emerges and embraces her.

I wonder how they met. It may have been a night like tonight. They go to dinner, they go to the cinema and to the theatre. She meets his parents and he meets hers. They share common attitudes and understandings intertwined by the need for both to find another of the opposite sex with whom to procreate. I feel jealous of the process by which they find out who they are and what they will be to each other. For there are so many things for them to consider; for all couples to consider - looks, money and status, which are so important in London - so many things I think, and somewhere within that almost indefinable mix there is the essence of man and the essence of woman - whether they feel that they can share their darkest thoughts, their darkest feelings, their fear of the outside world and what they believe it can do to them. They become a unit - two against the world revolving around the strength they give to each other. And finally they resolve their fears to each other and make the decision to commit. The ceremony ensues, they get their blessing from a religion neither of them has time for and they commence life together. It isn't going to be easy but they have moved from the familial of their parents and set up on their own.

And then it all goes wrong.

There is no right to happiness. My unhappiness lies in my isolation. These relationships are relationships with another, which Iris cannot know. No man has ever been with me. I have never been out on a date. I have never felt obliged nor have I wanted to take up any man on the numerous offers I receive wherever I go and whatever I do. Apart from biological function, I have absolutely no relationship with my body. I have no sexual desires. I have no inner urge to seek out a mate. I have no relationship with any other apart from those perceptions I have of others which always arise from an inner distance I cannot control. The outer world is a scientific one to me - I watch and analyse and I am no more a human being than a stone and my thoughts are as cold as the empty words I read in banking documents all day.

Looking at the remnants of the cocktail I cannot remember drinking, reaching once more for the bottle and filling the tumbler to the brim, I affirm that my perspectives can only be restricted to that of observation. No man will ever touch me. I will never touch a man.

V.

"I find these events so tedious. Come to think of it, I can't really
    remember why I am here. I was hoping you might feel the same
way."

I hear the words but it takes me a few moments to surface from my
appalling self-pity and register what has been said to me. It is a voice I do
not recognise and as I turn, I find a strangely languid man of medium height
with a highly toned body, a half-suggestive smile and deep eyes which could
offer intelligence. My immediate thoughts are of gentility. He is about thirty
but looks unweathered - his skin is clear, his eyes bright. In fact, his eyes are
beautiful - blue but tinged with green and shrouded by black eyelashes
which are thick and fall from his eyelids toward the floor, marking his
countenance one of sadness, of melancholy. He is clean-shaven though he
would normally be hairy and his hair is thick and sandy and coloured at its
tips by the sun.

"I hope I wasn't disturbing you. I can't enjoy the spectacle in that room
any more. Drunken toffs should stick to drunken toffs and I should stick to
distance. I didn't think I would fit in tonight and I have been pleasantly
unsurprised."

I smile, pleased to be on the receiving end of even this tiniest bit of
insight and cynicism. He watches me and I can see him searching for a sign
that I may view the world in the same way. This isn't an ordinary man; his
intelligence is too marked for that. I wonder whether he is talking to me
because he has been looking at me and wants what he sees, or, he is talking
to me and is actually genuine. Inebriated, I enjoy the confusion in my
thought.

Casually I agree.

He smiles back.

"A kindred spirit?"

He offers me his hand.

"Oliver Dauncey - afraid I cannot be responsible for the name my
pretentious parents gave me."

I detect an accent as I always do. Somewhere north. When I ask, he
congratulates me, fixes himself a drink and asks if I want the same. Tired of

vodka, I agree but am unsure when he cannot find anything other than red wine. I agree as I am too tired to disagree and he hands me a large glass of expensive Rioja.

"I tend always to migrate toward the kitchen at these events. Music tends to attract thoughtlessness and I prefer some element of conversation which lies beyond the banality of yelling above tired pop classics. The thoughtful always try to establish themselves where they can be heard, or better still, where they think they can be heard. There is so much out there which is disappointing, I cannot bear to be amongst it."

I suggest insincerity. Oliver laughs.

"Nothing is more insincere than the nature of interaction when alcohol and frustrated expectations are introduced. I like to sit and watch at times. But what I see generally disappoints. So I get tired and have to adjourn. Now and again I meet someone who thinks in the same way."

Once more he looks at me closely. Again he is searching. Of course I can't give him what he wants, which is an affirmation that his sentiments are similar to my own. Defences rise naturally and there is little I can do about it. At least he is right - there is a greater deal to learn by avoiding the slippage in thought brought on by alcohol and vulgar, cheesy pop. I decide to stay, deferring my normal trick of accepting inevitability by eloping into Iris's thought world. I quite like this man - he is unusual. His technique is to try and get under my skin by establishing himself as a sage and he isn't that bad at it. And if he is sincere, then he is good at being objective.

I find my curiosity interesting. Normally if I think I am being approached by a man with an ulterior motive and a sexual one at that, I extricate myself as soon as I can. I haven't moved.

Oliver Dauncey certainly isn't a lawyer, a banker or a trader. He is too perceptive for that. He dresses well and his shape, discernable as it is through his shirt and jeans, looks exercised. A degree of self-respect then if he goes to the gym - a degree of vanity too. But his face doesn't match that kind of analysis. He smiles beautifully. By any stretch of the imagination, although not my imagination, he is an attractive man. Maybe his evident boredom comes from the many circumstances where a man such as this finds himself on the receiving end of the wrong girl. I ask what he does for a living and take a gulp of wine.

"Accountant, frustrated painter - formerly a frustrated accountant. Just an accountant and easily bored. University was more a homage to the efforts of my parents. I felt as though I owed it to them. And I think I did. I was the dutiful son and passed all of my exams, did the appropriate interviews afterward and ended up as an accountant in London ensconced in a sausage factory for accountants.

"I despised the office from the first moment I stepped into one. No one prepares you for the indignity of being stuck in a shoe box with a gross weight of career monsters. No one tells you that all the achievement, all of the people you beat in order to walk into that office, is expunged straight away. The air becomes thick with young people who are, by objective standards, high achievers and is rich thereafter with those above who expect conformity, the eradication of any vestige of independence and total subservience to the collective. Like I said, I despised it."

I wonder how he got out.

"Well, I was sensible. My parents gave me a deposit for a flat and I made so much money on property by moving every few months that when I resigned and sold up, I had plenty left in the bank while I tried to make this painting and designing thing work.

"Unfortunately I don't find painting, or design, interesting myself, for it is predictable. I find myself, in isolation, without the voice I formerly thought was mine by right. Being just a number is for the shameful. Painting, at least in theory, represents a voice and an independent voice at that. But my misguided attempt at individuality when conformity is the norm was clear. I am a conforming individual, not an individual, individual.

"In my time, I have met three frustrated creators, as I call them. The first was frustrated because she couldn't paint, the second was frustrated because he couldn't get an agent and the third had forgotten that the vital ingredients - analysis and creativity, were utterly lacking, so much so that when she sat down at her computer and waited for that mythical spark, absolutely nothing happened. She was a management consultant again two months later."

I can think little of his words. I wonder why I am so stupid and start blaming this red wine. Tannin and grape, sugar and yeast, are playing with me. One minute I am on the thought straight and narrow, the next I let go and end up spewing that which I think is the right thing to say without thinking of the analytical thing to say. Save that I can say nothing.

"Would you have yourself as creative Iris? Do you look on trying as something to be regarded with contempt? Sometimes I wonder whether sitting back in the corner and watching the world go by is a derogation of humanity. I made the effort and tried. I refuse, generally speaking, to listen to anybody who doesn't at least try to do something, even if it is meaningless to the rest of us. Lawyers and accountants I find by the barrel-load in this city. I rarely find someone schooled in that way willing to put their middle-class head above the parapet and try something different."

Elements of Oliver Dauncey I like. Certainly his physicality exudes gentleness. But he is beginning to expose himself as more than that. I wonder if this red wine stops me from seeing what he is really after. For a man in London he seems to have his eyes wider than most. Still, I recognise now that I am feeling drunker than I have all evening and I have been drinking now, for a number of hours.

I excuse myself, feeling most unwell and take the stairs to the bathroom. Though I enjoy his company I hope Oliver Dauncey isn't there when I return. It is James who is upon my mind.

I look for James but cannot see him. I see Brodie instead who is engrossed with the same Chelsea girl he has been talking to all evening. I ask him where James is. He finds the distraction annoying.

"Gone home - winked at me on the way. Last thing I saw was your flatmate and the girl he has been kissing all night, heading into it."

Brodie smiles - a facetious, cynical curl of the lip.

"Pass him my congratulations."

He whispers it so that his chosen partner can't hear lest she sense that his objectives are precisely the same. I think nothing but ill of him, holding the thought in the bathroom as I notice my balance ebbing away - the first signs of total inebriation filtering through the alcohol and entering my rapidly denuding, thinking self.

I disbelieve Brodie. I am convinced he is lying. James is unlikely to go without me. He wouldn't leave without me, not on a school night. Feeling confused, I resolve to have a look in some of the bedrooms. James was horny enough to take advantage of the hospitality and utilise someone else's bed. And the woman he was with would have almost certainly agreed to do the same thing.

I flush the chain and stagger out of the bathroom. The corridor in front of me is long and dark and I can barely focus on the black and grey shapes marking the other end. Alcohol really has its grip and I try and be discreet though no doubt fail as I whisper James' name on stumbling past each bedroom door.

I take another flight of stairs. There are fewer rooms at the top of the house still I cannot find James and a reserve battery cajoles me into reason. Fine, Iris - take a taxi, telephone from the kitchen and get yourself home. You had enough to drink. You have just plainly had enough.

I almost fall down the stairs to the mezzanine landing. I feel nauseous. My attention is distracted by a light coming from one of the bedrooms. As I walk to the door I stumble slightly and knock into it. It opens abruptly and I dread what I am about to see. Yet the door falls away to unveil an empty room. I step inside and take a cursory look around. But my head is spinning; my brain is being wrung; my vision is blurred - so much so that on looking at a bedside lamp, its fogged outline separates until the object becomes two. I have to lie down. I have to get off my feet till the outrageous indignity I have brought upon myself has gone.

I totter to the bed, kicking off my shoes and fall down face first. Alcohol is now soaking all of my organs, sloshing inside like water racing through a sinking ship. I lie on my side and feel a creeping veil of nausea consuming me, from head to foot. Instinctively I grab then embrace my stomach, trying to coax it to remain still and inert and let the urge to reject the poison which has infused every molecule and every atom, subside. I start hyperventilating and can feel fluid beginning to collect at the back of my throat. Instinctively I know I am going to be violently ill unless I can let my body's rancour subside by passing away into a deeply troubled, alcoholic sleep.

And then, precisely then, I remember nothing.

VI.

As I open my eyes, darkness falls in.

What little light there is comes through the room door, which is half-open. For a few moments I have absolutely no idea where I am. It takes a great deal of concentration to even remember why I am here. All I have are visions - pictures in my head of James, Brodie, Edmund Rose and a man I cannot place.

I can still hear music from downstairs. I can hear voices.

I am lying on a single bed. I rest my arms to my side and look down. Momentarily I am at a loss to explain why I stare at myself then it dawns on me that I am partially clothed. My blouse is unbuttoned totally and my bra is undone at the back though my breasts are still covered. My skirt is on the bed beside me. I still have my stockings and knickers on. My shoes lie discarded on the floor and next to one of my shoes is an empty wine glass, which I presume is mine. I lay still for a second and can't imagine how I ever ended up in this state. My breathing is laboured and for a second I imagine I have been hurt. But I can feel no pain.

I sit up and reach for my skirt, which is by my feet and as I slide forward down the bed to get it, I feel pain in my midriff. No, it isn't my midriff, it is lower down than that, near to the top of my thighs. With my right hand I try to locate the area from where the pain arises but I cannot. But the pain is still there. Slowly my hand moves inside my knickers and as I touch my vagina I realise that the pain I feel comes from the outer hood. Disbelieving, I stop moving. Then I slowly insert the tip of my finger into my vagina and blench. I reach to my side and switch on the lamp adjacent to the bed. Still hurting, I stand up and stagger, for I am still extremely drunk - I stagger to the bedroom door and close it. I move back over to the bed and pull down my knickers. Inside the lining I see blood. I check myself internally once more and realise I have internal bleeding, with blood coming from the walls of my vagina. I do not panic nor do I dread. The only word I can use is disbelieving. Nothing dawns on me as I survey the damage inflicted upon me, though I am perturbed at the sight of the milky fluid which runs out of me. I also notice the blood which has stained the top cover on the bed. I realise that it is my blood. Now my insides are burning. As I

32

move my legs the dry skin of my vaginal wall rubs together and it is excruciatingly painful.

I get dressed as quickly as I can, with shock barking at me, demanding me to tell Iris what has happened. But the full magnitude is deferred until the shock of the moment has gone. How long that will take I am not in position to say. All I know is that I have somehow passed out fully clothed and have woken up to find my body has been soiled to the extent I am bleeding. Before I leave the room, I make one final inspection of myself and the room around me.

For some reason, I remember that each time I have inserted a tampon, the passage is blocked by my hymen. I put my hand inside my knickers and try and feel for that fold of skin - whatever it is. I feel nothing. It is a final confirmation that someone - something, has entered me.

Apart from the stain I leave on the top sheet of the bed, I leave no trace of my presence in the bedroom. As quick as I can, I get myself to the bathroom and splash ice cold water on my face. I need to sober up. I need to think. I want to go home. I want out of this house as soon as I can. I berate the alcohol clogging my thoughts for not diffusing through my system. I can barely keep my balance as I head down the stairs to the hallway. I am freezing cold and remember my coat. James' coat has gone. I reach for the door handle.

"Iris."

Through my stupor, I recognise my name, though I do not recognise the bearer of the voice.

"Iris – it is me, ."

The knot of Brodie's tie is hanging halfway between his belt and his collar and he holds on to the frame of a door for dear life. In his left hand is a bottle of Irish whiskey. I hide my face, just in case it is bruised and have little time for what he is about to say. Brodie is about as drunk as it is possible to be. His words are slurred and indistinct.

"Speak to me tomorrow Iris," he shouts, as I leave.

"I have something I need to talk to you about."

I flag a cab on the street. The driver suspects nothing of my condition. I, too, am practically unaware of my condition. I am numb from head to foot. I feel no sorrow, no pity, no sadness. I cannot bring myself to cry because I cannot feel to the extent that tears have become necessary. I stare forlornly from the window as Chelsea, Battersea and the outer reaches of Clapham go by. There isn't a soul about. I look at my watch and realise that I have to be up in about two hours. I resolve not to go to bed but know that sleep is the only way I can banish the thought of what may have just happened to me. Still I feel nothing.

James is awake when I get back. He has no time for me though, as I can hear him groaning loudly, along with his accomplice. Only then do I become emotional. Safely in my bedroom I remove my clothes and see in the light the full extent of the congealed blood, the bruises and the rapidly forming barnacle scabs clinging to me. I run to and stand in the shower which is as hot as I can possibly make it. The volume of the tears rolling down my cheeks competes with the volume of water soaking my body. What have I done to deserve this? Why me – a woman without the need for intimacy of any sort? Why should it be me that falls foul of man?

I cry uncontrollably and once cleansed of this act of evil, put every item of clothing I have been wearing, having doused the lot in bleach, into the washing machine. How that washing machine never stopped due to the amount of powder I put in it, I shall never know. I watch and I watch - round and round the cylinder goes, with my blank stare to accompany it, as the clothes which once protected my innocence are exorcised of the hideous detritus of life. Not once do I look away. Not once do I have a thought in my head. Iris becomes a somnambulist as Iris watches the purity of my past being discarded down the tubes of a machine and out into the sewer beyond. Not once do I think of who, or rather, what kind animal has chosen to do such a thing to me. Shock is disallowing me thoughts of retribution; shock is disallowing me thought. And I am unknowingly watching all the evidence the law requires to substantiate any charges I can claim being washed away. For my soiled clothes - torn knickers, blood and semen-stained knickers, are corroborative evidence.

Now they are no evidence at all.

VII.

Edmund reeks when I meet him. He is still wearing the same clothes and admits that he has not been to bed. I can see he is still drunk before he opens is mouth. He looks tired. Strangely he looks worried.

"Iris; I think I have made a colossal error of judgement."

The pain between my legs is so great I have a great deal of difficulty concentrating on what he is saying. He sounds sad and pathetic - a man caught up in his own rounds of selfishness firing off at a face his confused mind thinks of as friendly. Right now I feel as though I don't have a friend in the world.

"Why did I do it, Iris?"

Rose spits out the words and is on the verge of tears. I offer him a tissue before he realises how close he is to losing his senses at Heathrow Airport. Without knowing why, I place my hand upon his shoulder. Through my own pain, perhaps, I recognise the symptoms in another.

"If he chooses to, he can ruin me. Why did I take such a blatantly stupid risk? What will Brodie do now? With that kind of knowledge he can clean me out. I need to speak to him. I need to hear what he has got to say. I need to know what he is going to do."

There is very little I can say - there is certainly very little I can do. I feel devoid of all sympathy. I want to put myself first, as indeed, I should do. Here I am, sitting down with immorality itself and trying to console him when precisely the same kind of immorality has caused me so much suffering. I want to leave. I want to go home and cry myself to sleep. But I cannot leave him. As sad and as pathetic as the man is, I feel the need just to be there. In my isolation, I too, feel alone. We have no one but consequence. And neither of us can bring ourselves to face consequence.

There is little else I can do but move closer to a man I have previously chosen to despise. I feel unclean. I feel dirty. The temple I owed little to has been ransacked by another and I do not know who is responsible. In terminal two at Heathrow Airport, I choose to tell someone of my ordeal and the one man on Earth I could never have imagined being frank with is the man who sits in front of me now.

I want to be honest - through my unadorned words he will recognise we are both caught in a tempest which genetics has conspired to bestow upon him and upon men - sexual urges he cannot control and sexual urges bestowed upon others which, faced with the façade of my beauty, could not be avoided.

"Edmund. I must tell you something I cannot keep to myself. In the four years we have worked together, I have shown you little of my feelings."

Edmund looks up. He takes his hands away from his face and looks at me, searching for clues as to what I am about to say.

"My dear - what is it?"

I take him by the hand, leading Edmund toward the unoccupied ladies' bathroom while we fleetingly attract the attention of passers-by.

Edmund is incredulous.

"In here?"

I beckon Edmund to come with me and we enter a cubicle. I sit him down while I stand, and for the second time in six hours tears begin to well in the corners of my eyes.

"There is no denying I have found it difficult to work with you over the last two years, knowing all I know. For the main part, I have chosen to keep my mouth shut. But I have no one to talk to at this moment and we are both one and the same. Last night, at that house in Chelsea, I became very drunk and passed out. When I woke up a couple of hours later, I found these injuries and I found blood covering the bed. That blood, was my blood."

I undo the zip which loosens the skirt around my waist. Edmund looks uncomfortable yet realises that this isn't some sort of sordid joke. He can see from my tears - tears he would never have imagined, that I have sunk to a level even I have not imagined. As I hitch up my skirt he sees the bruises at the top of my inner thigh - the bruises which extend to my vagina. For a second, as I pull back material and show him, he just stares; for a second he is caught between nothing and knowledge as his mind slowly unveils the truth behind my tears. And slowly, as I stand there without saying a word, his eyes travel up my body as I let my skirt fall down around my legs.

"Oh my dear. I am most terribly sorry. I am most terribly, sorry."

I am trembling. Showing these wounds to another human being brings home to me the full gravity of what has happened. Shock has now subsided and been replaced with despair. I can barely stand up. Edmund Rose looks upon me, puts his arms around me and I fall into his large frame, feeling my strength ebb away as I dissolve into him, crying endlessly on his shoulder and he tends to me with a gentleness I should never have expected. After five minutes of his bear hug, he lets me go.

"I know this is difficult for you," he says, a snap of aggression colouring the tones of his voice, "can you remember anything of what happened; anything at all?"

"The little I have tried to remember of the minutes before I went upstairs to find James. All I can remember is waking up on the bed. My mind is blank."

Edmund pulls a handkerchief from his pocket. It is dirty, as I would expect, yet I draw solace and even a brief smile at the comfort and reassurance which takes over what would normally be repulsion.

"Listen to me, my darling. Let us get this day over with. I promise I shall help you. If I have spent my life being protected by my upbringing I promise you now that I shall do all I can with the power bestowed upon me to help you catch the man who has done this to you. Let us get through the day then we can think about what we can do next. I promise you, as I live and breathe, I will do all that is in my power to help."

I look up at him once more and the only sad, pathetic thing I can think of saying is, "thank you."

"Dry your eyes my dear. And remember your tears. We will never, between us, let this outrage pass."

I clear the tears from my eyes as we hear a woman's voice and Edmund remembers where he is. I open the cubicle door and cast my eyes upon a toilet cleaner who has just finished in the cubicle furthest away. She is dragging a mop and bucket into the cubicle adjacent to our own, when I appear, followed by Edmund. Her face is an oil painting, a photograph, a canvas, a still - half astonishment, half shock. Perhaps, so is ours when she looks at us, assumes the worst and shouts, after making the sign of the cross and in the most perfect East London accent - "it's a bit fackin early for that, innit?"

Edmund turns the colour of claret.

"Good morning, my dear," he replies.

"Sorry to have bothered you."

Outside, I laugh till my sides hurt. So does Edmund. Dark has lifted ever so slightly and I find myself giggling all the way to the aircraft. Only when the aircraft takes off, with Edmund fast asleep and snoring beside me, do I start thinking. Normally his snoring bothers me. Now it is a matter of benevolence on my part. In fact, I rather I enjoy it.

But my thoughts become dark again for, without trying to bring recollections forth, I get recollections in any event. I keep seeing a face, a gentle face - the face of a man I know I had a conversation with. I liked his smile; I enjoyed his conversation. I remember drinking red wine at his request and I recall going to find James.

As I look out over the English Channel, I begin to piece together what happened after I walked upstairs, looking from bedroom to bedroom. Room after room I stagger past and recall being at the top of the house. I remember walking down one flight of steps and light coming from a bedroom on the first floor. Finally I have it, rather I have the face of the man I had been speaking with in the kitchen.

I piece together a conversation. He tells me he is a frustrated painter, that he was an accountant, that he sold his house in London. He seems a philosophical man. I get an impression of gentility. But I cannot resolve the differences between my impressions and the very idea that it was he who took advantage of me in that hideous way.

As the French Alps approach, I look down upon the vast landscape outside, marvelling at the enormity of nature, the incalculable strength of the forces of nature and how we human beings are just passing victims to its power. I see birds below, content to follow the thermal winds lifting from the mountains and feel jealous of their simplicity. For each of the urges to eat, to kill and to protect that nature forces upon all of the animals upon Earth, one cannot blame them. This represents nature itself; this represents life. They know now not what they are. They cannot look down and know they are a bird, a tiger, a whale, an antelope, a fox, a heron. Nature imperils both the Earth and all inhabitants upon it, except one, to act according to a pre-programmed tapestry of cause and effect - of want and acquire. The one animal I think of which nature has thrown up, is the one creature of this idyll able to look down and around, knowing his place and being able to explain it. But just as the mountains rise up from the sea and the birds rise from the mountains, we too, cannot escape the imperatives which, in a final analysis, control us. The nature of the earth which I truly love, the nature of all animals which I love and respect, is not the only nature of man. The nature of man leads to destruction. Time and time again it is proved. We will fight for all that is meaningless in the face of nature but we submit to nature without realising it. As I look down upon the mountains, the forests, the valleys and lakes of Switzerland below, I castigate every living, breathing, fellow man on my planet. While I had, for better or worse, chosen to rise above the very fabric of nature and not give in to what I have been moulded into, I floated on air just like the birds outside. Now, with the pain between my legs, my injurious body and injurious mind, I have been cast down to dwell in the lower reaches of the Earth itself amongst the baseness and pervasive iniquity of mankind.

VIII.

Milan is dull. Time drags, elongating, punishing. Neither Edmund nor
   I have much to say. In our thoughts both of us are somewhere else.
During the meeting, which is just as I anticipated, with clouds of cigarette
smoke filling the room, suffocating each and every one of us and making my
head ache, Edmund and I cast each other glances as we try to sound
authoritative.

   I cannot bring myself to understand the quick Italian our banker client
fires at me. Eventually I insist that all conversation must take place in pidgin
English, much to our client's annoyance. Neither of us really cares and I
guess it shows. Edmund keeps yawning and I have to use every ounce of my
strength to stay awake. When the meeting is over we run as fast as we can,
not even stopping to say goodbye. If there are going to be repercussions we
do not care. All we want to do is go home.

   Back on the aircraft I can see that neither of us is able to sleep and as
business class is empty, I decide to ask Edmund a bit more about his past. I
realise there is a heart in him bigger than most and a sensitivity thoroughly
lacking in all the men I have known. I want reassurance. I am fully aware
that many of the stories I had been told about Edmund are hearsay. Given
that hearsay can't be relied upon, I want to tell Edmund what I know and
give him the chance of telling the truth.

   "They are just stories my dear."

   "I am tired of living in this cocoon and not knowing for sure. If you
choose to tell me it would help us both. I may be able to defend you."

   Edmund smiles. He seems happy to have someone beside him who
wants to listen. How, in his formative years, he must have yearned for
someone to speak to.

   I try to be judicious.

   "I can accept you whereas others, maybe can't. But there are rumours -
rumours of your tastes which lead to young men?"

   Edmund's smile evaporates. It is replaced by an intermittent reversion
to sadness and anger.

   "My dear, I have children of my own. I have a son and a daughter I
love very much. My relationship with the young extends only to those. Each

and every other word to the contrary is a complete falsehood. I admit that, although I have been a sinner in so many ways, I have sinned in this respect just once. And it was many years ago."

An inner caucus has opened up. I wait in anticipation, ready for Edmund to unveil. For four years I have suffered this man, never knowing for sure. This absurdity of place; this exposition I am about to hear carries with it a significance that to clarify, extends to and infuses all previous dismissal, prejudice, derogation and mental caprice on my part. I sit with bated breath.

"One evening I was leaving my club in St James. I had spent the evening with a couple of fellows from my days at Cambridge. Alone and outside, I was approached by three young men. Clearly they recognised that I had money, given from where I had just departed and I recognised them for what they were. However, I was unprepared when one came from behind and knelt down while the two in front pushed me over him. After they kicked me for what seemed like an age they rifled my pockets. My wallet was taken as was my money and my watch, which was a graduation present from my grandfather, who was a Bishop in the Church of England.

Eventually I passed out thanks to what I think was a particularly vicious kick to the head. It was dark and the streets of St James were sparsely populated at that time of night. I was left bleeding on the pavement, lying there for twenty minutes or more until I came around and tried to piece together what had happened.

When I opened my eyes and squinted into the darkness, I saw a figure I recognised as one of the street kids who had attacked me. Instinctively I curled into a ball so as to prevent further injury but he didn't strike me at all. In fact, he apologised and gave me a cloth with which to wipe away my blood. Then from his pocket he produced my watch, opened my hand and gave it back.

Part of me was furious and wanted to call the police. But part of me was touched that this child, who was a little under eighteen years of age, had shown sufficient remorse to help me and risked being arrested and charged with theft. In fact he helped me to my feet and when I stood up, I caught sight of a gentle face disguised by dirt and clothes fit only for a rubbish bin. While I tried to wipe blood from my nose and nurse the cuts to my head, his kindness mixed with no doubt a sense of guilt, assisted me to the extent that he accompanied me to the casualty department of St Thomas's Hospital, in Waterloo and waited with me while I received professional treatment."

I dare not pre-empt what I think I am about to hear.

"Iris; he turned out to be a wonderful man. He was kind and gentle with me and showed remorse beyond all expectation. I knew he was from the street and he had been as rough as one may imagine but I soon forgave him. He even gave me what he said were the only pennies in his pocket in order that I could get the bus home."

"You kept in touch?"

"Well, the dear boy was insistent and made me promise to see him again."

"And your homosexuality - it didn't bother him?"

"Well my sexual leanings were not at all clear to me at that stage. I guess I had sublimated them from an early age and was hardly in a position, with a wife and two young children to look after, to let what were residual inclinations arise. Life was complicated enough.

I grew to love that boy more than any other human being I have ever met. And yes, I suppose over time, my feelings for him turned to love, as did his for me."

"But did he ever make any proclamations of his feelings for you or for anyone before you?"

"Well we discussed it much later. I found out that Anthony had always had feelings for women and had never considered sexual relations with other men. So we both entered the relationship innocent in terms of the past and innocent in terms of the future.

You know there is a rumour that the day I made partnership I immediately told all and sundry at the firm that I was a homosexual, which then, as today, is taboo in this graceless environment we live in. The rumour thereafter turns on my relationship with my wife and the untruth that I went straight home and told her I was leaving. Well, both rumours are absolute falsehoods.

I spent many months agonising over my feelings for Anthony. Anthony, I know, spent just as many months agonising over his feelings for me. Only at a very advanced stage did I even contemplate taking the course of action I eventually undertook. And there isn't a day goes by without my heart being racked with guilt over the shame, the embarrassment, the very essence of the harm I did to my wife, my children and my family."

I want to ask the question - *the* question.

Edmund answers it for me.

"I swear on the life of my dear mother, that Anthony and I never put a hand on each other until the day he had turned the age of consent. Only then did I submit to my feelings. And nor have I ever laid my hands on any boy knowingly since. For me, he was the one and I miss him terribly."

It takes Edmund some considerable effort to carry on.

"Anthony and I thought the price of being together was too high a price to pay. Of course I looked after him financially, as I still do. I bought him a flat in Highgate where he lives, content but alone. I support him as much as I can and in many ways he is the brother I never had. But the relationship was never going to work. I had too much to lose and he had his innocence to preserve. Anthony and I rarely get together. And you see, my dear, it is a broken heart which has caused me to lead this double life, this duplicitous life where I pretend to the world at large that I am strong but am only too aware that my weaknesses, my need for attention from males without recourse to actually knowing those males, is both being the victim of a repressed sexuality I cannot control and of a society which has sought to repress my sexuality. I cannot pretend I do not have feelings when I have an abundance of them. Nor can I keep those feelings to myself when satiating my desires is so close and anonymously at hand."

Edmund Rose and Iris are opposites. I have no feelings toward the opposite sex in terms of sharing my body. But why am I so upset at being soiled by someone else against my will? Is it the lack of choice? Is it the inner invasion? Is it the desecration of an innocence I had so jealously guarded and reserved for myself? And what of the perpetrator's feelings? Was he overcome in that particular moment or was he calculating with no need for the kind of drunkenness which obliterates conventional morality? And is there a great deal in Edmund Rose which is within this criminal who has stolen my virtue? Both may have acted on impulse on a great many occasions. And both may have acted as slaves to their biology in letting their minds slip. But who am I to care of these philosophical concerns? It is my body which is bruised. It is I who is in physical and mental anguish. And the thoughts I hold today will colour me for the rest of my life.

"Iris; I had a choice. Anthony had a choice. Neither you nor my wife had any choice whatsoever. I followed my heart into what some may say is folly, hypocrisy - the essence of that dilemma between the blind desire nature still holds for us, and control. But the animal who has treated you so badly and the animal in me who had no choice but to treat my wife so badly, is one worthy of contempt. My story is sad because it is built upon weakness. You have to be strong now to overcome the weakness in others which has caused you so much harm. Don't be cynical nor bitter. One can't place the sins of one man upon the head of the rest of us. This is something I have begged of my wife and please God, I think I have succeeded. Please do not fall into the same trap. Let me take care of you over the next few weeks and I promise, I shall return the investment many times over."

IX.

At Edmund's insistence, I take some time off work. So does Edmund, which is unprecedented and a mistake. Brodie's calculus will be one of weakness on Edmund's part, though Brodie has become the unknown, his motives unknown, his thoughts, unknown.

I do nothing except watch television. I take in everything I can from the early morning to the late evening with absolute sloth, my enervating buddy. I see it all - the monstrous banality of that which passes for morning television gradually giving way to the downright idiocy programme planners spew out the rest of the day.

Sometimes I am actually interested, at other times I just stare, mesmerised by this preoccupation which infects the hinterland between thought and action. I see people and come to recognise faces and names I had heard or seen on adverts plastered on the inside of the tube. This is a playground for the mentally defunct and such temporary mental retardation suits me, just fine.

The only time I trespass through the front door of our flat involves trips to the supermarket. Even here perceptions are taken to task. Whereas all I had been used to as a professional was the professional, all I can see in Clapham are rough and tumble people mixing en masse with the Land Rover cabal.

For more than a month, I mutate, assimilate, delineate, erect and affiliate to a previously unknown sociologist, an amateur psychologist, a psychiatrist, an anthropologist. No doubt I have the perspectives of a bad novelist, an appalling zeitgeist apologist. Though I make no apology for it. Still I let prejudice sing inside my head, throwing socks at daytime talk shows on the television, hissing at the vile nature of these half-humans whose ego riddles them while they present me with entertainment based on the best way to boil an egg. There are celebrity chefs, ugly couples with chatterbox tendencies, inflated opinions, deflated invective, champions of the people, quiz shows with pre-school questions the public get wrong, discussions about tampons or pads, discussions about boils, do-good advise-badly doctors whose aftershave I can smell at home, charlatan lawyers, shoulder-pad women with square jaws coveting hats of hair lacquer, reformed thieves, bisexuals, active thieves, inactive homosexuals, debates on olive oil, bad actors, good authors, bad authors, fashion gurus, straight hairdressers, straight and gay interior designers, psychiatric counsellors, men with genital warts, psychiatric patients getting real time advice, repeats and repeats, re-runs and new episodes of some God-awful programme in which misery is the norm and all attention is focused on the local pub. I see films with no meaning; I see meaning dressed up as no meaning with no real meaning at all and I hear the same voices on the same commercials selling the same shit with different names that by the end of the second week a little bit of me is glad I have spent years discussing money with bowler hats in the City.

Then I'd walk through supermarkets snarling at passers-by for being just the type of person I'd associate with the audience of a morning chat show, snarling at incontinent women who push shopping trolleys around for want of a dog, at dogs mysteriously attached to the wrists of beggars by pieces of frayed blue string, at madmen, at sane men down on their luck. And all the time, as another mum with the perfect boy-girl set trundles past with the children oozing repression and sucking on chocolate, I congratulate myself on the redundancy of my thought - of the once in a lifetime, beautiful negativity of the whole process. For that entire month or so, I do not have a decent bone in my body. Everyone I see is deformed, deficient, disgusting and denuded by the insidiousness of my thoughts.

For my anger at my circumstance has chosen to direct itself toward those who have no idea of themselves in this black universe and no idea of my pain. I should have pity on them, congratulating myself on the fact that I am not retarded by my attacker or otherwise. I am not disgusting in my habits. I am not poor in mind. I am not decrepit and unknowing. I see and hear a million revolting voices. I see and hear a million examples which should make me, Iris, feel a million times better. How television throws up all that is bad about my race. How all that is bad about my race uses the London airspace during those times when I venture outside. I have a lot to feel grateful for and a lot to be grateful for.

Still, mental and physical pain colour all I think. I cannot sleep. I have insidious nightmares. I jump when I hear voices outside and as the key turns in the door when James comes home from work. What takes hold is fear - fear of the known and fear of the opposite. No matter how I try to rationalise, I suffer the indignity of not knowing whether I will rise from the depths to which my emotional state has descended.

Still, the overpowering urge, notwithstanding my fear, is to try not to give in to hate, to trepidation, timidity and concern. I had hitherto trained my mind and if not trained, been gifted a mindset which refused to look into this goldfish bowl of emotion and feeling but to analyse from the outside - to analyse the innards of others. Perhaps that very mindset will return while I reside within this goldfish bowl because I know what lies outside. I am too old to change and too proud to let circumstance change me. If I can direct my anger in the appropriate way, when the time is right - if ever the time is right.

The telephone rings continuously. I refuse all calls though one particular enquiry is from Edmund. Replete in my isolation, I confess I am touched he has made the effort with a plate as full as his and with what his imagination could be telling him. Other callers are mostly colleagues who cannot understand how I could dare to relinquish even a week of work - claiming that I am ill. I am ill, though not in the way they understand. Maybe I was in trouble clinically before the attack. Maybe the very essence of my thought processes have always verged on definitions of madness. But I didn't think so then, though I knew I was different. Now, though perhaps it is with hindsight that a definitive diagnosis can be made, I am troubled by a deep depression which causes me pain and reflects the pain I have suffered and which stores up pain - physical and emotional, whilst my body reflects the trauma and the utter indignity of the attack, the intrusion, the rape. I am living through clinical depression wherein I hack away at the environment and all aspects of the social world I temporarily perceive with the utmost disregard. I knew I was critical, cynical, dismissive and derogatory before the attack but in depression, I store and offload sentiments bordering on hatred. Should they subside of their own accord and in their own time?

James notices. Every evening he inquires as to my condition. Sweet James. He is the one human being in my proximity I have time for. I can see that my intransigence when questioned annoys him. He knows something is amiss - that something has happened. He has never known me to take so long off work, nor has he known me to sit in front of a television and do nothing else. I cannot tell him and do not want to. I need to keep James, like all of mankind, away from me. Protection lies in my psychological isolation, clarifying then classifying the issues for myself.

Save that time ebbs and my chemistry changes. I can sense it. I cannot feel it. Intuitively I know it has nothing to do with depression; intuitively I sense and then see the mutation, the change, the developments within which appear, predictably, given what has taken place given the mind to which they become apparent.

Mutations, excretions, release and catharsis normally arising at the time of each and every month, do not arise. As regular as clockwork, each and every month since I was thirteen years of age, I suffer as most women suffer, the pain that commences in the stomach, travels through the body and discourages the mind from any sort of rational feeling. I have come to recognise the sign that I am about to submit to biological inevitability, as madness takes over for a few days before it subsides and pain takes over when I begin to ooze blood.

Blood - yes, blood, consequent upon the internal fluctuations within a woman. It seems anomalous and is anomalous that I leak into a cotton wool pad for four or five days every month. Men have no such affliction and care not for their bodies in the way they abuse their bodies, thinking little of their physical selves until, by and large, it is too late. But women - for reasons of vanity in many cases and self-awareness from the youngest age, spend so much time over how they feel, how they are, both inside and out, how they wish to protect themselves, both inside and out; I cannot imagine a man doing the same thing - eating fruit because it is good for you; not getting too drunk because too drunk is bad for you; abstaining from challenge, mischief and physical violence because they see, through fragility, that they are at risk. For the majority of women, unknowing, it does not and cannot happen. It didn't happen to me save that I was conscious of my body for one week a month, save that my body was not conscious of me. Now my body calls me and speaks to me, beckoning Iris to its change, offering a lament to what it was and how it suffers, to how it alters. I can sense it and now, strangely, I can feel it.

I venture to the chemists. And meekly, I suppose, ask the advice of the worldly girl at the counter as to what I should do. To her credit she is most helpful. It is to do with the colour. If it turns a certain colour you are one but if the applicator turns to the alternative it is just possible that my biology has let me down and I am two.

Colour acts against me. I sit in my bathroom and stick to the written instructions. Slowly I look on as the appearance and the sheer irrelevance of the colour in relation to what it means, filters into my disbelieving and resigned outlook. I am looking at the first evidence that, not only have I been raped while unconscious, but also the seed of the rapist has been left inside me and is taking its first cakewalk-tentative steps toward forming a new life. In as much as certainty is apparent on a Sunday afternoon in a bathroom in Clapham, I look down upon a colour which confirms what each and every woman I hear in conversation on the subject dreads. I have been raped, and Iris is pregnant.

I try to take the information in my stride. I look upon my stomach and attempt to imagine what is going on there, at what chemicals had combined into what Cics declare is life. At first I cannot see it that way. I want whatever is invading me without permission expunged from my body - immediately, irrevocably. I think about doing it myself. But what am I looking for? Many old wives tales clarify the procedure and all end in disaster. With time meaning time without meaning I stare at my stomach and want that intruder taken from me and banished. This is evidence of greed. It is evidence of want. It is evidence of evil itself.

But Iris takes over. Gone is the depression which stalks then pounces - back to reason and control. I am pregnant but the process of having the position clarified by that little coloured tube gives my thoughts a sense of direction. I have decisions to make. I need to work out the character of behaviour required in order to resolve, to my own satisfaction, a direction, a destination and a conclusion.

I weigh my options. I have already decided on the futility of going to the police pursuant to my immediate stupidity in having washed and bleached the underwear which carried the DNA fingerprint of the assailant. Law is an irrelevance. There is only one question. Do I have the child or do I take steps toward having this pestilence sequestered from my innocent body?

Is it a life I withhold?

When does it become a life?

Would it matter even if I did consider it life for it is dependent upon me for its existence. If I choose not to eat, it will die. This germ, this seedling, has no life of its own. It belongs to me and I should be able to do with it what I like. However, like it or not, I, Iris, have put myself in a position through my own choice - to drink, to lose control, to attend that party in which circumstances arose where men could forget restraint. I have no right to blame the trappings of excess within. It is not this germ's fault. It was no fault of the intruder that I was negligent when I know only too well what men think and do. So why should I bestow upon myself the right to eradicate the blameless?

Yet cruelty does not and never did become me. Even as a child, I remember refusing to join the throng as consciously I made the effort not to hurt even the tiniest speck of life - animal or human. So why should I choose to do it now?

It is a misallocation of blame.

Still, there are consequences. I am utterly unsuited to the idea of motherhood and to motherhood itself. How can an obvious career woman even countenance the idea that a child is possible?

The reply is obfuscation for I would be using the career girl option as a way of disguising my true feelings, or, in point of fact, my lack of them.

Should I be listening to my feelings now?

What are feelings, anyway?

Feelings more often than not lead to the type of trouble for the bearer that I do not desire. The decision Iris has to make must have little to do with feelings. This has to be a reasoned settlement. I have to come down on one side of what was in essence, an academic search for the appropriate response.

Am I engendered with the attribution of blame for the innocent?

Will I displace my gentleness and take out the insidiousness of my pain upon the life which, in only a few more days, will have the form of a body - arms, legs, torso, head?

47

Upon this decision I know my life will change. Upon this decision I know I have to face the consequences which will live with me until I am not able to reason any longer. To have a child or not to have a child? Not so much a question but a definition of existence beyond the purview of a single mind, for with one summation of thought I may choose to bring into the world another who will live beyond me. There are far more consequences than immediacy and the near-sighted selfishness of my concerns. I will keep this child. I will not give in to hate, to displaced revenge. I am stoic and will accept these circumstances. I will let this little chemical live. I will not blame the outcome of the criminal act for the outcome is innocent. I will have this child.

X.

Six weeks after the rape, a gravy train pulls in. Iris is back on the
Northern Line; the Northern Line is back upon Iris and it is as if I
have never left. I stand from Clapham Common to Kennington. At
Kennington, as usual, the train empties and fills with the year-on year-in
output of English public schools, off to the City of London where daddy and
generations of housemasters have informed them that the streets are paved
with gold.

Two smartly dressed men stand to my right. One is white and roughly
shaven, the other is black. By design they do not work with us as one of us. I
have them down as the more respectable type of Londoner who chooses to
work in the back rooms or the post room of the banks or law firms in the
City. Most are very decent people in fact - very decent. But not these two.

A woman stands directly in front of them. On a crowded tube such as
this, there is little room to breathe - there is little room to do anything save to
pray that there are no delays and suffocation can be avoided. So I stand to
one side, stultified and controlled, huffing out of boredom because there
isn't a conversation to be had, until I see her purse hanging out of her bag,
presenting itself to these two friends, who notice.

I watch them discreetly. I see their eyes flit from one carriage occupant
to another and I see them weigh up their chances of success.

It is so, so simple. The purse is practically falling out and by the cut of
the owner, it is either stuffed with cash, or full of credit cards which might
not be missed until lunchtime. I know what they were going to do and in
some sense I admit - who can blame them?

I look around the carriage. I notice a smallish, middle-aged man nearby,
who, through the pattern of bodies, can see between people and understands
what is about to take place. His initial expression is incredulity; his instinct
is to hide and to read whatever of the morning newspaper he possibly can.
He knows what is about to happen. He tries to pretend it isn't about to take
place.

Then a hand protrudes discreetly from under a sleeve, taking advantage
of the jerks and jolts of the antique track. The purse comes free easily. It is
slipped from the bag from which it is hanging and slid into the open pocket

of a holdall.

I watch though I take care not to look at matters directly, casting my eye between these petty criminals and this gentlemen, so called, who, like me, sees it all.

What do I do?

I am caught somewhere between an analysis of everything about these tedious thieves and this extremely wealthy man who is privy to the theft. What are his thoughts? Is he thinking about saying anything to the lady whose goods have been stolen or is he reminding himself of a Londoner's duty to keep oneself to oneself, no matter what happens - inaction speaking louder than words?

For a second I imagine a young and pretty secretary at his beck and call. I imagine toadying acolytes built in his own image, listening and glorifying every word of supposed profundity to emerge from his mouth. I imagine the sound of a slap on a back when a mirror presents another master of the universe, or an indistinct reflection distinguishing the genius looking back from the clear glass partitions of some high-powered meeting room where multi-million pound decisions hang off his every word. The reality is a coward rising from the ashes of a reputation built upon façade. It annoys me. It annoys me.

As opposed to grabbing the criminals, who, with pounds stencilling their eyes seem smug and satisfied, I move toward this appalling little man and let rip, for he may take himself to work and arrive to a trumpet voluntary of sycophancy but when social responsibility calls, his ears, his eyes and his actions report missing.

"Do you not feel shame?" I shout.

"Do you not feel weak, unable as you are to raise even a scintilla of decency and confront these two thieves?

Do you not feel a sense of utter revulsion for yourself as you watched those two steal that women's purse?

You - pin-striped grey suit, blue shirt, grey hair and maroon tie."

I point at him and as my finger shows clearly the object of my wrath, the victim checks her bag and realises her purse has been taken.

"You will find your goods in the side pocket of that holdall."

Still my attention falls upon another.

"Yes, you. I am talking, to you."

I push a passenger aside and when I reach his newspaper, it falls with my graceless chop. Around me, two things happen. Those on that carriage - clearly not the public school, cricket-on-the-village-green type, stand up to see what is happening while those who are the public school, cricket-on-the-village-green type, whether they are adjacent to me or not, assume this altercation is an unfeasible discord to the slow pulse of morning solace.

"No doubt, you probably think yourself profound. I have no doubt you think yourself worthy. But how worthy are you as you watch an unknowing woman have her belongings stolen by two cheap, opportunistic thieves? Do you feel a sense of shame in not acting? Do you not feel any guilt that this woman could have suffered immeasurably because, deep down, you are a coward?"

Behind me, one of the thieves is trying to give the purse back to the victim. I hear him mutter an excuse, obviating himself of blame.

"Take no notice," I yell.

"I saw him discuss the possibility then steal the purse, while this paragon of virtue here watched. I mean I would have thought you had a bit of chivalry in that well-fed frame. I may well have assumed you had more than an ounce of decency. You are pathetic. Yes you - the man I am pointing at for the benefit of everyone interested on this carriage."

I turn to the victim.

"Are you going to have these two arrested? I am sure," I say, sarcastically and pointing at my victim, "this model citizen will be your witness."

A voice tells me to leave it alone. I turn to see a young man wearing round horned spectacles, bearing down upon me. He recoils when he sees the look in my eyes.

"Please, just…"

"And why should I do that?"

Sheepishly he looks at the floor, like a child admonished for speaking up but out of turn.

"I seem to have embarrassed you. Fine. Talk to a woman's back but turn to face me and all you can do is whimper away, frightened and tiny. Come to think of it - is there anyone on this tube willing to admit they are not embarrassed by a display of silence in the face of a blatant wrong?

"Which one of you defenders of the moral code by which you earn such a substantial living is willing to face up to what is happening here and defend this woman?"

I glare. I, glare. Only one speaks up. The bearer of the voice is the owner of the cowardice who watched the incident from the beginning. Through some sense of shame he feels his place to articulate what the others feel. His accent is pinched and upper crust.

"They made a mistake, that is all. It was an opportunity which simply presented itself and they took it without thinking. I mean all they did was to take someone else's property. It is hardly theft."

Speechless with rage, I turn and grab the woman who has had her purse taken, pulling her toward me, trying try to show her as a face indicative of loss.

"I am sorry to be so much trouble to you and I am very grateful, really I am. But I have my purse back now and I am sure they didn't mean it. I am sure it was just a bit of fun.

Can't we just forget it?"

Her face is pleading and her voice falters. I turn to the thieves who sense my cause is lost. They look at me and one smirks knowingly. The other leans over to whisper in my ear.

"Any chance of your telephone number?"

I open my mouth and a monologue appears, delivered quietly, so quietly that I bet no one else save for these two characters, can hear.

"I bet you never considered bravery when your hand entered her bag and you took her property. It was about what you and this hideous looking fuckwit could get away with. There again if you had considered your behaviour in terms of bravery you wouldn't have considered it, would you?

"Bravery is a man's answer to circumstances where he could take advantage but chooses not to. I look at you now and I do not see a man. You are less than a man. I see less than a man who calls himself a man but has failed in relation to every expectation ever placed upon his head, a man with nothing more than a job in which he is eminently replaceable and a pay packet earned for employment which wouldn't tax a monkey. But there again that is all you are - a monkey. A salaried monkey.

"I bet a little bit of pride is now beginning to surface in your brain. I bet the bravery reference gets to you the most as you think of all the opportunities you know you have missed with the benefit of hindsight. You have no courage. You have no integrity. You have no backbone - all you have developed into is the most despicable kind of rodent. You couldn't even resist asking me out, not because you thought I would say yes but because you felt superior to someone you knew was infinitely superior to your hideous little self. Brave you are not, pathetic you are. Take yourself off to your monkey-suit job, continue getting your kicks out of those cowardice allows you to take advantage of. Taking advantage of the vulnerable is the very definition of a coward itself."

I notice long before my monologue is over that eye contact has been lost. His eyes glaze as his supposed friend looks away. When the train stops, I stop talking. I stare right between his eyes as both of them leave the carriage. Only when the tube doors close does all of the anger welling up inside him, all of the pride his cowardice would not let him extol, burst into torrents of abuse.

"You bitch. You fucking bitch," he shouts, banging the tube doors.

"You fucking bitch."

When the train pulls away he grabs his crutch and squeezes it. I stand in silence as the intelligentsia carry on, pretending it is nothing to do with them. Every now and again one or other looks at me to examine me and establish who and what I am. I am a parasite, a leper, a runt. One is either a member of the club of silence or one is not.

"Tell me, which one of you feels superior to the man who stole the purse?"

Silence.

"Which one of you?"

Silence vindicates - empty vessels do indeed, make the least noise.

What of the woman whose purse was stolen?

She gets off the tube along with me. I follow behind but in front of the man who saw events unfold. She turns and she smiles at him. I listen closely as they exchange pleasantries by name, sharing a laugh with each other and at my expense. They know each other and they work with each other. I bite my lip and hide. Welcome back to the City of London, Iris. Welcome back.

XI.

Still quietly spitting, I arrive at work. On my chair is a note from
Edmund. I am to make an excuse about a client meeting and leave.
Edmund has invited me to lunch at The Maundeville, St James, as his guest.

All the excuses I need are in that note. I about-turn, slide my coat on,
leave the building and head toward Fleet Street thinking how beautiful St
Paul's Cathedral is and how enticing it is just to wallow in the early morning
streets of London, knowing I have deferred the need to face the life I have
chosen.

On the way, I pop into a little coffee shop I know and sit in the window
with a milky latté gratuitously loaded with Demerara sugar, staring down
Ludgate Hill at the swathes of money-hungry parasites as they head toward
their esurient good offices. Off the next train and the next train they arrive,
crashing onto the pavement in slow, inconsistent waves, pouring in from
stations adjacent to Ludgate Hill and Blackfriars, squeezed into a bottleneck
where Iris can compare.

Bankers are the most palpable. On Mondays the average banker will
adorn a pink shirt accompanied by a bespoke suit of the highest quality -
suits scored with luminous lining underscored with handmade shoes of a
type too obscure by name for me to recall. The right to luminosity is the
fiscal road to nirvana in the stale and staid world of the banker. Alas,
luminosity is a tangent for a dullard though vivacity is the message, loud and
clear. One banker carries a huge umbrella, even on this clear and sunny day,
just in case vanity and the water-weary fissures of the heavens conflate.

I count one banker for every ten men. Some turgid cross-sectional
survey informs me that one in ten worker drones in the City of London is a
banker - one in ten of these ogres stumbling past is the perfect catch for
someone whose life is built around the assimilation of the perfect catch.

Lawyers are similarly obvious, distinguished by their replica pink shirts
as nearly-men but not quite - replete in their jealousy of the hours bankers
work and the bonuses bankers earn while servicing the needs of the banker,
the company, the conglomerate, the multi-national, the financial whole.

There is no resort to appendage in the lawyer as all are comparative
block-heads without the necessary luck or the connections to get them to the

fiscal coalface. There are no handmade shoes, no college ties, no Ferraris at home in Chelsea. Social status arises in the English social landscape not with a professional qualification - one must have money to go with it. Alas, lawyers cannot compete and neither can they distinguish themselves by façade. All they are apt to do is follow the rainmakers without ever truly emulating the suavity which, as a matter of course, must accompany this new élite.

So then, what of old money?

Old money has little place among us drones. The march of the upper middle-class across the moneyed landscape has meant the departure of the classic Eton type, whose stupid brother lands at Sandhurst or Lloyds while he travels effortlessly through Oxford or Cambridge and attracts interest upon interest in a merchant bank. My colleagues are all minor public school or worse and to the chagrin of the ageing hegemony, sometime common achievers from the proletarian untermenschen - drinking cheap French lager, flashing money without class - with little decorum and limited taste. No wine, no port, no house in the country, no winters in the Caribbean, Gstaad, no summers in the South of France.

So too, do the back-room people walk by - the secretaries, runners, photocopiers, cleaners and waiters who service the service industries who service the prevailing system. They are easy to point out for they are shabbily turned out, with nylon shirts, polyester ties, pot bellies, an ashen veneer brought on by ritualistic nicotine and alcohol abuse, a wide gait, too much make-up, bad hair, shaved hair, loose-fitting shiny suits and incongruent colours. They talk incessantly and defer constantly to the great and the good without ever knowing why - concerned only with collecting enough money to indulge themselves twice a year in the Mediterranean and twice a week in a parochial nightclub with a member of the opposite sex. They are marked by little ambition, or if they are ambitious, they have neither the courage nor the imagination to actually make something of it.

I survey those I see and I pass off my opinions, superficial as they are, as the truth. I do not dismiss life but simply categorise so as to fit in with what Iris thinks is observational objectivity. It is, in fact, plain old prejudice. I do not see the tiny bits of existence they see. No; I am able to study them through the lens of a giant, self-invented macroscope and my acumen lies in my knowledge of how they all fall in with each other while their knowledge extends only to themselves and their kind.

Looking upon the dregs of my coffee cup and at the residue swilling around the bottom of this mug, I consider this dubious talent to be a waste unless I can put it to some use. I consider the child I carry. I resolve not to leave the individual I bear to work matters out for him or herself. I want to infuse this child with a knowing which blesses this child with a chance to feel and a chance to understand, too. Far too long have I been surrounded by those who feel and react only, or people who cannot feel but spend their lives trying to. This child will be neither a machine nor a reactive animal. It will have the best of both, unfortunate, worlds.

I look at this disparate commonality one last time. Analysis of their differences begins to bore me. Now I want none of it and consider ways to escape for the morning before I meet Edmund at lunch.

Should I go home?

I decide against it. I decide to take a walk toward Trafalgar Square and see how I can forget who I am, who they are and what I will become. But as I stare, present but not in attendance, a figure comes toward me, unmistakeable in its form and outlandishly different in its appearance.

Cutting a dash, even compared to the ubiquitous banker, he stands out immediately - more so with his incongruous physicality. His waist is high and his torso extends but a few inches above his belt line which is but a few inches below his armpits. With hair is as pitch black as ever, he has made a forlorn attempt to grow a beard. His beard, such as it is, serves only to increase the size of his head which has clearly outgrown the rest of his body, while his undersized shoulders and thin neck have not the right to develop the strength to hold such a bulb, up.

With male pattern baldness gracing his advance, he walks, leaning forward as he does so, with a peaked crown resembling an ominous black arrow leading the way - not that he looks down and forward only - he looks constantly at his reflection in the windows of the shops, checking his appearance and at intervals, slowing down to give himself more time to confirm he looks exactly the way he wants to before he gets to work.

When he is opposite, he crosses the road and heads directly for the shop in which I sit. But I feel safe for I know the tarnished glass of the coffee shop window and the low reflection of the sun means he can little distinguish me. As he comes closer, I can hear him. Each time his shoes hit the London pavement they give off a sharp click as the metallic heels he had obviously had a cobbler fit, make him stand out from the crowd. It draws my attention to his shoes. He is short, what I have not hitherto noticed is that he would have been an awful lot shorter had he not had the heels of his shoes built up so as to give him some extra inches in height.

There are some - some who try to distinguish themselves in the City by their dress. But there aren't many who are so insecure of their place but so aware of the minds of others who try and protect themselves by portraying an image developed on some far flung celluloid.

A cherubic Celt is playing to the message. He is not tall; he is tiny. He has no male physique as he has an utterly inexplicable physique. He has neither the dark, classical look nor does he have anything other than the jaw line of a child. And his hair, including the scrag which has fought its way out of his face, is neither natural nor befitting. It is the bosom of the bottom of an sabled inky bottle.

Could the barriers he has erected; could his arrogance actually allow him to see himself for what he is?

I doubt it. As he crosses the road he is oblivious for all he is doing is looking at his reflection in the glass. He is oblivious to who is inside that shop. He is oblivious to me.

I watch as he prunes his hair. I watch as he puckers his lips and gently scratches his neck, lifting back his head so he could check the progress of what could be loosely called a beard. I watch as he gives me a blast of his yellow-white teeth and I watch as Brodie, now satisfied with the gravitas he thinks he exudes, proceeds to put his hand inside the side pocket of his satchel, producing a pipe and a lighter and letting out a few puffs as the smell of rancid carcinogenic shag begins to fill the streets. He smiles at himself, turns and prepares himself for the glorious walk up Ludgate Hill in the direction of St Paul's Cathedral.

How many men have walked up that street - great men and infamous men? How many 'men' worthy of that epitaph, whatever it means, have stood on the corner of Ludgate Hill and bravely consigned themselves to their fate, King and commoner alike? How many have faced the gallows or the roar of the crowd? How each had a sense of place and that rare epitaph - power. How each compares to this hideous little atom who thinks so much of himself I dare not consider. All I know is that Brodie's evident insecurity aligned to his pride and his vanity has so much within to threaten me that a sense of foreboding fills. I so want him to leave. He is looking at me through the glass but all he sees is himself. It is all he wants to see.

Yet something or someone, catches his eye. It isn't me. The object is, in fact, a woman mixed and indistinguishable, like a chosen grain of salt shaken with multiplicitous grains of pepper. Her head is bowed; her eyelids seem destined to shield her eye line from looking up. But to Brodie her attention seems worthy of breaking his own attentiveness to himself and he breaches the crowd in order to pluck her from it.

A few words are exchanged. With her back to me I cannot see her face. And I cannot immediately pick her status because of it. I have her back and the black pony tail which swings around the back of her hat. I have hunched shoulders. I have the impression of deferral - Brodie seeming didactic, she seemingly unsure.

Not till Brodie returns to my window do I get a more coherent chance at estimation. Though her eyes are obscured under the dark shadow thrown by the hat's circular brim, I counter a solemnity in penitence as she stands next to him while Brodie continues to preen, that marks her for me, that picks my interest, that pilfers my thought.

Yet, as Brodie seems to ignore her, muttering execrables under his breath, I see her sharp in her observable eye movements, deferring and deferring again as she concurs and concurs to the multitudinous platitudes I imagine emanating from his villainous mouth.

Who is she?

Who is this woman who seems tied to his side, unable to break free from an illusory stranglehold and why the stranglehold in any event? She seems such a gentle creature, so lithe and graceful - a ballerina tagged to a troll held by his spell to the under-earth which envelops her. There is a gentle rythym to her repose. Brodie mutters, adjusting his tie, smoothing his follicles, carried to a constant pulse by her looks of solicitude which follow his words, waiting for her to agree, while her eyes dart to his façade then curtail and sink once more to the ground, accompanied by quick and nervy flicks of the eyelashes which sheath her eyes. She looks to be in fear of him and she looks in awe of him. He, certainly, is in control of her though he cannot seem to see her timorous frame, the shoulder blades bent around a collapsed sternum and a neck which falls into her chest.

If he takes two steps forward, so does she. If he steps sideways, so does she - it is the dance of a minion not a tango of the betrothed. The rythym of his words, the contiguity of her body suggest to me something deeply unhealthy and untoward. How does Brodie effect such control over such a plain, sweet-looking creature?

And why does she not object?

As he leaves, without a care for her attentions, he receives her attentions anyway. I crane my neck in order to watch them go. Her head remains bowed, he stops still periodically, once more to catch sight of himself in windows and glass doors. When he stops, this solemn woman stops just a few paces behind. She speaks only when spoken to - she defers, she defers. I am fascinated as they walk off together.

What is she to that man? What is that man to make her what she is? Impulses and twitchings attack me. It is the shroud which fascinates me - another pinching confirmation that I am confronted by less than a human being who feeds me fear. Yes it is the shroud - the hat which covers her eyes, the lashes which shield her eyes from recognition, the language of her body and the pretensions of her master that I think about until I have exhausted all my thought. Is this prisoner of circumstance his wife? If not, then who is it?

Who can she be?

What and who, is Brodie?

XII.

I spend the rest of the morning drifting in and out of shops in Soho. In daylight, the area is alien to me. I have set down on Pluto. As I stop to browse in bookshops, or sit outside, drinking coffee, I watch again - Iris forever watching. The area seems so full of life - schoolchildren speaking Spanish, Italian and French; designation people with mobile phones dipping in and out of sordid fetishistic iniquity; waifs and strays; down and outs; men selling sex to tourists and to locals alike - gay bars, gay restaurants, straight bars, straight restaurants. Traffic rams the streets with animate cars mixing freely with peculiarly animate people - media monkeys, immigrant London junkies; theatres packed to bursting; theatres picked to fail - the profane, the misfit, the vain, the sophisticated rubbing shoulders with flesh-tempting women selling their bodies as best they think they can.

How different to the City. Here there is an urbane charm although hedonism, creativity and a kind of cerebral élan seem bedfellows destined to divorce. Oh, such real-time rose-tinted spectacles. People are nice to me though they have nothing to gain. Strange, I know, but nicety is something I have forgotten. Nicety has forgotten me. Such rosey, blooming, tinted spectacles. What scratched, frosted, opaque lenses!

This is fatuous, simplistic fantasy. People are people are people. And money corrupts - oh, how it corrupts. And cynicism - my cynicism, leads to romantic thought and romantic thought is dangerous. I return to Brodie's moll. Intuition calls back a re-match. She seemed too nice to accompany him, yet accompany him she did. What lies within that face behind the shadows cast by the brim of her hat? She spoke of pain; she spoke of distance. Yet she held him close for fear of seeing him leave. Intuitions scream at me for secrets, that face, the face beneath the veil; the outer the lodestar for the inner - a surface bubbling with covert distractions evident if only to Iris and if only, to me.

I end my morning in the National Portrait Gallery. How Iris is so addicted to faces; how Iris tries to establish who and what people are. Each has a story realised - realised in every single stroke of a brush. But do they actually say anything? It is I who talks to myself in trying to establish what Leonardo was thinking? Is it Iris trying to guess Raphael's intentions towards a wealthy patron - the object or the subject? I grow frustrated. These paintings say little to me of the artist or the subject. They can be little more than oil on canvas, little more than a loose collection of glistening, coloured coagulant on a porous, forgiving slate.

Such meaning is mine alone and can have little relevance to others. Am I so wrong? Is the generality right? What perspectives can I have to fall foul of the masses who cannot see? I fight universal meanings like a rhino fights a lion. Where does Iris's world stem from? Why do I think I am so alone?

I walk down the steps alongside Nelson's Column feeling lost and vulnerable. Faces without meaning have been replaced by faces replete with twist and counter-twist. How am I to relate to them? How can they relate to me?

Analysis is valueless and a guide to doing absolutely nothing. Feelings are creeping up on me. This twisted vista; this mealy gestation has commenced so that for the first time since the rape, I have spoken out and failed to retain control. Now I feel alone. I have never felt alone before. Feelings creep like lava creeps to stone. Iris begins to seek a shoulder and I feel so desperately alone.

Am I so different from others who know not their differences?
Am I?

XIII.

At the doors of The Maundeville the concierge is polite. Edmund is in the building. Someone goes to fetch him. While I sit in the reception I look on the paintings which more than line the walls.

More bloody faces. But how different - each a well-known man, past and present - politicians, judges, actors, civil servants, businessmen. The Establishment is lining the walls. The great and the good look down upon me and I feel disgusted that one is either in this world or one is not. I am not, as are the majority. It is a clique by birth and profession. Those who rule, and those who think it is their right to rule, need somewhere to indulge their tastes far from the plebeian classes. What price openness and honesty when decision-makers feel the need to hide from the rest of us, and fall in with each other no matter whereupon the spectrum of thought they come from?

"Iris - lovely to see you."

Edmund looks drunk.

He is drunk.

"Come, follow me."

Edmund turns and stumbles. He quickly regains his balance, gives me a knowing smile and holds the door.

"Place for sinners, this. We are all sinners in some way. Here I can sin with impunity, as we all sin together."

He starts laughing.

"We'll sit by the window. The view can be quite glorious on a sunny day. It leads one to think that one is a master of all one sees."

Again he laughs.

"Place yourself there. The waiter will bring us something to drink before we order."

I sit in a dining room in which green leather and teak wood are embellished by the glint of solid silver cutlery and crystal cut glass. I catch sight of a Renoir on the far side of the room. On the wall above my head, is a Picasso.

Edmund is oblivious and hands me a starched white napkin. He looks unhappy and sluggish. I ask him what he has been doing.

"Drinking, my dear. More than usual, I am afraid to admit. But this isn't an occasion for dwelling. It is lovely to see you. And you look, wonderful."

I want to pry but guess the subject will arise naturally, perhaps after he has consumed another half-bottle of gin. I cannot wait that long for nicety. Seeing Edmund again reminds me vividly of those moments of honesty at Heathrow. Without any sort of control, the words are out of my mouth.

"Edmund; I am pregnant."

I stare and try to remain impassive. In truth of fact, I am, impassive. Edmund is quite something different. His facial expression turns from one of alcohol-fuelled jollity to disbelief to horror to one of complete compassion. A tear forms in a corner of his eye - a tear which rapidly becomes a trickle. His tears begin to make me emotional though I am determined to hide it.

"I accept and am resigned. I bear no ill-will to the child I carry. It isn't the child's fault. The fault in this room if there is any, is mine. It was I who put myself in this position in the first place."

"No my darling, the fault is mine. If it wasn't for my own selfishness, you would not have been in that house. How many people must my urges hurt before I realise that I hurt those I value most. I am most truly sorry."

Silence passes between us. What is unsaid doesn't need to be said as Edmund attempts to navigate his brain away from blaming himself and towards a more rational clarification of what we are discussing.

"Tell me what you want me to do. Tell me what you are thinking in relation to what you carry."

I take a long time to reply. Iris is unemotional and matter-of-fact.

"I cannot destroy a life which is a result of my weakness. I am going to have this baby for better or worse."

"You are sure?"

"There is nothing I am more sure about. I am not worried for the life I bear. My only hope is to retain the degree of strength I am going to need in order to come to terms with how the child was conceived. I have already suffered from depression, though I have come out of it."

"But you seemed so good at controlling your feelings in the past. I often doubted that you had any, my dear. Forgive me, but control seemed to be your greatest ally when you have been surrounded by those of us who are utterly weak."

"You thought that much about me?"

"I have always valued you more highly than most. Behind my actions which, for the most part, verge on prostitution, I am able, believe it or not, to see into people's eyes and make fairly cohesive estimations of what they are. I know I swaddle myself in alcohol and sexual excess, for reasons I have told you of, but above all else, I keep my thoughts about those closest to me in a world of clarity I sometimes do not project. For the years I have known you, you have been one of the few dependable creatures when almost everybody else in the City of London, and in my life, has let me down. I am sorry I have never told you before. You are, and always have been, very dear to me even though I was totally aware that you thought me a despicable man."

I pinch myself for being so blind and cocksure of my own analysis that I have failed to see through the jealousy of the storymongers who have done so much to harm this caring, sensitive man.

"I admit I have judged you in the past on the basis of the superficial things I have seen and a sexual morality I do not share. It has been so difficult to see you for what you really are, as you are so good at hiding it. It should have been obvious to me that I had every right to be frank with you about so many things and you had every right to expect it. Now, in these awful and adverse circumstances, we find ourselves with each other.

"I am only too pleased that we have become close. I am upset we were never close before. Two months ago, I could not have imagined having this conversation with you. In fact, two months ago I couldn't have imagined having this conversation with anybody. We have become friends through this adversity. You are my confidant whereas I have no right to expect anything from you. But all you want to do, is give."

I can see Edmund is genuinely touched by my sentiment. But sentiment gives over to reason. And reason gives over to Iris.

"But we both have a problem. Problems arise in the form of the man you yourself chose. If I may even tell you a little of my thoughts, snippets of thought, I have gathered since I met him?"

" Brodie?"

"You know I saw him this morning walking up Ludgate Hill, on the way to the office. Quite apart from anything else, the man is undeniably strange. His oddity is beginning to come out. I know I am only talking superficiality but I saw a man stop at every other shop window to check his reflection, I saw him sneer at other people he clearly saw as unworthy and I watched him in the process of the careful cultivation of effect. There are many superficial people in the City of London - even on those measures of effect, Brodie is extreme.

"Shall I tell you something else?"

I get into my stride, pleased with the opportunity to air my opinions without fear of retribution, internal or otherwise.

"His vanity not only consumes his opinions as to the exterior, it also controls him. He is dangerous simply because his arrogance precludes him from thinking that others may think in precisely the same way. It is as if he inhabits a world in which all of the keys to all doors lie within his grasp, and his grasp only."

Edmund looks bemused. I carry on regardless.

"Maybe it is his background. It seems to me that they preach, to those who actually believe in the good of the dissemination of hatred, as if hatred itself were some sort of universal good. Apply that writ large - there are those who are worthy and those who are not. Put the sentiment in the City of London where, again, there are those who are worthy and those who are not and he has two tiny ways of looking at the environment embellished by each other. Put him in a university like Cambridge where all we were taught was how much better than all others we actually are and the tapestry of élitism, fuelled by idiocy, is complete. Throw in the vanity too - vanity, pride, ambition, determination and ruthlessness. Brodie becomes the perfect City capitalist and the ideal user of people and situations solely for his own ends. It is unusual for a man you elected to employ almost as a equal."

Edmund looks out the dining room window and into the distance, formulating a reply while I simply follow his stare and notice Whitehall and the Houses of Parliament.

"Hindsight, Iris. A lack of judgement too. He is not of my breed, I know. I had to let instinct subside and familial loyalty pervade. Brodie is a friend of my son, though I wonder precisely what kind of friend. I wanted to show my son I could trust his opinion and I let Brodie through my exclusion net. I am not blind. I guessed that may have had a few issues to deal with. That is not to excuse myself. I made a gross error of judgement and I fully admit it."

"You hired him because he was a friend of your son and you wanted to please your son, feeling for so long that all you have ever done is displease him? So Brodie, the man, didn't matter?

"It seems to me that Brodie, as twisted as he seems to be, has no place in your affections nor has he any place in relation to your thoughts of the future? If I may say so, you simply chose to employ the man because he was there.

"That, is a start."

"My dear, I had hitherto not recognised any ruthless side to you. Your suggestion is that he is meaningless. It follows that, whatever may happen to him, should be meaningless to us."

Edmund sees motives in my words I have not suspected in myself. I digress in order to establish in thought what my intuition is telling me.

"Edmund; you misunderstand me. I don't want to hurt the man, at least, I don't think so."

"So you doubt whether you want to hurt him or not?"

"It is human nature simply to want to protect oneself from the worst excesses of those whom life puts up against us.

"Well, in some ways I could look on myself and say that I have every justification to hurt the man.

"Think, Edmund. I am alone in a house. I am drunk. I walk the rooms of some large terrace in Chelsea until I can walk no more. All I know is that my flatmate has been his usual, unwonderful self and disappeared. So I walk the corridors like a vagrant walks the streets, stumbling from doorway to doorway, looking inside bedrooms for someone long since departed until I end up passing out on a bed, waking a couple of hours or so later, having been raped.

"Who could have done such a thing?

"I remember talking to one man who seemed far too nice to even contemplate the act. I spoke to no one else. The only person at that house that night who knew me, was Brodie. The only person I think, who was capable of being able to guess what condition I was in, given the amount I had to drink, other than the man whose name and face I have forgotten, was Brodie. It could have been him."

"But darling, you can't make accusations like that."

"I can make accusations when I still have the bruises to prove the act."

Edmund holds his hands in the air and gestures for me to stop. I don't want to. I want to let out all of this anger.

"Iris; listen to me."

I continue to mouth words.

"No, Iris. Just listen.

"If it was Brodie who perpetrated this hideous crime upon you, then there is little constructive you can do about it now. There is little either of us can do about the man until he makes his first move. Neither you nor I know what has taken place in the office since we were there last and we certainly have no idea what his intentions are. He may even be a coward and seek to stay in line knowing he will always have something to punish me with should he not get what he wants. We cannot let this hatred gestate until we have some sense of whether we have an enemy or not."

"But it could have been him - you must admit it as a possibility. And if it was him then I have nothing to prove it, save for a child."

"The child is innocent. You have said so yourself. I suggest you drop the mental relationship you have with what is in your body and whoever put it there. Anger here is neither helping you nor me."

"But you can see it at least as a possibility?"

"I give up. Of course it is a possibility. But how can we ever prove it? One simply can't going around making accusations. Let stealth be your best friend. We shall have to wait and see. We have nothing else to go on."

Angry and shocked by the simple fact of my anger, I excuse myself and go to the bathroom. I am sick all over the bathroom floor. My stomach has turned itself inside out - a constitution upset because my mind is upset. But I have never had a relationship with my body. I, Iris, am as inert as a seaside rock. I am simply a brain and the rest of me is a vehicle for taking me to and from two points on a compass.

I look at my face in the mirror. My eyes are bloodshot and my hair is a tangled mess. I take a tissue from my bag and wipe my brow. I begin to cry. In my innocence I have never considered the possibility that Brodie is responsible. I am intolerant; I am addicted to analysis and thought - it just isn't me to let things happen. I am in control of my world.

What is happening?

What is happening, to Iris?

Floodgates to thoughts have opened and I cannot help myself. I have seen it happen so many other times to so many other people. Mine is not to give in to such febrile things as emotions. Emotions are for the many but not for me. Emotions are for the weak and I hate myself for becoming weak.

"Just in time my dear. I have taken the liberty of ordering for you. I hope you don't mind but the lamb today is simply going to be magnificent."

I baulk at the thought of food while Edmund opens a bottle of wine. Reluctantly I insert my fork into a well dressed tomato and dread the thought of throwing up where I sit.

"A drink?"

I refuse.

Edmund will not take no for an answer.

Behind me, I hear the sound of voices. Grateful for the interruption, I turn around, chewing slowly - deliberately, seeing two figures both of whom I recognise - both well-known public figures.

"Friends in low places, Iris. We seem to be honoured indeed."

Before he has finished his sentence, Edmund is out of his chair and shaking both men by the hand. He is on first name terms with each. I am utterly uninterested in meeting either of them and the interlude gives me a chance to collect my thoughts, save that I daren't collect my thoughts.

Nothing of any consequence flits into my mind. Feelings have turned themselves to thought inertia. I am now a somnambulist, sleepwalking without any idea where I am going. My body is still and lifeless, as is my mind. Emotions have turned and I have mutated from the inert to the highly charged to the thought void which seems to lie beyond.

"Was at Eton with both of them. Seems like they have made quite a name for themselves, although they have remained good friends."

"So they were never mortal enemies, being politicians in opposing parties?"

"Good God no."

"Oh?"

"Best friends, as far as I can see. Not really the leading type at school, if I remember correctly. But they had connections and in this world, connections are a huge and invaluable start."

I tell Edmund off for being facetious. He pours himself another glass of wine and tops up my glass. I feel much better and I look into the wine glass for some sense of consolation for the rumblings I feel inside.

The conversation drifts into general reflections on all manner of things unconnected to the reasons why Edmund and I are together. Edmund is good company and fills the next two hours with many amusing stories of the people he knows and the experiences to which he has been privy. As a raconteur he is first class and I can see that my grateful and attentive ear makes him feel even better about himself.

When I leave I feel giddy and pleasant. Gone is the foreboding of the morning, the anger of the tube, the upset at lunch. The rest of the day I indulge in television for one last time before my life starts again in earnest. I sleep well too. I sleep well for the first time since the attack. I sleep well, although I do not know why.

XIV

"It's Iris isn't it?

I have a fax for you."

· The accent catches me unawares. I am caught in between the document in front of me and gentle touches mithering Iris to consider the texture, the sound and the contortions of timbre around vowel and consonant undulating through the simple words at my door.

Still, I have work to do - many weeks of catching up. I try not to look up, accepting in compromise, a document slid under my nose. But I have to look up as the body comes near and something asks me to assemble the woman before me so that I can see who and what she is.

It is the black ponytail I see, falling about her neck as her head spins, her shoulders following as she tries to leave the room. I recall a pony tail at some point in the past. To whom it was attached and why it is germane, I do not know.

"Thank you," I mumble, reticent and closed.

"It's as well to say thank you."

The accent brings me around and awakens me to a guttural tone yet soft and somehow gentle. Its origin evades me. It is not middle England that finishes in my ears. It seems Celtic and familiar.

"Sorry?" I shout.

"I didn't catch you."

She stops dead. I imagine her reluctance to stay - she seems so bent on departure; as if there are million and one better things to do. A second or two passes as we look into each other. Her face is quizzical at first, then, for an instant, seems to warm. I think I recognise her just as I think I recognise the accent. Force of inquisition pits the need to look down at to my work against the need to put my mind at rest. I have to ask.

"I'm sorry, I don't think we've met. My name is Iris."

She seems reluctant to speak. It is as if she is weighing me up, classifying me, searching her mind for value; whether I am worth the effort; whether the effort is worthy of her. Perhaps a glint of confirmation comes to her eye.

"Helen Jenvey. Pleased to meet you."

Again she starts to turn. I need time. My choice of words is banal.

"You're new?"

"Not so new."

She smiles though still seems unsure. An inner discovery eludes me. I have seen her before but I haven't seen her before - for the body language is different, if it is different at all.

"Miserable isn't it - this office?"

"Offices are always miserable. You've had some time off?"

"Yes. The longer one stays away the more difficult it is to accept the truth and all this job entails. The atmosphere in here is about as enticing as a week in Siberia."

"Depending on who you are working with, Siberia can be a very pleasant place."

"And who do you work for?" I ask.

Her reply seems cryptic and displaced.

"I work for no one."

"I guess one can be very lonely then?"

"When one has little choice - yes."

The guarded reply interests me. So does the simple fact that I have learnt nothing. Though she has a physicality I have seen before, she has a manner to that physicality I haven't, and she has an intelligence I hadn't countered for with an accent I have, betrothed to a place I haven't.

"And who don't you work for?"

"Like I said, I work for no one."

"You work for no one, so you can't work here at all?"

She grins. So do I.

"Technically, yes."

"And in the real world?"

XV.

"Iris - this is Helen; Helen - this is Iris."

Helen's smile disappears immediately and her countenance becomes that of the woman - less than the woman - the skivvying inconsequence snatched from the crowd by Brodie. Jigsaw pieces fall into place and what was before is dissembled and what is now re-presents itself as the servile, meek and craven dependent stuck under Brodie's shoe.

Brodie's interruption, quite by chance as far as I can see, establishes before me the tenuous link his secretary has with the ability to express herself away from the umbrella which Brodie has opened above her. For a moment she was free; now she is a slave. Once I glimpsed a person; now I see a toad.

"We've already met, haven't we Helen?"

The question perturbs. Brodie stares at her intently, goading her into the right response. The right response is an empty response. Social intercourse is not allowed here - Brodie won't allow it. She belongs to him, is owned by him, is part of the recesses of his own psyche run by agencies of repression and subjugation. For her to break these bounds is treasonous. Brodie will not allow it. To give herself away is giving him away. His face is a snarl. Helen is its victim.

Helen's eyes flit between me and her master. The dichotomy subsides and she defers to his power. Whatever humour we shared has been cast away and the electricity running the machine once more pulses through her body.

"Sorry to have troubled you. I'll let your secretary know you have the fax."

As Helen leaves I watch her master watch her go. His glare follows her out of the room. She has dared and he has caught her. I hope I have not been party to circumstance wherein retribution falls upon her.

I decide to pry.

"Similar accent?"

"Similar to you. To my ear, Helen's accent speaks of a totally different place."

I defer, cheekily so. I have somehow made a point.

"Been your secretary for long?"

"Long enough."

The defence means something. There are keys here - keys to doors beyond which resides the funny, rather sweet woman who has just disappeared. There may even be keys to doors beyond which the past of this Irishman himself resides.

XVI.

"Glad to see you have recovered Iris. We were beginning to wonder if you had deserted us."

Brodie raises his eyebrow, suggesting deceit. It draws my attention to his face. Part of his beard has gone, replaced by a rather thin goatee designed to accentuate that weak jaw. Underneath the goatee falls skin, a morass of unwieldy skin marking the onset of middle age. The lines of hair marking hair from folds of flab are carefully constructed and angular.

"Not much of note has happened since we last saw each other. What a hangover I had the next day."

I eye him suspiciously. His eyes focus on mine for rather too long.

"Strange evening. A bit too much information all round. Information is the brick upon which careers are built, Iris."

I need not eye him suspiciously any more. Brodie closes the door. Machiavelli appears in his stead.

"The thing is, I have been here a few weeks now, and I am beginning to understand. From what I see there are many secrets in this department kept from the outside world. I know you are aware of them and you clearly have the countenance to take them in your stride. I don't, in fact, doubt that you have a degree of loyalty to all you see before you. For me, the discovery of this clique has come as quite a shock."

I play dumb.

"I suspect that, playing the games we all have to play, one is in a position where advantage could be taken."

Brodie laughs. I ask him what he is suggesting.

"I am suggesting nothing. I think I have a right to know precisely who I am working with and what they are. I think, actually, there is a moral case for me needing to know. I have picked up all sorts of tittle-tattle."

"What, precisely, do you want to know?"

Brodie wastes no time and comes to the point.

"I want to know the extent of the moral degradation in this department. It isn't too much to ask."

Should I tell him and so allow him to judge for himself on the basis of what I say? Or do I allow him to scratch around and collate misguided information so as to confirm what will be his worst fears. And who do I have to protect? Well I have to protect myself. And I have to protect Edmund Rose. But how do I protect myself and Edmund Rose?

"I am hearing all sorts of stories. There are tales of untrammelled sex with other men. There are stories that I have landed right in the middle of a department specifically devoted to the practise of homosexuality; stories that the head of this department has deliberately conceived a group of people who progress their relationships with each other; stories of sauna liaisons; there are stories of the homosexual underworld and even - I am not sure I can believe this, stories of his liking for children."

I choose my words carefully. I am playing politics. I despise the whole.

", this is an office. Gossip circles an office until it finds suitable prey. Rumours become truth when they have no right to do so. What you may accept and what others may accept as the truth is often very far removed from actuality. Stories abound wherever one goes.

I won't deny that Edmund Rose is a homosexual. I find it hard to believe you were unaware of that fact before you agreed to work here. As you said, you are a friend of his son."

"Not that close…"

"Edmund has told his family and those of us who need to know. It is only natural to seek to protect oneself if one is threatened or if one feels threatened by circumstance. Edmund has made the careful calculation to present himself without regard to his sexual proclivities. Call it hypocrisy if you like, but Edmund Rose albeit a homosexual within, presents himself as, for want of a better word, 'normal.' Can you blame him? Prejudice is everywhere."

Brodie's reply is sharp and again, to the point.

"I assume by using the word prejudice you are referring to me. It isn't prejudice to disagree with what someone does in public. And by the nature of the hole in the ground in which we ended up a few weeks ago, we were in public."

"But , your objection wasn't only to the public nature of the acts you saw take place. Even your conversation afterwards alluded to your disgust."

"I admit it. I find the whole process of homosexuality revolting. It is inhuman. It is against God's law."

Nerve endings start to fire. A call to arms within appears once more. To attack is to defend and I have not the patience to choose my words.

"This is a law firm in the twenty-first century. God's law has no place here. Your repugnance, if it is based on Christian values, has no place here either. We do not live in the Dark Ages nor do we live in the supra-moral land of hypocrisy from were you came. This isn't Ireland. To think you can use and abuse some degree of knowledge about what a man does in private to your advantage, is utterly repugnant."

"But it isn't in private."

"So these clubs are open to all?

Edmund is entitled to pleasure himself on one criteria only, namely that each and every other participant in whatever they choose to do, consents."

"But people do get hurt. Think of what I know already."

I laugh right in Brodie's face, consoled by the fact of my laughter. When he replies, the pitch of Brodie's voice begins to rise, his eyelids widen and he points at me with his finger.

"You are not on the receiving end of the want of these men. Think about what they think when a child is seen walking down the street. To some, children are the first vestige of innocence but to these people, they are instruments to be abused."

"Edmund has children of his own."

"When I imagine what is going on in the minds of those around me, I think I have every right to know how to deal with them and to know how to deal with them, I need to know precisely what they are doing. This moral repugnance has got to stop."

"But it isn't moral repugnance. These are consenting adults."

"They will infect all of us. The constant search for satisfaction with members of the same sex will make us all suffer. My heterosexuality shouldn't be a crime. But right now, surrounded by these animals, I feel victimised. I can see them staring at me when I walk past, I can hear them whispering about me when I leave the room. These people have taken over."

The uncomplicated stupidity, paranoia, contempt and psychoses of Brodie unravel before me. He must have a good brain, a logical and a rational brain. Why can he not apply a degree of reason?

But this isn't to do with reason. Like a child swatting at the dark for fear of the unknown, Brodie relies on the false morals of his church to try and make sense of the situation he imagines he is in. The best traditions of all organised restraint - the reliance upon mores of no utility dreamed up upon some skewed reading of the Bible, have led this poor man into a position where he cannot reason any longer. Answers thus lie on a tightrope where either side is moral oblivion.

", stop. You are talking complete rubbish."

"So I have to ask what is your position in all of this? Well, clearly you condone their actions, as you have nothing adverse to say about it. I hear not one word of criticism for the actions of these people, only justifications for the kind of morality which belongs in a human sewer. Assuming your opinion, which seems neither to criticise nor to encourage them, I must also assume that you have no inclination to agree with me, or support me in anything I decide to do about it. Law and the practise of office politics is one thing but what these men are up to steps beyond the moral boundaries of what is right and what is wrong *in toto*. These men are morally repugnant to all."

"And on whose behalf do you speak?"

"I speak on the behalf of the majority of decent well-meaning people out in the wider world who would have no trouble lynching these men and think little of the consequences."

Reason and anger collide. I listen to an idiot - a dangerous idiot. It is all I can do not to stand up and walk out. But I will not - I can not. I will stand my ground, not on behalf of Edmund but on behalf of all decent people who recognise the spurious nature of arguments based on the ephemeral. Brodie deserves only my contempt. But he gets contempt spliced with reason though he deserves contempt in isolation.

"You speak of facts. You have no facts. You only want to hear what you previously believed because it serves the idiocy of your prejudices. How many times do I have to tell you that the sexuality of such men extends only to each other. They do not impose themselves on anybody else and they certainly do not impose themselves upon minors. That rumour started as a consequence of precisely the same kind of stupidity you are passing off as fact. It is built upon an absolute pig-ignorance, an over-great association with difference from the norm and the darker side of human nature. Well no one in this department is anything other than decent, few of them have anything critical to say about anybody else which doesn't cross the boundaries of what is acceptable in inter-human contact and most certainly none of them has anything sinister underlying their natural state.

"In any event, what does that stupid phrase, 'decent well meaning people,' actually mean?

"Are you a decent person?

You make me laugh. In the brief moments I have known you, all you have tried to explain is how people are there to be manipulated for one's own ends. All you have done is denounce the freedom of consenting individuals because it doesn't accord with your own sense of restraint. And further, you have announced yourself as a hypocrite by being a married man quite willing to sit in a party in Chelsea trying your best to get an unsuspecting female into bed.

"Is that decency?

"What do you do when you go home at night?

"What do you think about?

"Well I know what you think about as you leave and enter this building, walking past shop windows trying to catch sight of your reflection, marvelling at your self-proclaimed hegemony over peoples you think unworthy of you. I have seen you preening your little barrel like body, combing that ridiculous beard, constantly changing your image as a consequence of constantly analysing yourself in a world you feel utterly unhappy in. The pattern fits - the need to be liked by some blind female in a bar, the need to confirm to oneself the deluded nature that hides within those hideous cherubic features; the hair you must spend hours combing over that fifty-pence piece at the back of your head, the three-piece suit when others wear two; the goatee; the heels which click as they hit the pavement so as to sound profound. Does that relationship with vanity and the need to establish control and difference from the plebs you choose to side with, give you the right to declare yourself the moral leader of people you actually despise?

"Even more to the point, who do you think you are defending? Are they really the moral majority? Or are these the majority whose morality is pedestooled while they always fall below it? How dare you even contemplate 'what you are going to do about this' on the basis of what you nefariously consider to be some objective truth. Surely the education you have had would give you some ability to let people who don't hurt others, be. My God, I can see why that pathetic little enclave over the Irish Sea is so riddled with depravity."

"Leave God's country, alone."

"I will not leave your idyll alone because its hideous face is sitting before me. You speak for no one. You act only for yourself. You have nothing in mind save to gain for yourself and the rest of you is bullshit."

"So we are enemies, Iris. It is your choice. I have been polite enough to give you the option of siding with me. I must take it now that you choose not to."

One last time, I try to reason.

"Tell me . Tell me if you can imagine what it is to be abused on the grounds of simply being none other than a culmination of biology. Tell me if you can really understand the objective truth that one can't change the fundamental facets of one's nature. Take yourself back to childhood. Remember doing things without thinking about them and being scolded for mistakes. Remember learning, little by little, what was acceptable behaviour and what was not. Catch sight of yourself being told off by your parents as their fingers punch the air in your direction, recall the fear of crossing lines to enable you to develop and grow. Mistakes follow error follows judgement which results in the ability to analyse, so taking ginger steps in the right direction and not the wrong one. It is how we learn, it is how we come to know others and how to treat them. Soon those first transgressions are lost in foundations as a matrix of judgements posits a structure, an edifice of character built upon counterpoint - action and reaction. Stop me if this gets complicated but soon reaction becomes action itself and those first blind instincts are lost, save for one thing - you learn that, sometimes they are wrong, sometimes they are right. And in learning that some are wrong, you, I and all thinking others never repeat, never transgress, never return to folly because it is so obviously folly. You are now a construct, an invention in

76

which you see yourself through the eyes of others and from your own, special, pre-determined perspective. But whatever lies at the heart of this perspective is instinct - nervous temperament, intuitive feeling, the first urge so sublimated by analysis over time that it is an urge indistinguishable and almost unknown and indefinable in its origins.

"That urge was never about choice. It is what bottoms man - urges that are within us, classify us and define us. Can you not see my point? Sexuality lies at the very essence of man, for it pre-dates choice and only learning portrays to the person whether society applauds it or denies it credence. More to the point, you cannot blame anyone or anything where the power to choose is not present. You cannot blame because blame is irrelevant. You must understand and through understanding, you can accept. You must forget about choosing to dismiss another man on the basis of reasoning, be that reasoning based upon religious values, social values or absolute self-interest. I am appealing to you just to consider what I am saying. Please do not make any rash decisions. Please remember that humanity is what distinguishes us, as does cruelty, as does greed, as do all other actions built upon choice. Please remember what bottoms choice and let this man go."

Brodie sniggers under his breath. Yet he sits in silence and I sense that he is thinking about matters far removed - a sixth sense tells me that he is considering, a sixth sense decides upon some inner conflict within this man I had previously not seen.

My words prove worthless.

"Make a choice, Iris. Eloquent as you are, you are incorrect. I will ask the question one more time. Whose side are you on? This is your career we are talking about; this is your livelihood. Choose and we will be enemies. Choose and we could be friends."

"I side with no one. To talk of sides is absurd. Can you not let these people be? They offer you no threat. Why would you want to threaten them?"

"My thoughts are clear. Through my naivety I have put myself in a moral-free zone. It is up to me to re-establish a degree of order."

If suicide is beyond the vale of hope, Brodie is beyond the vale of reason. Before he leaves, I decide to try and establish what he proposes to do.

"Well that is the point. What will I do?

"Now that things are in the open between us and I understand your position, I must choose my words wisely. I will consider my position over the next few days. But it is time others become aware what is going on here. Do not doubt me Iris, I will make them aware. And I will protect myself doing so. If I were you I would choose to do the same thing and not side against me."

I tell Brodie one last time that it isn't a matter of taking sides. But

Brodie is already half way out of my door as I finish my statement.

"Remember Iris. Your argument is simple. Find a man who cannot choose and you have no one to blame. Find a man who can and all the forces of retribution may fall upon him. You cannot blame a man who cannot choose - you can blame a man who does. You, must choose."

I sit still for five minutes after Brodie has gone - normless, lost. Half thoughts run around my head looking for completion and finity. Suddenly Brodie's last words hit me as does the tangent - the oblique relevance of my argument. Say I find out who has raped me? Say I find out that the human being who took advantage of me was, for a few moments of his life, just an animal and unable, on the sight of a beautiful woman easily compromised, to control the instincts which in his drunken condition, came racing to the surface as control, critical faculty and choice became scattered and indistinguishable. I cannot blame the rapist for the rapist cannot be blamed any more than I can, as both he and I, made the choice to drink into eclipse. Retribution cannot fall upon the blameless. I am not a victim - there is no victim.

But I am the victim. Feelings tell me I am the victim. The child tells me I am the victim. Fear tells me I am more than a victim. My body beats me and sends messages to my brain. My twisted logic falls flat upon my circumstance and deep within, I know that emotions are pummelling a segway to the reason which was so much of Iris and presently so little of me.

I clasp my desk with my hands, cupping my thumbs underneath and squeeze as hard as I can, trying to expel all of this abhorrence from me - begging Iris to return. Iris was so easy. Iris was straight and practical, untouched and sterile. Now I am unclean and no matter how I try and revert to Iris, I cannot, for a new person is taking over, infected and resiled to this social septicaemia. I pray for my thoughts. Accept the present, Iris and deal with what is in front of you. All is Brodie, all must necessarily be Brodie. Protect what you have. Protect and enforce the battlements Brodie has demanded. Think not of uncertainty and only of the present. Accept emotion and learn to grow with it. Accept the character and the words of the man who threatens you and disregard all else. For this is a thing of dread whereas the unknown is the thing of nightmares. The present dictates that the darker side of male nature, combined with ambition augmented by the vacuous tenets of religious bigotry, has conspired to create a character Machiavelli must have had in mind. But Machiavelli's Prince is too, a creature of imagination, a theoretical construct, a designation from the imagination, a model upon which the actions of flesh and blood can be compared. Little Princes are everywhere but the thing of dread is to find the perfect model looking at you, asking if you are for, or if you are against.

I consider his options in order to consider my defence. I consider Brodie's options as I have more than just myself to protect. I consider his options because I have no choice but to. All the advantages are with Brodie, all the sufferings with me - with us.

What of Iris? And the child I am carrying?

I am not one any more; I am two. My body is changing little by little and it is affecting my mind. Already I have noticed mood swings and the need to speak publicly whereas before I kept things to myself. I have noticed the violence in my reactions to what I think are injustices around. These may be the flowerings of one who is changing into a fuller adult with a reactive scale more akin to a mature person but to me, my scientific analysis of all around me is, and was, the best way of dealing with any environment within which I am misplaced. Yet I am still flesh, I am still bone. I realise this more and more as time goes by. I cannot but think of protecting myself in relation to Brodie and I must think of protecting my child more than any other.

Hm - if this situation at work had arisen previously I would have been able to deal with it coolly. I would change jobs, move to another firm, get myself out of this situation. I can still do the same but my loyalty to Edmund won't let me. We will face events as they unfold. But I must protect this child. I cannot live nor suffer an environment where my future will be at risk. I need to protect myself because I need money in order to provide for a lifestyle in which my child will flourish. Anything else would be anathema. Anything else has to be anathema.

So the paradox arises. In order to provide, I am reliant on money. In a world at least part of me detests, where the worship of money is the norm, I too, am trapped by its ugly face. Oh, how I wish I could escape - how I wish I didn't need to rely, as everybody else seems to rely, on the whole hideous concept. But it traps me as it traps everybody else. All of the weaknesses of man - pride, vanity, power, pain, lust, stupidity, arrogance, contempt and deceit have aligned themselves to me and to ice the cake, I cannot escape because I am trapped by the need to earn in order to provide. Whereas several weeks ago I was a free spirit - thinking and analysing about all but ascending above the earthly, I am embroiled in the earthly at the expense of the value of my mind. I must act wisely. I have got, to act wisely.

XVII.

I begin to accept my situation and the nature of change that manifesting within my body. Hitherto unknown thought-effects; hitherto unknown side-effects, rise and surface. The body which for so long I had no relationship with, forces me into thinking about precisely what it is and what it will become. It is not vanity. Like any great physical change, like any change which one has to imagine because of its inevitability, I think about it and yes, rather dread an unrequested mutation. But I dread it for myself, for what Iris will become, for who I am turning into and not, in any sense, through the eyes of others.

Then there is my job - my questionable status as an achiever; a machine; a lawyer who oils the wheels and greases the leathery innards of my own silk purse. Soon, the lump will show and Iris will have to leave - discarded, rejected, banished by a call to biology men have used against us since time immemorial.

I am pregnant - women get pregnant and though it may be the death knell to a career, still, women get pregnant. Contrast homosexuality - sexuality in the finance society hidden and underground - pregnancy in the finance community, hidden and underground. My exposure and their exposure are the same - men presently thriving and vaunted for their knowledge, acumen, brainpower, raw intellect are cut away - they too, discards from the church, having exposed that small fact - difference. Am I so different from Edmund?

Precipitation confirms all. There is only one place to go when one is excommunicated from the City of London. That place is down. Homosexuality, pregnancy, differences, differences from the norm, departures from the accepted, alternative colours of the rainbow - all delineate rejection.

I hear little of Edmund. Upon enquiry, quiet voices tell me he has taken to the law but continues with the bottle. Preoccupation means I do little to get in touch. Preoccupation necessarily means I keep myself to myself though Iris is constantly on the lookout for Brodie; what he is up to and who he is speaking to.

But Brodie is elusive and Brodie is contrived. He is rarely seen and even discreet questions prove to be of no use, for he tells his secretary little of where he is, only that he is contactable on his mobile phone.

On the odd occasion, I hear his laugh emanating from his room, like a church bell across a village green - the same cynical office laugh never meant sincerely, meant only to impress the recipient with its facetiousness. Perhaps a couple of times I hear it, resonating around the walls, punctuating a corridor marked by the silence of my fellows. I never actually see him. I cannot say he is out of sight out of mind, for his form, his voice and intentions are always lurking somewhere within my thoughts and the thought recesses of others.

I presume to know how his secretary must feel. Yet, on the occasions I walk the corridors in order to deliver work to my secretary, Helen Jenvey seems to elude me. It is as if she is teasing me too - my perceptions plied with food for thought, withdrawn when my appetite increases. I curse my inquisitive nature. Helen seems a little touchstone and a touchstone too far. Apart from Edmund, Helen and I are the only two women in Iris's proximity with at least something in common, though I little know what it is that Helen is so afraid of. Again and again and again the question arises - what has Brodie over her? What lies beyond that veil of subservience, the span of that wall of timidity, that dread, the unease, that apprehension?

It seems that I stare at a coin, balancing nervously upon its edge. To one side lies the face of Helen Jenvey, shrouded by an age of living within a penumbra of pollution, becoming, naturally, polluted herself. On the other side I see Brodie, grinning, grimacing, snarling - the pollutant of the goodness I know I feel within Helen - a listless, obscured face.

Intuitions tell me she is an oppressed soul – impure; impure and dishevelled flesh designed to cover the gentleness within. It is almost as if this strange hold he has and the brief opportunity I have had to see beneath it, gives my intuitions the feed to nourish imaginations to do with a greater understanding of Brodie, what he is and what he is capable of. For what is this man in a final analysis - less than a man rather a tempest of deceit, cruelty and manipulation.

How Helen Jenvey is so important to me. How I need to know this woman so catching the terms of the currency to which she is indebted. Could it be that Helen's subjugation is important if only for the reasons she submits, for it is the eyes of her master that I need, not the forced myopia of his moll.

For all my aimless thoughts, for all of the times I let my curiosity get the better of me and walk the corridors for a glimpse of this saddened lady, I always come back empty-handed and undernourished. Helen Jenvey is as elusive as Brodie. Perhaps she too, is contrived. Perhaps she too, follows the faces of the chameleon and the interminable distances of its nature. Yet in her absence she seems to be closer at hand whereas the dilatory perspectives of her colleagues make them ever further away. I need to see Helen Jenvey. I need to confirm or deny the credibility of my obsessive thoughts.

Finally it is to one of her number that I turn - to one of the secretaries adjacent to Helen that I turn to in plucking up the courage to find out where she is. Her reply is curt and dismissive.

"Brodie's secretary? Nothing to do with us."

"Oh?"

"That girl can keep herself to herself."

"But why?"

"She is worse than he is. Is that right girls?"

I look over my shoulder and see four very different faces, all with the same expression - distaste.

"She is really that bad?"

"Worse, Iris, than you could ever imagine. Helen Jenvey is possibly the most miserable person we have ever worked with. See for yourself; she'll be back in a minute."

Confused, perhaps, I hold back, trying to busy myself until Helen arrives. I grasp the subservience, the subjugation - for whatever Brodie has over her; I do not know why this third facet - this grating nature explained by the secretaries alongside her, bears any relevance to Helen's previous character. Why would the other girls ostracise her? It isn't in their nature to join forces against an individual. There are no careers to be had here. They type, earn and get the hell out as quickly as the tube can take them.

When Helen returns to her seat, I am polite when I ask a question. I am disappointed and annoyed with the answer.

"Who wants to know?" she replies in an accent which speaks of the same Irish brogue as her master - the same grating, disrespectful, deconstructive use of the certain vowel and consonant sounds of the English language.

This is not the sweet creature who spoke to me, controlled, as she is now, by some hitherto unnoticed voice within. This is not the nodding dog tied to Brodie's lead, either. The difference is palpable and the disrespect germane. This third creature – it is this third facet of her visage that speaks to Iris.

"Can't tell you. I'm afraid I am under instruction not to tell anybody where he is unless he allows me to. And in order for that to happen I must have your name and the nature of your enquiry."

"I am enquiring where he is, that is all."

"Well if that is the nature of your enquiry then you can't be told in any event."

Her eyes remain fixed; her stare, awry. Iris is now an enquiry, more than that, a difficult, confrontational, voice - not a person; I am unrecognised and trouble. I wonder what she will do if she realises it is Iris - the woman she shared a joke with, the woman to whom she gave a little away.

Alas, as she turns her head and continues to type, it seems as if she is utterly unaware that I remain right behind her. But I decide not to take my curiosity elsewhere for my curiosity is overwhelming. I try to gain some sort of pithy recompense at my failure to embellish my analysis of Helen's innards, by examining her façade.

Helen is attractive. She has blue eyes and freckled skin. Her hair is thick and naturally black, though tinged with a degree of red dye. She wears no jewellery of any kind and her clothes are dowdy and unattractive. Her skin is white, porcelain smooth and pure - so unmistakably Irish and so much a colour juxtaposition between her full and blood red lips. The skin, the freckles, the hair - her birthplace moves to the forefront of my mind, immediately.

The evidence is irrefutable in any event, for the accent is irrefutable. Not only is she Irish, the voice tells me is close in origin to Brodie himself. Given her abrupt manner and her rudeness I wonder whether they are related. But a family apt to produce a hideous pug such as Brodie would not have had so much genetic blessing left so as to create such a petite and exquisite creature. The relationship by accent with Brodie is still intriguing. Again, questions arise in my mind - why is she here? What makes her work for such an unbearable creature? What is her object in choosing to protect this malodorous man?

Suddenly unaware of myself, Helen is aware of me. I see the whites of her eyes reflected in her screen, like drunken fireflies skating across a grey, watery varnish - flecks of white reflected on the screen at which she stares. It is the eyes that give her away, just as before. Seconds ago she was thoroughly unpleasant. But her countenance changed for a scintilla - a brief respite from what I am beginning to see is a manufactured hardness. She looks full of sorrow. Her eyes speak of pain. Then she returned to the bewitched as the passages to Helen Jenvey are pushed behind the veil.

One becomes four - something funny, something a little odd underneath, something hard and protective presently, something weak and timorous with Brodie. There are reasons for all four though I know not what they are.

A call comes in from New York. I pick up the receiver in my room, happy to hear Edmund's voice.

"Staying in New York for a while, Iris. Nothing much in London for me to go back to. Think I can break out in these more temperate climes. The tentacles of the City don't stretch this far. Got to move on. In a few weeks' time there will nothing left for me in London. Got to start afresh. Got to create a new niche for myself. The tolerance here is markedly different. These people actually understand what it is to be different from the norm. These people accept me for what I am."

Save that New York isn't different from the norm. I have worked there often and Edmund's summary doesn't add up.

"New York and London are practically the same town. Bodies swap beds across the Atlantic for weeks at a time. Your reputation now is as high there as it is here. And once you are destroyed here it will follow as a matter of course that you will be eviscerated there. Why do you choose to ignore the truth?

"And you love England so much. Why give up all you own on the basis of a threat? You still have a home here. It will be the support of those who love you the most which will allow you to get through."

"Well maybe it is early morning gin talking - allowed to be weak you know."

"Edmund; weakness comes not in the thought, it comes in the actions which preclude thought. You have got to get away from the supposed solace which lies at the bottom of a glass."

For a long time the telephone is silent. I can almost hear him thinking. It pains me to think of Edmund trying his best to assimilate coherent consequential thoughts when he is drunk and so emotional. Eventually the silence is unbearable. I repeat his name continuously but the telephone remains silent.

"Yes of course Iris, you are right, bless you. I am a fool. Tentacles of excommunication will find me wherever I go. I am better off in London."

The line goes dead. Suddenly I feel cold. I don't want to be in the office anymore. I want to go home. I care not for Helen Jenvey now. I care not for the strangling potentiality of her master. It is all I can do to think of Edmund. It is all I can do to think of myself. Blow the rest of the them for I have Iris to think about and I have my child. I have all the forces of nature against me, the changes I am beginning to notice and the emotions intrinsic to that change. The Iris of old is gently slipping away and the countenance of this new face - my face, this new body - my body, requires all the strength I can muster just to keep my head above a watermark whose distance from the toes which stretch beneath me is ever further with each passing day.

Poor Edmund. I cannot bear to think that he is suffering. How our differences unite us. How I yearn for a sanctuary for the child I carry. How I wish I was Iris once more and change had passed me by. What do I hold? What do I have within? It feels not like a child; rather a millstone around my neck. From where do I derive the strength to look after both of us in this grotesque round of perversity?

To think of another, to have thoughts of Helen Jenvey, of Brodie, of Edmund, is as stupid as a teapot made of chocolate. Iris must protect myself and I must protect my child. Damn - I keep seeing his secretary. She has a key. She has, in that delicate frame, in that beautiful face, something - just, something. If only I could lay my hands upon it. If only.

She is as distant as the Sun, the stars. Only the content of my womb is close at hand. How will it change my mind? What is its relationship with my mind? Forget the face Iris, forget appearances, forget the transient changes as pregnancy progresses. The call to protect my child follows the linear progression of blood between my mind and my body - that once distant matrix of flesh and thought. Let not the flesh become weak. Let it become strong for it will need to be. Become strong and accept the inevitability of change.

Yes, I want out of the office. I so desperately want to go home. These four walls, this peopled, putrid rabbit warren, reminds me so much of Iris, so much of what Iris was and is, so much of what Iris has become and what Iris is up against, that to stay and feel the festerings of discontent swell to bursting, is insanity. Brodie is an irrelevance. Helen Jenvey is an irrelevance. Edmund is an irrelevance.

Maybe I'll stay at home and crawl back to the sanctuary offered for the weeks after the rape. No one gets to me there - a crowd imagined outside can but shout yet cannot assail the walls of my home. It is sanctuary indeed. To lock the doors, to draw the curtains, to sit in darkness having shut out all of the light, comforted by some cheap tome to read, soothed by the soft and gentle tones from the lamp falling quietly over my shoulder, I find peace. To Hell with the others. To Hell with all.

XVIII.

"So you are going to sit and read all night? How are we ever going to
get you a man when you resist all I can do for you. We, Iris, are
going out!"

James smiles. I love that smile; I love it for the way he half-cocks his
mouth and a cheeky face appears, full of life and mischief. Before I can
protest, James grabs my book and hurls it to the far corner of the room,
where it nestles amongst a random pile of his dirty clothing.

I try to resist but I can't. I need some sort of seclusion within the royal
grounds of alcohol - to escape maybe, yes, to escape. Save that a little of me
is concerned. I haven't been out since Chelsea. But why should I let events,
now passed, control my life today?

I change my clothes and decide against make-up. Who would I be
putting make-up on for? James enters my bedroom room while I am taking
off my blouse. For a second he sees my stomach.

"Putting on a bit of weight, Iris?

Bit of a tummy?"

I react.

His response is a mixture of surprise, banter and concern.

"A little sensitive in your old age?"

"No."

"Have I offended you?"

"No."

"Well what is it, then?"

"Nothing."

James puts me in a dilemma. James is, on balance, the only real friend I
have. I know him - he will return to the subject when he thinks I am tipsy
and my tongue loose.

Do I tell him I am pregnant? Do I tell him why?

James has a right to know. It is in both our interests that I unveil my
secret so that he can prepare himself for the arrival of my child and accept
the circumstances of its conception. In as much as this child will have a
father, James will be the closest man at hand. A better friend and a better
man I couldn't wish for.

Still, men are most unpredictable when confronted with something not previously dealt with. And these are emotions he will be dealing with here and men and emotion are a strange mix. I guess he will run off in a fit of anger if I tell him my progeny is the offspring of rape. Why shouldn't he? He is a decent and caring man, notwithstanding his roving eye. I will understand his anger, for the rules of the mating game count in the challenge, the sales pitch and submission or non-submission. One sees a product one likes, one sells oneself so as to allow the object the choice whether to submit or not and the quality of the sales pitch determines the sale. James loves the chase because there is an element of challenge and an element of choice. To be raped is vile because there is no choice. And decency demands always that there should be.

We leave the house and walk to Clapham High Street. It is eight o'clock and the bars are beginning to fill. Suits drift off to get changed replaced by those sensible enough to stave the urge to have a drink after work, now ready for the slog from early evening to the tipsy early hours.

"The Falcon?" James asks.

Situated close to Clapham North station, The Falcon is one of the few watering holes which has retained a degree of character the other local pubs cannot compete with. Its grubby innards and its lived-in charm have it adored because it isn't meant to be adored. The Falcon is staid, timeless and of the earth. Somehow, so are its occupants.

While I reserve a table, James heads to the bar, returning with two pints of weak lager. As he sits down he looks at me and I guess at what has already left in the first class post.

"Are you going to tell me what is wrong or are you going to keep that big brain all to yourself?"

Instinctively, I look around. We are enclosed and huddled in a corner. Somehow it feels safe and I feel a little uncomfortable, given the gravity of what I am about to impart.

"Well?"

Slowly, without feeling, logically, calmly and from the very beginning, I tell James what has happened in the preceding weeks. I refer James to that night when we started off drinking in The City, on to that homosexual club then to events later in the evening. To his credit James says nothing but listens attentively, giving little away save for the odd exhalation of air and the odd sharp intake of breath.

Finally, having told him of Brodie's threats, the imminence of Edmund's downfall, my precariousness, I tell James I was raped and that I am pregnant. And I tell him it is my intention to have the child.

After I have finished he swallows half a pint of lager. Now it is his turn to speak. Unpredictably he seems to remain calm and seems to take it in his stride. Unannounced he walks around the table and gives me a hug. When actions are out of place, men run off to compose words in order to replace their physical redundancy. But as a medium to convey they give men little - words never win wars, words paper over the cracks when a call to arms is so much redundant clarion.

Then, though he sits in silence, lost to himself and to thoughts he cannot see the end of, his first comments take me just a little by surprise.

"Iris. Why are you friends with me?"

"What do you mean?"

"We've been friends for many years now. In all of that time you have never questioned me. On the contrary you seem to laugh at my antics when you don't really share my outlook. What I mean is - do you not see? I represent in some ways the kind of behaviour, the outer edge of which is responsible for the terrible events you have just described. I don't get it. We are best friends yet we are opposites. And you forgive me whereas I don't sense you feeling the same way about anybody else."

Sweet James - intuitive, sensitive.

Selfish.

"It is a contradiction, Iris. Why do you not hate me? Surely I am just like the man who hurt you."

I look at James - James the centre of the universe, James beyond which he sees James. I try to smooth the lines which ruffle his outlook.

"Is it ten years? Remember when we roomed together? When we were eighteen? You were unlike anyone I had ever met before and when we were both away from home, me for the first time, it wasn't so much that I liked you as you were new to me. You are the only man I have known and though you have faults, we all do. I liked you because you were a front man for your own personality, hidden beneath that thick skull of yours."

James consumes more beer, pondering, considering.

"But my personality is everything I do. It isn't just what you think I am beneath the surface. Shy people, you know - the sort who are quiet but loud when you get to know them, they say they are shy, they say they are loud, sometimes. But they are both, though labelled one way or the other. I am all that I am on the surface and all that I am underneath. You can't look to one side of character and say that'll do for me. I would have thought that all I am is the thing. And bits of me must remind you of this awful circumstance you find yourself in."

"I don't forgive you for the perimeters of your character. I have learned to love those sides of you too."

"Am I not just like any other man?"

I find thinking about James uncomfortable. I can predict him. I can anticipate him. Why do I want to question him?

"You don't understand. Give me one occasion in the last ten years when your quirks and your wants have ever caused offence? You harm nobody."

"But the women?"

"Oh look, they are just games. I have no real opinions about your lifestyle. I know you can be cynical and manipulative but you manipulate those willing to be manipulated and the decision to react is theirs. You don't corral people, you do not force yourself upon them. And name me anybody who has had a bad word to say about you whether you have bedded them or not?"

"I guess I can't."

"You guess correctly."

"So why, exactly, are we friends?"

"Because we are opposites."

"Opposites?"

"Yes - opposites."

How little he knows me; how little has he thought.

"James; let me put it another way. Why exactly do you like me?"

"Because I can rely on you. Most people who know you, tell me they think you are strange. They always refer to you first on the basis of how beautiful you are. Then they make assumptions about how you must have this perfect life, a better life than theirs as they look plain - Iris must be so lucky; she has everything; she has it all. And they keep you at arms length for they are afraid of you. You never use your beauty, you never use your charm. You must have a gift yet you seem to defer always from using it. That, to most, is strange."

"But I am talentless."

"So are they. But you are beautiful and they are not."

"I don't get it."

"Iris; you always tell the truth. You never let me down. You never judge me even though I am deserving of your thoughts. You are reliable and decent."

"So why talk about my beauty - why through the eyes of others?"

"Beauty is all about greed. You suffer jealousy and distance; you are vaunted and rejected. Never mind that you have a first class brain, that you are a success. It is irrelevant. You know I have never seen you ever show any sign of vanity, arrogance or conceit. You are pure and to me, inviolate. It is an inner beauty I can't put my finger on. And I feel proud to be your friend, for you are a remarkable friend. I am distraught that greed has found its way to you and you must suffer. I am sorry that the greed of man has taken an innocence from you I adored. I am sorry for being a man. I am sorry for having shown the same traits as the bastard who raped you."

I am touched; I am sorry too. How little does he have even the slightest clue about this broken psyche. To disclose the way I think to my friend would break him. It is he who is innocent and not I. I am guilty because I understand. His innocence is his terminus.

"James; you are the only friend I have. I have no right to judge you. I am not even sure whether I can judge the man who raped me because I recall nothing - I have no face, I have no actions; all I have is residue. I am telling you because I love you for what you are, whether you think that there is little value in your urges or not. Your behaviour does not offend me as it natural and undeniable. You are humane and you care."

James continues with his tangent.

"Tell me, do you not feel angry at the way you are constantly harassed and dismissed, constantly the object of attention and the object of greed? It will never end for as long as you look the way you do. Can you not see that? Do you not scourge the environment for treating you so badly? Do you not, even in your private thoughts, scourge the genetic blessing of beauty for what it really is?"

James is getting closer - closer than he has ever been before.

I mix truth with lies.

"I get nothing from the way I look. I can not be cynical about what I can not control. Nor can I stay in forever and never let the world see my face. For better for worse I am a simple woman in a complex world, sometimes a complex woman in a simple world. James; I cannot avoid it. I have no choice."

"So it never gets to you?"

"Previously? No. It made me."

"And now?"

"It will get me regardless of whether it gets to me, wherever I am. My pregnancy will not change that. Nor will it change our friendship. Please respect me, James, for the decisions I have made."

"I can do nothing but respect you. I will, from this moment, do everything you want of me. I am only sorry that you must suffer. This world is such a shitty place."

Once more James touches me and holds my hand. Then, somewhat abruptly, he stands and stays for an aeon at the bar. His is a judgement as to how to act - what to do next. A wry smile pulls my lips east and west. How funny. How predictable.

James returns with a double gin and an orange juice.

"We can't have you getting drunk, now there are two of you to consider."

I ridicule him. I am serious too.

"Don't be foolish. I should be grateful I wasn't killed. As for your concern about me taking things easy, well thanks but no thanks. I can take care of myself."

I walk to the bar still grinning and about to enjoy a cruel little tease. I cadge a cigarette from a barmaid and return to my seat with a light lodged in the corner of my mouth, simultaneously gulping liquid as it bubbles and froths about my tongue. James turns green with anger. I turn green when the tobacco hits me.

"Iris; please stop."

"Stop what? I am just making the point. I am not stupid. I know what I haven't got myself into here. I am not going to jeopardise the health of my child. It is just a cigarette and a beer."

"But you have got to take care of yourself. If it isn't bad enough that you are going to have a baby, I don't think it is going to do you any amount of good by throwing beer down your neck."

I find James' concern amusing. Stupidly he tries a compromise.

"Alright. This is what we'll do. I'll stop this lifestyle if you will."

"And the girls?"

James pulls a face. I start giggling. James giving up the attentions of women is like a fox giving up the attentions of a chicken.

"I bloody well can. You just watch."

"Fancy another drink James?"

Absurdity circles the innards of his eyes as the muscles which surround contract to push his eyeballs inward toward an understanding of himself, as James slowly realises he would rather eat his leg than change. Still, he sees the funny side as he intimates his thirst by lifting his glass, pawing it and cherishing its latent contents until they slide uninterrupted down the back of his throat.

Once more I walk over to the bar. Six grubby feet are on the bar rail next to me trying to get the barmaid's attention. When they see me their knowing nods tell Iris I am about to be approached. I wonder which one of them is brave enough. I hear them whispering to each other. One of them mentions my chest.

Part of me is angry; part resigned; part blasé. Somehow the point to the evening, if there is a point to the evening, crystallises. Can I criticise this sexual powerplay, this masculinity unbounded? Can I criticise what is natural to them and sinful to me when I absolve James of the sin of being natural too? Sure, their timing is awful but life travels on and life travels on through my travesty. Blame somehow, has to be put to one side as they eye me up and I wait for the inevitable and the inevitable arrives.

The smallest of the three and the one who thinks he has most to prove, sidles over. With an irony unknown to him he tells me I am beautiful. I choose to ignore while I wait to be served. Redundant, spent and resigned, he slopes back to his friends.

The event amuses and enthuses a compatriot. Perhaps the tallest, he decides to hit me with his best lines so showing his clansmen the superiority of size and concomitant inclination. Should he fail however, and this is his real gamble, he will have to return with his tail between his legs knowing that not only has he failed for himself but he has brought shame upon the purported ascendancy of the bigger male over the weaker breed.

Stupid man - a man who cannot see or feel his way into the evident psychology of the moment. The woman in front of him understands more than he does. Rejection is the natural course of things. Upon his exile Iris receives a look of pure hatred while I pick up two drinks and return to our table.

James is complimentary.

"What can I say? Am I a sage? Am I a prophet? Greed - greed. Tell me I am not as obvious? We can but laugh. We have no choice but to laugh. Never fail do you? The surlier you are the more they seem to want to try their hand. To say I enjoyed the performance is an understatement. What is it with you Iris? The more disinterest you effect the more the trolls congregate."

"Effect is the wrong word. I don't effect a thing. Nor do I submit to the cheap nature of the moment. And they can't accept a woman who isn't interested in giving in."

James smiles knowingly.

"What am I going to do with you, Iris?"

"Getting me home safely would be a good start. You can get yourself home safely too."

James hasn't noticed. These rejected suitors, smarting and confused, have decided to stand next to us and pass off rude comment about James in order to alleviate their shame. They do not pass off comment at me. My immunity is given as a consequence of still being the object of their eye. Tactics have changed for what they now try to do is to impress me with an ascendancy over the male I have chosen. James is vilified simply for talking to me and is accused of homosexuality, cowardice, of being ugly, of femininity, of stupidity. What would a girl like that be doing with that idiot I hear. Look at him. Just look at him.

Slowly James falls in tune with their comments, being sucked into their trap. Should he let pride speak and stand up to protest, comments will turn to aggression. Pride then wins out as their pride at being rejected causes them to devalue James so raising his temperature so causing a fight. And when that erupts, with poor James not standing a chance, I am supposed to be submittal and impressed as the male ego triumphs and the strongest, the fittest, the proudest, the warrior amongst the protagonists gets his prize. And I, of course, will submit willingly for I am weak, I am female, I am there to won, there to be carried away, there to be ravished and rejected.

I stand to leave, telling James I feel unwell. Immediately his attention reverts to me and he extends his hand to help. Of course I am not unwell but just the whisper with which I deliver James the untruth is sufficient to let his pride abate. I do not counter for the ears of kinsman three - the only one of the three combateers who hasn't chosen to give me of his best. He offers me his hand. It is his humiliation and a very public humiliation when I reject his offer and something akin to dropping a match at a petrol station.

Offence has now turned ugly. As James protects my back and we leave the pub, we are subject to a volley of unwarranted abuse in which jealousy is the only winner. Even I am a target as these Neanderthal pugilists choose to liven their night and temporarily their existence at our expense. In the space of ten minutes I have gone from being the object of desire to a piece of meat one step away from the receiving end of a fist or a kick.

James looks upset. I too, for all my understanding, am upset. We walk up Clapham High Street once more while James apologises profusely for the offence just caused. I try not to blame, though they are, I have no doubt, giggling to themselves in the pub. And as we walk past another pub with testosterone hanging out the doors, I curse man under my breath.

"You know Iris, there is only one place on this entire street that can accommodate us tonight."

I can hardly hear James speak as an ambulance screams past taking its contents to have the glass removed from his face.

I know exactly where he refers to. I ask myself whether I want to stay out. Pride wells within me a bit. I will not have thuggery stop me from spending a little time with my friend, not tonight especially.

As we turn and cross the road, James slips his hand into mine. It is comforting, reassuring. With doe eyes and sunken shoulders and far from the earshot of any other James stops me in the street.

"I am sorry Iris. On behalf of all of the idiots out there, I am sorry."

XIX.

The room is dark and reeks of an attitude manyfold removed from the other pubs in Clapham. As far as I can see, though it isn't very far, men upon men line up and size each other, queuing as they are to get to the bar or the dance floor. In the immediate distance I see the dance floor itself, which as usual, is covered in dry ice and svelte men trying to out wiggle each other. No one looks at me, thank God. To this assorted collection of monosexiers, a woman has no place in a bar devoted to the consummation of relationships with those of the same biological stock. I am periphery, I am wallpaper, I am defunct.

James is precisely the opposite. Eyes crawl all over him. Men guess their chances by sight, dress and demeanour. Is he to be approached or is he to approach them? When they do approach, or come over for a closer look, their faces are friendly albeit expectant. But they neither evoke the testosterone-led masculinity we have just seen nor do they counter members of the same sex with such a jaundiced view of what to expect. James is a potential mate, of that there is no doubt but the challenge lies not in the near-sighted truth of dismissal once a sexual act has been consummated, nor do the Marys collecting and circling each other have the same desire to control, to diminish, to desecrate - a cadence to that before, a cadence to the accepted.

I fall into banal conversation pointing out oddities though in no way enjoying them. James seems relaxed, though I am not sure what degree of apprehension he carries within. Most would feel the threat of the environment and most should include my friend. Yet he chats nonchalantly as if the evening had been a normal evening. I cannot help but wonder what he has done with the tale relayed, the rape, the child within. Is it being processed or has it been processed and ready to gestate? I may expect no more than either. I shouldn't and have rightly seen inaction, for what else could James do? He is not one to deliver a tear, a sign or even a fist upon the table. Yet he still thinks as a male and wants to act as one. But he cannot act and the tale must be processed and sat upon until some call to arms is clear.

Of course, he cannot help me now nor can he be anything other than a featherweight caught in the random airflows of a circulating city breeze. His company is all I require. I know that should he be called upon, he will act. And only then will the depth and severity of the burn to his psyche become known. James is my best friend and apart from Edmund, my only friend. I have no worries that this is a man who, for all his weaknesses, will protect me and value me more than any other. I have no worries at all.

The music is horribly loud. It pains my ears and I cannot help but think that speech here is denuded by design so all that matters is the look of the other - physicality, attraction quotient, promiscuity; a montage of image rather than the delivery of the inner. Characters are touched at their edges in here. No one cares who you are. No one wants to care who you are. The physical is all and the offspring of the many. I stand next to James and he cannot hear me. He was never meant to hear me. This temple of excess reminds me so much of Edmund. Such places are precisely the places where he has misspent most of his time and where so many of his horrid relationships have transpired as he threw money around the bar and impressed no one who wasn't willing to be impressed anyway, by a willing mind and a subservient body. I wonder if he thinks the price, such as it now is, was worth it. What price openness and honesty if the alternative is all around?

My eyes begin to glaze. I notice James looking at me, wondering what I am thinking. I have obviously stopped observing and drifted into a world of my very own. His intuition lets him down.

"Stop thinking about it, Iris. It is done and you have accepted it. You have made the choice to have the baby - why dwell on circumstance any more than you absolutely have to?"

I smile in my friend's direction. At that moment, how wrong could he be? It is not me Iris thinks of. I tell James I am thinking of Edmund.

"You need only to be thinking of yourself. Edmund is not your responsibility no matter what you now think of him. And remember how much you despised him in the past. Remember what he has tried to do to you in the past; how much he made you work, how he transformed you into a sad reflection of one of those stupid financial documents you read all day. He has taken a good deal of what are supposed to be the best years of your life."

"Oh James. He did nothing of the sort. I made the choice to work in the City of London. No one has ever made me go and work in that horrible office, surrounded by all of those people. Edmund isn't to blame for the choices I have made."

"But what about the choices he has made which have had a direct bearing upon you? If it wasn't for the man's selfishness we wouldn't have ended up at that party in Chelsea a few weeks ago and you wouldn't have been the victim of such a vile act."

I remind myself that James doesn't really have the first clue as to how I formulate thoughts. How could he ever have the tiniest degree of insight as to how I qualify my actions and judge the behaviour of others? That saying, I do ask myself, in fact I question myself, why I am now so attached to the well-being of Edmund Rose, a man who James rightly points out was intensely questioned such a comparatively short time ago. And James is right; the only person, sorry, persons I should be thinking of are Iris and my child.

As James heads toward the bathroom, I take a look around. I wonder if I am the only female in the room. I squeeze my way through the crowd at the bar somewhat absent-mindedly forgetting that James is still otherwise indisposed, wishing to take a closer look at the dance floor, nipping through and jostling with expectant faces, past faces which curl around their hungry features as another body walks past, another opportunity until they see Iris - a woman and an opportunity lost. As I get closer to the dance floor all I unveil is one anaemic man after another; another orifice concentrate; another tart upon the altar ready to sacrifice himself to another man. What a relief it is to be a disappointment; an object of shame; an object but an object which remains untouched by the greed of man. Be I a leper, a runt, a discard in this church, I do not mind. I implore every man to ignore me, to disregard me and to reject me - just do not touch me. But I am touched - rather forcefully touched and tapped upon the shoulder. I imagine it is James, rightfully peeved at my absence. To my disbelief I turn with a smile to see a smile I have seen once before.

Yet she doesn't see me. She looks straight through me. I imagine her expectations do not extend to seeing me. I imagine her expectations stop, as do mine, at the locus of an all male world. She pushes me aside while I hide my face and the allegretto pulses of my heart start bouncing off my head. What can she be doing here? To make the choice to enter this colony of samesex poineers moves beyond the atypical. I am here for respite. Is she here for the same? And if her presence allows her to foil the sentiments I too, wish to foil, is this not one more touchstone of difference which marks her out and makes me want to speak to her even more, to find out, to actually find out?

Coincidence or fate? Happenstance or design?

I seem fated to think of Helen Jenvey wherever I go. And if I am not to think of her, she is there upon my shoulder, much the same as Brodie sits upon hers. Did she see me? Did she recognise me? And what further facet of character will I recognise when I lay my eyes upon her?

On looking around I see her talking while dancing - talking to and dancing with another woman. They seem friendly though not engrossed, chatting periodically while swinging their hips and yelling to each other while the monosexiers abound. They look so incongruous - two pretty things amongst a scrum of sylphs looking for slackened passages pursued by amyl nitrate, like two drops of blood in a cold bath.

"Do you have any idea how many times I have had my backside pinched? There was an old fella in the bathroom who wouldn't stop looking. Do you realise how hard it is to pee when another man stands next to you and looks at your penis down the length of your shirt? I had to tell him to look somewhere else, which, of necessity brought sideways glances upon me. Now I am a pariah in this club because several of its most sexually virulent occupants know I am not a friend of Dorothy."

"A friend of Dorothy?"

"A friend of Dorothy should be as obvious as a hooker in a nunnery. You are surrounded by friends of Dorothy. Alas I am no one's friend for I, by not being willing to be intimate with any friends of Dorothy, have selected friends of Dorothy as my enemy."

"You are not even listening. Here, have this pint of beer."

James waits for a response but knows he isn't going to get one. He sees I am distracted.

"Who are you looking at?

Isn't my humour good enough for you?"

Without looking at him, I sense his eyes following the same direction.

"Two girls. So what? One rather Irish looking, the other blonde and athletic. A pervert's dream. Probably lesbians in a club like this and no doubt here for a bit of peace and quiet from prying eyes.

"Why are you so interested in them?"

"Because the woman with the dark hair is Brodie's secretary."

James looks muddled.

"Don't all lawyers have secretaries?"

James screws up his face.

" Brodie? Poor woman. No wonder she has turned to a member of her own sex."

Gyrating males now surround us. Observations become obscure due to the unwanted imposition of a song sung by Shirley Bassey.

"Think she might be leaving the dance floor, Iris. And we are smack bang between her and the bar."

As I try, but fail to recede into shadow, Helen walks straight toward me. It is too late for me to move and as her hand falls upon my shoulder once more, she politely asks me to step aside, with, once again, no realisation on her face as to the identity of the woman she has just touched.

"She recognised you Iris," James tells me.

"I think she recognised you."

"We've met, twice. This is the last place on earth she would expect to see me. Tell me there was something to her face which told you she saw who it was - tell me."

"You know it and I know. She saw you alright."

I should be thinking politically. This woman is integral to the man about to ruin a multitude of careers. But I am not. Again I have that intuitive feeling about this woman; a sense, an inexpressible clarity that she is different from the characters making up the act. I feel strangely nervous about the prospect of speaking to her. Iris - I am cold and even-tempered, methodical in my thoughts and rarely given to a deal of excitement. But this is a feeling, another feeling, another sign of the slow change in my emotional temperament and in the relationship between my body and my mind.

"So this is where international finance lawyers escape to on a Friday night?"

I feel a tap on my shoulder. I turn around. Helen stands in front of me - the same size; eye to eye; drink in her hand and a slightly lopsided grin on her face. Caught by surprise, I am at a loss as to what to say, while I get an impression markedly different from the aggression I was in receipt of that very afternoon.

Helen backs off slightly.

"It's Iris isn't it?

"Sorry to pounce on you. I saw you just a few moments ago. I have been watching you from over there just to make sure it is you."

I look around. The club is a little rabbit warren offering a myriad of dusky alcoves this club affords from where I could have been watched.

"Iris; I think we should formally introduce ourselves away from that horrible office. And I think I should apologise for being so rude this afternoon. Working for that little runt means that I have little or no capacity for what he calls fraternising with the enemy."

Helen offers me her hand. I accept. Woman to woman, hand to hand, this is not the accepted normality in relation to a feminine greeting. It is a rather more masculine trait – Germanic, anal.

"Want to sit down?"

I look at James. James is looking at Helen's friend who is looking at James, while two men behind James are looking at James' behind. James senses his moment and leaves me to it as he skirts, then approaches, whispering in her ear, causing her to smile, leaving me with no excuse but to talk to Helen.

"Let's go find somewhere a little quieter."

I follow Helen through the crowd, squeezing in and out, trying not to absorb the sweat being secreted by the semi-naked bodies cavorting some in time, some out of time. As I gingerly take steps forward I wonder what the ensuing conversation will be; who will lead, what I should in fact do, whether I should lead, whether I should be relatively open, whether I should let Helen take the lead and see how she wants to deliver information if, indeed, that is her intention. She is, I remind myself, closer to the man who threatens me more than any other and is either for him or against him.

So should I trust her?

I implicitly should not trust her.

Should I let her into any of my thoughts about Brodie?

Probably not.

Should I impart anything other than the bare minimum?

Probably.

Helen leads me to a seat close to a servery in a back room. Colouring the innards of the hatch is a transvestite serving chips and all manner of fried food to the hungry, the insane, the earthy. Dorothies are deep in discussion. I watch flirtation and hunger coincide as conversations turn to performance with tongue, body language and the power of suggestion two-stepping with the salacious consummation of fried food.

"I've never seen you in here before Iris. I wouldn't have thought it is your sort of place."

"No, not really. Unfortunately we had a bit of trouble in the pub. You know, drunken men thinking they can conquer the world. They got nowhere and decided to turn on my flatmate. So here we are. These men only molest each other. Oh, and they molest James too. Fortunately he is able to deal with it."

"Respite from the world at large?"

"Men at large really, men at large with beer coursing through their veins."

"My sentiments too. I can't go anywhere without getting my backside pinched, a tongue in my ear, an arm touching my breast, a ridiculous comment meant to make me roll over and submit. If only men were a little more like women I think life would be a little easier for all of us. Especially men."

"So this is a haunt of yours?"

"This and a couple of the quieter pubs in Clapham. I'll let the futility of youth pack the main bars. I only go out to chat and dance."

"And your friend?"

"Feels the same way."

I wonder if I can get away with light conversation - if there is any need to refer to Brodie.

"Sorry about this afternoon. I have little choice but to do as I am told. It isn't as if I want to be sub-human but the man I work for has me over a barrel. I'm sure you understand."

"I'm not too sure I do."

The way Helen looks at me suggests that her sentiments represent something of a tale. She seems embarrassed and uncomfortable. It pricks my interest.

"He has you over a barrel?"

I can see she wants to explain her actions, her attitude, her feelings. In truth I want her to explain and perhaps it isn't just out of interest. Part of me knows that if I have as much information about the man as is possible, I can make informed judgements how to deal with whatever he chooses to throw at us. Yet intuition tells me that Helen is rather simple in comparison. Intuition tells me she is rather more honest. Still, should I defer from seeking information imbued with a cynical spirit of self-interest or am I actually keen to see the transmission of sweetness her eyes depict into an honesty she should not portray?

What has Helen over a barrel?

Why?

"How long have you worked there, Iris?"

"Edmund hired me a few months after I qualified. Almost four years."

"Edmund Rose. I think I've seen him. He is the one who hired isn't he?"

"Yes, through a spurious relationship with his son."

Helen is quiet and thinking. Her reply is more for her benefit than mine.

"That would explain it, then."

"Explain what?"

"Oh, nothing."

"You've worked for Brodie for how long?"

She seems to wince as if she is stretching - reaching for forbidden fruit.

"You don't have to tell me if you don't want to."

Helen looks at me and weighs me up - more than a cursory examination, less than a prognosis.

"Ever since I don't want to remember."

Her words are slow and pathetic.

I try to appease her.

"Well let's try and forget, then."

"No, no. You know I just have to be careful. You know what he's like."

"I guess he finds it hard to avoid being obnoxious. Put it this way; if I see him, I try to cross the street. I think I have good reason now too."

"Yes, well we all have one reason or another to avoid . Some more than others."

"I take it he isn't exactly a friend?"

I ask the question though I know the answer - a segway to a deeper conversation I intuitively desire. Sod the care with which I have run my life. Helen Jenvey is not a threat. I know. I just, know.

" Brodie? Doesn't have any friends. All that man has is enemies. I think he'd prefer to have enemies. He is predisposed to harm."

"Known him long?"

Again, she withdraws.

"Hm?"

"Known him long?"

I seem insistent. I am, insistent.

"Since I was a child. His parents and mine were very close. We attended the same school, were good friends when we were kids and have seemed to orbit each other ever since."

"But you do or you don't, get on with him?"

"Well that's the thing. I always did get on with him. He wasn't always as bad as he is now. A tiny bit of Brodie is nice, uncorrupted and gentle. Then he changed - things changed."

I wonder why Helen needs to explain herself to me. If she is threatened, why tell? I cannot but feel that the exposition to me aids her not one bit. So why expose?

"Our paths took a very different course once we left school. You can clearly see he is as ambitious as they come and he always was about as intelligent as they come. It is a scary combination."

"So what happened between you?"

I do not expect a response. I can tell that I am trying to intrude upon some private grief. What right have I, Iris, to run into this woman - a woman I barely know and expect her story? It was presumption to ask and presumptuous to wait for a declaration. That very evident fear of Brodie, a conscript to his whim, is surely enough to keep her tongue exactly where it is. If she had so much to hide and so much to be afraid of, if I were Helen, I would keep myself to myself.

Somehow I do not counter for her honesty. In fact, I do not understand her honesty and give her a bailout clause.

"You don't have to tell me, you know. You seem reluctant to tell. And why should you? We have only just met and whatever is between you and Brodie should, of necessity, remain so. I am not in a position to ask and if you do not want to, you should not put yourself in a position to tell."

Helen's voice lowers as she moves closer, secretively scanning the room for prying eyes, uncivil ears and mouths that will bear the story.

"Met, yes. But we are kindred spirits, too. I know Iris. I know about Edmund Rose."

It is my turn to hesitate.

"I'm afraid it is true. Nothing about Brodie should surprise you. I've given up wondering where it comes from. Rose isn't the first. has been screwing people into the ground for years. He only cares about himself and doesn't give two hoots about the sufferings of anybody else. As much as I feel sorry for your boss, I couldn't have told you about if I had been able to. I'm afraid that I, too know only too well what he is capable of. I too have just as much reason to fear him. Brodie is a unique little specimen - the most underhand, egotistical, selfish and disgusting man. Believe me, nothing is past his greed. And no one is immune to its potential."

I decide to bite.

"You speak as if you know yourself."

"Hm?"

"He has something on you?"

"He isn't happy unless he has something on everybody."

"So why are you telling me? You have something to lose."

Helen composes herself - the mutation from protectorate to complicity has taken ten minutes. She must have a great deal to tell.

"I don't know. Perhaps because we shared a silly joke. Perhaps because we share the punishments of an idiot; perhaps because I see in you, I saw and I felt in you, on the first occasion we met, an understanding and a strength I have rarely seen or felt. Even now, when I know I should keep my tongue to myself, I feel trust. See, I ask myself - what have I got to lose? We are both one and the same; we both have the potential to suffer harm at the hands of this man. To hurt me is to risk hurting yourself. Both you and I have little to gain but we can certainly do each other a great deal of harm. It is, as I have said, that I feel I can trust you, though I don't quite know why."

"He hasn't hurt me. I'm not sure he can."

"Oh, he will, now that you have sided against him. Believe me."

"Why put up with it Helen? What has he done to you?"

Helen twists her body to face me, shoulder blade to should blade, eye to eye. Stranger still, she slips her hand into mine.

"I expect you recognised that we come from the same community in Ireland. I don't expect you to understand what that place is like, apart from your general perceptions. Sometimes I can't fathom it out myself. But the truth is simple. Religion camouflages, enshrouds, conceals bigotry and hatred, both in my community and the Cic community. Each faces the other in mutual impasse, in mutual loathing - abhorrent to each other, abhorrent to everybody else.

What makes this tolerated intolerance worse, for me at any event, is that my father is a Protestant Minister who brought up myself and my brothers to believe that the Cics represented the very seed-bed of the devil. We were never to mix with them, never to share space with them, we were to despise and ridicule them, to hurt them at every opportunity, to dismiss them, reject them and subjugate them - all under some supposed moral authority from a higher place.

is of the same ilk, the same destructive self, the same pride, anger, the same stupidity. Quite apart from his intelligence and the drive which got him to Cambridge then to the City of London, deep down he represents the opposite of goodness and all that is feeble in the human mind when faced with opinions which are not his own."

"But surely you think the same way?"

Helens reflects for a while. She moves even closer.

"It isn't the same for me. I admit I once believed all I was told and all I was exposed to. All I ever knew, whether I was at home or wherever I was, was an insidious hatred of the opinions of others. And that barren and insidious redundancy did not just extend to the Cics - it extended to all things and all men who did not think or act in the same way."

"And you don't think like this any more?"

"I most certainly do not, for my eyes were opened in the most appalling way."

I feel teased.

" went to Cambridge, as you know. He had the time of his life and succeeded at everything he did. I, however, stayed behind and got on with my life. There wasn't much to choose from and as I had a general disdain for examinations, though I never considered myself as stupid, I signed up to do a secretarial course at a local college, which owing to the size of our town, was the only college I could attend. The position was the same for Cics.

For the first time, when I was a young woman, I was forced, much to my father's anger, to attend classes alongside people who, I had been told, were vermin."

"And I assume they thought of you in the same way?"

"Of course. They despised us. We despised them.

However it soon became apparent as I attended classes with them that what they hated and what we hated were mutated images of the Cic, the Protestant. I realised very quickly that the image which was so powerful in our minds, was not the same and did not relate to reality, which was that the people I met and the man I fell in love with, were not hideous ogres nor were they detestable. They were just people and had precisely the same concerns as anybody else."

"You fell in love with one of them?"

Helen smiles. Then she looks away.

"I fell in love with a Cic. He was just a boy in my class."

I begin trying to imagine scenarios in my head. I see Helen sneaking around, trying to catch moments with this suitor so as not to raise suspicion. How difficult it must have been. How brave she must have been.

"A Cic boy in a secretarial class otherwise totally populated by young women. Initially I thought he was a homosexual and in some respects he was effeminate. Yet the man I sat next to and got to know, then fell in love with, was kind, caring, sensitive, decent, innocent and brave. But he was a Cic boy and I was a Protestant girl."

Helen drains the dregs of her pint glass. Trying to find space, to buy time to think, I offer to buy her another drink, an offer she accepts. While I am at the bar I mull her story over and, indeed, why, though I am desperate to hear her conclusion, she is telling me at all.

What relevance does it have to me?

What relevance at all?

When I return Helen is lost in a very private world. I cannot help but think of the environment she had grown up in, the environment which had shaped her and the reasons why she is here.

"If you guessed, you guessed right. Each moment we had together became very precious to me - sneaking around, finding time in places were we couldn't be seen, risking excommunication from the people we loved most, risking the total and complete disruption of the very fabric of our lives, the very fabric of all we knew - it was a risk, but a risk worth taking. And when I say fell in love I mean precisely that, for you may think I was enamoured by forbidden fruit. That is wrong. I fell in love with the person, the man, his very being. It wouldn't have mattered to me if he were a different colour or struck with physical deformity. Corin was the world to me and all that was in it.

"And then I fell pregnant.

"Then we were betrayed by a friend of his and a friend of mine."

"Betrayed?"

"Betrayed to my father and to his."

"So what became of you? What became of the baby? What became of him?"

Tears start flowing down Helen's cheeks. She has begun to attract attention. I offer her a handkerchief which she graciously accepts.

"Well we were both excommunicated. My father excommunicated his own daughter. But that bastard waited till I gave birth before he banished me. Corin had no such luck."

"Betrayed to the community as a whole?"

"No. Just to our families in turn. When this happens, the betrayer has most to gain in utilising shame - shame being sufficient for the purposes of blackmail for the protagonist to name his price. Save that in Corin's case the protagonist never had the chance to. On finding out what their son had done he was exposed to his local community by his own family. Corin's body was found a week later. It didn't and doesn't take a brain surgeon to work out what had happened. He had been killed for being with me. And that is a burden I will have to carry with me for the rest of my life.

As for my child, I gave birth to a boy weighing seven pounds and six ounces. The moment I gave birth was the last moment I had with our baby. In the same clothes I wore when I gave birth I was taken away by my father, driven from the house in which I was raised, given a ticket to England and waved goodbye at the Belfast Ferry. I can never go back home. I have brought shame and odium upon my family whether the rest of our community knows about it or not. My father put religion before blood, doctrine before fallibility, bigotry before humanity."

I work it out.

"And Brodie knows."

Helen looks surprised then settles down, reverting to her tears.

"Yes. Brodie knows. The reason I work for the man is that he has threatened me with telling the community back at home why I left. If he were to do that, my family would be finished."

Anger wells up within me.

"Iris; this isn't your problem. I must confess, in a way, I don't know why I am telling you. However, before you jump to conclusions about me, thinking I am a hard bitch, that I am difficult and obstructive, you must understand that I am not in a position to object to Brodie for he knows too much about me."

"But what does he know?"

"He knows absolutely everything. My father told his father and the information was passed on to . told me that if I didn't work for him and do all he said then he would see to it that the whole community at home knows precisely all that has happened. And that will mean that my family - all of my family, meaning not just my parents but my brothers and sisters and all of my extended family will be ostracised and banished from the only community they know."

"So he is blackmailing you?"

"Yes. He has me and the people I used to hold dear, totally under control. And whether my father excommunicated me or not, I love them all too much for that to happen to them. It is enough for them that this happened in the first place."

The anger which I feel on hearing of the depth to which one human being can sink in relation to another, is all consuming. Helen's story represents the very essence of inhumanity. While I take stock of all that has happened to me, I am exposed to a story of a put-upon woman whose strength and decency puts me to shame. As I am slowly coming to terms with change, here is a woman whose courage is accepted in isolation and accepted in the subjection she had no choice but to accept - courage which runs far into the distance while I am standing still.

I resolve, through clenched teeth, to fight Brodie on his own terms. Iris is going to grasp the nettle and deal with Brodie in a way that is going to save this woman, this poor, poor woman.

I put my arm around Helen and hold her close. It is only the second time in my life I have ever hugged anyone. As she cries on my shoulder and tears run into my clothing, I look up at the people in the room, glaring at them and into them. I tell myself and by my visage, I am telling them, I am going to put all of the understanding I have gleaned about human nature from years of observation and deal with the injustice dealt upon me and those I hold most dear. And if that means descending to a level where I cannot avoid all I have rejected, then I will just have to do it. I now have a higher purpose and the greater good is at stake. Should Brodie represent in microcosm the intrinsic perfidy of man, then if I can extricate him to a world in which he could no longer harm the innocent, this tiny eradication may enable a few who are decent to live better and morally healthier lives.

"Helen; I think we should leave. This is not the place to let others see you in such a condition. I'll get your coat from the cloakroom. Please, come back to my flat. Let's get out of here."

"But my friend?"

"I'll go and find her. I'll tell her you are coming back with me. James will make sure she gets home safely. No doubt James is trying to take care of her already, in his own, unique way."

I find James in the darkest recess of the darkest corner, with his tongue descending down the throat of Helen's companion. It takes James a good deal of time to respond as I yell at them across a beer-soaked table. James stirs with a grunt and is only too happy to oblige when I tell them I intend to leave with Helen.

I pick up Helen's coat while thinking of James, of his undoubted good intentions of taking care of me, of helping me through the next few months and of being more than just a friend. How quickly that disappears as alcohol cuts him off from the capacity to reason and his lust for flesh gets in the way. I castigate him for being no different from all the other men I have ever known. I admonish him for being male, for being human.

XX.

After the long walk from the club to my flat, Helen looks in much better spirits. We say very little to each other as we take in the scenery late on Friday night in Clapham. There is plenty to distract for we see, in the fresh air, two men being sick over the pavement, a full-on fist fight across the High Street, a couple having sex in an alley with a man taking a woman from behind - both of them oblivious to the merest presence of anybody else and we see a man giving another man a blow job just fifty yards from my front door. And on arriving at my front door, we are just in time to stop a man in the process of unzipping his fly, from urinating all over the front of my flat.

It may read comedic. Perhaps the late night Clapham booze show is comedic as alcohol denudes typically English repression and all that pent-up desire released when brains collapse. But neither Helen nor I, seeing these scenes unfold, think they are anything other than pathetic and a warning of where dishonesty with oneself and the world at large can lead.

"I am so grateful, Iris. See, I needed to tell you that I am on your side when it comes to . But there is absolutely nothing I can do to help you."

"And Edmund?"

"I've known about that particular situation since became aware of his behaviour. Knowing he can destroy the lives of my family and that I can do nothing but accept, he tends to confide in me because I am not the slightest threat to him. So whenever circumstances like this have arisen in the past, and let me tell you he didn't get to where he is without resorting to all sorts of appalling behaviour, he uses me as a sounding board - someone to run ideas past before he decides to destroy another life before he goes in for the kill."

"Doesn't he confide in his wife?"

"I have never met the woman he claims to be married to, nor have I met his children. Yet he claims to be married and happily married at that. He tells people he is married and he tells people he has children. But I have no real evidence that he is married or that he has kids. All I know is that lives in Surrey, has a brother who is a professor of psychiatry and another from whom he is estranged. As for his life as an adult, I can't say what he does when he goes home and where his home is. It is a complete mystery to me and a complete mystery to everyone who has ever worked with him."

"In the same way as Edmund has kept the lie of his own sexuality going, so as to keep his career together, Brodie is doing the same thing? What, possibly, could Brodie be hiding? I don't think his sexuality is an issue. What else could it be?"

"You know, I asked myself the same question maybe over a thousand times. And the only answer I can come up with is that he has nothing to hide. Absolutely nothing."

"So why does he lie, if he does lie? If he does not, why does he hide? It doesn't make sense."

"It makes sense if you think that he has opted for a quiet life. Let's just say there is nothing sinister in this. Let's just say that he has worked out that if he tells people he is normal, whatever normal means, then he is, in all likelihood, going to be left alone. So whatever skewed paths he chooses to follow when he goes home, wherever that home may be, he can do so with absolute impunity and far from prying eyes."

"If we could see underneath the façade, then I would have a better opportunity to work out how to protect the people he intends to hurt."

"People have tried to get at him before. I remember when he was newly-qualified, one boss in particular took an instant and irrational dislike to him. was in an appalling position as he knew this man had the power to destroy his career. had to decide whether to leave the firm, which was the wrong thing to do at the time, or whether to stay and fight.

"Do you know what he did?

"He hired a private detective and had this partner followed. He soon realised, on the basis of the information coming back to him, that this man was having an affair with one of the trainee lawyers. He was also having an affair with one of the other partners.

" had choices and he confided those choices to me. He decided to expose all the people involved in such a way that his involvement as the messenger was completely inviolate. And when these liaisons became public knowledge, the senior partner, who Brodie knew to be a moral purist, demanded the resignations of all concerned."

"So he is willing to do anything to protect himself and to do anything to advance?"

"Yes."

"You obviously know what he plans to do in relation to Edmund Rose. Indirectly and then directly, that is going to affect me. I don't know what you think of Edmund. I used to despise him but recently I have got to know him, more out of adversity than anything else and I can tell you, behind all of the scurrilous gossip and the machinations of the rumour mill, that man is as kind and as thoughtful as one could possibly be. He is simply trapped by urges he can't control in a society which will not accept him."

"Like I was, Iris?"

"Yes I suppose so. Both of you have suffered; both of you still suffer at the hands of men.

"I know you can't help me, Helen. But one thing I can do is help you. In doing so you will be giving yourself the opportunity to be rid of the man for once and for all. I am aware it is dangerous. Brodie has all the cards in his hand and we simply have nothing to play with. I cannot say what he will do over the next few days or weeks to hurt yet more people, though we can both imagine. But while he waits to pick his moment, we have time and clearly the inclination to pick ours. What I need is as much information about the man as you can possibly give me. I need as much of his background and I need insight into his thoughts and motives. I know you don't threaten him so he confides in you. How would you feel about helping me in any way you can?

"How would you feel about stopping this hideous thing from ever being able to get to you again and so saving you and your family from what you fear most of all?"

I ask the question and in asking the question, I know I am making an easy decision. I have nothing to lose, for I will suffer at the hands of Brodie in standing idly by. The reputation of my family is not in question, I do not have the guilt which Helen clearly carries around with her - the death of her only love, the child taken away from her and the shame she has already visited on her family.

"You know Iris, there is one thing you have not asked me and I am surprised that you haven't."

I cannot imagine what it is.

"You haven't asked me whether I hate my family for treating me so badly. You can see that I am trying to protect them but you haven't enquired whether I bear them any ill will for what they have done to me."

"I assume you despise them. And you want to protect them because you assume there are higher principles at stake."

Helen's eyes light up with my reply.

"How would you know that? How would you be able to understand?"

I find Helen's naivety a little amusing. I tell myself off. I have to ask the question - how could she contemplate the way my mind works? How could she even know who and what I am?

"Womanhood has been very cruel to you. The man you love is taken from you and no doubt murdered, simply for falling in love with you and you with him. And the only good thing to come from it, being a child which bears the marks of both of you, is taken away. You have lost a child; you have lost your closest friend. Regardless of what is taking place in our office, I can see you are as well-balanced as one could possibly expect, given all that has happened. It would have been the easiest thing to tell Brodie to go to Hell but the very fact that you haven't means you have considered and chosen a course of action in which you have sacrificed yourself for the good of others.

"I cannot say that you have no malice. If it was me, I think I'd have every right to hate every atom in 's body. Who can blame you if you do? But I guess that you have chosen to disregard hatred. For myself, I see and analyse people for what they are – interaction, language, body language, motive, desire, lust, greed and all the rest of it. But I never feel part of it. I am as cold as those banking documents I read in my shoebox of an office. I want to do all I can to help you. And of course I want to do all I can to help myself for my very own reasons. Only you can answer the question whether you feel hatred for anyone. Like I say, I would be the last person to criticise you if you did. I think I, of all people, can understand."

I think my last comment through. Am I getting too close to what I, too, have suffered? My empathy with Helen has to come from somewhere other than my inner concern for this woman. My feelings, for that is what they are, have to have arisen from somewhere. I feel anger; I feel sadness and the desire to help when I have never been in the position to help anyone else before - anyone else other than myself. What a rosy life I have led. What a picture of innocence I could have been, for I have been as lucky as they come. Iris has lived a life as easy as the alphabet. I had never been tested in any moral way. I have never had to put my head above anything other than the mealiest parapet. Now I am in, I am amongst it and my spirit has been aroused - the one thing I thought I never possessed. Helen, Edmund Rose, Brodie and the man who raped me, have turned a hitherto barren emotional landscape into a form I am slowly coming to terms with via the induction of emotions I have only ever seen in other people. And how will I be able to deal with this progression from stone to a vibrant living entity? I have suffered pain and I have suffered torment. This is the biggest challenge a cold and austere finance lawyer with an eye for social detail has to face. And I use the word has in a quite deliberate way. This is not a matter of choice as so much is. I have no choice.

One question nags me. I look at Helen, across the living room floor and see in her an inner beauty and an external beauty I am privileged to share. I sense that we are already kindred spirits, bound by the very same contusions of immorality and bedevilled as a consequence of man. How much of myself do I give to her in order that she may trust me?

How much should I tell her and how much should I trust her with?

Can I trust her?

"Iris; I will help you as much as I can, although I have everything to lose. I think we both have everything to gain."

Helen stands up and sits next to me, staring at me from no more than six inches away. I see just how beautiful she is; how angelic her face is; how her eyes plead with me for help and how her very body seems to fall into my heart begging me to act on her behalf.

"I promise you that I shall do whatever it takes to get this man away from us. But I want you to promise me that you will never betray what I have told you. I have, in life, trusted only one other human being. And he has gone - taken from me. I don't want to suffer any more. I don't want to live the life I had previously accepted. I implore you - if I promise to help you with every bone in my body, I want you to tell me right now, while I look at you, that you too will not seek to hurt me in any way possible. It is all I ask. It is not too much to ask."

"You have my word. Together we will be strong. Together we will see this through."

Helen puts her head on my lap. I watch my hand stroking her hair. Within ten minutes Helen is asleep. I stand, trying not to wake her and lay her out on the settee, cover her with a duvet, turn off the light and leave her to the serenity of sleep. Within five minutes I am fast asleep myself, back to a thought world which cares nothing for the challenges my child and I, Edmund and I, Helen and I, and Iris, will have to face in the coming weeks.

XXI.

I slide out of bed and walk into the living room. Helen has gone. The duvet which covered her is strewn across the settee and on top of it is an array of female clothes. For a while I cannot focus until my numb mind realises that they belong to Helen's friend.

I pick up the telephone and call James' mobile phone, listening to it ring in James' bedroom. Then I hear faint sounds of movement through the bedroom wall – groans, sighs and expletives, as James searches his room.

"What time is it?" he asks, gruff and unaware.

"A fine way to answer the telephone."

"Iris; where are you?"

"Outside your bedroom door, waiting for you to come and talk to me."

"Can't it wait?"

"No it cannot wait."

As he walks out of his bedroom door, he throws a cheap towelling robe around his shoulders. Behind him I catch a fleeting glimpse of a half naked body and hear a gentle snore.

"Sorry Iris. Another lucky night."

"When you returned last night, was Helen here?"

James looks confused.

"Helen - you have just slept with her friend. When you got back was she asleep on the settee?"

"No. The living room was empty when we got home. That's right, I noticed the duvet but thought little of it. I thought you had decided to watch some late night television."

"So she left?"

"Who has left? Are you going to tell me who was here? And who left?"

"I walked Helen here. We stayed up for a while, talking and she fell asleep on the settee. She must have woken up, realised she was in a strange house and decided to leave. Understandable probably. I guess we can glean her address if we need to, provided you use your charms on her friend."

"I presume you and her hit it off?"

"You presume correctly.

"Alright. I'll do my best. I'm not promising anything, though. She seems very protective of Helen."

The telephone rings. As James bounds over the settee to get it, I snarl at him and he knows to leave well alone. I expect it to be Helen. It is Edmund Rose.

"Morning sweet Iris - such a lovely day."

I have no idea what kind of day it is. I check the clock. It is nearly lunchtime. Edmund's timing could not have been better.

"I do feel a rather splendid lunch coming on. We can take it at my club. Why don't you bring that lovely young man you live with? I'll hear no more about it. Late lunch. Two o'clock sharp. We'll take it with a view of the park."

Edmund hangs up and I see James eagerly waiting for a précis.

"Bad news. Lunch at two in Edmund's club, off The Mall. Shirt and tie. He won't take no for an answer."

"What? Both of us?"

"Both of us."

"I have no choice do I?"

"You have no choice at all. We have much to discuss."

James turns abruptly and heads straight for his bedroom door. Not more than thirty seconds later I hear peals of laughter, both his and hers, while I take to the shower and start to make myself presentable, letting hot water fall onto my head, soaking my hair, covering my shoulders and run all over my body. I reach for the soap and create a lather, gently cleansing myself. While I try to discard thought, I catch a glimpse of my body in the mirror and become curious. At the sight; at the mutated sight of my shape in the mirror, I examine my features. I have long legs and straight legs; I am not overweight in the slightest and I have large but rounded breasts which have not given in to gravity. My arms are graceful and my hair is blonde. I have always known that this is attractive to the world at large though I know that in a different age I would have been considered simply plain and average. As I swivel my hips, I look at my stomach side on, expecting a huge protrusion. There is no huge protrusion and I have to remind myself that I am only a short time pregnant.

I find it difficult when looking at my stomach, feeling my stomach and trying to imagine what is taking place inside my stomach wall, to accept that I carry a child. I find it hard to imagine I will grow and gestate and develop another life entirely dependent upon me while it is inwardly attached to me and outwardly dependent upon me for the formative years of its life. I consider, for a few moments, the sex of the child - be it a boy or be it a girl.

Should I want a boy? Why should I be responsible for adding to the sum total of human misery in presenting another with the potential to hurt and destroy? See, I may not be able to give a boy the outlook I so readily cherish. I may have to accept that a boy turns into a man and no matter what I have the potential to instruct, there are certain traits in a man nurture cannot control. I should want to give birth to a girl. I want a child and shall tutor a child to become an adult who fills me with pride and so makes up for the circumstances of its conception. I should want to give birth to a girl.

I pinch the fat around my midriff. I notice no particular change and I mock my own self-interest when I push my stomach out and use that image as some sort of lodestar in my vain search to classify what is going to happen to me. I tell myself off for wasting my time.

My attention turns to Edmund. What do I tell him? How do I present all that Helen has told me? Will he accept that we have little choice but to enlist the help of Brodie's secretary? I wonder without answers and decide that conjecture does me no good.

"Iris; you have a visitor."

I dry myself off and as I walk into the living room, James beats a hasty retreat. Helen is sitting upon the settee. She appears to be tired and is wearing the same clothes she was wearing last night and has obviously not been home.

"I'm sorry Iris, I couldn't sleep. I have been walking around all night. I felt I owed it to you to come back."

Conscious of the time and the exactness of Edmund Rose, I lead Helen to my bedroom and continue our conversation while I get dressed. Helen sits on the end of my bed and looks down, talking mostly to her shoes. For some reason the actions undertaken in getting myself dressed and applying make-up make me feel detached from the very intensity which marks Helen's words.

"I think of the resolve you are willing to show for me and for yourself and I want to help you. But the fear I have, which drives in and burns, is one I have tried to escape from but feel it tethering me so that I cannot help you. My mind is a list of 'what ifs'. And each question is to do with the consequence to myself and to my family should your proposal fail. Please be in no doubt that Brodie will betray me to the local protestant community should he find that I am involved with what you propose. He will betray me and he will destroy all I hold precious."

I consider very carefully all Helen says. I cannot blame her for her reticence. I cannot help thinking that she is hiding behind the potential harm which may befall her relations. I sense something deeper and I think I know what it is.

"Helen; if there is one thing in all you say, it is the one thing you have not said. The only person you have not mentioned since you first told me of what has happened to you is your child. It doesn't take a genius to work out your real intentions, sheltered as they are. It seems clear that after your child was taken, he was taken into the bosom of the family which rejected you.

Should your family be exposed, then it necessarily means the exposure of your child to a life which is, in fact, a non-life - a life where the towering animalism and bigotry of a whole community will fall upon and curse your child. That, I agree, is almost too high a price to pay, for what ultimately, you are seeking to protect is innocence. And while there is a scrap of innocence left in the body of that young life; while there is still a chance that the kind of maturity and outlook which you yourself manifest could be somehow passed on to that child, you have chosen to sacrifice yourself.

"But you need not do this any longer. I give you my word that we shall succeed in stopping Brodie from exposing you. You must allow yourself to trust me in a way that I shall repay you a thousandfold. We have more than just hope on our side. Brodie is just a man, though a man with all the forces of ignorance and information on his side. It doesn't matter. He can still be defeated. All you need is courage and the ability to trust."

"Oh Iris; how right you are. Of course I want to protect the only good that has come of my own sorry story. That boy means more to me that anything I know or am likely to know. And it is his life which is at stake here - not mine, for I had the privilege of making my own mistakes. If he is exposed, the excommunication of a child whose name I do not even know will make his choices for him. And what will become of the innocence I am trying to protect? My son will become a monster just like the rest of them, only he will become worse. Bitterness will follow him wherever he goes; anger will surround him and hatred will envelop him and hem him in. Why should I risk revenge when that is the price to pay?

"I cannot say I cannot trust you Iris. I have to say that I could and am sure I would trust you in other circumstances. But I cannot now and not ever, when it comes to the life of my child."

I weigh up my options. Helen must have complete confidence in me. In order to get it I must give. Mere empathy is not enough. Helen needs to know I am suffering and what my fate will be should I fail too. Only then can she trust me.

"Helen; I want you to listen to me. You say you cannot trust me. Well, what I am about to tell you should give you the ability to see that I can feel for what you have gone through, and I, above all others, have just as much reason to want this man taken out of my life and our lives, before he damages all of us. I want you to listen to what I have to tell you."

I commence with the evening wherein Edmund's homosexuality was disclosed to Brodie. I recall for her, in all its detail, precisely what happened, matters which I have already told. As I do so, I do so coldly, speaking objectively in much the same way as I used to think objectively. Clarity of description suits me, as Helen needs to make up her own mind without the need to fall in with the emotional outburst of another woman. Not only must she feel for me, but she has to feel without recourse to outburst, with a slow, ticking realisation that the circumstances which I describe are as much an injustice to me as were the events which have consumed her. There can be no spontaneous and cathartic delivery of feeling. She must see me as a kindred spirit willing to fight for myself and take just as much risk as she is in doing so. The only way that can be done is by planting a seed and allowing it to germinate within a higher sense of morality which I know Helen shares.

"Can you not see how we should be together? We need to pool all we have so as to protect that which cannot protect itself. We need to work together."

"Alright, I promise. We shall do this together. Once more I promise and this time I mean it. I shall do all in my power to help."

XXII.

We take a taxi to St James, just off The Mall. The majority of the journey is conducted in silence as we look out of the window at the passing London landscape. Rarely do I look at my city; rarely do I think of the city itself. One has so little time to reflect such is the speed at which London life is conducted, that The Houses of Parliament, which is to our right as we cross over Victoria Bridge, or the Tate Gallery or the numerous buildings wherein decisions have been made which have such pivotal status in the history of the English people, are apparent to us for what they really are.

I wonder if Edmund himself has the same perspective. He is, as were the generations of his family who did so well out of the way the English have chosen to order their society, a man destined to have his say, well, a say more than most.

I have no such pretensions nor should I have. My humble beginnings gave Iris the benefit of an environment where a good education was a rite of passage and my parent's kindness evolved a daughter who has neither the wit, the drive nor the talent to be anything radical, anything more than the ubiquitous norm. I am just a cog in an engine which will roar, long after I am gone.

"Impressive isn't it? Means something more than you and I - mere people. We are simply passing through history, James. This place is history."

James appreciates the sentiment. But it embarrasses him for it is so twee and he directs his comments to matters close at hand.

"It is hard to think of Edmund Rose as anything other than intimately connected with the fabric of the walls here. By birth and design he has been fizzing around power for generations. Why he has not chosen to call upon what must be a protectorate in order to avail himself of Brodie?"

"I think it is to do with the intrinsic nature of the class from which he derives, James. I know class is a dirty word these days and in reality, it may be that the ruling elite is now drawn from a wider background and a wider background than it has ever been drawn from before. I have no doubt that those who have the ability to command key decisions in practically every sphere of public life in this country are closely bound by ties of birth, education, perspective and some sense of history.

"Be that as it may, it has always seemed to me that these people have such a preoccupation with how they appear and by implication, a totally absorbing paranoia about the maintenance of appearance. The importance of the act should never be underestimated. It is about how one appears to be, not what one actually is."

"And this became a birthright - a generation by generation progression?"

"I think so. Well, yes - each generation embellishes the prejudices of the others until what may have been a simple tangent generations ago, mutates by degrees into a trait which, to an observer, is easily distinguished."

"Aren't we into the realms of cliché, Iris?"

"No; not cliché. I am not referring to a parody of the English upper class. History books are full of tales as to how utterly useless as an ilk those sorts of people are. They did have their uses, being people whose arrogance and wealth made them worthy of aspiration. No, I am talking of the functional underbelly - I am talking of people, like Edmund, who have accepted the Protestant work ethic and grown into the real holders of influence and power in their own right.

The only way I can reason with the realisation that Edmund Rose has not swotted Brodie like a fly, is that he is trapped by his own inability to face up to shame. This is the paradox he sees. His upbringing; the - sorry to be twee again - the triumph of form over substance which is such an integral part of the English way, stops him from seeking help from those who can provide it."

"But aren't they all as bad as each other?"

"I guess they probably are. You must remember that all of these people are human and they have the same general drives and emotions as we do. While we plebs look on at a distance, imagining what a privileged life they lead, we cannot see how the responsibility to be, rather than act, covers a multitude of sins. If we strip off our clothes we are all the same. For Edmund to strip himself bare would almost be a betrayal of everything which is different about the people he mixes with and something he will do at his peril."

"He is in severe danger of being exposed. Why does he not take the path of least resistance?"

"Maybe it appears to him like some sort of illusion - as if this really isn't happening. Maybe, having been a lawyer for so long, he sees reality in black and white terms. Maybe he has always seen reality in black and white terms. It is very difficult to feel and imagine that what is about to happen or may happen, will happen to you. A superiority complex is just that, after all."

"Maybe a man like Edmund Rose doesn't have the power he used to have. And maybe he actually realises it. Maybe Brodie, ill-bred as he may be, is the crest of a wave that has been enveloping England for a good few years - a wave both you and I sit on too and one which is so tumultuous in its weight that it sweeps the old guard before it. That is why Edmund is powerless to protect himself."

I wonder sometimes if this is correct. England has changed; Britain has changed, even in my lifetime. Edmund may be the very last remnants of a culture which has been slowly eroded until what was once hegemony has turned to impotence.

"Why don't we ask Edmund, Iris?"

The cab stops outside The Maundeville and I pay the cabbie. To my left, Helen, who has slept all of the way, gets a gentle nudge. I check her appearance while James takes her by the arm and leads her from the cab. Within a minute we are in the reception with Helen and James looking sheepish while I hold the fort for both of them.

We are approached by a rigid ex-military man who informs us that Edmund is already seated and expects us in the dining room. As we are led from the reception I feel Helen's hand squeezing my arm, discreetly but with a degree of force which reminds me of how frightened she is. Gently I stroke Helen's back. James too, seems to sense Helen's feelings. He turns around and gives her a sweet, a sensitive smile as we are led through a long dining room - the very dining room where Edmund and I had dined before, and into a huge garden conservatory. Set around us are several dining tables, none of which are occupied. Edmund is alone, reclining comfortably with his back to us. There is a bottle of chilled wine next to him and what looks like a gin and tonic in his hand.

As he stands up to greet us he casts his eyes upon me, looks upon James without, unusually, offering James anything licentious to say and bestows a rather puzzled eye upon Helen. Characteristically he offers her the most charming greeting notwithstanding Helen's evident nervousness and, no doubt, her secret amusement at Edmund's anomalous appearance.

I apologise for not advising him of a further guest. Edmund will realise that there are cogent reasons for this. I imagine his is mind already working towards a conclusion as to who Helen is and why she is here.

Edmund asks the waiter to set out another chair. While we wait we stand - Edmund regarding it as rude for us to sit down. In the interim he takes Helen by the arm and leads her to the window, below which is a long and beautiful rose garden.

"You will see Buckingham Palace in the distance, to the right. I think, if my eyesight doesn't deceive me, that the present incumbent isn't in today, as the flag doesn't fly on the flagpole. To your left you can see the many government buildings charged with running affairs of state. You can just make out the back of Ten Downing Street over there. These little fiefdoms are empty today as many of the occupants choose to spend their weekends in the country. In the week this club tends to be full at this time, filled with the many mandarins whose job it is to make sure the country runs like clockwork. The price they exact is that they escape from the society they create, two days a week."

I can see Helen becoming a little overwhelmed. Edmund's ability to charm tends to work best with those who are like-minded. How much further is this from the world Helen inhabits and the world which banished her?

"Edmund please - don't crowd her out. Just because this is all very normal to you; I think you should give Helen a little space."

"I apologise if I am a little overbearing. Well anyhow, come and have a seat next to me Helen. I insist."

This is, of course, very wise. He has realised that this stranger, who hasn't even spoken to him, must be very important. Accordingly he must hold her close.

We are each handed a menu. I watch Helen studying me. It is obvious she has never been to a formal occasion of this nature. She watches and copies as I take my napkin, open it out and spread it evenly across my knee. I can see her confusion as she attempts to read the menu. After several minutes she looks at me, lost as to what to do. Edmund orders for us - for all of us. I choose a main course then recommend my choice to Helen. As graciously as she can she accepts, trying her best to look as though she knew all along what she wanted.

Edmund orders wine and it is the best wine in the cellar. Each of us has, naturally, a choice of red or white and Helen decides to go with whatever I choose. When it arrives, in order not to have Helen drink too quickly and inadvertently embarrass herself as a consequence, I sip slowly. So does Helen. The same cannot be said for James and Edmund, who are evidently enjoying each other's company, with Edmund drinking profusely whereas James simply sees the episode as a matter of competition. I dread the prospect of having to hold James' head over the sink as he throws up his lunch.

Only after about twenty minutes does Edmund ask after Helen, thinking it rude to question her straight away. When he speaks, he speaks very gently and graciously. Helen seems happy after their first interaction and appears to relax. I too, feeling the wine infusing my system, relax.

"So my dear, as Brodie's secretary you must have a great many stories to tell. I gather, although only through hearsay, that he has led quite a life."

Before Helen replies I butt in, anxious to get to the argument before alcohol pushes it away.

"You are wondering why Helen has agreed to come with us today. I could tell you myself. I want Helen to tell you as the story is much better heard straight from the victim."

I look at Helen and she senses her cue. Nervously at first, knowing that the eyes of both Edmund and James are upon her, Helen gives a thorough account of all she told me through tears the night before. I sit opposite, dispassionate, or at least doing my best to appear so, watching the expression of the faces around me, seeing tiny muscle movements around the eyes, hearing the natural exhalation of breath when Helen reaches criticality. Again, tears begin to form in her eyes as she makes known the unknown fate of her son and what she risks if the cabal in front of her fails in our attempt to counter Brodie. Once more I am overawed by the sensitivity which the simple body language of Edmund conveys as he becomes emotional, choosing to stroke Helen by the arm when she reveals the depth of inhumanity to which she has been subjected. And when she has finished he is the first to take out a handkerchief and hand it to her, much the same way as he had taken out a handkerchief for me all that time ago at Heathrow Airport when I too, had disclosed the misery one human being can inflict on another.

When Helen finishes we all take a deep breath. It is James who breaks the ranks of silence. His voice, slow and deliberate, is coloured by anger.

"We must find some way to get back at this man. There must be something we can do."

"But we have a start," I reply.

"Helen is as close to the man as anyone we know. As he perceives her not to be a threat he feels the urge to display his motives and question his actions. From this we can deduce what he may do or has already done. And even if he hasn't spoken yet, we still have the opportunity to know what he may say next."

"But isn't there more we can do?"

"Well, it isn't so easy, James. Helen has told me she knows very little of Brodie's personal life."

"Yes, that is true. seems to have got away with simply stating what he is and never proving what he is. He has only ever told me and others that he is married. I have not seen his wife. He has told me he has children and yet I have not seen his children. 'Fine', you may say, he keeps his home life and his work life separate which is what some people choose to do. But I would, in the years I have worked for him, have been likely to have spoken to his wife or his children. It is the strangest thing."

Edmund moves in his chair. I feel he is about to say something but James, whose anger is evident, cannot help but explain this anger born out of frustration by speaking when he should be silent.

"So he has something to hide. He has something sinister about him which we ought to know about. We should find out precisely what it is. We need to establish precisely who and what he is. From that we may even be able to approach him and offer some sort of deal."

Edmund sighs.

"I can't hear this. I didn't bring you here to lunch to listen to such a descent into moral iniquity, so copying the man we so self-righteously despise. We talk of hidden behaviours, counter-blackmail, revenge. That is not an answer. Would it make any of us feel comfortable in bed at night knowing that another life has been ruined, albeit the life of this man?

"Look; it is not Brodie who has caused Helen to lose her child - it is the disjointed moral values of the community in which she and Brodie grew up. He is simply a leech who has decided to take advantage of her misfortune. And it is not Brodie who forced me to lie, declaring the life of a happily married man when I wasn't and spending most of my free time and most of my money having sex with other men. It is not Brodie who forced or imperilled me to have sex with other men. Again he is simply a leech who by luck and vulpine instinct, tarred too, with the brush of bigotry handed to him by the madness of Irish history, has chosen to hurt others in order that he may not be hurt himself. Yes that is a shallow constitution, yes, they are the actions of a weak man.

"Helen knew the rules - whether they are right or wrong is no matter. People follow rules and the leech will use them to his advantage. That, Iris, is why lawyers are despised, for we create nothing of value. If one cannot argue with the rules but by our actions we submit to them, we cannot complain when a moral-free zone comes along and punishes us. It is up to us to accept the situation. And ultimately it is up to us to realise that once we are hurt by our environment, we perpetuate that very same environment if we decide to descend into it. I cannot play Brodie at his own game. I cannot. I am not saying that you should not. I merely want to point out that there are higher moral principles at stake."

I am shocked. James is shocked. In rather a funny way, I think that Helen understands. I wonder why. I guess it is to do with acceptance. Edmund Rose has had many years to come to terms with what he is and how this relates to the world, albeit a narrow world, in which he lives. So acceptance of the failings of others becomes the norm. And the key to self-respect is not to join those who make you suffer but to steer clear of the very mindset which makes suffering the norm. It is a higher knowledge of a lower world in which acceptance of the failings of man with specific reference to oneself, engenders a reticence to try and disentangle the vicissitudes of the human spirit, replete with the knowledge that one can keep one's own human spirit intact by choosing not to indulge but to accept the very nature of the beast.

I compare this analysis to myself. I am cold; I am analytical; I am slowly changing. I have only commenced the change upon being subject to precisely the same suffering with which both Helen and Edmund have had to deal for a number of years; in Edmund's case, practically for the whole of his adult life. How under-developed must I be compared to the mature and experienced outlook of two thirds of my partners at lunch? How arrogant have I been as I watched and thought I understood the motives of man in all facets of his behaviour when I had never been subject to and suffered by a darker side I knew was there. I know I constantly make reference to the barren intellect of men, ruled by their sex drive and thereby commanded by that sex drive to treat me differently because I am regarded as classically attractive, but the arguments I established as a consequence of my own observations are immature reflections by one who had no right to feel smug about the value of anything. Rather than leading Helen to retribution, it should be I who defers to her. Well I can defer to Helen's outlook and I can defer to the outlook of Edmund Rose. But I cannot now control the anger which has built within me in relation to Brodie and I cannot defer to the arguments which countermand the very eloquent words Edmund has presented and the very sophisticated emotions presented to me by Helen and Edmund Rose together.

"Is there not a greater good to be obtained by trawling within the moral abyss and in taking on these very human weaknesses because not to take them on allows them to control and manipulate the innocent? You can say that Helen knew the rules but that doesn't mean that moral madness can be ignored. It is not good enough to accept them because acceptance discloses a degree of rectitude. We cannot dismiss something as absolutely wrong then stand back, accept it and let it overwhelm us. We four must be in total agreement that what has happened here is flawed. And we must thereafter be in total agreement that it is up to us to stand up for what we believe in. I am willing to do that now, whereas I was never willing to do that in the past. I used to watch the world go by; I used to watch men and women make the same appalling mistakes over and over again and somehow excuse their stupidity on the basis that they were flawed human beings. But there must be a line over which one simply cannot step. Like I say, I was a total observer, content to let all the idiocy of man take place all around me. We cannot let this happen now. We owe it to each other. We owe it to Helen's child. What kind of a person would I be otherwise? It might be too late to save some souls but it is not too late to serve the innocence of a child. If you do not agree then so be it. I shall take this man on, on my own. But I want you to reconsider the argument. Reconsider the argument not in relation to yourself, as you may see yourself as past redemption, but look on it as the opportunity to advance the protection of innocence. Flawed we may be. But that doesn't mean we have to accept the inevitability that has infected us, for it need not infect others."

I look at each of my lunch companions in turn, starting with Edmund. In his eyes I see a look of admiration.

"Iris; I never knew you had so much inner strength. I thought you such a gentle and quiet thing."

"Well I am willing to forego anything I used to be because I am right in the intimate middle of a world in which the idiosyncrasies of man have a direct bearing upon me. And I will not lie down."

I look at James.

"You know Iris, I think I am with you. I don't want to be seen nor do I want to feel as though I have given in. It is enough to fight whether we lose or whether we fail."

I look at Helen.

"I promised I would do all I can and I will do all I can. The time has come where I have to take the risk. I have been far too shy about what this man and what life has done to me. I want to help you in any way I can."

Edmund still looks uncertain. I can see thoughts behind his big red eyes and I can almost hear the debate going on inside his head. Still he doesn't answer and chooses to turn and look out of the conservatory window, out beyond the hinterland, beyond the institutions of London to the panorama beyond. It takes him five minutes to speak and as he does so, he still looks the other way.

"I am not saying that my feelings have changed. I am unconvinced, that is all."

"But what have you got to lose?" I ask.

"I suppose the answer is that this man has within his power the ability to lose it all for me. How much do I want to protect myself and not give in to this moral inertia I have so vigorously defended?"

"So you have nothing to lose, then?"

Edmund still looks the other way. Then he seems taken over with energy and enthusiasm.

"Well I do have nothing to lose."

"Why give in? Stay and fight."

"Yes, stay and help," Helen states, grabbing Edmund by the arm.

"Think of who is going to get hurt if you do not."

That does it. Edmund slowly turns around and smiles. His voice is gentle; his delivery soft. With his agreement each of us seems to relax. Privately, we each of us know that in aspiring to higher principles, we have to dwell within the lesser proclivities of man. Yet Edmund confuses me. What has happened to the man who promised to help me, to do all he could, to be my champion? Resolve seems to have left him and I cannot think why. He is now assisting through suffering – it is as though he has given in and has accepted that his fate is not in his own hands.

James changes the subject, directing his comments at Edmund.

"You know, one thing puzzles me. It would seem that you are amply protected by the accident of your birth. No, hear me out.

"It may well be that if I worked in the City of London these days, I may come from a variety of backgrounds. In the past the background of those who were seemingly chosen to work in that world, came from a very narrow social set. Without wishing to sound impolite, I would have guessed that you are such a person. And it follows that if you are, then you are socially betrothed to people who you have known from school and university and your status as a member of this elite is accepted. So, in these circumstances, when you are threatened by an outsider, would it not be a case of informing the appropriate people and closing ranks? Surely there must be more than you - people who you have known for years.

"On pain of sounding fanciful, it strikes me that by accident of birth and lifestyle, you have an awful lot of people you can call upon to help you. I can't understand why you cannot do that now."

"Yes; well; in the past - you are right. Once, say twenty and more years ago, we belonged to a small club of gentlemen. The City of London was a cabal, a collection of right-minded men who held all of the keys to the institutions which could make men millionaires and could cripple those it considered unfit. It wasn't democratic; it wasn't fair. But that was the way it was. Times have changed. I am no longer master of all I see - not that I am inert but the cabal has been infiltrated so to speak, by attitudes and ideas so far removed from what we used to know that the powers that once used to be are no longer. Of course there are phone calls I can make at certain times and to do with certain matters but you must understand that we are not dealing with an old boy network where a nod and a wink will do. We are dealing with something altogether different."

"But there must be others like you out there who have crossed the line between what is traditionally acceptable and what is not. Surely they are tolerated; surely they have come across circumstances like this before when their discretion has been unfounded?"

"Provided men were discreet, matters were quietly brushed under the carpet. Even if scandal transpired, it was known to just a few people who had a lot to protect by keeping it in the family. It was all very gentlemanly and orderly.

"But you have to look around you now. All you have to do is walk around the City and hear the accents, have a look at the names on brass plaques, listen to the conversations in the bars and restaurants. What is it called? It is called the global village. Before it was the Oxbridge village."

"Isn't that a good thing?

"Doesn't that work in your favour? Doesn't the idea that tolerance must have its place mean that you can proclaim exactly what you are without any fear of censure?"

"Your argument belies the real nature of the truth. You forget what we are involved with here. It is called capitalism whereas when I began working in the City, capitalism was a sort of high society closed shop. We made money and the means to make money was assured because we all knew each other by background. As doors opened and outsiders arrived, both as underlings and as overlords, they brought with them at least two essential elements of capitalism itself - competition and survival of the fittest. And just as importantly, they brought with them a whole litany of different mores which could be used against the person in the context of survival and competition."

"Is that not more honest?"

"Well, it leads to dishonesty. Think about Helen for a moment. Sure, religion is no bad thing because it teaches right from wrong and good from bad. But these things can be used by the unscrupulous as justification in eradicating people. So Helen's behaviour is defined as immoral because bigots decided to use the moral epithets of religion as a justification for the downright evil they delivered upon her. It is the same in the City. I am competition - only the fittest survive and one can utilise prurience these days in order to dismiss me, so when people hear of behaviour which calls into question the value of association with a man or woman who fails to fit the norm, that abnormality is swiftly used against you. In my case it will be my homosexuality; I will be culled not because I have habits which the majority find morally abhorrent; I will be culled because I overtly transgressed an imaginary moral standard which no one really believes in but, in the pursuance of the theology of profit, allows others to cut me loose. Thus the pool of competition is diminished, someone else steps into my shoes and I am excommunicated and quietly forgotten."

"But as far as Iris has told me, you chose not to unveil what you are from the very beginning, before you became a member of this human zoo."

"Quite the opposite, in fact. Those around me in the old days knew. Even my wife knew but in her own, rather sweet, stoic way she chose not tell - rather she chose to ignore what was more than suspicion. Maybe another part of it is precisely as you say - my wife is from the same coterie as myself and we have always pushed this sort of thing under the carpet. The English are very good at hiding and then pretending that a breach of standards doesn't exist.

"Well I digress somewhat. Simply put - the people around me, in that tight unit which used to run the City of London, knew that I had to pretend that I was what I wasn't. Those who were never privy to that environment, precluded as they were by their lack of access by birth and association, could never know. But now, well in today's society, a new hegemony finds out and I will be punished. I cannot rely on what was because what was, is no longer."

"So, Edmund," I reply, "with the process of financial and secular globalisation; with the intermingling of peoples, there has come into being a kind of standard morality allied to an accepted way of life which has dismissed the narrow inclusivity of the past. And the values of old, which were based upon hypocrisy - appearance being the paramount consideration, have been replaced by an alternative value system where appearance is still the norm, dissension from which gives the opposition the opportunity to destroy because the destruction of competition is the prevailing standard."

"Badly put, Iris, but precisely the truth."

James butts in.

"Hang on a minute. Can we not say it a little more simply?"

Edmund obliges.

"I am to be culled because I am different. We are all different. But we cannot appear to be different. We must accord even though none of us accord."

"But that doesn't make sense."

"No, it does not. Well, it does make sense - it makes sense because competition is all and money the measure. The accumulation of money, status and prestige, is the yardstick. Stupidly, there must be, though I don't know why, standards associated with the people who accumulate money. These standards are impossible to attain if one displays all the weaknesses of humanity. So presentation becomes the lodestar of first measure. Fall from grace in terms of presentation and the competition has its chance. The speed of descent thereafter depends on the gravity of the offence and the qualities of the protagonists. And in this case, rather in my case, Brodie, although I am not sure he fully understands the system which he has used so well, is as practised in the black art of people obliteration as any other champion of self-promotion. He represents the vanguard of a new age. One type of morality is replaced by another and the hegemony of the old ruling, professional class, is replaced by a culturally amorphous group tied to each other by another set of norms. One culture replaces another. Casualties arise along the way. I suppose that is why I am resigned to my fate."

I wonder how Helen has been formulating thought as she listens to this sophisticated analysis. I am surprised at the ease with which she appears to have taken it all in. She seems neither unfazed by the discussion nor at a loss for things to say in relation to the minutiae of our words. As I speak, I do so with Helen in mind.

"There is one further matter which we have already mentioned. The final piece in this jigsaw is religion. See we mention standards of behaviour and we rightly make the point that they are secular. The argument follows that secular standards are based on the refutation of religious mores. I would prefer to think that capitalism and religion have had a healthy relationship in the past and that relationship still remains. One only has to look at the convergence of politics and religion in the United States to realise that money and standards go hand in hand. But the overt nature of religious lines have been replaced, as the intrinsic but overt role religion has in life has been sublimated due to the movement away from the starkness and the impositions of duty religion puts upon us. Standards - what could be conceived of as religious standards, are still there but have been set in the background. None of us is overtly dependent upon religious standards any more in order to justify our behaviour. But they are, just the same, still there. We are just not aware of it any more.

"I don't think this is applicable to . Nor is it the case in Ireland. Religion, in relation to what we are discussing here, that is, what has happened to you Helen and what I think is about to happen to us, is the final piece of the jigsaw. Religion is how Brodie would overtly justify his behaviour on the basis of the immorality of my homosexuality. Religion, rather than a tool to help and assist, to inculcate decency and kindness, is thereby turned on its head and presents itself as a sentinel of evil.

"Yes; making Brodie all the more dangerous as he is no pragmatist looking to simply do the best for himself. At all times he believes he is morally justified. There is no end to which he will not turn in order to promote what he believes to be some sort of metaphysical commandment. He is akin to a madman. That is why he is dangerous and why I am afraid."

I want to bring things to a close. I have what I want already.

"The thing we need is information. Brodie has information he can use. What we should have is information to counteract him. Helen; I would like you to spend time racking your brains thinking of everything you may consider useful. We have never seen his wife; we have never seen his children. We do not know where he lives and we have no idea what he does when he goes home. I think we also need to watch him at work. We need to know where he goes when he is out of the office; we need to know who he associates with and what he says. On a daily basis, not at work, I would like you to tell me what he has done each day. Do not speak to me at work. Keep the dismissive act you have developed so as not to arouse suspicion. I suggest you see me in the evening at my flat, convenient as it is, for we live so close to each other. I also suggest that not one of us here breathes a word about this conversation nor our intentions to another soul. Excuse me sounding militaristic but there is so much at stake for all of us."

James butts in.

"We also need to imagine what he will do next. We need to put ourselves in his shoes. Some of this will be established on the basis of what he has done before and how he has reacted when he has had the opportunity to threaten. We also need to take ourselves away from what he has done in the past and work backwards from a worst-case scenario. Obviously he needs publicity. That is his main asset. The question is, to whom he will speak and how he will conduct himself?

He will, I think, have three possible methods of attack. He can go for a creeping denunciation where all is smoke and mirrors - denunciation, destruction by stealth - all completely unattributable of course; he can threaten publicity. He could, on the other hand, get others involved - others he trusts. I doubt he will go for the latter option because in some ways it could be counter-productive. I think the latter idea would be rather far-fetched in any event. Does this man, in fact, trust anybody he can't control?"

Edmund, who has been listening intently, has nothing to say. I can sense the conflict within him. He is resigned, I can feel it. But he is letting us go anyway. Still, what has he got to lose?

"I take it we are in agreement?"

There is silence around the table. Edmund breaks rank and reaches for a bottle of wine, allowing himself recourse to thoughts of a much more entertaining lunch than we have hitherto taken part in. And an entertaining lunch it is, for the alcohol in James and Edmund allows both of them to bounce off each other as Helen and I listen and laugh.

Periodically I look at Helen. At times she looks back and we seem a little frozen in each other's stare. I find it uncomfortable as I sense the feelings she extols though I cannot work out what they are. But there is little time for reasoning. As Edmund and James really get going I lose myself in their conversation and imagine Helen doing the same thing. Only much later am I able to come to terms with the slow process of realisation I have embarked upon, encumbered as I am by thought and trepidation as to how the following days, weeks and months will unfold.

XXIII.

Nothing happens - nothing happens save that each night at about half past nine, I hear a knock on the front door and find Helen clutching a satchel containing papers on which she has conscientiously made notes about Brodie - movements, conversations, actions.

But little detail.

Little, little, detail.

So we learn nothing about the man we did not already know. Brodie seems to have developed a sixth sense; a seventh sense. Whereas he used to give Helen rather meticulous accounts of what he is up to, he seems to have clammed up, giving to Helen on a 'need to know' basis. Helen is now as much a bystander in relation to his life as we are.

Nonetheless we have a fair idea of what he is doing but we have no idea of what is gestating within his mutant brain, nor can we realistically guess. It is as if he is punishing us for having the temerity to contemplate taking him on and it comes as no surprise to me and is all the more worrying for Helen. He has never incubated like this before she tells me - as soon as he has the opportunity to strike he strikes as soon as he can. Why waste time and let circumstance move against you? Why not push the knife in while the victim is defenceless and the knife is in your hand?

I spend a great deal of time calming Helen down while constantly doing my best to see any chink of light. But there are no chinks of light. James, on the other hand, is struck by inertia. He comes home from work with an expectant look in his eye, waiting for news that may go some way toward giving us the opportunity to call Brodie to account. But James is as disappointed and frustrated as we are. He feels like an outsider; he is an outsider. So James is inert and quiet, withdrawn and dissatisfied. I tell him and I tell Helen it will get better. They tell me it will be too late by then. We will have already lost.

Only Helen seems to listen and only when she is calm and only when she wants to encourage belief and the self-confidence that we can somehow salvage something from this appalling scenario. And as she does so she gradually opens up. Provisionally she comes to my flat to relay what Brodie has been doing. Pretty soon after it becomes apparent that he has done little of consequence so Helen and I start taking about all manner of other subjects, unveiling more than just feelings about Brodie. She tells me of things which don't really matter, of thoughts on many different subjects, and I too, slowly feel myself opening up, beginning to converse at a level in which nothing I say counts to any great degree - just flippant thoughts with miniscule conclusions; nothing finite nor anything other than the self-evident. Feminine conversations - discourse without beginning and without end; not quite a monologue but feelings rising through the intuition which arises as a consequence of airing thoughts to someone who will listen. It is most unlike Iris. I have never had a friendship where conclusions are drawn from simple conversation. I have always relied upon myself not to have half-thoughts which need resolving. I have never really had half-thoughts. The world was a finite place where everything made sense because I had the power to work it out for myself. With each conversation with Helen, I am progressively being sucked into showing and sympathising with trivialities which didn't matter to me before. And I feel comfortable doing so, with James beginning to notice, making comments about the impenetrability of the mealy minglings Helen and I share.

Somehow I am beginning to rely upon Helen and I know she relies upon me. Soon I realise that the situation which brought us together is to do with Brodie, yet the situation which keeps us in each other's pockets is nothing to do with Brodie. It is called, friendship.

I see little of Edmund. Although he has returned to work, it is in our best interests not to be seen with each other, other than on a strict working basis. I spend as little time in his room as possible and he spends little time in mine. If we do talk, it has to be absolutely necessary. We know that Brodie is watching. And when he isn't watching, Helen, his duplicitous concubine, reports to him daily.

Emotionally, Edmund is upbeat. As time wanders by he begins to feel, though he only intimates by suggestion, that all may have been an invention of ours and that Brodie has forgotten all he has learned and those threats of exposition were simply the spoutings of an egotist with nothing better to do than to throw his weight around without actually throwing his weight anywhere. I doubt him. For Brodie there is too much to lose by not sticking the knife in. It is just a matter of time and the more time goes by Edmund will lose vigilance. I refuse to be so foolish. I watch all like a hawk.

In a sense, though a very external sense, all does get back to normal. The cloud which hangs heavily over all begins to dissipate. Occasionally I hear laughter along the corridor. I can see how the weaker-minded tell themselves all is well. I can envisage the chain of reasoning - the credibility of their conclusions. But with my analytical head on, with Iris knowing so much more about Brodie than my colleagues, I know; I just know he will take his opportunity. He still has a long way to go before he gets to the top of the corporate ladder. And this is an opportunity only a fool would miss, albeit an opprobrious fool. And Brodie is no fool.

XXIV.

Two weeks and two days after Helen, James, Edmund and I took lunch at The Maundeville, Brodie dispatches an email to Edmund and Iris, asking that we attend him in his room. His secretary will be in attendance to take notes - Helen as Brodie's minion, blackmailee, overt ally and mute.

A sense of deja vu greets me as I depart. The last time I took Brodie's company, vitriol coloured the air, pleading infused speech and an appellation to reason was discarded. Now what lies behind his door?

I manage to get a brief glimpse of Edmund as he turns the corner into Brodie's room. For a nanosecond there is a smile in his eyes, then a cold exterior sweeps over him. Brodie has his back to us and is sitting down, talking on the telephone, trying his best to look and sound awe-inspiring, powerful, replete. Once more Edmund and I glance at each other. Once more and for a scintilla, our eye lines cross and we both know we are thinking the same thing.

Brodie makes one further call, bluntly instructing Helen to come in. When Helen, who studiously avoids all eye contact, is inside, Brodie tells her to take notes after ordering her to close the door. Only then does he turn around. It is theatrical and somehow comical - I am schoolgirl in the presence of a master; blind in the presence of a sage; victim in the presence of a criminal; pewter in the presence of gold.

Edmund giggles.

At first it is a nervous reaction. But it is an appropriate reaction. And it is an infectious reaction. Before Brodie can honour us with his profundity Edmund pegs the absurdity of the moment. This is no school admonishment - this is an appalling little man trying to act as dictator to a man far better than himself. If it is arrogant for Edmund to giggle, it is most certainly appropriate. And it is utterly infectious.

Once I sense Edmund doing his best but failing to squeeze the laughter out of his diaphragm, I too, catch the bug; I too, shuffle uneasily in my chair and battle the urge to let the air punishing my lungs free itself with fits of laughter. It gets too much. What starts off as discreet laughter turns to impolite laughter to peals of laughter ringing in the Celt's ears. We sit and roll around our chairs howling in derision at this pink, cherubic, self-important, vain and insecure shagsack - pointing and gesticulating at him, denuding him and all he thinks he is while he has no choice but to look at the enemy dismissing him for what he isn't - a valid, a viable combatant.

It is entirely the wrong thing to do. It feels like entirely the right thing to do. And so it continues, with Edmund, who isn't drunk, taking things a stage further, trying to stem his laughter but dismissing Brodie to his face.

"To think, that you, yes you, could actually warrant a threat to me. Look at you. You are possibly the most repulsive, odious little man I have ever seen. All your tiny life you have been rejected. To counter-balance you have taught yourself to reject. But why did they reject you? Just look at you. Your outer features are the key to the preposterously ugly little man you are on the inside. I never saw it before; I see it clearly now. With a face like that, how could you be anything other than the idiot you are?"

Quite why I laugh, I do not know. Edmund can't think of his verbiage as the truth. He is far too deep for that. My guess is his resignation in relation to his fate makes him indifferent. He might as well have some fun by poking fun. I too, am almost past caring. But I am almost past caring and care enough to watch Brodie closely as he changes colour, sensing the pressure building up in his head as the bloody molecules within the veins in his brain, boil, expand and explode. I so desperately want him to speak, just to round off our visitation. I know full well that he cannot say anything. The first word which comes out of his mouth will have us in fits of laughter. Whatever happens, his credibility is destroyed, his perceived superiority manacled. Whatever he says and whatever he chooses to do, will be coloured by this very afternoon. I fear him no longer and Edmund knows he now has nothing to fear.

Finally, Brodie, too long in silence, too long in suffering, speaks. We can sense it; we can see it coming. Edmund stops laughing in anticipation. I do too. We can guarantee we will not hear the end of his first sentence. Every Irish fissure in Brodie's repugnant head is screaming at him to respond - every corpuscle, every atom, every proton, every singular part of this man's being is telling him to defy the urge to remain quiet. I watch as his instincts fight tooth and nail with every possible combination of instinct and control wrapping themselves around the desire to retort, to do nothing, to respond, to remain calm.

But, as I watch and examine, indifferent to myself and the part I play, Brodie gives over to a more rational, yet conniving side. As the internal volcano which erupts, subsides, he seems to clarify the need we have to destroy and ridicule. In his silence he is storing the hatred he feels for Edmund and myself. He knows he has a strong hand to play. All he has to do is bide his time. He stands up and walks toward the door. In doing so he has to ask Helen to move as she is seated in the way of Brodie's only means of escape. It is upon Helen that he serves his anger. It is upon us that his rage is deferred.

"Get out of the fucking way you hideous bitch."

Edmund stops laughing immediately. Having realised that he has caught our attention, Brodie changes tack.

"As for you two, enjoy the moment, for a moment never lasts. And to think that I asked you here in order to give you one last chance. Your days here are numbered as is your reputation amongst all you know. Enjoy the moment, for a moment does not last."

That sets Edmund off again, reverting to fits of laughter as Brodie leaves his own room, slamming the door behind him.

I look at Helen. Seconds after the door slams, she crumples into a heap, sobbing uncontrollably. Edmund realises how out of place his laughter has become. He seems embarrassed and in a moment, he is gone. My final words to Helen are pithy and stark.

"Helen; be strong. I know you will bear the brunt of his tongue. But bear it well and never let him know what you really think. Like I have said all along, you have got to trust - you have got to trust me."

I hug Helen, squeezing her with all of my strength. I see her eyes close as her head falls toward my bosom. I close my eyes and feel for her in a way I have never felt for myself. As I leave Brodie's room once more I feel the resolve, the complete and utter determination to stop this man from furthering the suffering he had already meted out, if not for my sake any more, then for Helen and for my child.

XXV.

I stare at my screen all day. It is coming to half past five. At 5.30
precisely, I prick up my ears, listening for the chimes of the clocks
which ring out across the City of London - marking time, dissecting time,
killing time. The chimes aren't significant. They confirm that another day
has passed, another hour has passed; another hour - another hour in the life
of Iris has been consigned to my past in much the same as the hour before
that and the hour before that.

It is a glorious evening in London. I see St Paul's Cathedral become a
silhouette against the orange, tangerine and Raleigh-blue skies streaked with
thin, white cloud. I look down - down towards the entrance of our office
upon which I have an unrestricted view. As usual the roads are clogged with
rush hour traffic. Commuters sit bumper to bumper in order to escape this
unholy mess. I open my window in order to hear the counterpoint of cars'
beeping horns and the listing nature of time itself, as clocks chime all
around. Yet, above the din and above the cacophony of noise in the distance,
I hear the sharp wailing of a police siren rising in pitch. I think of terrorists
about to strike; I think of convoys of prisoners subject to the daily ritual of
being taken from the Old Bailey and back to custody. But I see flashing blue
lights below and traffic making all efforts to move to the side of the road in
order to let these police vehicles past. Save that they do not drive past. They
stop outside the office entrance.

From the first car I see four flak-jacketed uniformed policemen walk
into our building, chaperoned by nervous security guards whose
somnambulism has been shattered. I know something is wrong. As they
disappear inside I leave my room, heading toward Edmund's office. From
Edmund's room I can hear drunken rounds of laughter and I am presented
with the sight of Edmund Rose cuddling a bottle of vodka surrounded by a
retinue of acolytes. I know it is a matter of time. It is too little time. With my
disbelieving mind holding my tongue halfway down my throat, I hear, then
see, four large policemen accompanied by our Senior Partner, enter our
corridor, brush me aside and stride straight up to Edmund.

In the briefest second I see Edmund's face turn from one of welcome to
one of horror. Brodie has struck and has struck with all he has. He tries to

speak but anything he does say will be a futile and idiotic gesture. Sobriety hits him quickly as do the words of the arresting officer, who asks Edmund to confirm his name.

"Edmund Rose, I am arresting you on suspicion of buggery and indecent assault on a minor. You do not have to say anything but should you not say anything and later choose to rely on evidence which you give in court, your silence may be held as evidence against you."

The arresting officer asks Edmund to get his jacket and deliberates whether to use the handcuffs which hang from his belt. Our Senior Partner busies himself trying to convince the arresting officer that Edmund should be led through a back door to the building. The offer is refused. Edmund's charge is one of the utmost gravity and he is to be led to a police van which waits outside the main entrance. I follow slowly behind as Edmund is shrouded by three policemen and led down a maze of corridors toward the main entrance. As he walks his head is bowed and he tries to maintain a straight line. Somehow I sense his brain trying to come to terms with the indignity he is suffering. He must know that Brodie is behind this; he must know that a move such as this will not be undertaken unless it is thoroughly researched. Surely this untruth will come to nothing. All charges against Edmund Rose will come to nothing. But will they?

As Edmund is led from the building, colleagues for years line the corridors and watch him. Such men - one-time acolytes, sycophants, crawlers and users, having chosen to turn the other cheek for years, desert him. Edmund is a leper, a pariah, an outcast, an untouchable.

By the time he gets to the entrance there is only one person behind him Edmund would recognise. Even our Senior Partner has chosen to make a discreet exit and views the scene from the safety and the anonymity of a first floor window. The only person who stays near to Edmund Rose, as he is led to the street, is Iris.

Just before Edmund puts his first footstep on the pavement outside, I see him draw a deep breath. I see the arresting officer do the same thing, as Edmund's arm is held to his back. When Edmund appears steps on to the pavement, with an embolism of vehicles clogging up the street, with light from police sirens intermittently pealing off the windows and the walls all around, he is momentarily blinded by the immediacy of an offensive attack from the flashbulbs of cameras. Ten, maybe fifteen photographers take Edmund's photograph as he is led, still stumbling on account of the alcohol, towards the back of a police van and unceremoniously bundled in.

"Where are you taking him?" I ask.

The question is futile.

"Questioning."

My response is instinctive and embarrassing.

"What business is it to lock an innocent man up?"

I receive no reply. As quickly as they arrive, they whisk Edmund away. He is alone and alone to contemplate through the twisted eyes of drink, all that has befallen him, entering a world he knows little of. All of his life he has skated on the thin ice separating respectability and denunciation. His is a world not so much of black and white but of shades of all, mixed, co-mingling. Now he is reduced to the status of a common criminal where there can only be black and white.

I imagine him in tears; I imagine him trawling through all he has done and all he has been, considering the shame he has brought upon the family name, which had held firm throughout the past centuries. What shame upon generations of men and woman who have held steadfastly together through all of the trials of life, so developing a reputation second to none in a society where reputation is all. I can almost hear his sobs through the cold metallic interiors of that police van, sobs giving way not to light, but to darkness. I imagine the mutated sounds of the world outside passing over to the stillness and moribund surround within. Here is a man without friends and a man who will give up all semblance of hope.

As the convoy leaves I turn around and see Brodie standing next to and chatting to our Senior Partner. Brodie does not speak to me. It is our Senior Partner who approaches me - another coward, another vainglorious welk.

"I think it is in your best interests to leave well alone Iris, that is, if you want a career here after this whole debacle is over. It doesn't bode well to show any concern for a man like Edmund. He hardly helped himself. I really don't think you should be helping him in the alternative."

Behind I can see Brodie wearing a half-grin, his mouth half-cocked to one side and a self-congratulatory glint in his eye.

Anger wells. I refuse to give in to my anger. I will not give Brodie the satisfaction of seeing my temper. I make my excuses and leave, careful to let Brodie see the whites of my eyes, but trying to deliver a strength to my face so as to make him sense fear, to feel fear, to know fear, to see in my self-control that I too have something to offer, wanting Brodie to think of Iris as the next protagonist he will have to eradicate. I want this man to think of me as his next target; the next enemy he will have to grind down. For in the process of coming after me, he will have a great deal more to deal with - I promise him that; I promise myself.

In the look I give him, watched by all around, the inward-looking woman I am - was; the inactive, the watcher, the analyst of all, stands aside for a strength Brodie will find almost impossible to counter. How can he? How can he find anything to use? In all the years I have kept myself to myself, I have never envisaged it as being of any use, save to help me understand the world in which I live, so avoiding the mistakes as others. Insularity is my only weapon. Brodie cannot attack me as a consequence of who I am, only what I am.

Three quarters of an hour later and I am at home.

James bursts in through the front door.

"Iris; have you seen? Look - he is headlines everywhere."

Looking at the television I see the entrance from where Edmund Rose had been spirited away. Then, with a reporter standing by, speaking over pictures as Edmund is taken from the building, I see Edmund himself. And it isn't good. Images of paedophilic excess through mug-shot eyes displayed on the front pages of the national press over the years, do not betray this image of a drunk, grossly overweight, hideously ugly and what is more, rich doyen of the City of London, being branded a child molester. The picture plays to every conceivable social prejudice and Edmund looks like the one thing he isn't.

"They have really done their homework, Iris. They must have had time to do their homework. Whoever fed the police the information must have tipped off the press. Edmund is being systematically taken apart. There were photographs of him when he was a young man, a biography of his illustrious career, pictures of his family, pictures of a boy I do not recognise. There is even a biography of your law firm."

"Jesus Christ. I didn't know he had stooped to such levels."

Even James is sucked in.

"Don't be ridiculous. You know that the man wouldn't harm a fly. He is the victim in all of this. There is absolutely no doubt that there isn't a shred of truth in what has been portrayed here. There isn't a shred of evidence."

James doesn't hear me, though, as if on cue, it seems as if the television does.

I see for the first time the basis on which Brodie has taken his time, so weaving the strands which make up this most unbelievable ensemble. Pictured is an interview with a man who looks about thirty years of age - boyish and handsome, clearly homosexual and standing outside a picturesque house situated in Highgate, North London. The interviewer, whose face remains obscured from the screen, begins asking questions about the house behind.

"Yes; he bought me this house for services rendered - his expression. Edmund bought me this house when I was nineteen years of age."

"When did you first meet him?"

"I met him when I was fifteen years old. I was homeless and destitute and on the streets. He approached me in Piccadilly Circus. Edmund asked me if I wanted to have sex with him, which I did, in a flat in the Barbican Centre."

"Did you have any idea who he was?"

"Well, you never ask questions do you? Believe me he is not the only one I have seen. He was a good customer until things started to change and I became scared. But he kept giving me more and more money and introducing me to more and more of his friends."

The interviewer fails to ask the question - what was there to be scared of? What, precisely, had Edmund Rose done wrong? Everything is implicit, subliminal; Edmund becomes a monster by implication. This is trial by television; trial by half-truth.

"So there were others?"

"Yes, there were others."

"Can you tell us who they are?"

At this stage and only at this stage, does a lawyer present indicate that his client is not at liberty to answer any more questions. It is so convenient. The allegation is made and mud has stuck.

"My client has agreed to be interviewed by the police in connection with this matter and has agreed that upon full disclosure to them, the matter will be closed from the public until such time as the police decide to formally charge Mr Rose.

"Thank you gentlemen."

One further piece of information is placed before the camera. These are the deeds to the property in which this complainant resides. They show clearly that the owner of the property is Edmund Rose and that the property had been leased to the complainant, whose name is given as Mr Anthony Down.

I have seen all I need to see. As I get used to what I am forced to ingest, my thoughts turn from outright shock and back to analysis. I have no doubt Brodie is behind the whole thing but I begin to question how much of what Edmund has been accused of is the truth.

How has Brodie managed to dredge up this man - this Anthony Down? Is this the man Edmund described as his only true love? And how has Brodie subtly manipulated the forces of order in a democracy so as to destroy a life? Is there really some truth at the bottom of it? And how has Brodie remained unscathed, unseen, ethereal?

How has he managed to impart this information without giving himself away?

How, once the information had been disseminated, has he managed to manipulate the press so quickly and how has he been able to allow them to gather their sources so quickly?

"You know Iris, in some ways it is best not to stew on the reasons why this has taken place nor what forces the man has been able to marshal in order to manipulate events in this fashion. I would accept it all."

Disgruntled, I ask why.

"Because it won't change what we have to do even if you had some sort of answer. Edmund knew what was going to happen to him even if he couldn't have imagined that this was going to happen. He knew he was finished. That was why he was so resigned when we met him at lunch. For him all hope was lost and he was really only playing devil's advocate when you tried to prove the value of a fight.

But the argument - your argument is still valid. You cannot save Edmund from the fate which lies in store for him but you can still take this to Brodie. He has nothing on you. Only you and I know you are pregnant and only you and I know why. Helen is still inviolate for she knows nothing. Accept Edmund's fate and respect him by taking this back to Brodie. There will be no prouder man alive if you do. It will represent a degree of strength he, in his weakness, was never capable of."

XXVI

I call Helen very early in the morning. She is scared out of her mind but stoical. Though she has internalised her fear, she is still able to make sense of matters and knows perfectly well who is behind the whole train of events. She can recall nothing remote, close, substantive or germane. As much as Helen is forthcoming with her recollections she exposes nothing - nothing.

I hit upon an idea. I ask Helen if she has ready access to Brodie's office.

"He has no choice but to leave his room unlocked. If you remember, there are no locks on any of the office doors. And today he has meetings - external meetings all day. You will not arouse any suspicion by simply going into his room. You are his trusted secretary. There is nothing anyone can say in relation to what you are proposing to do. I know this is risky, though we can offload the risk.

"Do you think you could, on the pretext of looking for something, make a search of his room? It will probably come to nothing but at least we can try. I don't think it will do any harm."

Helen is reticent, understandably.

"The man is obviously extremely clever at covering his tracks and his senses will either be heightened by the events of yesterday or they will be dulled. I think we should assume the former. Check everything you touch for signs he is on the lookout for unwanted eyes. Be very careful to keep everything exactly as it was. Don't tell anyone what you are doing unless they ask and then only say you are checking for some errant document. I can't see how anyone will question you. Why should they?"

Somewhat defensively, Helen asks me what I will be doing while she is risking her neck. It is a fair question. I give little thought to the answer, originally intending to go to work.

"Do you not need to see Edmund? Do you not think he will be alone?"

"I'll visit him in custody."

James appears from his bedroom while Helen is in the bathroom, wiping sleep from the corners of his eyes. Still in slumber, his resurrection is slow and lacks deliberation. Once he comes around, he is as prescient as ever.

"I would like to go with you."

"Why?"

"Because not only does he need support, I think you do too. You may be taking this on your shoulders as if a Trojan, but in all the mêlée and this awful turn of events you have forgotten one fundamental fact - you, are pregnant.

"And you think I haven't noticed the changes you have shown in the last weeks. Come on Iris, since you told me, the few thoughts I do have in thinking of your behaviour add up when I do.

You have changed. Formerly, as you readily admit, you were like a stone - impervious to consequence. Now you are more emotional by the day. Whatever changes to your body you may be denying, they are still happening. And they are still affecting you."

Once more I try to brush James off. Once more he is prescient.

"So I am a man and men don't understand. Tell me to mind my own business if you wish but I'll keep after you until you realise that you have to take account of what this could be doing to you. You are not the island you once were."

I defer and give in, if anything, for an easy life.

"I'll take care of myself, then."

"No; take care for both of you."

James points at my stomach. I smile back and extricate myself, grabbing my coat and briefcase. Before I go I round off the conversation at my front door.

"Thanks for the offer. I really must see Edmund alone."

To find out where Edmund is, I have to call the police. Edmund is being held in custody at Snow Hill Police Station which is just a stone's throw from where I work. He will be allowed visitors if he wishes. I ask if anyone has come see him already. Just one, I am told - our Senior Partner.

Snow Hill Police Station is located near to the Old Bailey. Once, Snow Hill stood out as a hive of activity, home to those who enforced the law and to those who outnumbered them. Today, Snow Hill Police Station is obscured by the march of progress, the growth of capitalism and the architectural excess which grows daily within and at the boundaries of the City of London.

I ascend the steps outside and ask myself whether I have ever attended a police station before, which I have not. Politely I ask if Edmund Rose can receive visitors. I give my name. After a couple of minutes I am led through some reinforced iron doors to the cells.

How undignified that a man like Edmund Rose should be banged up here. Outside is a world which belonged to him; inside is a world in which all individuality is lost.

Edmund is located at the farthest end of the corridor. The custody officer produces a set of large keys which seem hard and inhumane and bangs on the cell door, struggling to pull it to while shouting the simple word, 'visitor.'

As the cell door swings to, I am left alone. The only sound is that of the custody officer whistling as he walks away. I think of what to expect when I first lay my eyes upon my friend.

What will he look like?

What will he be wearing?

What will his feelings be?

What condition will he be in?

As I look at Edmund Rose, all becomes clear. It is not a man who stands before me but a child; a helpless child - lost, confused and disorientated. At first, I do not notice the blackened eye. Nor do I see the blood which has crystallised and circles his mouth. All I see are huge, red, elliptical eyes.

I cannot speak, nor do I want to. I fall into the cell and embrace him. We hug for ten minutes as he holds me like he is hanging on for life itself. As I hold my head back and look at him, tears are falling down his face.

"My dear, what have they done to me? What, have they done?"

I have no answers. I just hold him. Actions are all; words mean nothing. With this man at his lowest ebb, all I can do is simply be there for him. There is nothing to say.

I lead him to the iron bed on which he has slept. In the corner there is a chamber pot which is nearly full. The room smells of urine. I check the contents of his chamber pot. Edmund's urine is coloured with blood. Somehow instinct takes over. I sit him back and take a close look at him, asking him to remove his suit jacket which he is still wearing.

Like a child he protests. Like a mother I ignore his protests. I protrude my finger and touch his ribs. He screams in pain and moves backwards, cowering, frightened.

"Afraid it is my lot, Iris. A pariah has no friends. And the police have just as much truck as any member of the public. Who doesn't have children who need protecting?"

"And you accept it?"

"Iris dear; I have no choice but to accept. My voice has disintegrated as quickly as my reputation, as has my career."

"You know you are all over the television and the newspapers?"

"Yes."

"And that they have been hounding your family?"

"Well I wasn't sure. My wife refuses to speak to me. My children have refused to visit me. You are the only person to stand by me."

"So I take it our Senior Partner wasn't here to offer his legal advice?"

"He was here to tell me that, officially, I have been disowned. I am on my own."

"No you are not. You have me."

"It is as I told you, Iris. Whether or not there is a shred of truth in the accusations, I am finished. My life is spent."

"But these charges are false - they must be."

Edmund remains silent for some time. His silence worries me. It is as if he is summoning up the courage to admit complicity. I decide to beat him to the admission.

"You know the press have interviewed a man called Anthony Down. He told them you used to pay him for sex when he was fifteen years old. He told them you were part of a ring of men who, though he didn't admit this in so many words, used to abuse him."

With my reference to the name, Edmund's face changes. I can sense thoughts curdling with emotion.

"Is this true?"

"My God. I don't know how they got to Anthony. Of course it isn't true. When I met Tony he was young but not a child. And I certainly didn't introduce him to anybody else. I wasn't involved with anybody else, Iris. I have told you the truth all along. Homosexuality isn't a crime and I have never committed a crime. Anthony Down was a young man, yes, but he was a young man I fell in love with - he is the only man I have ever fallen in love with. I can't understand why he has chosen to betray me. Even when we realised that we had no future I provided for him and have always provided for him."

"And the house? I've seen the title deeds with your name on them."

"Yes; the house is mine. I bought it for him to live in, to give him a home, to give him a chance. You know Anthony is the man who attacked me then looked after me. Anthony is the man whose history and my love for I explained to you on the flight back from Milan. I just don't understand - the betrayal, the betrayal of all I did for him, of all we did together. The house was just a statement of how much I cared for him and how much I wanted him to succeed. I can't understand it; I don't want to understand it."

"I kept watch on him, content to see what a success he had become, happy to see him settle down with someone else. He was an honourable boy - why should he fall from being an honourable man? He has all he needs."

"The press and no doubt, the police, will see the house as some sort of bribe or inducement to have sex with you.

"If you are so confident in his loyalty, how then could he even countenance destroying you publicly? Wake up Edmund. Brodie has got to him."

"But how would Brodie have found him?"

"Come on. Discreet digging is all that is required. Brodie has spent the last few weeks gathering and collating as much information as he can. And he must have something on this Anthony Down too, or his partner, so that he can use all the information at his disposal in order to close a net around you.

With you laughing in his face yesterday, the time was judged right. I have no doubt that, after he left the room he went straight to the nearest phone, a few calls were made and the whole chain of events which has you sitting here, beaten, ridiculed and destroyed, commenced.

Even the people you imagined being able to rely upon have disappeared or betrayed you. If a neutral observer knew what we surmise to be fact, he would have to admit that Brodie has played this beautifully."

"And for me there is no way out. There never was a way out, Iris - there never was. You know I haven't even been interviewed. I do not know what evidence they actually have. I can't see how they would have any. I have done nothing wrong."

"Then it will be made up. Brodie clearly has so much that he has conjured up the potential for perjury in order to get to you. He now has the police on his side. The forces of the state are lining up against you."

I kick myself for being so tactless. How stupid of me to remind him of what he must already know.

"I am afraid, Iris. For the first time in my life, I am lost. Nothing here reminds me of who I am. All the people I have taken care of have deserted me. I had no idea that appearance and the preservation of status was so endemic in the psyche of my class, and in those closest to me who would rather run the other way than support me - a man who has looked after them all their lives. What have I done to deserve this? How has society treated me?"

"Oh Edmund; society – society; it means nothing. The word means nothing. In a final analysis, we are always on our own. English people - the English people you know, have no backbone. It is a world turned upside down. Morality has no place where appearance and its preservation are all. You told me that. You told me it is the English way."

"I hoped it was rhetoric."

"You knew it was no such thing."

"In here, what I know; who I knew, means nothing. Whether these charges are true or false, I am ruined. It is not others who have betrayed me, it is I who have betrayed the sentiments of the society in which I lived - a society which treated me so well and which I abused so badly. What chance do I have now to evade and escape the shackles of ignominy whether I walk free from this cell or not? These four walls, just like the four walls of my office, retract and contain not just a man but a spirit, a conscience, a soul. It is best that they stay here, for if I step outside and if I am allowed to step outside, nothing can give me back what I have in isolation inside this cell. It contains me; it contains all of me and is society enough for this man. I just cannot face what others will cull me for. My real face - the real man beyond the face shown sparely to you and to others, has been taken away. And now, as I realise that I have become an invention notwithstanding the truth, I understand that I was a sad and sick invention anyway. What is my name and who am I? Yesterday I was a name and an impression. Today I am a name and a totally different impression. Yesterday no one cared for who I really was. Today no one cares for me either. Each day of my life has been a lie - my, lie. Now each day of my life will still be a lie but it will be a truth in the imaginations of the multitude outside. Oh Iris, whether or not I have done little to deserve the fate which brings me to this cell, I have done everything to deserve this emptiness and the hideous realisation that when I had the choice to face up to all I truly was, I could never summon the courage to do it. I am better off in here. This cell marks me for what I am and what I will be. What a waste my life has been. What a waste it would be to continue. I can never reveal my true identity and no one will ever, ever believe."

A sharp metallic bang on the cell door and a pinched cockney voice tells me time is up. Edmund is going to be taken to the magistrate's court shortly, where he will be formally charged.

I hug and kiss him as I leave and as I walk along the corridor outside I hear the cell door bang shut and an echo grating like tooth on wool. There is a finality in the echo which stays within. A door has closed on a life, on a person, on a human being. Cast upon himself, Edmund's loneliness I understand. His loneliness is suffering actual and through the eyes of Iris is no substitute for suffering actual. Momentarily I despair of the human condition. Far better to be an animal and not have the capacity to choose. Blame cannot be allocated without choice. I cannot blame the innocent for they do not know the difference. To eat, to sleep and to propagate however time and environment coincide, seems to me an impregnable state. The folly of humanity is the paradox of the very word. Humanity with all of its ills isn't humanity because of them. Pettiness and self-preservation in a world of excess falls into the lap of the manipulative and provides a playground for the weak.

How it has dragged me back; it drags me down. Humanity hurls me into a corner of a capacious ring in which the fight for survival is all about choice now that basic need is catered for. I have all the material things I need. Brodie has all of the material things he needs and so did Edmund. So the need to fight travels from the basic to the sophisticated, mutates and wraps itself around objects, in this case, status and money. Edmund made other choices. But sexually he had no choice. I cannot blame Edmund for his biology. I can blame Brodie for not listening to his.

Outside I look up and see the Old Bailey. How many of the great trials which have taken place in there have involved the supposedly sophisticated taking vengeance on those who acted without choice? A judge confirms guilt when handed down by a jury. The very concept of guilt implies a choice. But who can criticise the failing of man if he is heeding the call of his biology? And who can but manipulate when the calls of biology are not respected any more.

I know my thoughts are confused. One could feasibly argue that competition extends beyond the basic needs of the human body. No matter how much we have we always want more. That is the crux, the nub of the argument: Brodie, Edmund Rose, Helen Jenvey, James and myself are just a microcosm of the whole. And be it me or anyone else I know, we will be hurt. It is basic. It is banal.

I remind myself of my promise to get involved; to get my hands dirty. I consider once more how I can protect myself against Brodie. I do not seek revenge. I seek protection. Maybe the Old Bailey is poignant - revenge, protection, retribution, justice, equity. These are all maxims of the law. They are maxims of a supposedly moral law, of Gods law. But I seek only protection and justice. I seek protection for myself and my child and justice for Helen, and though it is almost certainly too late, for Edmund.

XXVII.

Once more, I hear police sirens. I see an ambulance in the distance, crawling through Holborn Circus, along Holborn Viaduct, coming toward me. Eventually, as cars move aside, it flies up the road and takes sharp left down Snow Hill. I turn and attempt to see where the ambulance has gone. It is parked outside Snow Hill police station.

I approach the station entrance - the entrance I have just left, to be told that I cannot enter. I do not remonstrate, for what is the point and sit on a wooden bench on the opposite side of the road. Oblivious to consequence I wait and I wait. The thought doesn't strike that I am waiting for anything in particular save for the sustenance of plaintive curiosity. And I do not make the connection which seems so vividly apparent now as I reflect. I am transfixed by this scene in which nothing takes place and from which I draw no conclusions.

I hear, and then see, another ambulance. As soon as it parks - though it hardly parks; it is rather slewn across the road, I watch a uniformed doctor and a paramedic jump out and run up the steps to the entrance of the police station. Still, I make no connections and sit in my own world until finally, a nondescript car arrives. Two photographers and another, with a notebook, step out and onto the pavement, seeking information and are politely rebuffed by a policeman who seems to be guarding the entrance. More people follow, obviously reporters. As the slow wheels of anomie turn inside my head, I begin to understand what is happening.

A camera crew arrive and only then, after an aeon, does the doctor I saw running into the building, walk slowly from the building, flanked by two policemen. He looks solemn and withdrawn while a scrum forms and the doctor, who is a young man with a lisp, shuffles around in his pocket trying to withdraw a piece of paper. I stand up and hurry across the road. Suddenly I have a sense of what I am about to hear and feel sick. With the words of the doctor, my fears are orally confirmed. His delivery is matter of fact, though the teasing of his lisp is painful.

"At 10.35 this morning I, along with my colleagues from the ambulance service, was called to attend Snow Hill Police Station to attend Mr Edmund Rose. Unfortunately we were not able to revive Mr Rose and he was pronounced dead a short while ago."

A fury of cameras click as soon as the news arrives. Reporters jump up and down, trying to call the doctor to answer questions, which he does the best he can. But no one asks the question. No one asks *the* question. It is left up to me, a small voice from within the crowd.

"Can you tell me, sorry, us, what are your first thoughts as to the cause of death?"

He looks unsure whether to answer me. Momentarily I am the centre of attention.

"My conclusion from the scene of death was that Mr Rose died of asphyxiation."

"And the death itself?"

I can hardly articulate my words. All I want to know is how he died. Once more the doctor looks reticent.

"Without wishing to pre-empt the judgement of any investigation as to the circumstances of death, my own view is that the deceased committed suicide. I cannot say anything further and emphasise that this is only a preliminary conclusion. A full conclusion will be disseminated after the autopsy."

The doctor now has to deflect a supplementary volley of questions. He refuses them all and is escorted inside. I walk away; I barely hear it. Edmund is dead. That is all I hear.

I cross the road on Holborn Viaduct and an articulated lorry nearly hits me. Luckily I am grabbed by a man whose quick reactions and instinctive bravery save my life. He asks me if I am alright. My mumbled incoherent reply tells him I am not alright, but he doesn't have time for me and walks me to a coffee shop. I barely remember asking for coffee nor can I recall having much idea of how much sugar went in. I sit in the window and for all I know I look like a mannequin. I am numb. I am lifeless. Time is frozen as all around me falls away and I am left without perspective, without motion and without a care for anything. The man I hugged half an hour ago is dead. Edmund, is dead.

In the distance I see a stretcher being carried down the steps of Snow Hill Police Station. The paramedics have trouble carrying it and I know it is Edmund's body. Behind me I hear Edmund's name. I am stirred from my own world as I hear and recognise the speed at which bad news travels.

'That is the body of that pervert. He's gone and killed himself.'

'Best thing for him. Pity they didn't castrate him before he died.'

A tear falls down my cheek and nestles between my lips. Cameras whirl as Edmund's body is slid into the back of an ambulance.

I curse Edmund Rose. He has died a guilty man, a selfish man, a monster. I think of his wife and his children. I wonder if they ever had any feelings for him that could not break out of the stranglehold of appearance. I bet they have not been told. The moment Edmund Rose was arrested he became public property. His death is told to all before his loved ones but not to them. For if a man is a monster no one can imagine him being loved, cherished, cared for. Forget that he is innocent before being proved guilty. Remember only that he is a pervert who preys on young men. There is nothing else to remember. He is guilty. He did to himself what every thinking and unthinking person in the country would have done to him, given far less than half the chance. But his death isn't justice. His death cheats the man on the Clapham omnibus - the public and those who have turned their back on him.

Why?

Because there is a finality about suicide which robs the human of the need for catharsis. Without the ability to wash one's hands; without black and without black and white, each human being has an opinion as valid as any other. Only the moral majority cuts this away. And only when the arbiters of morals proclaim, can the issue at hand be consigned to completion. Justice after all, must be seen to be done. Edmund Rose was guilty as he was unable to face the world that was about to castigate him for the crimes he has committed. Yet justice - catharsis, is unavailable, so our reassurances are denied. All the public have left, is sly castigation over coffee at a bar.

XXVIII.

On the day following Edmund's death, several Latino cleaners walk into Edmund's office and empty it of its contents. The gifts which have piled up - gifts from happy clients and gifts to do with all manner of ground-breaking transactions, are swept from his shelves into a black plastic bag. His drawers are opened and the very personal contents - letters and personal artefacts, are similarly swept into the same bag and carried away. His books - mementoes of a lifetime, are cruelly piled on top of each other and placed in storage, where they will never been claimed. Even his furniture is removed until, by the time I arrive at work, there is nothing in his room save for the innards of the four walls and a small lady without a word of English to her name, noisily cleaning the carpet.

Every trace, every ounce of that man is carefully and systematically erased from that room. It is as though he never existed. He has been purposively eradicated from the centrality of existence itself - that we are defined not only by what we say and what we do but by what surrounds us in the course of all we say and all we do.

I pay for and am the only person to attend Edmund Rose's funeral. Despite trying to get in touch with his wife, she refuses to return my calls. I accompany his body from the morgue to a cemetery in North London and I watch a Roman Cic priest commend Edmund Rose to the ground - finality, exorcism, decomposition, dust.

In the days before, I draw up a speech which I read at his side. I read out loud but no one hears me. I read it to myself after his body has been interned and earth poured all over him. As I read, it begins to rain and so runs the ink which counterpoints my paper. Within seconds I cannot read my own words and think of giving up. But I carry on speaking from a heart Edmund helped give me. I speak of a man who was misunderstood but misunderstood himself. I speak of a man without choices in a world of choice wherein the inhumanity of man ruined him. I speak of confusion and dissonance - people groping around in the dark and grabbing the lowest for ease of reach; of those sometimes pure, sometimes impure, whose weakness necessarily makes those different suffer. I recall a man, who I too, have misunderstood but who stood by me and showed what it is to accept but never to give in to prejudice, to bigotry and to hatred. Edmund Rose, I tell myself; I tell the damp oak tree caressing the wind next to me, made the best out of lifeless, barren earth by not letting the lie of the ground be his undoing. But it was his undoing; People were his undoing - inhumanity was his undoing. Still, I thank him for giving me a glimpse of how, even in weakness, and Edmund was weak in many ways, it is possible to develop and retain a heart no matter how forces fall upon you. I thank him for allowing me to change from a stone to the cusp of life itself, able to counter the iniquity of man by not being afraid of the iniquity of man. Though Edmund had reticence - reluctance to act as his ally; knowing that times have changed and a master of all he was not, he gave me the strength to realise that I too, must change. As the social landscape becomes ever more convoluted, Edmund's reluctance to fight came from the satisfaction that he had been benefactor of many good times as well as bad. But he did not discourage me and he did not discourage my friends. He opened a door to insight which is presently closed to most. His death will not be in vain for I speak for two new lives - my own and that of my child. I stand alone but I am not alone: grey sky, blue sky, wet earth, dry - let all the seasons come upon me, for I am not just Iris any more. Iris was buried along with her master. His ashes proffer a new life and I, and Iris, will honour him. Edmund Rose did not die in vain. He did not die at all.

"Iris I need to see you. This is important."

I crawl over to the side of my bed, squinting at the digital display. It is quarter past four in the morning.

"Helen; it is extremely late. Can it not wait?"

I sense the urgency in Helen's voice - pinched, squeezed through her glottis - undulating, high-pitched and croaking. It confuses me; she confuses me. I have never heard such excitement in her voice before.

"Where are you?"

"In a taxi around the corner from your flat. This really cannot wait."

Helen hangs up. I almost curse her. I am extremely tired, having felt inexplicably tired all the previous day. I put my head back into my pillow hoping it is a dream. But her words sound alarm bells within and I roll into daydreams until I cannot sleep. Ten minutes pass and there is a knock at the door. As I flick the catch, Helen bolts and almost slams me down in her wake.

She speaks immediately - excited, quickly, disjointed. But I cannot concentrate and ask her to stop, offering her a hot drink. When I return she looks a little calmer and a little tired as the adrenalin which held her actions, trickles away to a more functional display. Reluctantly, she seems to realise how unimpressed I am at this hour.

"I am sorry Iris. I know it is late. I had to tell you."

"Tell me what?"

"Remember you and I having that conversation a short time ago before Edmund died, about taking a risk and searching 's room?"

My recall is sketchy; patchwork at best.

"Yes."

"I was asked by to work late - he has a deal which signs this morning. negotiated the documents and gave them to me to be amended. I got the final versions last night, to be ready for a signing ceremony at eleven o'clock. went home - he has been up for a couple of days without sleep. I know he went home. I know because I called him a taxi and he asked me to carry some papers to the cab. I watched as the cab drove into the distance.

" looked demonstrably tired and explained that he was on his last legs, that without some sort of sleep he was finished, that he was physically broken, that he couldn't remember a transaction as intense nor as tiring. He has been holed up in meetings or in his room for a couple of days - two straight days without sleep and the whole place is an absolute mess.

"It was therefore the best opportunity to have a look through his things. Even Brodie wouldn't be able to decipher that paper mountain for differences even if there was movement amongst the numerous piles of redundant documents and discarded drafts in his room. I could make no sense of it. I doubt a man as knackered as he is, could either.

"So I waited and waited, getting on with the typing amendments required of me, counting time, nervous and unsure, resisting the urge to call you, adamant I could do this by myself. Eventually, in the small hours, when other lawyers had drifted off and I was left on my own, I tiptoed into 's room and as carefully as I could, began the process of picking through his things.

"I did exactly as you said. My actions were slow, meticulous and methodical. I studied the position of every object I moved before carefully placing it in such a way that I would disturb no other, moving through items of interest systematically, trying not to dislocate any papers, never underestimating 's deviousness or resource. Still, I assumed and I think, reasonably assumed, that legal papers strewn in such a haphazard fashion across the room had been placed without thought, without design and naturally, without reason. They hid nothing, if indeed, they were ever meant to. But that didn't mean I assumed anything other than order. Why would I take that chance?

"I turned my attention to the drawers of his desk. I took to his drawers and inspected the outside of each before I approached. Do you know, I am so glad I did. Subtlety and do not mix. But for this I have to give him due regard. Boy, must he have a suspicious mind, for in the gap between each drawer was carefully strewn one of the hairs from his head. So, if a drawer is opened, it dislodges a hair and on simple inspection he sees that, either by design or by accident, someone or something has misplaced one or more of those precious dyed black hairs."

My mind begins to race. Imagination takes over but pillories as I grow frustrated, for I cannot articulate intuitive imaginations and guesstimates are of no use. What has she found? What has caused Helen to turn up at my flat with a story to tell?

"I tried all of the drawers to the right hand side of his desk. Each contained nothing of note - precisely the sort of stuff one would expect to see in any lawyer's desk - pens, notepads, stationery. However, in the lower drawer on the left hand side, I placed my hand inside and found at the back of the drawer, extremely well hidden and disguised, the following."

Helen places her bag on the kitchen table. Without taking her eyes off me and unaware of the elemental panic I am trying to disregard, she puts on a plastic glove and searches inside, producing a clear plastic bag no bigger than an inch square and what looks like an address book or a diary.

It is the bag which catches my attention. Inside there are granules of white powder, like icing sugar or talcum powder. I ask Helen what the substance is. Helen laughs.

"You mean you don't know?"

"Should I know?"

"Oh, Iris, what kind of a life have you led? The substance in that bag, is pure cocaine."

"Cocaine?" I repeat, stupidly.

"You have never seen cocaine before - never taken it?"

"Are you sure?"

Helen looks incredulous.

"My God. You really have had your head stuck in a book. This is almost pure cocaine; not the sort of stuff you buy in nightclubs, not the stuff you buy at street corners. This is high-grade cocaine."

Am I stupid or naive? Am I the lesser or greater for knowledge of criminal substance? To be sure, I am lost. Consequence doesn't hit me - it passes me by without regard, like a gentle summer's breeze.

"How do you know?"

"Corin's brother was closely connected to terrorists in Ireland. They used to import cocaine and sell it to the locals, who, in turn, put some of it up their nose or sold it adulterated to their friends. Drugs used to fund terrorism's gun running and everything else they did. One night, I tasted it. This innocuous white powder on this table is as close as I can imagine. I have had plenty of inferior cocaine in my time and know what it should and should not taste like. Take my word for it, this is the highest quality - uncut, unadulterated, unseen by the market."

Part of me is elated. We finally have something - he uses drugs and hard drugs at that. I do not get the significance of the quality.

"The higher the quality of the drug means the closer one is to the source of production. Suspend your intellect - this isn't rocket science. Pure cocaine is produced then constantly doctored until, when it gets to the average white man, they are sniffing rat poison, talcum powder, ketamine or worse.

"This isn't inferior; quite the opposite. Whoever supplied this is extremely well connected, meaning that is close to someone or knows someone clamped to the nether slopes of the narcotics supply chain. Without regard to the simple fact that here we have a City of London lawyer actually buying and taking this drug, we are in a position to know that his connections and his lifestyle isn't the bed of roses and familial bliss we may have believed, had we chosen to listen."

"But is that a fair assumption to make?"

I swear I see condescension, largesse and magnanimity.

"He buys drugs unadulterated to the same degree as the populace - does that mean more than the simple fact of buying and taking it in the first place?

"Isn't that enough?"

"You could argue it either way."

Helen taps her finger on the address book.

"Not however, when you have a look inside this address book."

Taking a seat next to me, Helen opens a little black, slightly tattered, fake leather address book and we leaf through the pages together. The first thing to strike me is the meticulous way the names, addresses and the telephone numbers have been scribed. Whatever Brodie is, he most certainly has an organised mind, though an anally repetitive one - the same pen, the same ink, the same careful scribe with equidistance and equality between each entry.

I study each name and each address carefully. In themselves they seem to mean nothing. I recognise some names however - those of lawyers and bankers in the City of London. Nothing unusual in that. Then, as I try to think a little more deeply about the coincidence of identities, Helen makes the point.

"Boy, Iris, you are slow tonight."

"Should I be any quicker?"

"Alright, let me make the point for you.

"Remember the discussion we had with Edmund at lunch, in which you talked at length and I listened at length to your conversation in which you spoke of kinship and the ties between people by marriage, politics and outlook, and all the rest of it. You recall that my very own community in Ireland isn't that much different than that Edmund was a member of. We too, are held and bound together by a similar outlook and ways of looking at the world. And it struck me that , being from the same community as I am, left that community in order to descend to the Olympian heights he has scaled today."

I laugh.

"Sometimes you are more cynical than I!"

"Iris; please. Please listen.

"So, thinking it through, when a man whose morality is closely bound with that of the community in which he lives, leaves that community, then, if we consider him weak, which he most certainly is, my guess is that he tries to replace one community with another. And the obvious place to look is the very environment he left Ireland to become a part of.

"So what I did was to go to one of those reference books. It is called 'Who's Who in the City.'"

"I know the book - a hollow guide for the vain of the vain."

"Now who is being cynical?

"Anyway; I assumed you did. It discloses the names of those who are at least halfway up the ladder to the top of those venerable institutions in which we work - bankers, insurers, lawyers, accountants and all the rest of them. I checked the names in Brodie's address book against the names in that tome. Each of them is there; each of them is bound by one single fact - every man in that list is the same age, give a year or two, and each of them is a former member of the same college at Cambridge."

I remember the college - one of the smaller colleges with neither a bad nor a good reputation. Of course it isn't Kings College or New College but one of the oldest, one of the closeted, one of the profane.

"All were at that college at the same time. Each of them would have known each other and each of them has ended up here in the City of London and are doing very well, thank you very much. Look more closely, Iris. Like Brodie, not one of them attended English or Scottish Public Schools. They are men from the upper-middle class, yet they do not belong to the group in which Rose was so immersed.

"I remember something else from lunch, too.

"I remember Edmund saying that he was the last of his own. A new order has taken over - notice how borders-actual have gone, country borders have shrunk and withered till nationality is but a by-product of birth and little to do with how business is conducted and how people are marshalled. Notice how money movements have created this new challenge to the indigenous and reformed the psychology of the City of London itself.

"Suppose therefore, I guess for a moment. Let us say that Brodie *et al* came down to London together. They either explicitly or implicitly recognised that they were lucky enough to be this new order. They realised too, as would be natural, that the ties of kinship which had taken generations for families like Edmund's to attain, did not bind them and they were faced with threats to their own, new, gestating, growing hegemony. These are a new breed. They are also insecure. It is natural that they seek out each other for the comfort, the assurance they need in the face of what may seem like almost insurmountable odds. They become closer until they cannot but rely on each other and only each other. Brodie and this conclave of interlopers become an unseen, an unknown cyst which pulses an opaque poison yet a translucent veneer and a new breed of creeping control.

This and these are Brodie's friends. He has successfully replaced one community, that is, my community - the community I betrayed and that betrayed me, and chosen another. These names represent the only people Brodie feels he can rely on. That very sentiment is implicit in the way he has chosen to hide and contain these contact details."

I can deal with the premise. But I do not see its relevance.

"There is one more important piece of information contained in that address book."

I leaf to the last page, unsure what it will unveil.

"Do you know what that is?"

It is another address and meaningless in isolation.

"That is Brodie's home. The oddest thing is I have seen it many times before, for every now and then Brodie has parcels hand-delivered there though he never explicitly states who they are for. I know now because those parcels were meant for him - that is where he lives. It could be no other place."

Helen sits back, relieved to have got all of the information out in the open. My head is still unsure of its value, whether it has value.

"Iris; can you not see? What did we know about the man before tonight? You know because I have told you that he is from a hard-line Protestant community in Ireland. That is all. Now we know where he lives, we know who he trusts and we know that he isn't averse to breaking the criminal law. We have information, Iris. We have hard information which, if we think creatively, we can use. The discovery of cocaine in his desk we can certainly use. We are now limited only by our creativity."

A penny drops into the wrong slot. It isn't the penny Helen wants.

"And in sitting here, having removed the very artefacts Brodie would look for first when he gets back to work - looking at them, analysing them, mulling and scheming, we have just, if he finds out they have been discovered, given him every bit of notice he needs and every bit of notice we do not want him to have."

Shock comes across Helen's face. She realises her mistake immediately.

"Oh my God. I just brought them here without thinking."

I look at the clock. It is gone five in the morning.

"What time is he due back at the office?"

"Six."

"Oh my God is right. Get your coat."

XXX.

I throw my clothes over me, grab James' car keys and leave the house.

We drive through the uncrowded streets - through Clapham, Stockwell, touching the edges of Brixton and bisecting Kennington, till we reach Blackfriars Bridge. In the distance, dark and ominous and eerily still - a counterpoint to the shifting blackness in the skies beyond, looms St Paul's Cathedral, towering above the chaff buildings all around and dwarfed by the canopy beyond. I park the car in the basement and we rush upstairs.

My heart beats the walls of my chest - a timpani awakening realisation; a pulse serving an ensemble about to display. We run up the stairs to our floor and along an adjoining corridor. It is still dark outside though it will very shortly be sunrise and I check along the corridor to see if artificial light comes out of any of the rooms, especially Brodies.

I tell Helen to run to the photocopier and tell her to copy every page of Brodie's address book. I wait, delivered by the darkness, recoiled in the shadows outside Brodie's room, counting seconds. Far away I hear the sound of doors opening and closing. Sound - the increasing volume of swing doors opening and closing, tells me he is getting near. Helen appears and is sweating.

"As quickly as you can Helen, place both of these packages where you found them - precisely where you found them. Brodie is only seconds away.

"But the hair which covers the outside of the drawer, I cannot find it."

"We have no time."

Helen darts into Brodie's room. She appears seconds later and I drag her along the corridor and into my office. I leave the door ajar. Helen is behind me, holding me. Exposing the corner of my face to the frame of my door, I look into the corridor, expecting to see Brodie at any moment. Eventually, I see the door which leads to our corridor open and I see a cleaner carrying a blue plastic bucket over which, disorganised and ready to fall, lies an acrylic rag and pink rubber gloves.

I take a deep breath and tell Helen. She collapses, almost fainting. I have little time for her; all I want to do is get over the adrenalin rush which bubbles in my veins; the timpani throbbing the temple robbing me of air, starving me of oxygen.

"But he will see that the drawer has been disturbed.

"Iris; what are we going to do?"

Anxiety infects. I do not have an answer to placate. And then the answer comes to me.

"Helen; we will not replace that hair. We will let him think someone has been through his drawers and could have discovered the cocaine and the address book. We will let him think and watch him think. His mind will turn and turn, and turn, and turn. But he will have no proof. Brodie has no idea that you have even spoken to me. Brodie will suspect me alone, but with little or no evidence."

"But he could have had you followed."

Briefly I consider the possibility. I discard it, throwing it away for the unsubstantiated speculation it is.

"If he has had me followed he would have discovered you immediately. You practically live in my flat. And all he would have had to do was to pick up the telephone and call Ireland, delivering the threat with which he controls you."

Looking along the corridor once more, I see the cleaner busy tidying one of the rooms. I seize our chance, and taking Helen by the arm, we sneak back the way we came. All we can hear is the sound of this little cleaner humming an indistinct tune, badly. And then, once more, we hear doors opening; we hear doors closing.

Without taking any chances, we dive into another room along a corridor which adjoins our own. It has a partial glass door and we can see out. Suddenly the corridor lights up as whoever is walking in our direction causes the automatic lighting to charge. It works to our advantage as exterior light reflects off the glass - whoever is walking past will only see a reflection of themselves as they go by.

Once more, Helen stands behind me. The door is slightly ajar. Dust infused shards of light cascade to the corner while we recoil in the darkness, well back from the glass. We hear the sound of movement along the corridor, as cloth brushes against cloth - shoes periodically and rhythmically hitting the polished wooden floor.

There is something to the tenor of the sound, to the actual rhythm as each shoe strikes the ground, that I recognise. I think back to that morning when I looked up and down Ludgate Hill watching people walk by until Brodie himself goose-stepped past. I remember the click of his heels on the pavement - those metallic heels on the bottom of his shoes hitting then sliding off the pavement. Rythym, sound, metre and memory - the man walking along the corridor is Brodie. It has to be.

As he draws near I stiffen. Helen can sense it - she can feel it as she grabs my arm, sliding her arm around the small of my back. Both of us look, transfixed by the light which illuminates the corridor, waiting for him to

161

appear.

When she sees him Helen closes her eyes. He spares not a glance for the room in which we are standing. I only catch a glimpse of him. Once more he is leaning forward, following his peaked crown, hell-bent on getting to wherever he is going without the slightest care for the hinterland on the way.

In the few, turgid, elongated seconds after he passes, I relax. Helen opens her eyes and I can sense her looking at me. But I hear no footsteps after I see him; I hear no movement after he has gone. I stiffen again as the light unveils a hand shrouded by double cuffs and cufflinks of gold moving towards the door handle, grabbing the door and yanking it to. The sound of its snap almost catches Helen who tries not to scream. Even if she had screamed Brodie would not have heard a thing. I have my hand clamped over her mouth.

After what seems like an hour, I venture towards the door Brodie has rammed shut. With Helen still holding my hand, I peer around the corner. Everything is clear - seems clear, though the light in the corridor is on and we can be seen. But we have to take the chance of being seen. We have no choice but to take that chance. So I quietly open the room door and both Helen and I run as fast as we can towards the stairs to the basement car park, careless about noise, careless as to consequence.

We get back into James' car and drive home in silence. The sun is just coming up and it promises to be a beautifully clear day as streaks of light set the sky orange, rose and intermittently blue. Once more St Paul's Cathedral provides the counterpoint to the skyline as I look in awe at the majesty of nature and the beauty of that building, at the beauty of its architecture and the beauty of nature intermingled. What great things nature and humanity are capable of; what awful things both are capable of conjuring at the same time. What a pleasure it is to be a part of a race capable of producing such majesty; what a dishonour it is to be embroiled in nature when it can cause so much harm.

The streets are just beginning to show signs of life, as traffic builds up and the City once more springs to life. Occasionally I look at Helen, who still holds my arm. I feel her grip relax and I see her somnolent eyelids falling heavier and heavier as the need to sleep consumes. When we arrive in Clapham she is fast asleep, waking somehow on hearing the noise of the ticking engine stop.

"Are we back?" she asks.

"Yes."

"Should I go home Iris? Should I go home and get ready to go back to work?"

I look at my watch. Ordinarily I would have to be up in an hour and a half. So does Helen. I can stay awake. I cannot see Helen managing it.

"We have a little time to sleep."

"But should I go home?"

Helen looks at me and her eyes plead. I cannot let her go.

"You can stay with me until it is time to leave."

"And clothes - I can't return to work in the same clothes."

"I'll give you some clothes I never wear. No one will recognise them as mine."

We stagger from the car and into the flat. James is still asleep and unaware that I have borrowed his car. I replace his keys and upon entry to my bedroom, I see Helen lying there, fully clothed and fast asleep.

Frustrated, I shake her but it is no use and my heart goes out to her for her exhaustion, for the strength which takes her timid temperament beyond duty and for the courage to act for both of us. Gently I try to remove her clothes. But she has crawled into a foetal position; a baby snug to the walls of the womb and no matter how I try and assemble her arms and legs she snaps back into position like a coiled and taut elastic band.

I take off my own clothes and slide under the sheets beside her, turning out the light. As I turn out the light I notice the light which cascades through my curtains, unveiling the inner sanctuary of my own room, telling me, unwelcome as it does so, that daylight has returned. I roll onto my side, using my pillow as a cover to shield the light and to give me the temporal peace of darkness. Helen, still fast asleep, seems to unconsciously sense me and no sooner do I find myself feeling relatively comfortable, when her hand and arm move in my direction, circling me, surrounding me and enveloping me.

Reactive and confused, I sit up straight, moving Helen aside. She mumbles a few words, tries and fails to replace her hand - to surround again, to permeate, to infuse. I watch and gently reposition so that she cannot reach. Her face contorts, my face contorts too, as I think of how ridiculous this situation is. And how unique it is, for I have never in my life shared my bed with anybody. Poor Helen - I remember her telling me of her brothers in Ireland. How she must miss their companionship. How she must remember the times when she was a child, when the brothers and sisters were thrown into bed together and told to make do. What fights they must have had; what bedlam. What affection must have been extolled once the competition for places had given way to acceptance, to sleep and the natural tendency to search for signs of life and affection with the comfort siblings have for each other.

Alas, I can only imagine such feelings though there is a tiny bit of me that yearns. But is this what Helen offers?

And am I so stuck with this heart of ice that I can't reciprocate?

She begins to snore. To hear the soft flesh of the palette vibrating over and under air squeezed through an aperture reluctant to give way, brings a smile to my face. Helen doesn't - cannot annoy me. I find it amusing - alas, I cannot sleep in the face of someone who can do nothing else.

Am I the lucky one or is she?

What takes the ice, which freezes my heart, to thaw, so that my heart and my head touch then relate?

Doubtless Helen would say she is unlucky. I disagree. She has had the opportunity of companionship. Helen's luck is having touched that evasive; that spectral slice of humanity. I, on the other hand, just criticise the very concept of humanity for it hides from me - an impenetrable maze I cannot follow. She has had her fair share of misery too and a misery which even I find difficult to analyse and comprehend. When Helen was formed, gestation and due process were given to dealing with emotions and feelings denied Iris, for I have never had that chance, save for now.

I wonder about how my life has changed and indeed if I have, changed. I am a more emotional person. I am prepared to fight. It would be a lie to say I didn't, in some small way, enjoy the evening for I had been party to a beating heart, to fear and anticipation, to adrenalin.

When have I ever led myself to that before?

Is it the injustice of the situation I react to?

Is it the fact that I am pregnant?

I run my hand over my stomach. I have come to think of the child inside me whenever I am at rest. The inclination and the desire to think of the child is becoming more prevalent with each passing day. I have contrasted the innocence of the body inside me, to the evil at its extreme. I have thought; I over-think of the world into which the child will be delivered. I have contrasted and compared all I know and related that to all this little ball of chemicals in my stomach.

Have I done the right thing in keeping the child?

Is employing another life on the face of the earth the right thing to do?

Surely this little body will be no better nor worse than those I have to be with and those I see every day. Of course I have made the right choice in bringing the product of rape into the world. It is not the child's fault. And to kill the child would see its termination as the resolver of the sins of the bearer and the protagonist. Displaced guilt cannot be right. I must have the child and teach it everything I have learnt.

Am I being self-righteous about all?

I know I am. I know this represents such conclusive arrogance. Who am I, Iris, the social retard, the social scientist, the social pariah, the social non sequitur, to speak ill of others? The answer is as conceited as the question. It is not their fault for they are not aware of what they do, why they do it and what they become when they do so. This is the way I am - that is the way I used to be.

I have changed. I am more emotional and I am less of the person I used to be. I do not want to ask whether I am more of a person now. Have I more of the humanity I have watched and despised? Have I lost the coolness and the essential objectivity which to Iris, marked me out as different? Maybe. I just do not know where I am any more and who I am. Is this because I am now two or is it natural to feel and to hate and to want to feel and to hate when the vagaries of human nature rise up and attack? I have never been attacked before so how would I know for myself, regardless of what I know about others?

Do I really know what my feelings are now?

Helen is on the move, trying again to take hold of me. Once more I move her arm to one side. Once more she pulls a face and settles back into a deep sleep. Helen is perhaps the best example I can think of in answering the question. I have known Helen for days. But she was so open with me when I met her - so honest, so decent and so unfortunate. I have no choice now as I look down upon her. She has put so much trust in me in a city and a culture where you are told to trust no one.

I know and how could I not know that my feelings for Edmund Rose have grown too, and it is, in part, more than a discreet cousin to the tragedy which has affected them both, that I have the resurrection of feeling I scarcely remember as a small child.

And I have the rape, too.

To be cold, to become warm and to move toward some semblance of inner compassion requires extant emotion - some would say, upheaval. I have no recollection of the event. If the rapist met me in the street or stood next to me at a bar, I would have no idea who they were. That is not to say that having my insides breached by this man isn't the grossest intrusion and the vilest act. It has affected me more than the unwanted gestation of a life. I have changed - I have. But how much of this is attributable to the act of rape? It could have been different had I been awake and terrified; had I been beaten and left to die. But I wasn't and my thoughts keep coming back to my actions during the event itself. Rape is the act of sexual intercourse without consent. How much did I move? What did I say if I said anything while the event took place? Is it possible that as I lay there, practically unconscious from the effects of alcohol, that I somehow predisposed myself towards the rapist by not contesting his objectives? And what of the rapist himself? Somehow could my thoughts have become confused? One thinks of a rapist as a cold and calculating animal who has stalked his prey and in cold blood, executes his want over the resistance of the victim. Could the protagonist have been as similarly drunk as I? It doesn't seem unreasonable when I think of that party in Chelsea at that time in the morning and with that much alcohol having been consumed; it doesn't seem unreasonable to think of the rapist as a man who similarly could not distinguish between right and wrong such was the amount of alcohol in his veins. Perhaps he can't remember either. If such was his confusion and mine, then neither of us can remember that the act itself was not one of intent but of folly. So who can I blame?

Can I blame the individual?

I have chosen not to blame the individual but have slowly come to blame the male *in toto*. But I have been dragged into the abyss when all I ever wanted to do was to watch those within it. For that and that alone, I have every right to be angry. My body and the physical features I have been graced with have been a singular point of contact for men without respite. I had managed to avoid the suffering which men unveil upon women until the very worst vestige of masculinity unleashed itself upon me. Whether or not the rapist was drunk; whether or not he exercised choice; whether his mind was as addled as mine, that, finally, means little to me by way of excuse. As I lie awake, looking down upon Helen who has suffered both at the hands of man and the society led by man, I have stopped excusing the opposite sex for their behaviour, no matter whether I have spent a lifetime almost admiring it and certainly understanding it. There can be no excuse for what has been done to me. There can be no excuse for what was done to Helen. By their actions are they known. By my reaction, which sadly, has been forced upon me, do I feel every right to feel indignant to my very core, to the very epicentre of my being, to the heart of my identity as a woman.

XXXI.

I tell - I demand of the clock by the side of my bed that it changes; that it changes quickly. The more I look the slower the hands move. This elasticity of time annoys me. Why am I anxious for time to advance?

Helen is still asleep. Should I wake her and unveil a sentient mortality she seems, in so many ways, unfit to handle? I cannot do this without her. This is not to say that I rely upon her. Iris is alone as we are all alone. Reliance is not me, is not what I am used to, is not for me. This morning, once again, Iris is all I know.

Helen looks sweet as she opens her eyes. She doesn't know and can't comprehend where she is. I watch the lids of her eyes close and open slowly, a half-smile colouring her lips. I see comfort and reassurance in her eyes and her arm once more reaches towards me. She squeezes my arm and mumbles a few words. I guess these small words mean a lot to Helen, as they do to me. I am comfort; a friendly face; water on fire; comfort in dependance. She feels confident in me; she trusts me; she relies on me. I feel responsible but somehow happy with the feeling. My thoughts flit to my child. Will it be the same when a baby's face beams at me - a sweet innocent child knowing nothing of the world and the circumstances in which it was created? What responsibilities will I have then? What strength in these weary shoulders?

"Time to get dressed. I've laid some clothes out I think will fit you. There is a towel here and the shower is around the corner."

Helen refuses to acknowledge me. Mumbling like a baby, she rolls over so as not to face me. Sleep may give the mind its own pressures but compares to nothing when one considers what Helen has to face. It is no wonder she prefers the sanctity and the darkness of sleep to the ignominy and cruelty of awakening.

I push then poke her in the small of her back. As she turns once more to face me the smile has gone and ill-understanding replaces serenity - 'why can't you leave me alone, for I am content? Why do you want to disrupt what I have with what I do not want? I am comfortable. I am at peace.'

"Take a shower Helen. I'll be back in a minute."

I leave my bedroom and Helen to the slow-burn truth that she cannot avoid waking hours and all that waking hours entail. While I make breakfast

I hear the bedroom door open then the shower running. Helen has not given up. We cannot afford to give up.

James is pottering about in his bedroom. I look behind me at the photocopies of Brodie's very private address book. What will James make of it all when I tell him?

He too slumbers his way into the kitchen, sitting down at the breakfast table, waiting to be served. Cheeky bugger. His mumblings involve the provision of caffeine and the supply of sugar. Then he hears the shower. Immediately he thinks the occupant of the bathroom is a man. A sly grin comes to his face but he forgets the simplistic on perusal of his faculties, realising who he is looking at and alive to the potential of insult.

"Who is in the shower, Iris?"

"Helen."

"But she lives around the corner."

I place two strong coffees on the table.

"Helen has turned up something which may mean something but may mean nothing at all."

"What?"

"You remember I told you I asked her to search Brodie's room, if and when she had the chance. The opportunity arose last night."

James picks up the copied addresses, found in Brodie's desk. He looks at them without comprehension.

"She worked very late, at Brodie's request. He'd been up for two days without sleep and had to go home. Helen was left behind and searched his room. He cannot lock any of his drawers so he places pieces of his hair across the drawers of his desk. If anyone opens those drawers the hair falls away and he can see his desk has been tampered with."

"A bit James Bond," James says, sarcastically.

"Helen found that list of names and addresses and a small quantity of a drug she tells me is cocaine."

"Cocaine?"

"Yes, cocaine."

James laughs. I ask him why.

"I just can't see it - stiffs in the City of London taking recreational drugs? The cap doesn't seem to fit. Put me in the West End of London on a Friday night and there are handbags; there are pockets full of cocaine. Put me in a lawyers office in the City of London and the worst I thought you would have found is paracetamol."

"But does it mean more to you than the obvious?"

"Well, he is breaking the criminal law. But cocaine is everywhere."

Finally James gets the point.

"Yes; I see. Why would a man like Brodie have a drawer containing coke? It doesn't sound like recreational use to me. I suppose the real question is where is he getting it from?"

"That's the thing. Helen, who says she knows a lot about this drug, tells me it is just about as pure as one can get. She once tasted cocaine this pure in Ireland when her boyfriend, whose brother had dubious friends, gave her some which had just been processed somewhere in South America."

James catches on - articulating my half-thoughts with street thoughts.

"And if he is taking almost pure cocaine for whatever reason that twisted bastard takes it, whoever is getting it knows someone or is connected to someone who knows someone in the supply chain."

"Precisely."

"So who would Brodie know, in the world he lives in, who could provide him with high grade cocaine? Is that the question?"

"Well if he isn't buying the stuff from a normal dealer, who cuts it and adds all manner of vile substances to it, that has got to be the question."

"But how would you find out? The man is paranoid to the point of exhaustion. And he is clever. Surely he would take any steps possible so as not to render himself culpable."

"I've thought of that. And to a great degree I can't think of what the answer might be, save for one thing."

"And that is?"

"Helen found an address book next to the cocaine. You are looking at a copy of it. They are just names to you but I recognise a couple of them. Helen checked them against a book of the great and the good in the City and each one of the names, bar a couple of exceptions, is a man and a contemporary of Brodies from his days at Cambridge. They are all Cambridge and what is more they are all members of the same college."

"Which one?"

A wry grin comes to his face. James studied at Cambridge too.

"I knew that place was a little odd. They seemed to keep themselves to themselves - stupid of me not to recognise they were up to something. So they are Brodie's present friends or acquaintances from a long time ago."

"Well if they are just acquaintances, why take the trouble to hide their names and their addresses next to a bag of cocaine stuffed in the bottom drawer of your desk? Though I am not entirely sure why, the very act of putting those names next to that drug has got to be suggestive of something."

"So you are developing a theory?"

"A half-theory at best - Helen's theory really."

James embraces his chair, all child-like and expectant.

"Accept that in the world in which we live the days of the old establishment have gone and we have a new but insecure and weak hegemony. The ties of these tender new tyros are first developed at Cambridge. These men get to the City of London, they see an opportunity, strike and events fall in their favour. However, with competition for control being everything, they stick to each other like glue. They are mutually interdependent, they arrive and embellish a bunker mentality in order to protect themselves from every perceived threat imaginable, whether that threat is apparent or not. They were close and they stay close. But they wish to keep their identities as capitalist siblings only to each other."

"Very good as conspiracy theories go."

"It is not a conspiracy theory."

"A Cambridge clique taking over the City of London?"

"You heard Edmund himself explain how he was part of the last vestige of a previous class. One is simply replaced by the other."

"This is all wild supposition. What if it were true? What good does it serve knowing this and not being able to verify it?"

James has me. I cannot complete the analysis. It is conjecture and obtuse.

"Well; that is the question. But you have to agree that the cocaine and the list of names kept in what amounts to a secret location is more than a little suggestive."

"Well, I agree but like you said, you have very little to go on. Still, you do know one thing - Brodie is not as pure as the driven snow. You know enough now to be able to come back to him if you think he is going to go after you, which I suspect he will."

"If I were to tell him I found the cocaine, he could deny it as utterly implausible. And what would I have as proof? The cocaine was put back where it was found."

"Helen put it back straight away?"

"No. She brought it here."

"What?"

"Yes, she brought both the sachet of powder and the address book here."

"My God. So how did it get back into Brodie's office?"

"I'm afraid I had to borrow your car. We just had enough time to replace his things before he returned. It was the closest shave imaginable. And we may have made a mistake.

"Helen failed to replace the hair which separates his drawers. If he is not half-asleep and delirious with tiredness, I think he could well notice.

"It may be no bad thing if he has, James. See, the way I am thinking - what better than for Brodie to start thinking suspiciously? What if he does notice? He knows exactly what he has to hide. If he thinks I have been involved or any of the other assistants who worked with Edmund, it could be a way of flushing his intentions out."

"He could assume it was a careless cleaner."

"Well that is no bad thing either, because it sows a seed of doubt inside his head."

"I suppose so."

"There is one other thing which I need to tell you before Helen comes in. If you look at that list of addresses in front of you, you will see that not only does it disclose the names and addresses of Brodie's friends - or co-conspirators as you may consider them – but also, there is one address there which is unique."

"I cannot see."

I reach over and find the right entry.

"See? You know what that is? That is Brodie's home."

"And?"

"I've told you before - no one actually knew where the man lives. No one knows anything about him - not even Helen. He says he has a family and is happily married but no one has ever met his wife nor seen his children. This is partly why this whole discovery process has been so difficult. Now we have his address, we have his friends and to some degree, we have his habits. It is a start."

"It is more than a start, Iris. Let me have a note of that address. You know I have felt inert and useless since this all began. My assistance has been non-assistance. All I have been is an observer. Of course, I have been supportive but unable to help. I think that can all change now."

"What do you mean?"

James takes a pen and makes a note of Brodie's address.

"Let's just say that, today, I will ring in sick and tell them have an upset stomach or something. You and I know I am not medically unwell and no one else need know. I don't go to work, I get washed and dressed then take the car to this address. And I watch the home of this madman until something, if anything, gives.

"I can meet you here tonight and can tell you what I discovered."

"James; that is too much to ask."

"My best friend is raped, falls pregnant, is threatened at work to the detriment of herself and her child. Her friend has suffered almost half an adult lifetime of tyranny, partly at the hands of the same man and certainly, at the hands of the mindless religious bigotry that man calls his own and all I have asked of myself is to sit in front of a property and watch what is going on. Do you seriously think that now I can help, I am not going to?"

"It could be dangerous."

"Dangerous to who?"

"You."

"Why? I have met Brodie once. And you forget, while I sit and watch his house, he will be in your office doing whatever it is you lawyers do. Unless I am seen by the occupant, if there is an occupant, I cannot see how I could possibly be spotted. I think you should give me a little more credit. I am not going to wear a placard saying 'I am watching you'. I will be very careful. I will be so discreet that not even I will know I am there."

"Well, if you are sure."

"It is the least I can do."

Helen enters the kitchen. She looks remarkably fresh. James has the good sense not to continue our conversation, aware that Helen might not be so pleased with what he is proposing - the riskier our behaviour gets, the more she is likely to worry.

"I think we had better stagger our journey to work, Helen. We don't want to be seen walking in together."

"You told James, then?"

James is still looking at the copied addresses.

"Iris has told me what you two escape artists have been up to. Sounds like quite a night."

"Scary is perhaps a better description. I just can't think what I was thinking of bringing those things back here."

"You weren't, and I can easily understand why."

XXXII.

I work steadily in my room, glad that I have a few short hours affording me the opportunity of concentrating on something else. Process slows me down and isolates the one task in front of me, allowing me to collapse into a vacuum discarding worries I cannot control or want to consider.

My door is closed. I hear laughing outside and peer through glass to see Brodie looking at me. Gingerly, politely, he knocks on the door. To say I am intrigued is to understate my feelings.

I smile, though I know not why. And I am pleasant, more out of practise than design.

"I'd like to introduce you to the newly appointed accountant in charge of partnership finance. This is Oliver Dauncey."

Behind Brodie but standing considerably taller is a man whose face seems familiar though I cannot place him. I seem to recognise his name too, though I cannot place his name.

"Pleased to meet you."

"Iris is one of our best finance lawyers. Don't be put off by that smile. She is as hard as any of the men on this floor and tougher than most in this practice. One to beware of, I assure you."

Brodie laughs, as does this Oliver Dauncey. I feign laughter too though I know precisely what Brodie is referring to. Dauncey himself is unaware, no doubt thinking that Brodie is a bit of a cad and a charmer.

"Anyway, glad to have met you Iris."

Conventionally handsome, there is something to Oliver Dauncey's manner, to his delivery and in the way he articulated the few words he spoke, which is reminiscent - the City of London is such a small place. I brush the thought off, brushing off the whole interlude and carrying on with my work, speaking to nobody during the course of the day. When I get home tiredness gags me, envelops and blankets me. I fall into a deep sleep but am woken, not this time by Helen but by James, who is at my bedside, fully dressed and wide awake.

"Wake up, Iris. Wake up. I have something to tell you."

We are in the kitchen. It is now my turn to listen to James' story through a fogged, a confused, an exhausted brain.

"I suppose this could have waited until the morning but I just wanted to tell you as soon as I could."

James is excited and giddy. Growth covers and colours his neck and his chin. His trousers look damp, his knees are soaked with mud as are his elbows. Dirt colours his fingernails as mud stains his hands. His hair is damp, his breath is musty and sour.

"I decided to drive. So I mauled my way through the London traffic and into Surrey. I drove through Croydon and Cheam and ended up in one of those faceless stockbroker belt villages which circle the tips of South London. Boy, has he done well for himself. The man's house is enormous - beautiful in fact and set well back from the road; so far back from the road that I couldn't get a clear view of what was going on inside.

"The best thing to do was to sit in the car at a distance and see who came in and who came out. I sat there all day and not a soul came in and not a soul came out. I stayed until it went dark. Only when it went dark could I see lights inside, intermittently going on and off, though I couldn't see any movement. So I had an idea. Rather than come away with nothing, I decided that the best thing to do was to find some way of scaling the high wall which surrounds the property and have a closer look.

"Waiting until it was pitch-black, I left the car, still a safe distance away from the house and walked around the property looking for a suitable place to climb. Do you know that the entire perimeter not only has a large wall keeping the public and intruders like me out, it is also topped with razor wire?"

"Razor wire?"

"You don't know what razor wire is?

"Razor wire tends to surround army establishments, army bases and the like. It is incredibly sharp and extremely difficult to get over unless you can use your nous."

"I take it you used yours?"

"Well let's not go into it."

I look at James' hands, seeing at their innards, cuts which look deep and painful. I notice his shirt, which had been torn.

"It really is a beautiful house - Georgian I think.

"That is by the by.

"After about an hour, with the interior lights still going on and off, I began to think that Brodie had one of those security devices which trigger the lights at intervals, giving the appearance that someone is in when no one is in. Until, at last, I saw some movement. There I was, lying in mud and sodden grass under a tree, getting extremely wet and cold, when I caught sight of an occupant."

"His wife?"

"That was the funny thing. It wasn't his wife at all. From what I could see there is absolutely no evidence that a family lives there at all. If he says he has children then why did I not see any? And if he has children but I didn't see them, where was the evidence that they exist? I saw nothing that would remind one of children - no toys, no children's books, no playroom, no evidence of children at all."

"And a wife?"

"Nor a wife, either."

"He says he is married."

"If I were married I would expect to live in a house which showed the signs of life of both sexes. Call me a bigot if you like - there is always something intangible but nevertheless distinct about a home in which a woman lives. It may be décor, it may be organisation - whatever. I am certain that you too, could tell immediately if a house had a woman's touch."

"How far away from the house were you?"

"I scanned each room with these."

James pulls out a pair of binoculars.

"Where did you get those from?"

"Toys for boys. Not relevant."

"So tell me who you did see?"

"I saw only one figure - unmistakably the figure of a man."

"What did he look like?"

"I only saw glimpses of him. In fact I couldn't see very much. He seemed to be in his mid-thirties, though I am not the best person to confirm that. He had dark hair, which was receding slightly and was of average height. He was well-proportioned and I would have said he goes to the gym. From the very briefest glimpse I got of his face I would have said he was a handsome man although he looked effeminate."

"Effeminate?"

"Yes, you know - effeminate."

"How can you tell if someone is effeminate, James?"

"Come on, Iris. We have both seen enough people on the street and in those rotten clubs Edmund used to take you to, to know when someone looks effeminate. My impressions were those of effeminacy."

"Did it look like it could have been his brother?"

"Not at all. He does have a brother I recall - Brodie told you that himself."

"But what Brodie says…"

"I know. All I am saying is that he didn't look like Brodie's brother."

"Go on. Sorry for interrupting you."

"Time was beginning to drag by now and I had to force myself to stay and see if Brodie himself would show up. Two more hours I waited. It began to rain heavily and I began to freeze. But I hung on just in case."

"Did he?"

"He did. Don't worry Iris - he didn't see me."

"Was he alone?"

"No."

"With his wife?"

"No. He arrived with another man - bugger nearly parked his car on top of me - so close in fact, that I could hear what they were saying. Boring mostly - conversations about work. I took it that they were colleagues at your place."

"Did you hear his name? Did you see him?"

"Yes I did and it was only when I heard his name that I remembered who he was. And do you know it is the strangest thing? Normal conversation like I said then Brodie called his name and I remembered instantly where I had seen him before - it was at that party we went to in Chelsea, on the night you were raped."

"And his name?"

"Oliver Dauncey."

XXXIII.

My stomach turns. I see Oliver Dauncey in my mind's eye. His face conjures up missing images, splenetic resurrections of perfidy as the memory of that night starts slowly and then, ever more quickly, comes back to me.

"But how can it be?"

"Do you remember him?"

James looks at my face and realises that my memory has been jogged. I unfurl without checking the balance between consideration and uncritical exposé. The discovered flows from my mouth as it appears in my brain. What appears in my brain unveils then uncovers without recourse to censure the genesis of a landscape in a once lost, new world.

"I talked to Oliver Dauncey in the kitchen, while you were in the living room talking to another woman. I remember him now, because he seemed pleasant and interesting, telling me he was an accountant who had given up the rat race in order to paint. And he had given up the painting in order to join the rat race again, saying that the whole escapade was a waste of time.

He struck me as a decent man - funny and articulate and not at all like the type one would normally meet at those occasions."

"And?"

"I was in my office this morning. Then who should knock but Brodie and with him, Oliver Dauncey. Dauncey has just been appointed as the partner's finance director which is an extremely responsible and rather powerful role."

"And do you think Brodie actually knows him?"

I think hard. James finds the answer for me.

"I think we should take a close look at that list of names Helen photocopied. I bet you he is in there. If he isn't, I think we can rule him out of anything other than a simple working relationship with our man."

James finds the list and begins to read through it.

"Found it."

Unusually, for a man as obviously organised as Brodie, Oliver Dauncey's name has been added in a haphazard fashion. James reads out his full name and an address in Mayfair.

"I'll bet you that he is in the same cohort as Brodie. Strange though, Iris - his name has been added recently There is no original entry as with the others. And the name is entered with a different pen. I would have said the name has been entered in the not too distant past."

"Do you think they met again, not so long ago?"

"It is possible, Iris. What was it you said? He was an accountant who gave up the rat race. That would have seen him disappear from Brodie's sphere of importances. I wonder if they didn't meet by accident at that party and swapped telephone numbers. And moving on from there, if you say that he has just been appointed as the finance director of your firm, it is at least feasible that the appointment was engineered by Brodie afterwards. I mean, if what this list tells us is that there is a little cabal of ex-Cambridge graduates who attended the same college, then this man fits right in."

I try and fail to consider what James is telling me. My mind is elsewhere. I know I have seen Oliver Dauncey somewhere else. I cannot put my finger on it.

James' attitude suddenly changes. He moves closer and lowers the pitch and the volume of his voice. He appears tentative at first, as if he doesn't want to say.

"Iris - do you think that it could have been him?"

"Him what?"

"You are not making this any easier for me are you? Do you think it was this man who raped you?"

Again my stomach turns to knots. I rebuff James immediately on the basis of what my head tells me to do and not my heart.

"Of course not. I remember a gentleman."

"I am sorry, Iris. It seems only right to me that you should be naturally inquisitive. Surely you have had thoughts as to who did it?"

"Should I have a moral responsibility to think about the man who raped me? Does it actually make any difference? I have been raped. I cannot get to the man who did it because I do not know who did it. Even if I did, there isn't a shred of evidence to link him to the crime he has committed."

"I wanted to ask the question because seeking out that criminal would be the first thing on my mind. And there are only a limited number of people to choose from."

"Don't go on James."

"But I think we need to talk about it. The way I see it, there were only ever about four men at that party in any sort of condition to even stand, let alone anything else. One was Brodie."

"James."

"I can't see Brodie being that sort of man. He has far too much to lose. He may be many things but I don't think his acumen would allow the possibility of tangibly hurting someone. He is too much of a coward for that.

"There was another man - the man who owned the property. I can't see that, either. And the only other man in any fit state, besides me, was this guy Oliver Dauncey. But you said he was far too nice. Are you sure you are not mistaken? Whether you are mistaken or not, it seems to me that this man is in with Brodie.

"Can you see what I am saying?"

I confess that I cannot.

"Let us forget for the moment you cannot remember anything about that night, which you can't. Let us then assume that this man, Oliver Dauncey, can and knows what he has done or was as drunk as you were and had no idea he was taking advantage of you when he was taking advantage of you.

"So it happens and he goes home. And let us say he can't remember what has happened when he wakes up the following morning. But when he looks down when he bathes and sees he is covered in blood. He could remember at that point or the whole action could remain a mystery. But he is man of the world and he knows that he has had sex with someone."

The knots in my stomach tightens. Once more I speak out loud as pain forces me to unveil and the immediacy of pain estops all else reasoned and rational.

"Damn. I remember where I've seen him."

"That night?"

"No. I knew I had seen him afterwards. I have been trying not to think of it in the hope a place and a memory would coincide. I saw Oliver Dauncey on the very day Edmund died. I saw him right outside Snow Hill Police Station. That is it.

"James; I had crossed the road and was nearly run over. Oliver Dauncey saved my life. I was so confused and upset having just found out that Edmund had committed suicide, I couldn't really work out where I was. This gentleman took hold of me and walked me to a coffee shop and made sure I had regained some control of my senses. I remember who that was now. It was him. It was Oliver Dauncey."

James looks incredulous.

"And?"

"Well something and nothing. How could a man capable of such kindness stoop to any other level?"

"Iris; will you listen to yourself? You, above all people, know that a man is capable of anything when he is drunk. And look at you. Take one look at your face and see why, wherever we go, you are the centre of male attention. Stop for a moment being fanciful and get back into the real world.

"Right.

"So, as I was saying, even if he is Mr Nice, he wakes up the following morning and he is covered with blood. He realises he has had sex but he cannot remember anything. And now as he is sober and a moral pulse has started throbbing in his temple and he begins to worry if he has done anything wrong. What else would the sight of blood do to him? Blood always makes people think immorality. Blood thus become our ally."

"An ally in what?"

"For God's sake - it was you who a few weeks ago began talking about the need to fight in order to protect oneself - remember - at Edmund's lunch? Remember Edmund saying that he didn't have the stomach for it and you pushing his words back down his throat. You are now playing with fire Iris and you have to be prepared to burn.

"Think; think about this man - he can be used."

Intuitively I know this is wrong. From what I recall and from what I sense, Oliver Dauncey is not a man capable of rape, no matter what James says.

"James; it wasn't him. Why would I want to drag him into this? The man saved my life."

"He is a friend of Brodie. You cannot guarantee he isn't playing along with Brodie. The ties which bind him and vice versa are strong, at least where Brodie is concerned. They are of the same ilk and from what we know of Brodie, he trusts no one, save for very few. And Oliver Dauncey is one of those few. You wanted to get dirty; you wanted to play with fire - well you are right in the middle of it now, Iris and there is no turning back. Think of yourself; think of that child; think of Helen, for God's sake -she is relying on you."

"But…"

"There are no buts Iris. This is what you will have to do. You assume the worst. You assume it was Oliver Dauncey who raped you when blind drunk. He can't remember a thing, neither can you. His inability to recall you, which is evidenced by the assistance he gave you without any acknowledgement of knowing you on the day Edmund died and the way he simply said 'hello' to you yesterday morning, means he will be walking around with guilt riddling his head without knowing how he ended up with blood all over him after having sex with someone but not remembering who she was or precisely where.

"So you approach him. You do it discreetly when you have an appropriate opportunity. You look at him and try to establish if there is even the slightest bit of recognition in his face. Either way, if there is or if there isn't, you hit him with it. You tell him you remember him from the party his memory wants so desperately to forget and you explain in graphic detail what he did and all he did. You have already pointed out that this man has a conscience. You need to prick it. You need to start manipulating him; putting him into a corner. Tell him you still retain the evidence; that you have semen-stained clothes; that you reported the incident to the police; that the offence has been registered, though not sufficiently investigated. Accuse him of the crime and see what he does. Then tell him you will report the matter to the police. Tell him that it is only a short step from the physical evidence in a rape trial to the pictures and medical history of bruising you encountered, all of which would be unveiled in court. And that it is only a short step from physical evidence to forensic evidence which will confirm traces of his semen staining your clothes, traces of his skin and sweat staining the insides of your legs. Give him these details - as much detail as possible. Put him in a corner, which is where the bastard should rightly be if he is guilty anyway and see which way he wants to jump.

"That is how we get to Brodie."

"Through Oliver ?"

"No, through blackmail."

"And Oliver Dauncey?"

"An unnecessary evil."

"But James; I cannot do this. Suppose he is innocent. We will be no better than Brodie."

"To use that argument, Iris, makes you a hypocrite. And what are you seeking to defend?"

"Well…"

"The man is almost definitely in with Brodie. They are all necessarily tarred with the same brush. By definition Oliver Dauncey is not decent like you or I. By definition he is one of the very monsters you and I despise. Alternatively, think of Edmund. If you want to think of the betrayal of innocence, think of that man. It was the sick psychology of Brodie that indirectly caused that man to die. Oliver Dauncey, whether or not he is made of nicer stuff, is guilty by association.

You have got to put yourself first, Iris. All you have to do is put pressure on him to disclose what he knows about Brodie. We already have an inkling as to what Brodie is really like. We have the address book and the drugs. We have his strange living circumstances. You are simply honouring Edmund's memory here and protecting yourself, your child and Helen. Oliver Dauncey need not get hurt. If we play this correctly he should be made to feel guilt for what he has done. But we are not seeking to expose him as we cannot expose him. We are seeking to knock someone down who is going to knock you down sooner or later and will have a good laugh about it afterwards. From where I am sitting, you do not, as I have repeatedly said, have a choice."

I defer a choice if I have any. I cannot contend with the force of James' opinions any longer. I tell James I will think about it. The answer isn't good enough.

"Remember, Iris. You are not just thinking of yourself any more. You have sacrifices to make."

XXXIV.

I cannot follow James' reasoning - that this Oliver Dauncey deserves to become a part of something he may know nothing of. I understand all James says yet I cannot relate the man I remember with the fact of my rape. I do not feel that Oliver Dauncey and the perpetrator of that crime could be the very same being - reasoning and feeling coinciding - this fire and ice; these protons and neutrons colliding; a meeting of curve and line; an abstract date with firmity - my being, my soul and their sufferings unveiled by the sharp, unbending lineage from bow to arrow to impact; little to do with the Iris I know and everything to do with what I have become - little to do with what I have become and everything to do with Iris.

James won't let it drop. He is insistent; he is damn well insistent and uses all his powers of persuasion to get me to put a call into Oliver 's secretary to arrange a meeting. I submit reluctantly and promise to make the call. Now I have an hour to kill. He wishes me good luck; he tells me I will be brilliant. But the pus which feeds the wound oozes from my mind and I am practically shaking as I snake the long and faceless corridors to Oliver Dauncey's room.

Eventually I turn a corner. I see Oliver Dauncey's door. Just as I am about to enter the corridor on which his office is situated I hear laughing. Once more, I hear laughing and I recognise that laughing voice - that turgid snicker. Its grotesque timbre and its hideous knack, deflates me and saps my strength. I stand around the corner waiting for Brodie to leave, trying to recuperate while attempting to stay hidden.

The laughter dies and I see the back of Brodie's legs tender a thrusting advance - a drill sergeant-major under orders to act. From an unseemly conversation to the work-world beyond, I haven't heard him do anything but laugh since Edmund died. The sight of him and the sound of him angers me beyond all comprehension. Brodie is the prize and Oliver Dauncey is the patsy. Brodie is my object and Oliver Dauncey is ephemera, if ephemera at all. Suddenly I can see that James has been right all along. Whether or not Oliver Dauncey is a decent man, whether or not Oliver Dauncey is the man who raped me, I have got to go into his room and use him.

I knock on Oliver 's door. He looks up and flashes me a smile, enthusiastically beckoning me in. Standing as I enter, busily travelling from behind his desk and nimbly shaking me by the hand. His enthusiasm for me seems unbounded as Iris returns and I analyse him for the way he looks at me as an object - so much meat, so much fodder.

Would he treat an ugly girl the same way?

I think not.

Would he treat others the same way if there wasn't the opportunity to get something out of them?

I think not.

He offers me tea and I see him eyeing me with concern. I wonder if Brodie has talked to him. I wonder if he can grasp the significance of my visit. I wonder if this is the man who raped me and the man whose child I carry.

Do I carry this man's child?

Should I carry this man's child?

"So glad you popped down for a chat. I wonder what it is I can do for you. I have so little contact with junior lawyers. Partners by their very nature are dull in comparison. I wonder what comfort I can offer you?"

I hesitate before I open my mouth. I haven't considered what I will say. The detail is woolly and the devil is in the detail. I am unprepared - Iris is unprepared. Do I fall into Iris wherein precision is all or do I follow feelings now that feelings are so much to the fore?

Words comes out of my mouth. I haven't got time to analyse them as they appear, until I settle down and once more the Iris I know - cynical and cold Iris, detached from all, is both my persona and myself. The rest comes from a heart the old Iris still doesn't recognise.

"I would like you to think back. I would like you to think back some time, to a Monday evening. Whether or not you can remember immediately is of no consequence as I am sure you will remember once I have jogged your memory.

"Like I say, it is a Monday night and you have attended a soirée in Chelsea. You have had a nice evening and it is getting late. And you have had enough to drink but I think you want a bit more, so you walk into the kitchen in order to get some wine.

"You manage to bump into someone you haven't seen for a long time, someone you went to university with. In fact I bet you hardly recognise each other as the years have rolled by. However you recognise the unmistakeable manner which has hardly changed and the thick accent which has probably got worse.

"He has black hair, though he is now receding. He has the same build, round and small and he has the same manner, aggressive and to the point. Across the room alarms start ringing as you finally recognise Brodie as a fellow student from your days at Cambridge."

Oliver takes a sip of his tea. He starts fingering the porcelain edges of his teacup. Skin and friction conspire to produce a tentative note and recollections, and a ponderous lift of his eyebrows offer an inner trail. I wonder.

"And he recognises you. He always was renowned for having an astonishing memory for names and faces. Anyway you circle each other for a while until you both feel the time is right to enquire. Your suspicions are proved right. Indeed; the man you thought it was is actually the man himself. Brodie meets Oliver Dauncey - you greet and you exchange a mutual past. Eventually the conversation moves on and not wishing to be impolite you agree with Brodie to meet at a future date after swapping numbers and falling into commonplace small talk about the guests milling, dancing and drinking.

"You'll remember that Brodie told you he is with two new colleagues from his workplace with Brodie making it clear that he is a partner and a resounding success. Incidentally you may have asked Brodie what his new workplace is like. You may have been surprised by the negativity he portrayed. For present purposes that is by the by.

Yes - you will recall that Brodie told you he has come with a man and a woman and that the woman is very pretty and bright. The man is her flatmate. You decide to seek out the pretty face in the kitchen, for that is where Brodie thinks she is. In fact, the journey has the potential to serve two purposes as you can fix yourself a drink and get away from the canoodling couples you find distasteful. So, into the kitchen you walk where you find a blonde woman on her own swirling around the remnants of a drink at the bottom of her glass, seemingly lonely and even a bit drunk. You, by the way, are feeling more than a little drunk.

"However, you raise your game and approach the blonde, doing your best to entice her with a potted history of yourself and why you find the evening distasteful. You recall the story of your time away from the dull and listless life of an accountant working in the City of London, through an episode which was a romantic ideal which bore no fruit. At least you tried, you say, and that is enough.

"You cannot stop talking about yourself, fed by the eloquence at the bottom of a glass. Yes, you do understand a little of the world - you understand enough to know you didn't want the awful office life which so many of your contemporaries have settled for. You feel you have no choice but to be sucked back into it. You are not dull when you speak; you even show off a rather dry sense of humour which to this woman shows a sense of intelligence and insight. You are not dull or inert. You amuse, you interest and you show the ability to step outside the environment and have a look over your shoulder. In essence, that is attractive. It is attractive for its differences.

"You offer the lady a drink; wine I think it is and both of you proceed to chew the fat on this subject and that until circumstance conspires against you and you have to go your separate ways. Perhaps then, your overwhelming feeling was that you had met more than just a blonde with a big chest but without a vacuous brain. She too was interesting in that she could hold down a half-decent conversation. But that, like the rest of this story, is pure conjecture and one wouldn't want to impugn you with thoughts you did not have.

"You drink on and join in several more conversations, less and less in contact with your sober self, as the wine starts to take hold of your system, confusing your thoughts. And as you look around and you see more and more intimacy you realise that you have brought none of this intimacy for yourself. You are jealous and naturally, given how much you have had to drink, your mind begins to wonder about the lovely-looking, and increasingly more interesting, blonde the kitchen.

"As you stagger towards the kitchen door, your alcohol-riddled brain starts to close down. One by one, each section of your brain shuts up shop - balance, speech, coordination, coherence, control. Sentience is leaving you faster than a bullet from a gun and you cling to the few cogent thoughts you have left, which rely themselves on your misguided notion of jealously, simply because you are not one of an intimate throng. Where is she you ask yourself? She is in the kitchen around the corner. Once you get the charm going again, the charm which has sadly left you on account of how drunk you are, then you too, will have the privilege of intimacy.

"When you open the kitchen door she has gone.

"She is now your mission in life - finding her is your mission in life. You stagger around the downstairs rooms buffeted by a non-existent wind, swaying back and forth, pulled then rejected by the ground beneath your feet. Briefly you wonder if she has gone home. You ask a few discreet questions; you realise she is still in the house - she is still somewhere in the house. Upstairs you go, moving from room to room until you are barely conscious. Then you find her.

"The pretty blonde with the agile mind is on a bed in one of the bedrooms. You call out to her but you cannot remember her name. What is in a name anyway?

"She doesn't answer, though you may think because you hear a slight noise, she recognises you. So you call out again and you hear the mealiest sound of recognition - she may have mumbled something as she lies there and to you, that is all you need. You move closer and your blurred vision inspects what to you, is a vision. This pretty creature is on a bed and there is no one around. You have confused her sleep talk with recognition and affection, and recognition and affection are what you seek. So you climb on the bed next to her and put your arms around her. But by now your head has started to spin and you are barely able to control your thoughts. The only fixed point you can hold onto with your eyes and then your mouth, is her face. In fact you cannot control yourself any longer and the closer you can get without being rebuffed, means the closer she wants you to get to her, precisely because she hasn't rebuffed you. The deed is therefore as good as done when you kiss her on the lips and receive an instinctive reaction. But you are not interested in heavy petting. Your addled brain has been taken over by your biological urges. Your face moves away from hers and blindly you start kissing her neck and moving your hands towards the forbidden innards of her top. With no rebuttal, this is a green light.

"Your confidence is now increasing. You have stopped gambling with your advances. Your arm movements become more and more deliberate and you move your hands toward the outline of her large breasts which have only one option - to look inviting, to be grabbed, to be cleansed of isolation. So you knead and feel and stroke her breasts in an entirely clumsy way for you are too drunk to do anything different. Again her natural reaction causes her to sigh and a further threshold is breached. Anticipation and need now work in synchrony. You feel an erection and your only thought, if indeed you are capable of thought, is to free yourself from the constrictions of your own clothing. However, you have to think of her clothing and whether you should undress her first. Yet you choose not to do so because your body is telling you there isn't time.

"Your hands then move down to her knees and the hem of her skirt. You start moving your hands inside her skirt till you find her moist and another green light is found. This is no time for foreplay and you begin to unzip your trousers, exposing yourself.

"On top of her you climb and with your legs you manufacture a space between hers in which you can lie. You still have the problem of her underwear, though as you hitch up her skirt, without regard to the face of the lifeless creature below, you pull away the gusset of her underwear while you move closer to her entrance. You don't even notice how her body hasn't moved so as to receive you nor do you care. While you hold her knickers away from her vagina you cajole yourself to enter her, becoming frustrated at how difficult it is. Eventually you manage and first you notice how tight she is inside. That is beside the point as you lunge backward and forward on top of her for no more than a couple of minutes until you can control yourself no longer and you ejaculate, somehow telling yourself to keep quiet at the moment of ejaculation lest anybody walking past should hear.

"You are now out of breath as the oxygen supplies which were forcing themselves to serve your brain are now having to serve your lungs and your heart. You are light-headed and limp. You withdraw and try to make conversation with the woman but you realise that the mumbled words you offer are futile. In fact they are so futile, as are you that you convince yourself, now that the moment has passed, that she has fallen into a deep sleep.

"Half of you wants to lie there beside her. But you regain your senses and you realise that now you have serviced your biological need there is simply no requirement to wait around. She wasn't interesting anyway and you have conquered her; you have shown the couples downstairs that you too, are worthy. And you have no other conclusion to draw than to leave the sleeping blonde where she is.

"Still drunk, you are now entirely aware that, with all other challenges eradicated, you do not need to be in that house any longer. Once again you stagger and you stumble, you loll and you fall till you get outside and manage to get yourself a taxi. Once at home and without a care in the world, even with a smile on your face, you fall into a deep drunken sleep until you wake late, the next morning.

"And I can see you now. You awake with the most God-awful hangover. Your head physically hurts as you move, though you fight the pain and drag yourself to the bathroom. You undress and almost fall into the shower. You lather soap on your hands and reach toward your midriff in order to cleanse your body. Only then do you notice the colour of the shower water as it hits the hair around your genitalia and runs blood red down your legs. As blood disseminates you panic and instinctively check your penis for signs of injury. As you wash the congealed blood away from your pubic hair and you inspect, your mind is blank and you have no idea how you have woken up to find yourself matted with blood when you have no physical injuries. Still, you wash all of the blood away and only then do you sense the creeping feeling that you may have done something wrong. But your mind cannot tell you what may have caused your skin and hair to be soiled and you have no idea save for that nag, that feeling that you may have inflicted harm on another.

"You get out of the shower and inspect your clothes. You can see that blood has stuck to the material which surrounds your zip and the surrounding material. You cast your mind back to the night before but only have shadowy reminiscences of it - brief conversations, the lights of London as they stream through the taxi windows, a bed, the onset of sleep. You have no idea how you have come to be covered in what you almost know is the blood of another but you sense that it is to do with sex and it is to do with how horribly inebriated you were.

"Maybe you have cursed yourself for being unable to remember you actions. Perhaps you couldn't have cared less. But you must have been drunk that evening for the sight of that woman, even though you had saved her life, gave you nothing by way of recollection, of memory, of your past.

"So time has ebbed and old acquaintances have been renewed. The evening in question when you renewed your friendship with Brodie, led you to this very firm where you have swiftly forgotten the cynicism which would have coloured your speech and thoughts previously. You have found kinship and a community within a community you know will protect you from all - a community which will give you, a failure, the chance of a successful life. You have found all of this here and you have found all of it by a chance meeting in Chelsea.

"Let us just say that all I say is true. Let me say it isn't fanciful or some creature of invention. Let us say that you are the man I speak of in my story. Have you cared less for your victim over time? Of course you have, because in a sober world you have convinced yourself of your status as a gentleman and a gentleman could never do anything so awful as to mine a defenceless woman's body. Your mind has control, whereas for a few moments of madness, your body had all of its own way.

But what of that woman?

What of a creature who wakes up to find herself bruised and bloody, her insides damaged, her vagina torn at its entrance, her inner thighs bruised, her body racked with pain?

"And what of her mind? What do you suppose you have done to innocence when you have so cruelly taken innocence away? Would one not feel shame? Would one not feel remorse and the manifest heaviness of guilt? What would be the relationship now between the mind and the body of the perpetrator if you knew that a woman's mind had been destroyed by the coincidence of the attraction of her form and the inability to recognise desire and protect herself.

"On the night of that party in Chelsea, you, Oliver Dauncey, talked to me in the kitchen of that house. I went upstairs and fell into a drunken sleep on a bed. I was the woman whose blood soiled your clothes. I was the woman you so cruelly and selfishly defiled. I was the woman whose insides were speared by your greed. I was the woman who bled and was bruised. I was the woman you abused. I am the woman who has had to come to terms with the psychological destruction of the few decent thoughts I had about man and I, the very woman who sits before you now, am the woman who kept every tiny scrap of clothing, of sheet and of garment upon which is splattered my blood intermingled with your sperm and your detritus. I am the woman who had swabs taken at the police station and photographs and filed an official complaint.

"Rape is sexual intercourse without consent. The law casts doubt upon a conviction unless there is corroboration. I have all the corroboration I need. I just didn't have you. But now I remember who you were and I know who you are.

"I want to tell you what I am going to do before I do it because I want you to put the detail upon the feelings of guilt you had the following morning. This brain and my flesh is what you destroyed on that night.

"When I call the police I shall have you arrested. I will give testimony at your trial. You will be sentenced to several years in prison, no matter who your connections may be, for I have every scrap of evidence I need in order to convict you. I wanted to tell you because I wanted you to see my face. It will be a long time before you see another woman's face in the flesh. I wanted to give you the benefit of seeing mine in the flesh as opposed to being unable to recall nothing about me. I hope that you rot in jail. I hope that you rot, I hope, that you, rot."

I stand to leave. I am shaking. Cumulative anger has built until my mere frame has to shake in order for it to fall out. At the same time I study Oliver Dauncey's face, knowing inside that the anger at what had happened to Iris is mixed with this embellished story exposing untruths designed to convince this man I have him bang to rights. Iris the old mixes with Iris the indignant new, the truth mixes with tangents and tangents mix with lies.

Dauncey is anaemic. I guess and rightly so, that my story and its delivery have got as close to the mark as I could possibly imagine. And yet I stop short of asking him the question - the question. The point is that his punishment will be his manipulation. I have a child to protect. I have to protect myself. I have Helen to protect. Oliver Dauncey's punishment will be ignominy forever, whether he chooses to accept the offer I am about to make, thereby exposing himself as a coward and a traitor to his imaginary friends or whether he acts like a man in myth and gives himself up to the police.

And then, as James predicted, Oliver Dauncey becomes a coward. I watch and listen as he wriggles into life and squirms at my feet - equivocating, equivocating, equivocating - asking my forgiveness though he claims he cannot remember anything he has done, admitting being covered in blood, though he doesn't know why it was there, telling me he will do anything to help, though he knows he can offer little recompense.

His cowardice saves him. His words save him. And I and Iris - the words are now interchangeable, mouth the offer. The price he must pay for his behaviour is to Brodie and if it so happens, those of the cabal of which Brodie and Oliver Dauncey are part.

"Whether you regard it as a choice or not, you really do not have a choice in the matter. If you do not do as I say now I give you my word I will inform the police that the man who raped me has commenced employment at this office. Your choice is to do all I ask, otherwise you will go to prison

"You must be asking the question as to what I could possibly want with you. It would be an entirely appropriate question to ask. You must also be sifting through all I have said to give you clues in relation to what this woman in front of you, who has every right to see you punished under the law, wants.

"See, there were clues in what I have said to enable you to draw your own conclusions; there are names and circumstances with which, in the last few weeks, I have become familiar. The one name I have mentioned in particular is that of the man who left this room not so very long ago. Once more, I shall take you back."

XXXV

"I shall take you back to Cambridge University, to your college days and the faces which became the personalities who became your friends. I want you to remember the journey to London when you arrived in The Square Mile. There you see the very faces you got drunk with, grew up with and laughed with. You have shared interests in that you face the world not singularly but with a specific outlook and a very particular perspective, inculcated at Cambridge, inculcated in you and those closest to you allowing you to pick and choose within the system we live under.

"Ever since, that collective in your college keep popping up in your life as you always gravitate towards what you know. That is the reason you ended up in Chelsea, through a friend or a friend of a friend, all with a shared outlook and suitable attitude. And as luck would have it, you run into one of the very group you grew up with at university - Brodie.

"You swap numbers; you promise to keep in touch. Then, out of the blue, Brodie calls and tells you about an opportunity. Brodie is now in a position of authority, having made all the right moves and destroyed the right people. And he trusts you; he trusts you implicitly. How could he not trust you?

"The opportunity is the position you hold right now and you accept, happy that the network has served you again when you were at a low ebb. You are back in the fold and you are among friends. Now you are protected, you are bound by trust and interpersonal commitment which transcends simple friendship in a world which is increasingly hostile and disparate.

"Brodie introduces you to all of the group. You renew old acquaintances very quickly and catch up. The feeling is comforting and you are impregnable once more. There is no better place to be than in a hegemony against the world.

"Invitations follow. Your social life and the calibre of people you meet improves. And the trust which was once implicit, remains implicit. You are privy to lives and lifestyles which may have been fledgling when you were young, now advanced with all of the traits of youth being embellished. You do not mind the idiosyncrasies of your friends, because the common belief system you share offers you no choice. It may take days; it make take a couple of weeks but once more you have arrived at the vanguard of the new order.

"And your former worries are now long behind you. Forget the pettiness of existence - you once more have a higher purpose in kinship and being. You can forget all - you can forget that unknown blood, you can forget excess, you can forget worry. You are now protected. You are now privy or will become privy to the very information I want which will destroy the one man central to your rehabilitation - Brodie."

"Why do you want Brodie and not me? What has he done to you?"

"Don't insult my intelligence. You know why I want Brodie. You know damn well that he is at the bottom of the death of Edmund Rose. You know damn well that before he is finished, Brodie will destroy the lives of other innocent people who get in his way. He will destroy me, too."

"But how can I help? lives a clean life."

"Let me put is this way. You have no choice but to help. You will help or you will go to prison."

"But how can I help you? I have only recently met the man, having not spoken to him for years. How can I have anything which could help you?"

"Don't give me the clean life rubbish. I will tell you exactly what you will do."

Dauncey shuffles uneasily in his chair. I wonder if it is right to let the cat out of the bag. Is it right to unveil what I know about Brodie? Will he guess I am bluffing about the evidence I have, or will his sense of morality, his conscience and his cowardice get the better of him?

"I know you are close to Brodie. You will now get as close to him as possible. I want to know everything you know about the man. I want to know how he lives and who he lives with. I want to know who the person he lives with is or whoever he lives with. If he has a wife and children, I want to know who they are. If he lies about his habits, I want to know what is real habits are.

"I want to know how often he sees his friends. Believe me, I know exactly who they are. I want to know what they do when they are together."

I take a deep breath.

"And I want to know about the criminality."

Oliver takes a deep breath.

"What criminality?"

"I would like to think that you are telling the truth. Well let me tell you, I care not whether or not you tell the truth, as it makes no difference. Brodie and your friends are in receipt of almost pure cocaine which is used both at work and wherever they socialise. I want you to tell me who they get the cocaine from and in what amounts."

"If I find out, provided what you say is true, I will be exposing myself to precisely the same criminality you accuse them of."

I snap back.

"I have already told you - criminality and you are confidants. I only have to make one call and your friendship will be consummated.

"If you do not know already who supplies them with this drug and let me tell you, I know it is someone very senior in our drug infested culture - I want to know in minute detail the times and dates of all of their liaisons. You will tell me almost before you have registered the fact itself. Every facet of Brodie's life will become known to you and thereafter, to me. And you will breathe not one word of this to another soul."

I try to sound stern but just a little of me feels ridiculous. Iris returns and the relationship with emotion is strangled once more at the point of departure.

"You know this is blackmail, Iris? You know you are now no better than Brodie and the rest of us?"

"And what gives you the right to point out the moral high ground?"

"I was merely pointing out a fact."

"The facts are plain whether or not I have chosen to get my hands dirty. I will give you just one day in which to think about what I am telling you to do. I will return here tomorrow, in this very room and I want an answer."

"And one final thing. I want you to confirm to me that Brodie was behind the downfall of Edmund Rose as well as the other half-breeds who have conspired with him for all of these years.

"Understood?"

Dauncey nods.

"Tomorrow."

I get up and leave, slope around the corner of Oliver's door and rush along the corridor. Suddenly I feel sick with nerves - my head is spinning; I can barely stand up if I try. I hold my head in my hands and a mixture of incredulity, nausea and panic colours every thought and every action I have. At the back of my mind are Oliver Dauncey's words... 'you know you are now no better than Brodie and the rest of us.'

Is he right?

Is the first casualty of immorality one's self-perception?

Have I chosen to become what I loathe?

Am I closer to my biology, mentally and physically?

I feel all of my worth unravelling before my eyes. Nerves and exhaustion have taken control. I cannot think in straight lines any more and my body is rejecting me. I have just enough strength to get back to my room. I barely have the strength to put my coat on. My only thoughts are to leave and go home.

XXXVI.

I guess I could say I simply opened my eyes. I didn't just open my eyes, they were opened for me by Helen - by Helen kissing me on the cheek.

I remember falling into bed; I remember being alone. I look at the bed in which I slept. I did not sleep alone, for at some point during the previous fourteen hours, Helen has chosen to fall asleep beside me.

Did she mean the kiss in a simple and affectionate way or did she mean something more?

Morals listing - morals following arbitrary associations tethered to arbitrary forces of motive rising then falling between ill-defined axes' disregarded. Is my destination ever less in control? Am I in control any longer? A simple kiss into which I read a reliance beyond the random fall of cards dropped from the hand; beyond the certainty that fall is dictated by gravity; beyond simple rules between Helen and I. This penumbral protectorate lives somewhere in the dreams I had before I awoke and somewhere within the normlessness found upon opening my eyes.

Beyond the Iris of old, I fail to see because everything is a new experience – everything - a kiss, disorder, anomie, a trough from where the bow is indistinguishable from the stern. Helen is not a person by association; Helen is becoming part of me because she has to. I am letting Helen become part of me because feelings dictate little other choice. I cannot push away forces which trap and swaddle my arms and they cannot relinquish their hold for all the power of that which is natural is behind them. Helen is not by design and upon that kiss, my response is beyond manufacture. Truly, Iris is being subverted. Iris ebbs away. Iris, is ebbing away.

"Once more, we three conspirators meet over breakfast to discuss yet more titbits from a strange new world. Nothing is tangible; nothing is real. What people you have made enemies of, Iris. What singular people.

"What a day I had yesterday.

"What singular people!

"Morning Helen.

"What a day!"

James beams at both of us - a Cheshire cat; a strangely unattractive face when marked with a degree of triumph, self-evidently marked with some undisclosed victory. The chemical mix in my head cannot contend, just can't cope with people, albeit people I love, with their faces pointing at me. I convey a certain lack of enthusiasm, shuffling around in dressing gown and slippers with the bad breath of exhalation indicative of the reaches of the slow poison within and without.

"This is rather more than a fair mile beyond my perception. If I didn't have something tangible, you would have told me it was poppycock. Quite startling and unforseen."

James looks at Helen.

"Startling - not even remotely foreseeable a few weeks ago."

Helen seems ready to accept the inner excitement in James' voice. I am phlegmatic to the point where I want to fall back into reverie and depressive fancy.

"I spent the daylight hours outside his house. Nothing happened. I waited until it went dark and scaled the perimeter fence. There, once more, I lay in a damp bush - the same little moisture collection point I had camped in the previous night. And like the night before, I had to bide my time.

"Then, at about nine o'clock, Brodie drove into the grounds. He was not alone. Previously he had been accompanied by a man we have identified as Oliver Dauncey, who Iris will no doubt explain to you, Helen. This time he was accompanied by the man I had seen inside the house when Brodie returned with Dauncey.

"I am sure Iris has told you I saw an effeminate man inside Brodie's house. So Brodie and this man drove into the grounds and up to the front door. I heard them talking though their voices were too quiet for me to hear precisely what they were saying.

"The lights went on in the house and I saw them walking about, chatting, laughing and thoroughly immersed in each other's company. It started to get late and they watched a little television. After about an hour, Brodie got up and drew the curtains in the living room and proceeded to move around the house, drawing curtains wherever he went. To lose sight of them was to lose everything. A waste of our time.

"I stood up and sneaked towards the window, trying to catch a glimpse through the curtains. I'm afraid this was pointless as Brodie had been his usual very thorough self. Then, in a moment of pure vaudeville, I was privy to the one breakthrough we need. Not more than ten yards away the kitchen light went on and into the kitchen walked Brodie and this unknown man. They laughed and then, in a moment of absolute tenderness..."

James starts laughing out loud. For a few moments he laughs hysterically.

"They started kissing each other."

He stops laughing and looks at both of us, trying to see what kind of reaction he has created. For my part, I feel disinclined to speak. Helen says nothing, either.

"Oh, come on."

James implores with his hands outstretched as his chin is sucked towards his neck, the corners of his mouth fall back toward his earlobes, his lips pucker and his eyes bulge.

"I tell you it wasn't just any old kiss. It was a full on, one to one, tongue swapping exercise, a movie kiss - the leading man getting his way with, well, the leading man. And then Brodie started to remove this man's shirt, taking it off and kissing him all over his chest - oblivious, absolutely oblivious."

James starts laughing again.

"What are you laughing at James?" I ask.

"I'm sorry, Iris. This hideous bastard is deserving of so much odium for all of the things he has done and for all of the spurious justifications he has erected in order to act, and then I find out and in this comic book way that he is morally flawed by his own sanctimonious standards. Hypocrisy isn't a big enough concept; these circumstances are so averse to reality to me that I just can't help but laugh. I find it so funny because it is so sad."

"And why are you laughing, Helen?"

"I guess it's because I am relieved. Do you not see what this means, Iris?"

"No, I do not."

"In all the years I would never have guessed. We have him precisely where we want him. Laughter is relief; laughter is freedom."

For a second I lose my temper.

It doesn't show.

"Yes but hold on. Are we not forgetting one rather large and overwhelming point?"

James refuses to stop laughing.

"James be quiet."

He suppresses his laughter by putting his hands over his mouth. Helpless diaphragm contractions force out air. I lose my temper and bare my teeth. This is juvenile and pointless.

"For a moment, the pair of you shut up. Just shut up. You may have failed to notice but I haven't. What James saw means nothing. Why? Because he saw it. Why? Because of a simple concept called plausible deniability.

Sure we have established that Brodie is a homosexual and indeed it is shocking that the man passes himself off as something he isn't. But we cannot prove it and to approach him would lead only to one conclusion - he would simply deny it, and plausibly."

Helen realises I am right and falls onto herself. James carries on laughing.

"James will you shut up for God's sake."

"Iris; how wrong can you be?"

"Take a look at this."

In James' hand is a digital camera. In the camera is a tape. James presses play and shows us the contents of his film. The images are crystal clear and Helen and I crowd the image and watch, as we see a dark wall in the middle of which is a window from which light streams onto the garden. Two figures appear one of which is undeniably Brodie. The other is a languid man and unconventionally rather handsome. He is certainly pretty.

We see Brodie approach his partner starting to kiss. And as James had described, these are not kisses which could ordinarily be mistaken for friendship. This is affection between men which is undeniable and beyond dispute once they start to remove each other's shirts. Only when Brodie walks towards the camera and draws down the blinds does the image stop.

James looks triumphant and emblazoned with significance - man as a doer of deeds; man as the repository of action.

"Got him," James says.

"Oh, we have surely got him now."

Within the tender walls of my stomach I feel something move. It is the slightest movement, almost a stroke. It is a kick. It is, a kick. The child in my womb protrudes a boot against the walls of my womb; a frustrated intern devoid of escape; an animal trapped and helpless, and I can feel it. As Helen and James proceed to hug each other, I sit down for I am scarcely able to take it in, clenching my stomach, trying my best to come to terms with biology chronicling my mutation by the day and by the hour. I am not one; I am two - two against this perfidy and one striking out for the piecemeal victory at hand. I have something which may help ease the burden on all our lives and the life of my child - my child has something on me; an instinctive insight; a funnel from my brain leading right to the cranial nerve centre of a child without speech, without sentience but nevertheless, with all the timing on God's earth - a blow struck for the chance of justice and a kick respecting justice itself. What a child this will be, for it knows already. It already knows.

"We have got him, Iris. What cannot speak cannot lie.

Iris?"

I try my best not to show the significance - the significance of what a flick of the foot of a foetus finds in this fallow gestation of fortune. What is without has affected me within. The child has realised an important moment in its life has passed and with that kick, reminders of existences overcome.

"Iris; are you alright?"

I smile.

"Never felt better."

The truth is that I had never felt. Now I am overwhelmed with feeling. I feel insecure; I am, insecure. Where will all of this end? I feel the unknowing; I am the unknowing. What are we going to do with this tape and how are we going to use it? The materials of a tapestry are coming together and we are about to see shape and form emerge.

"You are not having second thoughts, are you?"

Helen could not be more wrong.

"By this afternoon we will have all we need."

"You seem distracted."

Distracted I am; confused too when thinking of the way and of the moment Helen kissed me when I woke; distracted as a child kicks at the inner wall of my stomach, confused and distracted until I can think through what we have to do and the way we should do it.

"We have to get this right. We have to make sure that there is no way he can get back to your community in Ireland and tell them about you. We have to make the man so fearful of consequences that he dare not even stick the tips of his fingers above the parapet. There are only two ways of doing it in theory and the choice we make dictates the future for all of us,"

I look at James - "save for you."

A shrug of the shoulders; an inflection of the ego; of pride; of an inner happiness at being part of the whole. Then a reminder of a false and a fraudulent modesty.

"I don't think so. It dictates the future for me too, Iris. For I am with you though he could never touch me if he tried."

James could be right. I decide not to think about it.

"What choices do we have?" Helen asks.

"If Brodie is a criminal and we can prove it, we can make sure he is sent to prison. If Brodie isn't a criminal, though there is every indication he is, he has committed an offence which, at the very least, could see him banished from the legal fraternity. The cocaine he could plausibly deny at this moment. However, what we can prove is that Brodie has systematically lied to all about what he is. If we choose to expose his homosexuality, his career would be finished. This is presently our trump card. Do we expose him and finish him off or do we let him know that he is exposable and let the threat linger?"

James is instinctive.

"We expose him."

Helen is taciturn.

"I'm not sure."

Iris is reason.

"Probably not the best tactic one could choose, James. See, upon his denouement Brodie would have no one left to answer to and nothing left to answer for. When he is finished what does he care if he reverts back to your community in Ireland?"

"But Iris; he doesn't know I am involved here."

"Maybe not. But he isn't stupid and could put two and two together. And if he is exposed and has nothing left to lose because he has nowhere else to go, he could choose, out of spite, to expose you anyway.

"In my opinion, the best way to treat the man is to blackmail him. We should let him get on with his career but should extinguish him as a threat. This necessarily means that we have to declare that you have betrayed him, otherwise he will take you along for the ride.

"But should he stay in London?

"What should we have him do?

"The choice is to make sure he stays within the firm, where we can watch him, or we can demand his resignation and see him go somewhere else."

"Can't you have him transfer to New York or somewhere like that?"

"That is a possibility. For my part, I do not want to see that man's face ever again. To put him out of harm's way would be ideal for all of us."

"How do we approach him, Iris?" James asks.

I think the question naive.

"This is, necessarily, something I must do alone. Only I can face him for I am the only one he sees as the enemy."

"So when are you going to confront him?"

"Depending on what I learn about him today, either this evening or tomorrow morning."

"And what do we do today?"

"Both of you do nothing. It is another day as usual."

I turn to James. Reason disappears with the speed of an arrow and Iris recoils to the shade. My heart falls from my body and from my mouth I mutter words of intense gratitude to my friend. Perhaps it is more of a speech than a thank you.

"On behalf of both Helen and I, and Edmund, I thank you for being so brave and putting yourself at so much risk. I promise I shall never forget it."

James smiles and looks at my stomach.

"A pleasure, Iris. An absolute pleasure. Now go and get him for all of us and let's get on with our lives."

XXXVII

Brodie is already in his office when I arrive. I can hear his voice flowing from his room, travelling like middle-earth lava down the corridor - singeing, burning, scalding. He sounds agitated. A little bit of evil takes over. Maybe he suspects; maybe he knows.

I see Helen walking past, making her way to the booth outside Brodie's office. She is late, though not excessively so, and pays not the slightest bit of attention to my open door. I thank her for it and busy myself with the paperwork in front of me. Through the silence, or rather, through the anodyne chattering of keyboards being punished on account of their secretaries filling screens with words, I hear Brodie yell at Helen the very moment he sees her. I poke my head around the corner to see Helen glance down the corridor before she turns, still with her coat on, and walks into Brodie's room. I hear a raised voice and his door slams shut.

I stop what I am doing and consider her actions and the meaning in his voice. I have never heard Brodie shout like that since the day he started working at this firm yet there he is, passing off his anger to his secretary. There is something very wrong.

What is he ranting about? I know the answer as I ask the question. Brodie must have discovered that his desk drawers have been opened, as the tiny little blackened follicles he guarded them with have gone. I guess that his mind is beginning to race; that he is considering whether it happened by accident; whether it had been done on purpose; whether his things have been searched. How could he be sure either way? There is no way of telling. He will see that nothing has been removed. His stupidity was leaving items so compromising in a drawer which could not have been locked. Now he is trawling all scenarios in order to establish which most fits his paranoia and his prejudices. Helen is simply one of the prejudices he has to eradicate before he can move on to another.

What can he be saying to her?

Will he threaten her when he has no real suspicion that Helen has anything to do with me?

Even if he regards Helen as an enemy, with the information he holds over her, surely Brodie realises that Helen is far too afraid to tell anybody or speak to anybody. I wait and I ponder. I receive a call - an internal call from a number I do not recognise. I hear Helen's voice, trembling with fear. I try to calm her down when I sense her losing control. I ask her to meet me in the building, but somewhere we cannot be seen nor discovered. Describing our destination, I tell Helen to meet me in ten minutes in a room in the bowels of the building, two floors below ground. I explain very carefully where it is and leave straight away.

I am now consumed with what Helen has been told. What can Brodie have said that has caused her so much upset? Logically he cannot have accused her of anything, for he has no evidence. So has he accused her at all?

Helen is already waiting for me when I arrive. She is in tears and visibly shaking. For a moment I feel nothing but compassion. But Iris takes hold. I need to know straight away. As much as I want to hug her and tell her she is not alone, Iris controls the need to get all she has gone through out of her. Compassion must take second place to discovery. Maybe then, compassion can rise.

"Tell me slowly, Helen. Tell me precisely what he has said to you. I need to know every single detail in as much detail as possible."

With the strength of my delivery and unsympathetic body language, Helen knows I am not going to be generous. She can sense that now is not the time for us to be weak.

"I have never seen him looking so nervous, so edgy and so angry. He didn't sit down once and walked around my chair, yelling into my ear, wanting to know if I had been tampering with his desk; whether I had been through his drawers; whether I had seen anybody in his room going through his things; whether anybody had even expressed an interest in his whereabouts so as to afford themselves an opportunity to go through his things."

"And you said?"

"I told him I had seen no one and that absolutely no one had made any kind of request as to his whereabouts. I told him I had seen nothing."

"So what did he say?"

"He changed tack. He was so angry. He started smashing some of the business awards he keeps on his shelves, accusing me of being responsible for going through his drawers, accusing me of betrayal and, for all the innocence I pleaded, he refused to let it go. I started to cry and the more I wept the worse he got, until and without explanation, he sat down and was very quiet, so quiet that, whereas I didn't dare look up while he screamed at me, inquisitively I looked up to see what he was doing."

"And what was that?"

"He was just staring at me."

"Staring?"

"His jaw was clenched shut and he was just looking at me. Then he spoke, quietly and controlled."

"He told me that I have until tomorrow morning to tell him all I know about the people who have searched his room and what my relationship is with them. If I do not tell him the truth, I will be fired and he will tell my community about my past and my son. If he does that my family will be ruined. And I will be ruined."

Helen starts to cry again. Iris recedes and compassion takes over, feeling nothing but pity, for Helen is just not made to fight on these terms. As I put my arms around her, I think of Brodie.

If he is bluffing, then he feels weak. If he feels weak, then he is going to be difficult to predict. If he is difficult to predict, then Helen is at risk. I have to act soon. But do I have enough to approach him with? I do not. All eventualities now hang on what I am told by Oliver Dauncey. If he can provide, then I can save Helen. If Oliver Dauncey cannot provide then Helen is lost. And it will be my fault. I must act quickly. I must, once more, be strong.

"Helen; listen. Do not worry. Remember how far we have come. Remember what we have learnt about him. If we are resolute and strong Brodie is in for the shock of his life. All along I have asked you to trust me; all along I have said that I would not let you down. You must cling to that, Helen. You must remember all that you have said. It isn't only your life which is at stake now, or that of your family."

"I must look after you. We must look after each other us and…" I hold my stomach, "I must look after my child."

I can see it in her eyes and then I remember - Helen has no idea I am pregnant. I have never told her.

"You - you are what?"

"Pregnant; Helen. I am carrying a child."

For a moment Helen looks at me in disbelief. She goes limp. She tries to mouth words she cannot articulate. Her face crumples and contorts. Her eyes catch light and reject light as blood floods into her head and drowns fences and stockades erected to dam the elusion of tethered memories of pain, of loss, of the wrench of giving away the child she was not meant to have. Oh why did I tell her? Where was Iris when I needed her? Speech without control and emotion without restriction - the foil of my replenishment. Did I not realise? Was I not aware that poor Helen - poor Helen who has fallen in with me, falls into a woman with a child unwanted whereas she has lost a child? It is I who has committed a treasonous disclosure to a woman forever on the cusp of losing all she holds dear. Poor Helen - Helen who has risked all to be by my side, facing her own denouement every step of the way. At the very moment when her despair is greatest, when the reality of her loss is at hand, she recoils from the horror of learning that the rock she clings to is merely a porous lump of earth. Strength ebbs from her limbs; strength ebbs at my side. Helen collapses, passing out into my arms. She falls into me and away from me. Love and hate have clasped each other within and fought until the inner sin of conflict causes the body to submit. I understand her kiss now - Helen's family, Helen's life; a kiss - just a physical gesture; a kiss and the display of the needy. What Helen had, has gone. This heavy, lifeless woman in my arms; a kind woman and a woman robbed of all - betrayed by her biology, betrayed by the gift of love, betrayed by morals screwed and twisted into the mind, betrayed by man and betrayed by the God she believed in, is alone, whereas the woman - I am less than a woman, who holds her, carries the seed of life and the only object of Helen's desire. What more could she take if she knew what circumstances had brought this child to bear? If I told her perhaps she would understand; she may not understand - for why should she? What woman understands another when conception is the product of rape and the child is allowed to birth? Rape is the desecration of the innate character of womankind and its offspring a desecration of choice. Helen surely, will not understand the child's innocence and its distance from its circumstance. I carry something that should not be wanted - she carried that wanted then cruelly snatched away. What more natural to blame me and my child for her own tragedy?

She opens her eyes and her lids seem to lift so slowly, as if pulled to their resting place by drunken muscles. Helen murmurs my name. She blinks and the slow close pushes the liquid filling and obscuring her view onto the lower lid to the cheekbone beyond. She murmurs my name again, drunk on the sound of it, on its hypnotic tick. There is no substance in her voice, there is no substance other than that liquid as it falls from her eyes. What have I done to this woman? What must I do to make amends?

"I'm sorry, Helen. I'm sorry."

My pitiful words make no mark. Helen neither forgives nor admonishes. Unaided she stands up, deliberately but tentatively. Incredulity shades her visage and sorrow colours her movement. Yet she says nothing. I let my arms fall to my side and can say no more. I turn and walk five yards backwards. She inspects me for a friendship she thinks is misguided and for the person she thought I was. To my core I feel shame and to my core I feel an obligation to this woman and an obligation to her distress. I am speechless. I know not what to say. I fear what I will say but I know that I have to say something. I cannot imagine what.

"I wanted to tell you and I wanted to tell you all. But in these circumstances I thought it was the wrong thing to do. I knew it was the wrong thing to do. I only hope you can come to terms with it."

I turn and flee. I am upset - so, so upset. I skirt along the corridor and out of frustration and out of a displaced anger, from a nucleus of disgust with myself and disgust with the world, I predispose and put time to its essence. I will see Oliver Dauncey immediately. For it is he who is to blame for events. Without his imposition in my life, empty as it may have been; without his greed and his jealousy, nigh on all of this pithy turn would not have taken place. I want answers now in order to assuage my guilt for disclosure. I want without consideration. I walk, a woman possessed; I walk without regard. Each door I walk through I throw open. I care not for the attentions of others who see me as I go; I care not to say anything to those I know who try and say 'hello'. I want answers. I want catharsis. I need information to set Iris to work on the basis of emotions of which I never knew I was capable. I want suffering and revenge for all the ills I have seen, all of the ills which have been foisted upon me and those I have grown to love dearly. It is time to leave Iris behind and accept the changes which I have never asked for, but nevertheless accept. Iris will have one last resurrection. I will be cold and calculate. I will be hard, scientific, logical and controlled. I will then let Iris go. She will leave me and this new person I have become since I was raped, will be the woman I am. I shall be that person no longer. For my sake and for Helen's, for my child and for the memory of Edmund Rose, I am going to defeat the madness of man and the ignominy of destruction. I shall clear all decks so that I, Helen and my child, have the chance to cleanse and be cleansed of this evil, this hideousness, this vile pestilence which soils and infects which neither creates nor destroys but renders incapable the passage of a moral life untrammelled by the virtues of the insanity of people.

XXXVIII.

I know it is a mistake. I do not care. I shut the door behind me and sit
    down. I look at him and I can see that he knows he should start
talking. I make the point anyway. I am not going to be messed about. I am
not going to be toyed with.

"Do not play games. I will spot them before you have finished one third
of each sentence you deliver. You have information I want and you will give
it to me in a slow and informed manner. I will stop you every time I think
you are deviating. I will stop you every time I sense subterfuge.

"Now start speaking."

I care not for my delivery. I care not for the impression I give.
Information is all I want. I owe this man absolutely nothing. I am totally
focussed on what Oliver Dauncey is about to say. I am totally in control of
all he says. It will land in my head and it will remain.

"You asked me several questions," he begins.

"I don't know precisely where to start so I'll tell you all I know and all
I have found out."

Dauncey looks sorry for himself. I have absolutely no doubt that he
does.

"Perhaps I should start historically.

"Yes; you were right. I first met Brodie while we were students at
Cambridge. You were right in relation to the college we attended - the same
is true of all who still remain in touch.

"We were very young. You, are a graduate of the same place and you
will remember what it was like - a new world draws people together and
pitches out all others. Brodie was one of a number I met while my ideas
were still being formed and one of a number of people whose lives have
become inextricably entwined with my own. If you work in the City of
London it is very difficult to escape the Cambridge connections as we all
end up moving in the same circles and drifting back into those very circles,
even if we have had some time apart, which is what I did. I refer you to our
conversation the first time we met, when I told you I was the world's worst
painter.

"And you were right to think that on that evening in Chelsea I ran into

206

for the first time in a few years. I hardly recognised him he has aged so much.

"Look; you have to see that when you are confronted with a room of faces you may want to get to know and then you see a man who knows you intimately because he watched you turn into the man you are, it is inevitable that you gravitate towards that man. So and I renewed our friendship and promised to keep in touch. Several weeks ago he called and invited me to lunch. At lunch I explained my predicament - I needed a job and wanted a challenge. I was aware that Brodie trusted me. How could he not trust me after all we had been through together? It was simply a matter of telling him that I needed a job and letting the network speak for itself.

"The interview was a formality as were the ensuing invitations to meet some of the other chaps. I was part of a club again and a club which had done very well for itself in the City of London. We are all in positions of control and responsibility; none more so than Brodie himself.

"We meet frequently and in private places, though we are to be seen in public. It is human nature to seek out those with whom one feels comfortable and I am no different from the rest of them.

"The interview got me the job here. It wasn't really an interview as Brodie introduced me to the Senior Partner, who understood. Thereafter it was a matter of crossing the Ts and dotting the Is."

"And its relevance?"

"Its relevance to you is that I am simply confirming your opinion that I am part of an élite clique of men who have attained, through cohesion and being around at the right time and in the right place, a degree of social status and power which most could only dream of, provided their imaginations could grasp it.

"See; we are dealing here in a world of powerful people whose sum adds up to a whole lot more than its parts. Brodie is just one of the group, though I may say, he is one of its driving forces."

"And Edmund Rose?"

"Yes; Brodie set him up. All he did was to use connections and the very fact that everybody has secrets they would rather hide. Edmund was hardly discreet and the rest just fell into place. Thereafter it was all a matter of timing. And Edmund Rose precipitated that timing by bringing matters upon himself."

"So you knew all along?"

"The group trusts each other. We have common understandings. It is the one place were Brodie feels he can be himself and that goes for all of us. The rest of the world out there is the enemy - bunker mentality, you may say but we all have some sort of phobia in relation to others. We just use each other in order to protect each other."

"And me?

"Presumably, as I am most closely associated with Edmund, Brodie is seeing to it that I am exposed for my weaknesses?"

"You are an entirely different matter. From what I know you have led an exemplary, excruciatingly boring life. You have no interests, you have no vices, you have no past; you have no enemies and very few friends. You are a robot, a machine, a brick in the wall of society; reluctant or indifferent to the normal idiosyncrasies of the human being. You are almost impossible to get at."

I think of Helen. I think of James.

"And my friends?"

"There was one I believe something could have been made of - the man you live with platonically. By repute he is a bit of a cad but utterly harmless. Besides, Brodie thinks you are so cold that you wouldn't care for him if he tried to use your flatmate's past against you. Brodie thinks you are a cold-hearted bitch."

"And my house; my lifestyle? Am I being watched?"

"Brodie decided not to have you watched some time ago, I think. There are far more subtle ways of trying to deconstruct the lifestyle of an enemy."

I breathe a sigh of relief. Not that I show it.

"Are you telling me that in matters of conspiracy, you discuss intimate details as to how you choose to ruin the lives of others, who may or may not, get in your way?"

"Some take a full part. Brodie is certainly one of them."

"And morally?"

"I know some think it wrong. There are many ways of chipping at morality. For my part I choose not to take part as I choose not to make enemies. But I cannot be outside the group for the group would become my enemy if I were. I am integrally bound to the lives of people I grew up with. I accept as there is nothing I can do to get away from it. And, of course, it has its advantages."

"Like ruining the lives of the innocent?"

"Innocence is a perception. Innocence does not post-date original sin. All are therefore fair game. Those are the rules. It is better to abide by the rules of the group than risk excommunication. The group always wins."

"Go on."

"Brodie is therefore unsure how to get to you. I think he has decided he will get to you through work. He will force those who control your life in this office to see you as a liability and a loose cannon. I am not entirely sure whether he has formulated the best way to do this though he sees it as a long-term process - a creeping process undertaken via stealth. Over time you will be given more and more work and suffer more and more pressure, until you crack. Every human being has a breaking point and you too have yours. You will resign and move on. He will remain intact."

I cut to the chase.

"But he will not remain intact will he, not if you are about to expose him on pain of being exposed yourself? We both know you have little choice."

"Yes well…before you go on, I have one question to ask you. We are both aware of what happened that night. I want your confirmation that it was you who raped me. I want your story."

"But Iris…"

Dauncey assesses his situation. He is intelligent, though weak and must realise that he has little choice. For my part, I begin to question the digression. Is it morbid curiosity? Is it confirmation that my intuitive sense is precisely as I imagine it to be?

"You were remarkably close yesterday. I could not remember anything precise about the incident. I was as drunk as you were. Yes it was me who entered that bedroom, annoyed at being left out. It was I who was consumed by my own greed. I can remember you lying on the bed and I can remember approaching you. I had no idea you had passed out as I climbed on top of you and I took the noises you made as I moved around to be confirmation of consent. I have very little recollection of the act itself and I had very little recollection of it when I awoke. You were right when you stated that I looked down upon your blood the following morning. I have had only half-thoughts about the incident since then. It wasn't until you reminded me yesterday that I could offer some sort of recall. Of course I had suspicions but with the passage of time and the movement of my life, I let events filter from my memory."

"And when you saw me?

"When you saw me on the day Edmund Rose died and you helped me?

"You could not recall anything on sight of your victim?"

"No."

"I could remember nothing. And I am so very, very sorry. I cannot beg enough forgiveness from you."

"Cut the forgiveness. It isn't you I want. I want Brodie and I want you to start being specific. I want detail. I want personal detail and I need evidence of the criminality. That is how you make amends."

For a few seconds I think of myself. Is it right to let the vile nature of this man's action transmute into revenge and protection? And is he truly sorry? In fact, can he be blamed at all?

But I am not here to mull over the past. I am here to protect myself in the future. I have got to learn more of Brodie and I have so little time to do it. The clock is ticking and there are lives to consider and protect.

"Tell me about Brodie."

Dauncey clears his throat.

"I am not sure how much you know."

"Assume I know nothing."

" is probably the most secretive of all the people I have ever come across. He takes his privacy so seriously I think it encumbers his actions. In any event, I suppose that given his background, he has a great deal to be wary of and a great deal to think about.

" is from a diehard community in Ireland. His background, as with most people I suppose, colours all he says and does. When I first knew him he was very quiet and remained quiet for almost six months. Looking back on it, I think he was feeling his way into this new world he had entered. Of course we all spoke with accents he was unused to and looked at life in different ways. His world-view was the most serious and he was and is, a very serious man. As you know, he is also a very ambitious man and that was clear right from the very start. I think it was his insecurity bordering on paranoia which gave him the drive to succeed while belittling those he couldn't understand nor wanted to understand, along the way.

"He had other reasons for being so strange. During those early years we would hang around the college bar and drink ourselves stupid. did the same. However, when we were drunk, our minds inevitably turned toward members of the opposite sex. Seemingly his didn't. I cannot recall a single occasion when he took the slightest bit of notice of a woman though his very aloofness and evident intelligence made him attractive. We didn't question it at the time and I guess, if we had, we weren't going to be too sure whether the conclusions we would draw were appropriate. So he was quiet and mistrusting and a little different from those of us who are still his close and only friends.

"I must mention his ambition, too. He talked often of what he wanted to be and how he was going to be someone. I can remember not really caring for this call to achieve and it was only much later, when the childishness had gone, that the rest of us began to catch up with his way of thinking. By then he was already well advanced in his chosen career, which, as you know, is the law."

"Why law?"

"I asked him the same question one day. He considered his answer for some time, then told me that law represents impunity within the middle of things. He could understand, at its nucleus, precisely how the world works, with money being the real God of all. And once he understood life at its essence, he could learn to control and understand the weaknesses and strengths of all people. Logically, if he understood the nuclear relationship of people to money when most people didn't, he felt confident he could manipulate the world to his own ends. He was a power freak, even then, and certainly a power freak now.

"On a personal level he was always difficult to know. The two forces I mentioned, which seemed to run him, were his background and his need to control. He has no other fundamental qualities and in my opinion, has always been rather dull and tiresome. That does not mean one should get on the wrong side of him and we all used to make an effort to keep him sweet, for he could and can, be ruthless. I wouldn't say that is my ideal companion. He is just there. He is just, I suppose, ."

"You are not telling me much at all. I have worked a lot of this out for myself."

"After we got to the City and we needed to be a more cohesive unit, given the real and imagined competition, I got to see both at his worst and his best. He still remains a strange man and a man of contradictions. His biggest contradiction is his sexuality. It took us many years to learn that he was a homosexual after we had listened to his rants about the immorality of the whole thing. I understood as soon as he told us, why he was so secretive in the past and why he was so reluctant to chase women. In the architecture of his brain and its relationship to the structure he was taught, he must contend with competitions of forces which are so severe that the inevitable result is a confused and illogical man.

"Save that he isn't illogical in many ways. I think he realised he would have to come out to those he trusted most of all, for he knew that one day we would need to protect him. I remember his face the day he told us, the child fighting with the ambitious man so contrasting the feelings he could not control and every instinct he was given. He need not have bothered you see, for most of us had worked out that his tastes were a little different. And we promised to protect him if he promised to remain private, which he has done to this day.

" has a long-term partner he shares a house with. His partner is discreet too as he has to be. They make an interesting couple for the man shares his bed with has as much reason to hide as does. And I guess you know, plays his part to the full in that he tells the world he is a happily married man with children. He is, I agree, not unlike Edmund Rose although altogether more paranoid. In some ways I can understand what did to Rose as the kind of punishment would like to mete out to himself. I think , knowing that he cannot accord with the moral precepts he pretends to follow, somehow turns the idea that he should be punished on its head and found in Edmund Rose someone whose denouement would make up for 's own very particular analysis of his own inadequacies. That is not to excuse him for his behaviour and I know that you have every right to blame him for Edmund's death. And I can see that 's sexual failing does not preclude him from representing on many occasions, the essence of immorality. He will do whatever is necessary in order to promote himself and does not give a damn about anybody who stands in his way. Whatever you say it is a tactic in this highly competitive environment which works, provided you can deal with being a lie to the world, full in the knowledge that if anyone ever found out your secret, you are, in turn, open to the very tactics which you use yourself. Provided, of course, it can be proved.

" Brodie knows this. Both he and his partner live in a very private house. They are hardly ever seen in public and knowledge of their relationship is strictly limited to us. To get to him, you have to break down that barrier and you need evidence. If you have no evidence then he wins, for he can employ the concept of…"

"Plausible deniability?"

"Exactly."

"There is one matter you haven't mentioned yet which absolves you of the whole notion of deniability. I think you should come clean."

Dauncey appears hesitant. He is no fool. He knows he must talk.

"Brodie dabbles in cocaine - that much you have established. And you are right that it isn't the sort of stuff bought on a street corner. In fact there are those in our group who also take the drug and others besides, some for recreation, some because the feel that they have no choice. I fall into neither category, for the record."

"And the supplier?"

"The supplier is a barrister, believe it or not. The cocaine is procured through a criminal client who is at the top of the pyramidal criminal structure in London. It is almost pure for this reason. In terms of consumption I would say that is about the biggest consumer. He procures it for two reasons: the first is simply to keep him awake during those long evenings he has to endure as a lawyer, the second is purely recreational in that he takes it with his partner, presumably for sexual reasons as well as the need to leave one's ordinary senses and enter an alter ego."

"It seems he has a lot to escape from."

"The question you have asked is whether there is some way you can prove that he procures cocaine - some proof, some evidence you can use against him and so protect yourself. That is not so easy. I have had to think long and hard about the best way of doing this and I must admit I have found it difficult to imagine circumstances in which it is possible to pin him down. In fact I have concluded that it is impossible to pin him down directly.

"However, there is one option you may consider. He is very close to the barrister who supplies him. Of the group I would say they are the closest. The way to get to Brodie is through him."

"Go on."

"Believe it or not, Iris, I am a very careful man. During my time I have seen so many decent people disregarded as rubbish that I have always been fearful that it could happen to me. So I have recorded my conversations with this barrister and in those conversations I have made a point of asking him to supply both myself and the others, including Brodie, whom I mention by name, with a quantity of cocaine."

"The process is still deniable. It is only a tape."

"I have thought of that. However, whether there is tangible evidence of procurement or not, which there is not, what you have is the voice of an eminent criminal lawyer, in clear terms, agreeing to the procurement of illegal substances. And just the attachment of Brodie's name to the conversation should be enough."

"I don't get it."

"If you approach Brodie with the tape, he could deny all knowledge. He would be lying but he can still deny. What cannot be denied is that he is still connected to a conversation in which a senior and highly regarded lawyer agrees to procure narcotics. Follow my reasoning - if that barrister hears that tape recording, he will realise he is in a very serious position for not only is his voice, as well as mine, evident on the tape but also, the name of the supplier is represented audibly. And if that tape were to fall into the wrong hands - say the police, connections could be made between this supposed bastion of responsibility and the higher criminal fraternity in London. If those connections are investigated, relationships would then be exposed and a chain of reasoning may ensue. From the barrister's perspective, he would be spotlighted and if brought in for questioning, may crack and tell all. Would you, if you were Brodie, be willing to take the chance that you would be subject to scrutiny by the police even if they had little to go on? For my part, I would think it was too much of a chance to take and Brodie is almost maniacally averse to chance. There is nothing he despises more."

I think for a moment about what Oliver Dauncey is proposing. One point confuses me.

"You clearly realise that your voice is on that tape. You would be opening yourself up for scrutiny too, if it was presented to the police. And in any event, I thought you said that the tentacles of this group ran far and wide. Surely this sort of thing could be brushed under the carpet?"

"You make the point, Iris. By giving you the tape I am exposing myself both to the police, if matters ever got that far and I am leaving myself open, as any halfwit would realise, to the accusation that the tape came from me."

"And your price?"

"Two things.

"I want your assurance that you will never go to the police in relation to what happened at that party. You have stated clearly that it is Brodie you want. Now that I have given you the means to get him, I want your agreement that the provision of that tape into your possession precludes you from ever stating your case."

"And the second?"

"I want your protection to be engineered so that you protect me too. With that tape your hand is strong. With that tape in your possession, my life will be destroyed by these people once they realise who you got it from. In protecting yourself I want your assurance that you make it explicit that the hold you have over Brodie which I assume you will keep as a threat and not anything other, will keep him from seeking to punish me. I want your assurance that your need to protect yourself extends to me. I cannot say it any clearer than that.

"And if you do, though I know that you owe me nothing, I want your word and I will trust that I will not have to worry on the future. Brodie's leverage with respect to both of us, must be nil."

"And the alternative?"

"If I do not have your assurance I keep the tape to myself. You can do with me what you will. Without your assurance I will be made to suffer either way."

I weigh up Dauncey's ultimatum as quickly as I can.

"The tape, Iris? I have your word?"

His hand moves toward mine. I take the tape and look at Oliver Dauncey for one last time. I stand to leave, trying to defer an answer to the question. Sitting before me is a man I have every reason to despise beyond all the trellises of meaning. Under man's weakness have I always suffered yet the man before me is not a concept, he is not a construct, he is not simplistic and the translucent veneer of motivation Iris sat and watched, sat and analysed and almost admired. Oliver Dauncey is opaque - flesh, blood and bone and warrants attention, not on grounds of prejudice but on grounds of biology and the simple fact of being. It was Iris who would have dismissed him but Iris rises ever more to an air of realisation - a realisation that I have a choice to make and a difficult choice at that. All along I have thought of this man as a rapist with all the negativity associated with the concept itself. And now I am being asked to protect a man, a rapist, a criminal, an underling of morals with no right to feel the sustenance of preservation - the father of my child. What is it I am being asked to do? Is it that I am being asked to forgive the man for the crime perpetrated upon me? If so, is it the man I am being asked to forgive or men for being men and for being less than an apparatus of choice; a slave to the instinct which bottoms them all?

This man I do not know. Men, I understand. This child I carry is the product of this man. All men fall into this one man and this one man pushed all men into me. This one man diseased Iris - the incubus of all; an incubus representing the many. Why should I protect him?

To forgive acknowledges the wrong; to protect acknowledges my culpability. If I had not been the sacrifice; if I had not made the choice to drink myself into unconsciousness then I would not have to resolve this horrible choice. This man had sexual intercourse with me without my consent. But what was my lack of consent? From whose perspective? I was free to drink as much as I like, so was Oliver Dauncey. Should I have to answer for the twisted perspectives of a fellow drinker who saw consent in my unconscious mumblings? Yet it was I who gave Oliver Dauncey the opportunity of mistake. Was it a mistake? At the time, drunk though he was, if Oliver Dauncey honestly believed I had consented though my sentience had long since left me, then the freedom to alter the conscious should, upon sober judgement, be taken into account. In the opinion of a drunken man, a drunken woman who makes no positive remonstrance but who responds to her own instincts and expressions of satisfaction upon being touched, is allowed to rely upon his own instincts and follow them without later circumspection - the consent of biology to the promptings of instinct. If true, there is little blame to be attached. There is little I need consider.

But what of inner leanings - my anger at being defiled? I did not, in full consciousness, consent. But Oliver Dauncey did not, in full consciousness, consent. Should he have sought consent safe in the knowledge that I was aware, or do I have to retain awareness in order to object? Does hindsight give me the moral high ground and a sober analysis of a chosen and plied environ? Or must I cut to the scenario itself and consider it in isolation? Sexuality must bottom me too. So must instinct. Can I blame Oliver Dauncey for living off his instincts and sexuality whereas I, unconsciously, responded favourably to my own? I fear I do not know the answer. I am a ball of anger covered in rage. I am a ball of reason who finds it difficult to blame. The man in front of me, if I rely on the power and intuitive emotion, has done wrong. Upon analysis, though has he acted so, so badly, am I completely devoid of guilt? Emotion dictates his punishment and reason dictates withdrawal. What do I do. What, do I do?

And there is, finally, the higher purpose. Should I suspend any conclusion until Brodie has been put to sleep? For this is the ultimate object. This is my goal. While I have no answers I cannot make a choice. Oliver Dauncey shall have to wait, though upon his contrition which I think is real, his worry is that his sacrifice to me will posit a nil return. He will still have to wait. Perhaps he should be made to suffer a little bit longer. I must concentrate upon Brodie.

"There is one last thing Iris.

"The people I speak of are due to meet this evening. It is a regular event. They meet at the chambers run by the barrister who supplies cocaine. Meetings usually involve a meal in the chambers' private dining room followed by discussion - social conversations and the like.

" Brodie never misses these evenings. He positively looks forward to them. On each occasion he makes a point of arriving as early as he can. For the purposes of dramatic effect, I would have thought that by confronting him there before their evening commences, will bring it home to him how close you are to being able to expose him.

"It is up to you."

"And the address?"

"Lamuel Chambers, Temple Row. You can't miss it. Lamuel Chambers is the oldest building on the square. Say you are there to visit Basil Roget Q.C."

"And the time?"

"Be there before half past six."

XXXIX.

Iris and I are colliding. I have to dispense with feelings in order to treat Brodie with Iris' logical, scientific mind. Yet I am consumed with feelings, fearing I will be unable to control the anger and the aggression I can sense welling up within me. What happens if Iris cannot lead and outburst, indignation and the madness of emotions follow?

But I cannot call on Iris in isolation any more. I could never call on Iris in the past - I was simply Iris and no one else. Time has gestated and as I look back I can see feelings creeping, then falling away, creeping, until a little attaches and a little less falls away. That cynical creature; that woman in physicality only, seems a memory, save a memory I need to call on now. What have I become and what will become of what was? I little understand myself any more and wonder if ever the bearer of feelings should ever question. Does Brodie question? Does Helen? I question everything - everything I saw and everything I am, trying to understand. How I ache from it all; how I want Iris back and Iris alone, giving me the strength to confront Brodie. Is this womanhood I now embrace? Was Iris ever anything other than a woman?

Periodically I close my eyes. I try to see Helen's face. I try to remember those last moments Edmund Rose and I spent together. I have barely a couple of hours to assemble myself before I confront this nemesis and put the misery which he has bestowed upon these innocent people to one side. How will he come back at me? What will he say?

And who will respond? Pray, I hope I am Iris whether I am Iris now or not. This is madness; simple schizophrenia - caught between a lifetime of reason and a few months of tender, realised emotion. I must be Iris, for Iris is all Brodie knows. Exclamation and emotions will give him a peephole to my psyche and a slender opening he could use. Brodie - less than a man, a creature, an inveterate player and inconspicuous destroyer of life, cannot be allowed to destroy this life - my life. I will not give in. Iris will be, one last time. Whatever she was; whatever I used to be, will be consigned to oblivion when this is over. That cynical woman; that precursor of an unnatural state, can be no more. She must be for a little while longer. She must be for whatever she was, is all Brodie thinks I am.

What of Helen?

What thoughts must that poor, confused woman have for me, knowing that I will soon give birth to a child when her own child was so cruelly taken away? Should she feel anger for me or pity that I carry the offspring of rape? This I must put to one side. This is not about me. This is not about Iris, either.

Actions must follow the best interests of my child no matter how that child came into being. And my actions must be in the best interests of Helen for no matter how she feels, I have promised to protect her. And Oliver Dauncey? I wince at the thought of being a friend to the man who took my innocence away. What do I owe him, save that he has allowed me the opportunity to get to the one man at the centre of my life?

Is my assistance a price worth paying? Is he innocent or guilty? Do I blame him for being as drunk as I was and simply letting his biology take over his capacity to reason? I have watched men all of my life - stumbling from one mistake to another while I have coolly sat by and taken mental notes. Did Oliver Dauncey simply make a mistake, forgetting that indulgence often comes at a price? In a moral court and not a court of law, should a person being predisposed to act in certain ways, like Pavlov's dog, be guilty for following that predisposition? No one blames a leopard for killing an antelope - why should blame be allocated to man if his actions are beyond his capacity to exercise control?

Do I protect him for being an unwitting slave to need, or do I destroy him?

What I cannot do is fail. What I cannot do is let the mental image I have erected of this man, Brodie, turn into a constricting fear so that I strangle my words and denude my actions, thereby rendering me ineffective. I cannot be ineffective. I cannot fail.

Butterflies fill my stomach. I look to the palms of my hands and notice a greasy film which disgusts me. I pace incessantly, running over control methods I have been using since Iris was a child. I have never felt nerves before these last few weeks. Iris wants them to go away. Iris wants rid of these awful feelings which diminish my power of thought and defer analysis to instinct. Each thought has a meaning far in advance of the cold thoughts I used to refer to. Seconds are turning into hours and hours into days. What power does this man really have over me I ask myself?

What can he really do to me?

But the time for such questions has gone. I was committed the day Helen met Edmund at lunch. I have descended whereas Iris point blank refused. Will Iris return once I reach the light and Brodie's power is consigned to a past chapter of my dull life? Do I want Iris back? Did being Iris make me happy? Was Iris ever aware of being happy or sad?

The clock on my computer flicks to five o'clock. I have an hour and a half. I try and listen for the sound of Brodie's voice. I open my room door to hear the voices of the secretaries outside, the very secretaries whose mistakes with men make them human, the very secretaries Iris secretly dismissed for simply being fallible.

Was Iris better or worse for being infallible? Do I want to remain infallible or do these feelings make me as fallible as the others? If the answer is yes, then Iris learnt nothing – I, have learnt nothing.

I get my coat and realise I have made my mind up about very little. I feel weak and sick with nerves. What must this man have over me? What must this man, be?

Once more I am outside. London is going home. London - a collection of peoples; eclectic and self-centred; bilious and narcissistic, grabs the opportunity to emancipate itself from the drudge and grind of a mill that turns for millions and has no foreseeable end. Again Iris classifies them by their dress, by their words and their body language. Why do I think so much about the way people look? Was Iris ever really right when I made comparisons and decisions about the way others thought and acted? What was the point - was it to understand the world as it is and was my understanding ever a reflection of the way people are? What was the point anyway?

It is about value, I convince myself. How do I value my own actions against those weaknesses I see every day. Am I better for having never hurt anybody else when I have watched for years, as peoples upon peoples continue under the banner of humanity, hurting one another, scheming and lying to one another? And what have I become, now that I am about to try and cull a master at the pretence of morality who falls so far behind the morality he espouses.

I look at a tramp on Fleet Street selling a newspaper meant to offer him some residual income so as to get him what will no doubt be a urine stained, flea-ridden bed. Why must he suffer as a pin stripe walks past without the moral credulity to look a vagrant in the eye and dismiss him so obviously as he does so? With the axioms these human beings revolve around being so similar, can it be right that one walks to a car worth more than an income the other will pick up in a working lifetime? For what reason does one human being have the ability to dismiss the insignificant other? All want to love; to share a smile; to be happy; to make decisions others will laud them for; to grow old in comfort; to grow old being loved and cared for; to be treated with respect, honesty and discourse without illusion. So what is the difference between a tramp and a City boy doing well? Is it connections, birth, intelligence, reason, emotion, intuition, creativity, logic, luck?

Gradations of peoples follow me, some overtaking and some falling behind. Accents and expectations may differ but need and want may be the same; calling and result may be different but fundamentals never change.

And, alas, weakness pervades, for the ability to love; to think; to care, express and create is counterpoised by the ability to not to think; to give in to hate; to manipulate and to destroy. Take Iris - beautiful, blonde, without obvious external flaw and vaunted for the luck of being what others think is attractive. Compare it to those who fall way short of an impossibly high water mark and watch the simplicity of people's dismissal when it is known that dismissal is anathema to most, who just want to be loved. What have I learnt and what are these people telling me - the secretary with the adulterer; the banker with the balance to die for and the arrogance of a king; the lawyer with status written over the lawyer's smug face; the entrepreneur, safe that the risk has been worth it and laughing at others - accountants, doctors, policemen, judges, politicians, clerks, venture capitalists, management consultants, musicians, artists, bar staff, waiters, chefs, miners, nurses and so on and so on and so on until I run out of occupations to think of. They are all around, judging, classifying, analysing, scheming, lying, cheating, controlling and dismissing while seeking virtue, love, happiness and calm. How can I, Iris, having lived in a world of hypocrisy such as this, without taking part in the dark side of mankind and coming so close to being so unscathed, possibly survive on finding myself called in? Iris was happy when the world was seen through a looking glass; through a television screen; through a lens and beyond the reach of the immorality dressed up as goodness all around. I have come of age - called back in needing to fight for the right to find myself loved and cherished one day, fighting for the rights of those closest to me. I feel; I can be hurt. I will be hurt for I am now mortal. Whereas I floated above the throng, levitating in the weak air above the mire of humanity, I have been restricted and caught by a man who thinks he is different; thinks he is above these people heading home to their wives, their husbands, boyfriends, girlfriends, children - people, just people, just, people. Was Iris ever truly better for being without feeling, without emotion, without love, without a heart?

I have no answers, only more questions as to why people treat each other as they do - why they cannot break out and speak for themselves with due regard for others. The world is spoilt and with too much to be consumed and humanity demanding competition to feed the right to consume, the worst in all peoples becomes the common denominator with separates all. Does this tramp know this? Does this pinstripe know this? Do I really understand the world in which I live while Iris has spent my life trying to find answers in the actions of others in all that they say and do? Can I ever really know for sure?

And now that I have had to descend into the abyss and fight can I ever really drag myself back out?

I think of my child in this very inhuman world. I think of the future. I cannot control people and I cannot really blame them for themselves. For sure I have been touched by this inhumanity in a deep and incomparably hurtful way. I have been gifted the offspring of inhumanity and I know I can make the world into which my child will arrive no better than it was a mere few months ago, when I was Iris and Iris was alone.

Can I create a better world for my child and what stands in my way? As Iris and I walk past peoples who see the dividing line between themselves expressed in money and the very character of money itself expressed in them - its division, its greed, its power to corrupt the corruptible, I know that in a few short moments I will face the nemesis I had hoped never to face and I will be taking my life and my understanding to a man who represents the very essence of inhumanity, of immorality, of the *de facto* reality of humanity itself. For the paradox of humanity and all it means is simply that humanity is inhumanity. Brodie is inhumanity itself - a living contradiction and a version of every Londoner I pass on Fleet Street making their way home. If I can in a small way, strike out for myself; if I can absolve myself from a world Iris wanted no part of, then at least I and my child, and Helen, have the opportunity to walk away from hypocrisy and hatred till it calls on us again. This is why I must meet Brodie. It is why I need to descend before I can elevate myself and float once more above the morass of hideousness which colours all. Surely I will be a better person for it for I know I will am able to fight on terms I never wanted and in the process learn too that I can walk away from inhumanity as it affects me, leading to a higher calling and a calling from where I can build structures, meaning that I can love and show to others by example what can be done if fairness and honesty prevails. It is Brodie who stands in my way. It is Brodie whom I must desecrate in the process.

I turn to my left, about a third of a mile along Fleet Street, having come to a decision that will colour the rest of my life. I ring the bell that leads me to the reception in a building built in the year 1744. What generations must have walked through these environs and how insignificant is the confrontation I am about to have in the pantheon of history. I am a meaningless part in a world which I will not let control me. The following thirty minutes will dictate whether the man in this building can ever control me; whether the man in this building derives from the pleasure of destruction; whether I can rise from the slumber that was Iris's calling and set in train a new life in which I am happy that Iris remains and this new person; this woman I have become can live together and try and create something for those I am close to which transcends the predictable banality and the paradox of humanity itself.

XL.

I am politely asked to come into the building and directed to the reception. The reception is on the second floor. A bright young man shows me to the waiting room, asking me my name and the purpose of my visit.

"I would like to speak to Brodie. I believe he is presently in the company of the head of chambers."

I am received with confusion.

"When you speak to Mr Roget, tell him Iris Silkin is waiting to see Brodie."

I am asked to take a seat and left alone - an unwanted solitude for I do not want the time to think and revolve around thought now it is time to act; to do; to be. Disquiet creeps all over my body like a relentless rash. My mind is squarely caught between the control of Iris and the screams and fits of the woman I have become. Which has dominance in my mind? Which should have dominance in my mind? Is it to be the synthesis of Iris and myself? Has Iris changed? Do I still have the right to call myself Iris? What should I think of myself and what I have become?

Brodie keeps me waiting. Perhaps it is a choice designed to make me uncomfortable. Maybe his senses pick up the threat and he can scent this unforseen danger. He considers; he is considering. And I wait and I wait. Brodie will be asking how I have found out about his presence. Only a fool would not realise how important the address book is. He will know I am here to confront him; to warn him off. And he will feel confident there will be nothing I can say or do, so rendering me a tangible threat. The names and the cocaine mean nothing without proof of association with anything more sinister. He will be unaware I have spoken to Oliver Dauncey. He will not know of the evidence with which I can destroy him. I have a pack full of aces whereas he thinks I have a nothing hand.

I take a look at the room I am in. What strikes me is the very similarity of the faces which look down on me; the portraits which adorn the walls of men past who will no doubt correspond to the walls of The Maundeville - a past age but with such a heady resonance for the future. There is a continuity of control and dissonance here, which, no matter what the social upheavals of this new, global world have brought, presents the apotheosis of man.

Accident of birth has been displaced by the synthesis of education and connections in this confusing environment. However, it is still controlled by the essence of man dressed up as morality, designed and defended by the law and the control of ethics and hiding the real nature of man I have mentioned almost to distraction - greed, envy, pride and such other sins; sins which are not only deadly, but also provide the very sustenance which feeds the desire to control and defeat all that those epithets - morality, law and ethics are supposed to stand for.

All I see in the faces of the old are the faces of the new. The environment may have changed; the City of London may have changed; the social fabric of the country in which I live may have changed - money the giver of life, money the divider, money the delineation between us and them - status the justification; status the cloak which covers the real nature of the powerful; status the arbiter of the English calling on the new to follow the dark side of man. I could not be in a more unholy place for I peer in on the particular and am smothered by the general. Brodie is but one man but in that man, that very particular man, is a naked representation of all this world represents. I cannot defeat this world but I can ensure that Brodie cannot defeat me, and in doing so ensure that I strike back for a few people who matter. If only others could do the same. If only others could see the need to do so.

I feel a hand on my shoulder. It makes me jump.

Behind me, with an insouciant smile beaming all over his face, stands Brodie. He eyes me closely, letting silence pervade the air, pervading for just a little too long so as to unnerve me. He may be smiling but his arms are crossed. The real nature of his thoughts lie in his body language which is defensive, though he passes himself off as friendly. Yes, he knows the significance of the meeting, as do I. It is time for each of us to bare our hand though I know he has very little to bare.

"I would be a liar if I said I wasn't surprised to see you here, Iris. I would be a liar if I wasn't at all interested in how you knew where to find me."

I say nothing. I too, want to play this game - a simple matter of human nature - Brodie is curious and needs to know. This reception is the wrong place in which we should be speaking. He knows it, as do I. I wait for the invitation.

"I rather think this is a conversation we will need to have in private. Follow me."

He leads me into a large and antiquated meeting room. In the centre of the room is a large mahogany table surrounded by oak panels, green leather and ornate though masculine artefact.

"This chambers has the benefit of some of the most luxurious rooms in

London. It is like stepping back in time, like being at Cambridge and sensing the provenance of history. Please, take a seat."

I sit at the head of the table. Brodie walks to the other side of the room and sits at the opposite end, about six yards away. Nothing separates us save for six yards of highly glossed, antique wood. The room is silent. I can hear nothing outside - no traffic and no signs of life. It is as if the present has failed to pervade the all.

"With the passage of time decadence becomes the norm. Time, Iris, follows each of us, stands in our way and surrounds. They say time is constant but history and yesterday are the same thing. And all that has happened in time is always at the back of the mind. Tomorrow is always the same distance away."

I despise the conversation immediately. I want to get to the point.

"Both you and I know why I am here."

Brodie plays phlegmatic.

"Do we?

"I am not too sure what we have to say to each other. I take it this isn't a friendly call. There must be some strategy to this pleasant visitation."

Yes; strategy. What was it? Not plans but intentions strategy - the art or science of the planning and conduct of war. A particular plan for success, especially in politics or business. The art of objective; the art of objective in obfuscation. To hide and yet to claim. To claim and never to unveil. Strategy in deed and strategy in action.

How his words spur me on; how redundant will his strategy be now. I have no strategy for I have the truth. I will not hide. I have no plan. The truth has no hostages. Strategy indeed. I will unveil. My strategy is, to unveil.

"I'm not too sure you understand what friendly means. Anyway, what I have to say will take place without interruption. You can make up your own mind, as it is you who should be listening."

Brodie looks slightly uncomfortable. I can tell that he understands the charge, though he convinces himself there is no threat he cannot eradicate. Deluded self-confidence precludes the notion of defeat. Behind the veil, the doubt and behind the doubt, the man. Bravura will attempt to canter over the perilous, until I stand up to claim the prize. How undeniably masculine to believe in oneself and underestimate these difficult odds. How stupid.

"This is not going to be an argument. What is done will be what you will live off for the rest of your life. You will either choose to listen or you will suffer, for I will take from this room all that I know and I will destroy you in much the same way you have chosen to destroy everything and everybody which is and isn't you."

"Hardly strategy, Iris. You cannot beat me and you haven't been the first to try. Look where you stand. Look where you are. Rain falls all around me and little do I ever get wet. If I choose to stand up and leave this very moment...?"

Another precious nugget - only the knowing can dance between the raindrops. But to know is not to falter. And to falter is to fail. Odds arise once more and another pin begins to sink into a sullied visage.

"Then you will fall into the same grave which you have made for so many others."

"So knowledge is power?"

"Words without value; shape without form. My knowledge is power. And the power of knowledge is what you do with it. Whatever you know cannot harm me. But you can still harm me in the future."

"Take a look around you, Iris. Look at these walls and see the faces that look down upon you. These were men of another time with one thing in common - togetherness. Their strength lay in numbers; a shared outlook; the same values; the same needs. What can you do today that will defeat me when I am of the same ilk? You are just one little aperture whereas I hold the keys that unlock the many. How can you, a lone woman, hurt me?"

"That depends on whether you are willing to listen."

"I am not willing to listen to insignificant words. Your reach cannot extend beyond your grasp and a touch does not imperil the element."

My stomach contracts. The muscles around my eyes seize and force open my eyelids. This cheap language; this galling display offends my ears till they want to close and banish, folded away like a deck chair at dusk. I reach within to pluck the truth from its hiding place. A voice inside me is screaming; voices inside me converge. It is time to consign this wordplay and these empty gestures to the wall.

Brodie stands to leave. His challenge to produce is accepted. I let him walk towards the door.

"I've said you would be ill-advised to leave this room. There are so many subjects I want to talk to you about. Let us start with homosexuality."

Brodie stops dead. His mind starts churning - a raindrop has landed on his smooth head, gingerly wetting him with detritus mixed and of his own making. He looks down and I see his eyes tentatively moving from side to side. He begins to question and he begins to think.

"Take a seat ."

Brodie takes his place. I can sense his interests unfolding. I may even sense his fear. Iris demands explanation without feeling whereas hatred fills me and I demand a delivery designed not to inform but to punish.

"An allegory is best. Yes; an allegory. See, there was once a young boy, now a man, of sorts. Probably the best way of describing him was confused. He came from a small town riddled with hatred and anger, by accident of history more or less, in which generations had taught children to obliterate what they didn't understand and what they didn't want to understand. See, hatred was ingrained and hatred was justified by the use of

God and all the misguided notions of God and morality which this feeble misapplication of man could offer. Denunciation of the unknown was endemic in all the populace. It is easier to hate than to love, after all. And hatred filled this man too - given to him while he was a child, and he believed it with all his hollow heart. Save for one thing.

"The vestiges of morality applied then and now, by that and this society, was something he could not live up to. The course of his life was different. The matter of his feeling was different and different in a way which went against all the insidiousness of his teaching. This, of course, created a contradiction. So what did he do? Well, he tried to ignore his feelings and follow life in the way he had been taught. He followed what he was taught knowing that deep within, he was the opposite of what he was supposed to be. It was a recipe for the twisted; the disjointed; it was cruel and led to the precipice of evil itself where it fell upon my subject to find some way of dealing with the self-diagnosis of a fundamental flaw.

"It was more sinister than that. The values which he had been taught, notwithstanding his crucial differences, made him see the world as a continuous threat, a world to be conquered; to be slain; where all was the enemy and all was to be eradicated unless of course, it became known and trusted. But who could be known? Who could be trusted? These are values with foundations of weaknesses found in religion, in unknowing and in the young. But who was young and how were they got to?

"Still, our boy and our man did as he was told and by semblances of luck he was intelligent and successful - so successful in fact, that his brainpower and determination got him away from the town in which he grew up to an arena where bunker psychoses were the norm as the occupants of this new world sensed their differences with society and as a consequence, they fell into each other's arms. In some way there was a subliminal connection between these young men slowly flowering into adults. So this man, for that is what he thinks he is slowly becoming, finds an integral trust with those around - a feeling of togetherness against the world at large and thereafter, entry into that very world, with strength in numbers as a most potent ally.

"But fundamental problems remained. The curse of the innate cut away the pleasure of the learned and the twists of fate designed a man taught to be another and never his true self. And the art of obfuscation cast upon a soldier and strategist of deviancy fuelled the strategy but never becalmed the man. From his waking moments till his tired eyes pulled him to sleep, the secret nagged and it gnawed and it pummelled his mutant psyche, damning all profoundly different because it was not him, though it was him, though his presentation was never him, though it was, him.

"You may ask from where this man came and where he ended up. I shall tell you. He came from a small town in Ireland. At the age of eighteen he travelled to Cambridge and the University of Cambridge, which as both you and I know, is a clenched fist against the world and from where generations have moved on and taken to history itself, moulding it, shaping it into a form they recognise as their very own.

"Cambridge was good to him. The unknowing was overcome and there grew a senseless ambition which sought to control a world he could not control and to grasp the exterior in order to quell the tempest within. He found friends; he found enemies; he found friends against the common enemy and the common enemy was all he could not quell. This clique of correspondence - a clique of minds powerful yet ultimately flawed, founded boundaries between them and others, denying others a chance. Anyone who got in the way was neutralised. Anybody with the temerity to question the fuel which drove this many headed-beast to achievement, was destroyed. Man followed man followed boy into man and front against the imagined was set. The only question to resolve was where would this calling take place? Where would this self-service at the expense of all arise?

"He and they arrived in the City of London. Once a small boy and now, with the combined strength of those around him - sure he is a man; a man amongst men and a lawyer, set himself down. Now the object was to attain in a world which he imagined could not be conquered without the destruction of those bedevilled with immorality, who were all around.

"And he was successful. He seized his chance whenever he could and with this purported strength in numbers, picked and chose those to obviate as he ascended ladders in the dawn of a new age, where family and birth were not the key to success but connections, pure and simple, are.

"Yet the problem persisted. For the world which he has chosen to inherit still demanded certain standards, as did his background. Alas, he could not escape the contradiction between those standards and an inner fabric which failed to unravel, no matter how the stitching was picked. A man has value in the City of London for all that he is and little value if all he is, is in some way flawed. What does one do if one is in some way different when if differences are seized upon, they could signify the end? What does weakness dictate? What do the standards of his past, dictate? What do standards of the present, dictate?

"A mask required; a mask retained.

"He lied to all but the closest few and passed himself off as respectable - a man with a loving wife, a man with a family, with children, with all the trappings of the present world's ideal of normality, save that in his heart he could not escape the urges, the feelings which told him he wasn't normal, he wasn't welcome; he wasn't worthy.

"And he intrinsically knew he could not breathe a word. What was this pestilence which filled him which could destroy what he thought he really wanted? What was this disease which raged unseen and unwanted, which sequestered motive and desire? It was a question he has asked in every quiet moment he has had ever since he became aware of the urge and of the knowledge that he is in some way different.

"Why me?

"Why, me?

"Why, am I a homosexual?

"Why am I, a homosexual?

"How the mind was unwilling; how the flesh, was weak."

I smile a thin-lipped cruel smile - twisted; a twisted smile. Brodie knows and an ego within enjoys the punishment. Pins are entering his body, pushed slowly and deliberately. Still his self-confidence precludes. But aggression begins to infect his voice. Pride picks at Brodie the closer I get to displaying the stakes which will finish him off.

"Interesting story, Iris. Get to the point."

The admission speaks. He knows I know. He knows I cannot prove it, save that I can. I am vainglorious; I delight in delivery. I could be slapping myself on the back as I begin to descend into self-aggrandisement. Punishment is fun, pleasing me, pleasuring me. The attractions of undoing are manifest. An eye for an eye; a tooth for a tooth. How gratifying. How dangerous.

"Oh, you hid it so well. You found a touchstone so hideous you slaked your thirst for yourself by killing another man for the sins of a life you have led. Therein lies the contradiction - the cruelty you declared upon another who was precisely the same as you. The complete and utter desecration of a man whose only sin was in some small way, having the bravery to confront what he was and declare it, dismissed by the folly of your cowardice, your pithy disregard for others - your vain, syphilitic conversation with all that is sinister and repugnant about man."

"Rose declared nothing. He lied to the world and expected the world not to bother."

"In the end he lied to no one. You lied on his behalf. And as a consequence you took his life. His blood is on your hands. What price the resurrection of truth in this unholy state? What price the death of one good, decent man, for a nugatory, uncivilised, thug?"

"I have no idea what you are talking about."

"Fine. You play your little games. Now I have your attention I can play mine."

I lift my bag onto the table and produce a digital camera.

"Forgive me. This will take a minute or so to set up."

I press play on the video cam and just before it starts, I slide the machine across the table, scratching the surface of the highly polished table, so that it rests in front of Brodie leaving behind the exposure of the innards of an antique. He does not want to look at it. I know he has no choice.

"You will of course, recognise the exterior walls of your house. You will see the recording has you in your living room talking to a rather effeminate looking man. You are laughing and it seems that your friendship is close. Follow the camera now as one can clearly identify you as you draw the curtains. Of course there isn't an element of culpability here as you are simply talking to a friend. But watch closely. There you are walking into the kitchen. But you are not alone, for he, the unidentified other, follows you in. And then...."

I pause deliberately.

"*Res ipsa loquitur*, ."

"What?"

"The thing speaks for itself."

I watch his face like a hawk. Nothing, changes. In his heart he must know. It is, indeed, all over.

"I am sorry it was necessary to invade your privacy. The rules are yours. These are the rules you have chosen to live by."

Brodie removes the tape from the machine.

"If that is the only copy then you have the evidence I need to declare you. But can you afford to take the chance that I have been so stupid? Can you really afford to take that chance?"

I am in for the kill. I hope he is suffering like he has never suffered before.

"You represent a degree of hypocrisy the likes of which I hope I never have to come across again. And there is more. You asked earlier how I came to know you were here. You are not a fool. You are now sure I have the answer. Until the moment you saw the contents of that tape, you have lived off the concept of plausible deniability. Now you know that is not possible.

It was I who found the address book and a small amount of high quality cocaine in the bottom left hand drawer of your desk. You may have already guessed though you knew there was very little I could do with it. Still, you profess to uphold the law while you break it in a profound way. When I found that cocaine and discovered it was pure, I realised that this was a purchase made not from a minion in the drugs world but from a man who had connections or a member of the criminal underworld himself. I have since discovered that the supplier is a very senior drug dealer in London and the purchaser is none other than the host for tonight's soirée."

"I can deny that."

"Can you?"

"Rather a knee-jerk reaction. Fine; deny it. But think - think. I want reason. Think, reason. You could deny all knowledge. You could say I am incorrect when I make the assertion that, whether for pleasure or addiction, you and your little cabal purchase, through a man formerly a client of your host, illegal substances which allow you to forget who you are. What you cannot stop me doing is going to the very criminal who supplies these drugs and telling him that his trade has been discovered. Now I am sure this gentleman will not be as reasonable as you are going to be and will get to thinking that if the purchaser - your best friend, Basil Roget Q.C., could be subject to investigation, then so could he. And this criminal mastermind isn't going to trust a man of the law to have the same band-of-thieves honour as a bona fide criminal. And this will set him thinking - if arrest follows and prison is the likely consequence, then questions are going to be asked and actions taken. And who will suffer? Well, you will suffer. Roget will suffer. Can you really trust anybody not to tell, ?

"See; you could be investigated, as would the lives and habits of your illustrious partners in subterfuge. You are guilty of having possession of and procuring narcotics for yourself and your friends. You are as guilty as your best friend and you run the same risks should my knowledge be imparted to the extremely violent man you have purchased these goods from.

"Again; are you willing to take the chance that I do not have the name of your supplier; that I have knowledge of precisely what that man will do to you if he thinks there is a possibility you will squeal? And, of course, you know that I have all of the names of the men you call friends - the very men who will be here in no time at all. I can finger all of you and you will betray all of them if you do not do what I say.

"The choice is one I do not envy. Take one path and deny all and you will betray and condemn yourself and your friends. Take the only other option I present and at least you will have a chance."

I can see that Brodie is lost - lost in an ether he has never encountered before. I have put him in a corner where not only he, but also his friends are at stake. He must know that I can expose all of them and in doing so, ruin the lives of those Brodie actually has some feelings for and those he has known all of his adult life. What does he do? What can he do? He knows that his denouement rests on his response. Does he fight, as I am sure he wants to, or is he intelligent enough to know that he cannot fight, for he has nothing to fight with?

Calmly I wait, without demand. I simply look at him whereas he cannot summon up the courage to look at me. I consider the repugnance I feel for the man and how the wheels of social justice have turned. I console myself that, not only Helen and Edmund would be proud of this moment but so too would the countless souls this amoral man has discarded. I have won. Iris has won. We, have won.

But at what cost?

Brodie is almost matter-of-fact - blasé.

"Alright, Iris. It seems that I have little choice. What is it you want of me?"

He gives nothing away - nothing. And here's the rub. I have no plan. I have no time to think. This is impulse; this is biology; this is, finally, me.

"I want assurances from you with respect to these matters I will explain.

The first is simple. You will return to the office tomorrow morning and you will tender your resignation. Dress it up how you want to but you will announce your departure from the firm on terms acceptable to whomever you have to negotiate with. In doing so, I want no reference to me nor to any of the people who you have associated with me, or Edmund Rose. If, in the days, weeks, months, even the years ahead, I get the tiniest rumour that you have sought to scandalise or brutalise those poor bastards who have run scared of you since the day we first met, I will deliver to whoever I need, all the information I have.

Once you have announced your departure and should you wish to stay in the law, you will give me an assurance that you will never practise law in the City of London again. I am not stopping you from going to any other commercial centre, however, if I find that you have taken one step to within one square mile of where I work, again, I will expose you. You can work in New York, Hong Kong - wherever you small talents take you but you never come back to London and practise law."

Brodie nods, looks down and remains silent.

"The next thing I want has to do with your secretary."

Brodie looks up and speaks. His voice is pinched, unsupported by his feeble lungs and carries little air.

"Helen?"

"Yes, Helen."

"She, too?"

"Do you think you could have a hold on that poor woman forever? Do you not feel even the tiniest bit of shame for what you have done to her? You are part of a tapestry of ruination that has clouded her every waking hour, her dreams, her nightmares, her very existence. The evil in you is almost incomprehensible. Helen is with me and she will remain so.

"To think that you did that to her makes me want to kill. Helen has earned and deserves the right to a better life. So I want a further assurance that you will never breathe a word, as you have threatened to, about anything which happened to Helen, all those years ago. Today Helen walks free and her family is set free from the threat of exposure. If you speak, I will tell all."

Brodie is slumped in his chair, his limp body pulling him earthwards towards a heavy and despised acceptance. He cannot object to me. He cannot resist. He must just simply sit and take it.

"Anything else, Iris? Now you have pushed the knife in half way, you might as well finish me off."

There is no humour in his voice. Only self-pity.

Am I supposed to feel for this wretch? Upon which side do I place the weights to balance the scales? This creature chose and chose again to put others to his sword. When he is put to mine he asks for clemency? I can only hate all the more. He makes up my mind for me. I will spare Oliver Dauncey. I will forgive Oliver for acting without choice and I will punish this odious pug for consummating his.

But should I spare Oliver Dauncey? Do I save the life of a rapist? Is he indeed, a rapist? Or do I let him rot, knowing that Brodie will work out that Oliver Dauncey and Oliver Dauncey alone is the traitor? And if I let Oliver Dauncey go on the grounds that he cannot be blamed for what he did to me, for he was a victim of his own biology, who, then, is speaking for me? Is it Iris? What are my feelings? If I have no feelings, then Oliver should suffer like the man in front of me, for Iris will have spoken. But if it is me, then Oliver must go as he cannot be blamed for following his urges, his instincts.

Can one blame nature, if one cannot blame a bird for flying, a tiger for killing a man, a crocodile for eating its prey? Can one blame a man for choosing to hurt, for choosing to harm, for choosing to maim and for choosing to kill? If thought precedes the action, I will slay the thought without. If action precedes the thought, then the action is without largesse. I cannot blame a man. I can blame the mind of a man. Brodie will suffer - Dauncey cannot.

"There is, another matter. Tonight, one member of your little group will not be here. It was he who told me everything. You would, in time, have worked out his identity. You will know who he is this very evening. But, upon his discovery, you will not harm him. He will remain as inviolate as I am, as Helen is, as are all of the poor people your hideous nature has chosen to harm.

"Agreed?"

I can see Brodie getting angry. All that he trusts and all that he is, has crumbled to dust around him. He knows he has been a fool to trust anybody, including those closest to him. The rules which he has utilised to destroy others, have conspired to deliver him the same fate.

"Do I have any choice?"

"No."

"And that's it?"

"No.

"One final thing. From this day forward you will declare yourself to the world. You will say to all who ask, 'yes I am a homosexual - accept me or destroy me.'"

"But...."

"No. You will offer yourself honesty in the hope that it may do you some good. Wherever you go and I do not care where you go, to be frank, you will stop this insidious life you lead and you will grow to be honest with the world around you."

"But I will lose everything."

"You have already lost everything. I hold all the cards which give you the chance of a better, a more decent life, or a return to the pitiable existence you have hitherto chosen. Either you come out or you will lose all. I grow tired of repeating myself."

"And if I do, you will lose half of your leverage against me."

" And if you do not, the tape becomes you.

"In any event, your crimes are sufficient to keep you away. If you are honest with the world, you may even be surprised at how honest the world is back."

"You ask too much."

"I ask nothing. I am telling you."

"I have no choice?"

Brodie turns away. He daren't look at me.

When he turns around, he is crying.

"You ask too much. How can I speak this truth, for I cannot? How can I change, when I cannot? You ask more than I can give; you want more than I am. Do you realise what this will do to me; where this will take me? There is one thing I cannot do and that is tell the world who I really am. It will destroy me; it will be my end. Please not this, this one thing. I will be a discard. I will be eradicated. Please, Iris - I am begging you."

Brodie leaves his chair and walks towards me. Pride falls away like boiled meat from a bone, stripping dignity to the skeletal. Tears are streaming down his face. He gets on his hands and knees in front of me. The tears are real; the body actions, real. Brodie kneels before me, a prostrate beggar summoning words and emotions in this last attempt to protect himself, from, himself.

"Iris; I beg you. You don't understand what it is like. No one understands. I can do all you ask but I cannot do this."

I am cold. I feel nothing for this weak man before me. Nor do I enjoy the power. This is no negotiation - this is arm's length, albeit this is a man's only chance of respite. If Brodie doesn't know it, he soon will. I stand resolute. I stand firm.

"It is just reward for the lives you have taken. I don't expect an answer. I do not expect any sort of response. By the morning, when I get to the office, I will hear rumours of your resignation and they will be confirmed by lunchtime. I will never see you again, neither will Helen. If I do hear of you it will be because you have resurrected yourself as an honest man, not a duplicitous man. And if I ever think you have repented and changed, I will let you back into the City of London. Otherwise, our business here is done.

"If you do not come out; if you do not declare your homosexuality, I will. You have no choice. For the first time in your life you have the opportunity to be a man. I suggest you take it."

With Brodie crying into a handkerchief, I leave the room; I leave the building. Before I go, I have one last thing to say.

"Remember , the truth has a way of turning its head to face all of us."

From my bag I produce a brown, manila envelope. I place it on the table and pick up the digital camera and the tape. Whether Brodie ever opened that envelope I shall never know. And whether he understood the words inside, if he did, should I ever want, to know…

Why, I can smile, and murther whiles I smile
And cry "Content" to that which grieves my heart,
And wet my cheeks with artificial tears,
And frame my face to all occasions.
I'll drown more soldiers than the mermaid shall,
I'll slay more gazers than the basilisk,
I'll play the orator as well as Nestor,
Deceive more slyly than Ulysses could,
And, like a Sinon, take another Troy.
I can add colours to the chameleon,
Change shapes with Proteus for advantages,
And set the murderous Machiavel to school.
Can I do this, and cannot get a crown?
Tut, were it farther off, I'll pluck it down.

XLI.

Opposite the chambers is a bench - just a park bench. Covered in the gentle anonymity of falling twilight, I sit down and watch the entrance to Basil Roget's chambers. One by one, man after man arrives, ready to meet Brodie as old friends against the world. I recognise some of them. Others I cannot know.

I wait and I wait but see no sign of Oliver Dauncey. I hope Brodie is clever enough to hear my final words, for my sake, for the sake of my child, for Helen's sake and for a man whom I and not Iris, have given a chance. Yes; I have given Brodie a chance. And for a few moments I am rightly proud of myself. Though Iris is still in me, the logic monster I used to be is now balanced by the woman I have become.

As for Oliver Dauncey?

Only time, will tell.

A woman is created from the stale, sexless persona of old. I can look forward now. I can be strong. I can show who I am - not just through the empty analysis that used to be Iris, but through the emotions I have attained at the lowest moments of my life. Through the eyes of Iris was life through the bars of a cell. My emancipation has come at some cost yet I can see how that cost was worth it. I have learnt to act and to feel. Maybe I will start making the same mistakes I so criticised in others. Maybe I am going to make mistakes and fall below the impossibly high standards I once set for myself and for all of the people around me. Maybe I won't.

Still, for a few moments, I am happy. I have every right to be happy. I am not just Iris. I, am me.

XLII.

Brodie resigned the following day. When I arrived at work his departure was the talk of the office. His room was cleared the previous evening and I was shown an empty box where once this creature sat and schemed his way to a status he little deserved. I guess that on leaving him to mull in that room in Temple, his insidious brain worked out that he had little choice but to accept defeat and save for himself the remnants of what little he had left.

It was many weeks before he surfaced and many weeks before I learnt of his fate. I knew he had left London, as James - cheeky James, took the trouble to drive to Brodie's house in Surrey once more and check for signs of life. But there was no life there to be had - the house had been hastily sold, so he was informed and the former occupants, a rather strange couple according to a neighbour, had departed to an unknown destination.

Brodie surfaced in Singapore two months and two days later. He commenced work as a partner in a satellite office of an American law firm in a market he knew little of and in a city whose impeccable standards and regimental moral spectrum marked a difference with the man that was and the man I wanted Brodie to become.

And Brodie became that man. Without obvious explanation, Brodie explained to the market that he was not a family man; he was not a father; he was not what he had previously portrayed himself to be. As one may imagine, when I found out, it was all I could do to stop a wry smile coming to my lips. Still, there was an air of self-congratulation to be had and I admit, I did allow myself recourse to thoughts of satisfaction when I heard the news and I followed with interest the events which subsequently took over Brodie's life.

In the beginning, it was exactly as Brodie had anticipated. Clients deserted him, fellow lawyers deserted him and if they didn't desert him, they certainly questioned his motives and the veracity of a man who had systematically lied to the market for years. Times were tough, so I am told, but once the information was out, as was Brodie, it was absolutely clear that there could be no going back. If Brodie had little moral character previously, if Brodie was as hideous a human being as I can portray, then I am happy to

236

play a part in the resurrection of a man from the ashes of that pug. As time went by, and the leaves of Autumn which fell around his feet were slowly brushed away, Brodie lost the make-up of the past and faced the environment cleansed of the face that portrayed a face that portrayed a face that portrayed a face. And in doing so, he managed to develop a career, picking up clients - different clients who somehow recognised the courage they saw in a man facing up to the realities of his sexuality and the gamble he took in proclaiming who he was and is.

I sometimes wonder, if I were to pick up the phone and speak to him what I would find at the other end. I am told he is now an eminently relaxed individual; that he laughs out loud when he should be laughing out loud, that he is willing to be made to look the fool; that he laughs at himself and understands the needs of others. A fellow lawyer I came across, who worked for Brodie for a short time, had nothing other than nice things to say about him. He is nothing other than a genuine man so I am told, and carries a sense of humour as a gift and a wit second to none. The question is, as I sit here and put this information to paper - these disjointed ramblings to paper, whether I should take on an air of self-congratulation for my part in the downfall of what was and the renaissance of a man without the clothes of ignominy which caused so many to suffer.

Perhaps the best way of describing my feelings, is that they are cold and non-committal. Is it not true that Brodie is responsible for the downfall and the death of my friend? Is it not true that Edmund Rose deserved not the fate which became him and the perpetrator of that fate lies happy in bed at night, in a far-flung city more than halfway across the world? As Brodie gets on with becoming a better person, I find it difficult to contend with the simple fact that a far better being decomposes in the ground, unattended, neglected and, apart from me, hardly missed. Can I blame Brodie for the sins of the man he once was?

Blame is the wrong emotion. To blame implies that there is a corresponding outcome to blame and that I look into a fellow *Homo sapien* and see a resolution to my anger - to my rage in the import of the wish of suffering onto another. I do not. I recall instead, an anger misdirected as it was, in yelling at two cheap, opportunistic thieves on a tube. Such men and the man and woman who were both their victims and my victims, cannot suffer the indignity of the allocation of blame in isolation from the crimes of those all around, who simply let things happen. The sins of the many are evidenced by the actions of the few. In microcosm one has the clues to the answer which helps me resolve the difficulties I have in seeing Brodie as a man of inconsequence, whether or not his life now belongs in a hall of commendation. To this extent things haven't changed; the nature of man and woman hasn't changed and as I look around me now, while I still reside in London, am surrounded by London and avoid as much as I can, all of the infections of London, the appalling unknowing and the acceptance of what isn't inevitable is the locus of where I should be placing the finger of retribution. And yet I do not. I cannot.

The paradox is that I cannot allocate the sins of the many to but a few. And I cannot allocate the sins of the many anyway, for they are not sins at all. Who am I to judge in any event for I would be a hypocrite in doing so. They are not transgressions of a moral line drawn by all in the face of all. If they are not; if the way we treat each other are actions drawn from a well whose passage is unadulterated and unknowing, the behaviour of all in relation to all, is nothing short of the real nature of man - the real nature of woman. To put it another way - the paradox of humanity is inhumanity. But it cannot be inhumanity if there is no appropriate measure of humanity itself. If we know our actions are wrong, then we know we can put them right. If we cannot know that our actions are wrong because they are processes we all adhere to, they cannot be wrong in any event. I cannot blame Brodie for the sins of his past, for he never saw them as sin, just as much as the motives and manner of all around cannot fall below a parapet which for the majority, doesn't exist. I cannot blame a man and I cannot blame the all. So I am cold; I am indifferent. Analysis may be a guide to inaction - it is also a lodestar of understanding. To pick on a few; to fall in with the few, is putting a shovel into the earth and thinking that the small crumbs of poisonous soil removed sanitises the earth *in toto*.

What then, of Oliver Dauncey?

Here too, I have few words of congratulation and a few words of consolation in relation to the decisions I have made. True enough, I carried his child. True enough he took advantage of me by following instincts which took advantage of him. It follows that if I cannot blame Brodie, then I cannot blame Oliver Dauncey either. Both followed urges - in one case, innate, in another, learnt and innate. I cannot blame the ape who placed himself upon me to satisfy the blindness of his urges. In taking away the innocence of my life, in a strange and oblique way, he gave me life - he gave me a life I had otherwise never had. For if it wasn't for the act itself, the words articulated here could never have been written.

Of course, this isn't an argument about the value of what Oliver Dauncey did to me. Any sane, rational and reasonable analysis of those events on that night in Chelsea must come to the conclusion that standards between human beings were breached, and breached in a fundamentally hideous way. I know that in a society; in any society, what happened to me was wrong, incontrovertibly wrong and should never have happened. To defend the circumstances of my pregnancy, to defend the disgusting manner that I was taken advantage of, is not the purpose I espouse. There are no imaginary moral standards when it comes to the taking of sexual advantage against the will. There never can be. The finite lines drawn with respect to the defilement of women are real and tangible. As applied to all of us, they cannot and should never be breached. My own sufferings do not change that - the truth was inherent before I was taken advantage of. Rape - the act of sexual intercourse without consent, is an act of evil. And it will forever be so.

But am I saying that I was raped on that night when my innocence was sequestered in a most vile way. Did I knowingly consent? Did I knowingly reject the advances of Oliver Dauncey?

Had I not drank myself into oblivion the answers to these questions would have been obvious. But I made the choice to eviscerate Iris and so leave myself to the winds which sweep across the grey and indistinct moral hinterlands where there are no answers.

If all Oliver Dauncey said was correct and if my analysis is correct, then we both fell upon the sword of our biology as we both discarded, through the twisted anonymity which befalls all who drink to destruction, the capacity to choose. Consent, in these circumstances, falls well below the manners of perception. Whatever movement I made on that bed and whatever signals Oliver Dauncey took them to mean, did not revolve around the mills of analysis. As a cat becomes feral when left to the world alone, so does man - does woman - left to the pitch the body brings with it should it cut the umbilical to the mind. The concept of consent does not arise, for a body without a mind has no choice but to go where it should follow. Though I cannot defend Oliver Dauncey, I cannot defend myself. Though I cannot blame Oliver Dauncey, I cannot blame myself. The only thing I can do is to look to the consequences of my actions and not to the actions themselves.

I have not seen Oliver Dauncey since I confronted him. He resigned on the same day as Brodie. To where he has taken his life, I am unaware. I am uninterested in finding out. I take from his presence in my life, very little. I take the consequences of his presence in my life in an altogether different way. To see a light from the shadows of my past, I can see that upon the moment of my pregnancy, a new life was created from the stale and staid persona of old - the innocence of a child for sure, but the emancipation of its mother. Oliver Dauncey, unknowingly, gave to me the ticket which commenced the journey which resulted in the words you see before you now. Without choice he gave me life and with choice, he saved my life on the day Edmund Rose committed suicide. If I should be grateful, I should be grateful on these two counts - he saved my life by pulling me away from an oncoming vehicle; he saved my life by pulling me away from the distance Iris had placed between the world in which I live and the distorted psyche which vilified and rejected that very world. I cannot blame Oliver Dauncey. Whether Oliver Dauncey thinks in the same way, I cannot tell. I do not want, to know.

XLIII.

I do not live with James any more. He stayed with me for the full term of my pregnancy and was as helpful, as delightful a human being and a friend, as one could hope for. I cannot put words on paper which give justice to the feelings I have for a man to whom, for some and certainly for Iris, a friendship should never have been offered. But, when I really needed him, when the need to act was the answer to my ills, it was James who acted; it was James who grew up and out of the circumstances of my pregnancy, of the circumstances of Edmund's fall and of the circumstances of Helen's past. To James both Helen and I have to be eternally grateful.

I know, as I look back on these notes, I have captured James as vain, as, in some ways, devoid of character; of being shallow and egotistical; of being flippant and easily led. Of course he was and still is all of those things. I remember him telling me, in The Falcon, in Clapham, on the night when Helen first told me of her past, that he was not just a man made up of the inner leanings underneath his flippant and easygoing façade. He was and is all one sees and all he is underneath. What was the example he used? Yes - a shy person who is quiet, then loud at other times, is both shy and loud. The face of the man gives way to another face, yet both are the same and one cannot be held distinct from the other. It is a lesson I should learn and a mistake I should not have made. James is not a front man for his own personality. He is more than a veneer and a man who is the sum of his parts. That I did not describe his features; that I did not describe his looks, is appropriate. They are irrelevant to the purposes of this memoir. James came of age because, in a final analysis, James, like so many men, is a being composed of actions which give little to my world of reflection. When he needed to act, he did - taking risks to establish who and what Brodie was, so giving me the strength to take the risk of speaking so forthrightly to Oliver Dauncey in order to establish the truth of his past and the truth of mine.

James is not a complicated man. He is not a straightforward man, either. His locus lies somewhere on the continuum between these two polar extremes. Though there is a cynical side to him, his values are worthy values, and I have the utmost respect for him.

He left my flat a couple of weeks ago and lives around the corner. Not long after Brodie's departure, he went out in Clapham with some friends from his office. That evening he met a small group of women who, for some reason had chosen the pubs in Clapham for a hen night pub crawl. One of them - a quiet woman from what James told me, he liked immediately. She was nervous and seemingly indifferent, weary and uncomfortable. Still, she spent the evening with James and he made her promise to see him again. They went out a few times until she felt comfortable with her own story - she was a widow with three young children; that it took her all of two years to get over the death of her husband.

Some men would have run a mile at this juncture. Not James. Over time he fell in love and the love he feels has led him to her doorstep and the greater responsibilities of looking after three children which are not his own. And he is happy - I can tell he is happy. Though he never looked for purpose, he has a purpose now. It is a responsibility he tells me he relishes.

If only Edmund could have been the same. If only Edmund Rose could have had the courage to face up to the responsibilities of answering the call to respect one's nature. I look at James sometimes and wish upon him all the luck in the world. When I think of Edmund, I cannot help but feel a despair that he made life more complicated than it ever needed to be.

When I have time; when I need to make time, I visit Edmund's grave in North London. Placing flowers upon his headstone, I inspect the graves all around. Each is tended with a love and respect which shows the human capacity to love; to love even that which cannot hear, or speak, or see. Memories live long in the psyche - memories of people past upon whom love was bestowed and from whom love was a gift to others. Edmund Rose has no such privilege. Only I know where his remains reside. Not once has his wife, or his children, even Anthony Down - his former lover, ever enquired as to the whereabouts of a man to whom they owe so much. In death, as in life, Edmund Rose cultivates the affection of no one in isolation of the gifts he bestowed upon them. It is as though he never took part upon this earth; as though his place amongst the billions upon this planet has been washed away by the tide - an excrescence forgotten, discarded, dismissed and denied a place amongst the worthy.

And yet, what place does he deserve? He showed no one what he was until it was too late. He defended neither the right to be himself nor the benefit of letting others make their mind up as to what value the real Edmund Rose had. In one sense, he was nothing of what one saw, though, if James is right and we are all we are in presentation and in the truth behind the veil, then he was everything one saw and all he was inside. But who saw? Who was able to look into him and realise that the act wasn't all? Who looked beyond the veil, apart from me? No one. It is fitting then, as some may argue, that his headstone is attended by no one; is tended by no one except me; is left to rot by the forces of nature to which we all must submit.

By the sword did Edmund live and under the sharp, brilliance of the sword will he never be remembered. The truth resiles with his duplicity. His duplicity will be left as a gift to all. Only I realise the duplicity and it is left to me to understand that duplicity is what caused this man to fall. Edmund knew this - his very last words to me, in that cell in Snow Hill Police Station, made the point. His life had been a waste because no one knew who he really was - no one knew him before he was arrested, before a label had been placed upon him. And no one, after the label had made him a pariah and a pervert, would ever want to know anything other than the label. Only after the event did Edmund realise and only when he realised did he have to contend with the fact that the realisation was too late.

As I sit at his headstone and I mull this over, I resolve always to honour the memory of my friend. I resolve too, to learn the lessons of his life. To hide; to secret away in the face of an imagined strength, is not to accept the indiscriminate hand. Let not the imagined wiles of others place before oneself the need - the absolute need to stand up in the face of what one is. Accept it and deal with all the blows which society, whatever that society is and has to offer, pushes in one's direction. The alternative is ignominy; of having lived but never having lived; of having touched but unknowing as to touch, of perspectives without perspective and of the whole without the sum of its parts. I have got to learn to trust just as Edmund could never trust. I have got to learn to love just as Edmund tried but failed to love. I owe the resurrection of my person to a man who tried in life to help me but failed. Now, in death - a senseless death - a wasted life, his gift is unseen and unknown by others and is an example to me which I swear, as I stand above his grave and shed a tear for the memory of my friend, my confidant and a rock when I needed one most, I shall never forget, just as I shall never forget the memory of Edmund Rose.

XLIV.

Finally it is to Helen that I turn. It took Helen two weeks to speak to me after I had disclosed my pregnancy. I am not sure whether it would have been longer had it not been for the efforts of James in getting Helen to see that her absence and her sorrow when faced with the pregnancy of the woman she relied upon more than any other, was misplaced and selfish. When she knocked on my door and when she unveiled the courage to knock on my door, it was all I could do to accept her as I had done before, indeed, as she had accepted me at the very beginning.

I had found a place in her heart, she told me, that she would find difficult to replace. I had saved her; I had salvaged what she had left in life when all that life had thrown at her had caused her so much harm. For her absence she was most truly sorry, though it was an absence I understood. For what else should this woman have been made to suffer? Her love is murdered; her child taken away. She is banished from the community in which she grew up, rejected by the very values she had been taught to respect. How that place is so twisted; how the mutations of man make all suffer when mutations forget the one fundamental truth religion should never forget - it is impossible to steal away the nature of people which rises above the predictability of the animal. We can love; love knows no boundaries; has no rules; has no face which cannot change; has no time upon which to lay itself. Far from condemning a man; far from condemning a woman and her child, it should be to Helen that faith should be applied. Her love crossed boundaries put there by those who regard hate as a virtue.

The proof is in the minutiae of Helen's story - how she protected the very individuals who treated her with a disdain riddled with hatred and unbended bigotry. She looked after the family which disowned her; the community which excommunicated her; the child taken from her and at the expense of years spent at the beck and call of a man using these rules to his own perfidious ends. I embarrass myself when I talk of forgiving Helen. What place have I to forgive when she has sacrificed so much to those who could never forgive?

I could, at this time, tell you that I went through my pregnancy alone; that I eeked out an existence through a lonely few months as my body expanded to make room for my child. I could tell you that I did this alone. I did not. Through the six months till the birth, Helen was my left hand and my right. She selflessly guided me through all of the trials of womanhood in its fullest account. I am not going to bore; indeed it was never my intention to bore with detail unless it was absolutely necessary. I had a fairly unremarkable pregnancy, uneventful other than the expected. Still it was hard and I have Helen to thank for getting me through the times when I thought I could not face the responsibilities my decisions had forced upon me. She was my strength; she got me through the challenges of body, leaving me free to digest and question the challenges of mind I knew I would one day have to undertake. And Helen helped me without regard to herself and without regard to her own loss. She claimed she was just happy to be free - to be free of the shackles of Brodie. I have no reason to doubt her.

But I doubted myself. Could I, on giving up work without telling the powers that be the reason for my departure, ever face the call to womanhood in a way which befitted the child I carried? And if I could not, what better than to look upon that child as a gift to the woman at hand? I thought long and I thought hard about who I had become and who I was. Was I really suited to motherhood? Could I bestow upon my child the love which may always be marked by the circumstances of the child's conception?

I had been given a second chance in life, though through circumstances I wouldn't want to wish upon any other. That chance was not to do with the child in isolation - it is to do with what the child did to the relationship between my body and my mind and how it awoke me to my biology whereas all I had been before was a stone. For that I have to be truly grateful. I could not say for certain that I was going to be able to love the child without qualification, and the innocence of life itself requires love without respite, lest that innocence be compromised and one more individual be added to the sum total of misery inflicted upon each within the whole. I know; I knew I could not take that chance. I was not ready. I am not ready.

I gave birth, at home, to a baby boy weighing seven pounds ten ounces. No one knew I was pregnant, save for Helen and James. No one knew because for the latter half of the term, I stayed at home. There was no midwife in attendance; there was no doctor on standby if things went wrong. I am very lucky, as is my son.

I cannot deliver onto this page the love - the immediacy of the love I felt for the child I bore. And I cannot know what the future will bring. I cannot know that the private tears which I shed, which have stopped, or whether the pain in my heart which I feel no longer on giving my son away, will ever return to follow me wherever I go. But I have more to be grateful for than just a son I have no longer. I have a son whose mother will look after him more than I ever could; a mother who will cherish him beyond call.

When I agreed with Helen, who did not ask or initially approve of the idea, that I should give my son to her, I knew that it was for the sake of the child. I knew she was the best person to look after my son. And look after him she does, though I know not precisely where.

We agreed it was in both our interests that our contact, apart from cards on birthdays and Christmas, should be minimal, if at all. It was best for both of us and best for her son. When I do get a card, the letter is stamped in London, so I believe Helen is living relatively close at hand. And her son? Corin will just be beginning to teethe.

I cannot say I have no regrets at losing Helen and at losing my child. I think of him occasionally and wonder how they are. I hope, however, that in my sacrifice, I have given two people on this earth the chance to benefit from the happiness once denied to Helen and in some way, denied to me. If there is recompense to be had, this is recompense enough.

On the morning Helen left, I asked her the one question which I have not referred to and which had prayed on my mind ever since the first occasion we met. It was always a matter of concern to me why Helen should choose me to open up to; how she made the decision to speak to me, of all people, about her past and how controlled she was. When I asked the question, I was afraid - afraid of the answer. Iris was so hard; so cruel; so indifferent - how could anyone see beyond that?

"Iris; it didn't take me more than a second to see that you were kind. Kindness is a gift we all know we should aspire to. Yours is the face of kindness, as is the woman who lives within."

In my life, it is the nicest thing that has ever been said to me.

XLV.

I am now on my own. In fact, when I am not at work, I spend a great deal of time on my own. In my isolation, I have had the opportunity to think over the last months and all that has happened to me. To say that my isolation involves a loneliness I didn't have before would be to misstate the truth. Life as Iris was life through the bars of a cell. The life I lead at this moment, with the benefit of a hindsight denied to many others, is as an enriching experience as any.

I do not now, though I did to exclusion before, look upon others and see them only for their weaknesses. I do not see them as weak because of their humanity, or indeed, in spite of it. Wherever I am, be it on the tube, be it walking the streets; be it at work and surrounded by those I despised for so many years, I look afresh and content myself that I have the opportunity to discard the old, frosted, opaque lenses. I do not classify as once I did; I do not blame as once I did. Yes; Iris was cold; Iris was as inert as a seaside rock. I am not Iris any more. If there is an epitaph to my life, it should read that salvation came to the interned through experiences not to be wished upon any other. I should make clear that those very experiences proffered a break from the cynical, dismissive, inhuman attitudes which marked Iris and the world in which she lived. In writing this, I should look upon this as an epitaph for Iris and a mission statement for me.

There is a depressive negativity about this memoir. But I look upon the life I fashioned for myself not with anger but with mellow reflections on the waste of it - the empty magnitude of thoughts designed only to create more thoughts which failed to correspond to action. At least Brodie; at least Edmund Rose had life - embraced life. Iris embraced circumspection, unable to see that beyond circumspection lies more of the same. For the fact of my pregnancy I should, in some rather perverse way, be grateful. I may even say that if it were not for the circumstances of my insemination I would not be here today following the logic of existence with these few words designed to explain all.

See; far more good than bad has come of events. Of course I have regrets - I have regrets because my innocence was taken from me, by Iris, by Oliver Dauncey and to some degree, by Brodie and Edmund Rose. Mine was previously a refusal to get involved, to get my hands dirty, to hover like so much burnt paper above a flame; watching and understanding the wiles of those whose only choice was to periodically get burnt. Today, I do not consciously avoid further scenarios in which I could get hurt and I do not ridicule those who cannot be the watcher without ever descending the ladder to humanity. In any event, relating to humanity is not a ladder to be descended. I am not better for thinking I am better - the misguided notions I took on never established their veracity. I thought I was entitled to a twisted vista because I imagined I was the only one who understood. How wrong could I have been? It was only through my own circumstances that I got to know Edmund and to know Edmund was to realise that he too, understood and understood in many ways which were far more profound than my own. No one makes the choice to get hurt or even to hurt others. And just because Iris saw the mistakes of the many through a microscope and a macroscope - be they lawyers, accountants, bankers, runners, secretaries and all the rest of them, this didn't make Iris a better person than they were. To assume Iris was advanced, as I once did, is to adopt an arrogance in inverse proportion to the profundity of the idea. I am glad of the lessons I have learnt. I am happy to see those lessons becoming part of my future.

Still - what of my future?

Presently I take each day as it arises. I still work at the same law firm in the City of London. I am still doing the same job. I look on my employment now with more interest than I ever used to. I realise that I am lucky to have something which stirs my intellect away from the concerns documented here. I have also taken on more interests than I ever used to. I have taken to sport and to the theatre; to culture in some small way - culture with a small 'c'. London has thus become a different landscape for me and I see it less for what it was to Iris and more for what it does for me. There is so much to offer here, and, approached with the right and not the wrong attitude, little to detract.

As for my feelings; well, I am happy to admit that I have feelings. As for the future of my feelings - I am sure they will find a home. I am not consciously looking for a relationship, though it may in time, arise. I am not a bad person. My hope is that I am recognised as kind, as gentle and thoughtful; as one who can laugh and feel and make at least some of the mistakes of my fellows. I am sure; I am certain that one day my nature will be recognised as opposed to my face, my chest, my legs, my hair - and the content of my character is fallen upon and cherished, not my reflection in the mirror. Of course I understand this to be romantic and maybe I always was a romantic whose frustrations lie at the bottom of the twisted pile on top. Still, I live daily in the hope that I too, may find happiness. I pray that when it arrives, if it arrives, I have the courage to adopt the risks that make it worth the while. I hope I can recognise it, too.

Iris Silkin,
12a Gladstone Road,
Clapham,
South London.